THE Hot Scots

PREQUEL NOVELLAS

Other Books by Anna Durand

Dangerous in a Kilt (Hot Scots, Book One)
Wicked in a Kilt (Hot Scots, Book Two)
Scandalous in a Kilt (Hot Scots, Book Three)
The MacTaggart Brothers Trilogy (Hot Scots, Books 1-3)
Gift-Wrapped in a Kilt (Hot Scots, Book Four)
Notorious in a Kilt (Hot Scots, Book Five)
Insatiable in a Kilt (Hot Scots, Book Six)
Lethal in a Kilt (Hot Scots, Book Seven)
Irresistible in a Kilt (Hot Scots, Book Eight)
Devastating in a Kilt (Hot Scots, Book Nine)
Spellbound in a Kilt (Hot Scots, Book Ten)
Relentless in a Kilt (Hot Scots, Book Eleven)
Incendiary in a Kilt (Hot Scots, Book Twelve)
Wild in a Kilt (Hot Scots, Book Thirteen)
Unstoppable in a Kilt (Hot Scots, Book Fourteen)
Valentine in a Kilt (Hot Scots, Book Fifteen)
Lachlan in a Kilt (The Ballachulish Trilogy, Book One)
Aidan in a Kilt (The Ballachulish Trilogy, Book Two)
Rory in a Kilt (The Ballachulish Trilogy, Book Three)
Brit vs. Scot (A Hot Brits/Hot Scots/Au Naturel Crossover Book)
The American Wives Club (A Hot Brits/Hot Scots/Au Naturel Crossover Book)
A Novel Secret (A Hot Brits/Hot Scots/Au Naturel Crossover Book)
The Dixon Brothers Trilogy (Hot Brits, Books 1-3)
One Hot Escape (Hot Brits, Book Four)
One Hot Rumor (Hot Brits, Book Five)
One Hot Christmas (Hot Brits, Book Six)
One Hot Scandal (Hot Brits, Book Seven)
One Hot Deal (Hot Brits, Book Eight)
One Hot Favor (Hot Brits, Book Nine)
One Hot Bash (Hot Brits, Book Ten)
One Hot Moment (Hot Brits, Book Eleven)
Natural Obsession (Au Naturel Nights, Book One)
Natural Passion (Au Naturel Trilogy, Book One)
Natural Impulse (Au Naturel Trilogy, Book Two)
Natural Satisfaction (Au Naturel Trilogy, Book Three)
Fired Up (standalone romance)
The Janusite Trilogy (Undercover Elementals, Books 1-3)
Obsidian Hunger (Undercover Elementals, Book 4)
Unbidden Hunger (Undercover Elementals, Book 5)
The Thirteenth Fae (Undercover Elementals, Book 6)
Cyneric (Undercover Elementals, Book 7)
The Immortal Falls (Undercover Elementals, Books8)
The Complete Echo Power Trilogy
The Psychic Crossroads Series Collection
Passion Never Dies: The Complete Reborn Series

ANNA DURAND

THE HOT SCOTS PREQUEL NOVELLAS
Copyright © 2024 by Lisa A. Shiel
All rights reserved.

ISBN: 978-1-958144-53-4 (paperback)
ISBN: 978-1-958144-54-1 (ebook)
ISBN: 978-1-958144-55-8 (retail audiobook)
ISBN: 978-1-958144-70-1 (library audio)

Manufactured in the United States.

Jacobsville Books
www.JacobsvilleBooks.com

Publisher's Cataloging-in-Publication Data
provided by Five Rainbows Cataloging Services

Names: Durand, Anna, author.
Title: The hot Scots prequel novellas / Anna Durand.
Description: Marietta, OH : Jacobsville Books, 2022. | Series: Hot Scotsl, bk. 3.9.
Identifiers: ISBN 978-1-958144-53-4 (paperback) | ISBN 978-1-958144-54-1 (ebook) | ISBN 978-1-958144-55-8 (retail audiobook) | ISBN 978-1-958144-70-1 (library audio)
Subjects: LCSH: Highlands (Scotland)--Fiction. | Man-woman relationships--Fiction. | Scots--Fiction. | Americans--Fiction. | College teachers--Fiction. | British-Fiction. | BISAC: FICTION / Romance / Contemporary. | FICTION / Romance / Romantic Comedy. | GSAFD: Love stories.
Classification: LCC PS3604.U724 H68 2024 (print) | LCC PS3604.U724 (ebook) | DDC 813/.6--dc23.

THE Notorious DR. MACT

<h1 style="text-align:center">Chapter One</h1>

Iain

I march across the campus of Nackington University, head held high, shoulders back, and ignore the taunts and jeers erupting around me. I expect this reaction whenever I dress like a true Scotsman in a heathen country. I'd never been to America until I flew in last week, in preparation for assuming my new job as a professor of archaeology and ancient history.

"Whoa, dude," one young numpty shouts. He points at my clothing. "Do you wear lace panties too? They'd go with your plaid skirt."

It's a kilt, not a skirt. But I won't waste my time explaining that to any of these morons. Not everyone disapproves of my attire, though. The lasses love it. I see groups of them gathering to watch me stroll by and to whisper to each other while they give me appreciative glances.

Another laddie points at me and laughs. "What a dweeb. Did you lose a bet and had to wear a skirt to class today?"

I reach down to pat the hilt of my *sgian dubh* which pokes out of my sock. "My knife is bigger than yours, laddie."

Aye, I say the word knife as if I mean "dick." The laddie understands, I think, since he rolls his eyes. I prefer the word *slat*, since that's the Gaelic term.

My march through the asinine world of college laddies ends when I push through the double doors into the humanities building. The students milling about in the hall glance at me sideways but make no comment on my outfit. The lasses, naturally, cast me appreciative glances.

I find my classroom and walk up to the lectern that's been set up at the front of the room. The space is not large, but then, archaeology courses aren't normally the most popular ones. Still, I should have about thirty students this semester for my course on Celtic history. Aye, an American university offers a class like that. They created it this year just for me because I convinced the curriculum committee that the university should expand its offerings. They were keen on the idea. Very keen.

Turns out the grandparents of the committee chairman emigrated from Scotland.

And now I have emigrated too, though only for a while. I've been given a one-year contract with the option to extend it if everyone likes my work here.

I set my bag on the floor beside the lectern and get set up for today's class. Someone walks into the room just as I'm finishing. I see the figure peripherally, and since I'm still organizing my papers on the lectern, I speak without glancing up. "*Guten Morgen.*"

"Uh, good morning?"

The female voice bears a note of uncertainty.

I lift my head and see a bonnie lass standing halfway across the room. She's more than bonnie. The auburn beauty transfixes me with her voluptuous figure and her classical features. Since I've confused her, I say, "*Guten Morgen* is German for good morning."

"Oh. *Guten Morgen*, then." She moves closer, halting an arm's length away. "You don't sound German, though."

"I'm Scottish." I step sideways, away from the lectern, and offer her my hand. "Iain MacTaggart."

She slips her hand into mine. "Rae Everhart."

"A pleasure to meet you, Rae." I step behind the lectern again. "I learned some German phrases while doing field work in the Saxony region."

"Wow. That must be amazing. To work in another country, I mean. I've never been anywhere except America."

"You'll get to know Scotland in this class." I wink. "It's a very romantic country."

Am I flirting with her? She's a student, an undergraduate, which means she cannae be more than twenty-one or twenty-two. A thirty-seven-year-old man should not be making romantic advances toward a lass fifteen years his junior.

More students begin to file into the room.

"Choose a seat," I tell Rae. "Class will start shortly."

She sits down three rows back, directly in front of me. I don't watch the other students as they choose their seats. No, I can't stop staring at Rae. Her eyes are the most entrancing shade of dark blue I've ever seen. Her lips have just enough fullness to make them enticing too, and I know I could kiss those lips for hours. But I won't do that. Getting sacked for sexual misconduct on my first day at Nackington would ruin my career.

I can be mates with a student, though. Can't I?

Once everyone has taken a seat, I set my hands on the edges of the lectern and begin. "Good morning. I'm Dr. Iain MacTaggart, your teacher for the semester. Welcome to Celtic History 401, the Story of Scotland from the Paleolithic Era to the Union of Crowns." I raise a hand just as a lad raises his hand to ask a question. "Donnae worry. In due course, I will explain the meanings of those terms and many more. By the end of this semester, you'll be experts on all these subjects."

"Cool," a blonde lass declares. "I love your accent, by the way."

"Thank you." My gaze gravitates to Rae. The second our eyes meet, she smiles. "Let's dive into the first lesson."

Her lips tighten more, carving out dimples in her cheeks.

Bod an Donais, the lass is lovely. Kissing her would be…cause for my dismissal. Aye, I *should* curse myself in Gaelic because only an erse would think about kissing a student.

I clear my throat and focus on the class. The girls all watch me with rapt attention while the boys thumb through their textbooks or scribble in their notebooks, though I suspect they're not taking notes. Aye, getting and keeping the attention of college students is always a challenge. Before I can begin my lecture, I ask for the names of all the students and write them down on the diagram of the classroom that I made last night. I also inform them they should always sit in the same seat because that will make it easier for me to remember their names. And aye, one sarcastic young man asks if I have senile dementia and that's why I need a chart to remember the students' names. I shake my head and do not respond.

Stepping out from behind the lectern, I gesture at my clothing. "I'm sure you're all wondering about the way I'm dressed."

"Yeah, what's up with the skirt?" a cheeky sod asks.

I feign disappointment. "Apparently, none of the lads in America know any other way to insult a Scot. You all say the same thing. I expected better from seniors who will graduate in the spring and go on to exciting careers in the fast food industry."

The laddie clamps his jaw shut and puckers his lips, staring down at his notebook.

I take hold of my kilt and lift it just enough to reveal my knees, though I didn't do it for that purpose. I meant to draw their attention to the garment. "This is a kilt. Not a skirt. The kilt I'm wearing features the MacTaggart clan tartan. Every clan distinguishes itself with a unique plaid design." I pull my knife out of my sock and raise it for the class to see. "This is a *sgian dubh*, a type of dagger used as a weapon by Scots in the old days. Today, it's strictly for ornamental use. The word *sgian dubh* means 'black knife.' No one knows why, but that's what we call these blades."

Rae raises her hand.

I nod to her. "What's your question?"

"Do you have a big sword too?"

When a few laddies make suggestive noises, Rae bows her head.

I glare at each snickering *cacan* in turn—and they all haud their wheesht. Wee shits always crumble under pressure. Now that I've silenced them, I focus on Rae. "Aye, I do have a sword back home in Scotland. My cousin Lachlan gave it to me for my birthday last year." I squint at the laddies who had ridiculed Rae and speak in a menacingly soft voice. "My sword is called a claymore, and with that blade, I could take the head off anyone who causes trouble."

I wave my *sgian dubh* in a threatening gesture.

The laddies pick up their pens and pencils as if they now mean to pay attention to the lesson without harassing anyone. Maybe I enjoyed terrifying them a bit too much, but I cannae stand for any man harassing a woman.

Rae tentatively raises her hand again.

"Go on," I say. "What did you want to ask?"

"Um…" She bites her upper lip. "I was wondering about your shirt. It's cool, but it doesn't look old-timey."

"No, it's not. I didn't have a traditional shirt, so I improvised." I wink at her. "If I can find a Jacobite kilt shirt, I'll wear it to class one day."

She smiles shyly, and it's the sweetest thing I've ever seen.

"All right," I say, stepping behind the lectern again. "It's time to dig into our first lesson for this week—the Paleolithic Era. Does anyone know what that term means?"

A laddie, identified on my chart as Andy, thrusts his hand up.

"Tell me your definition, Andy."

"It's a pail of lithic. You know, like a bucket full of, uh…lithic stuff."

"Afraid not. Anyone else care to try?"

No one moves. Most of them stare at me blankly.

Then Rae lifts her hand. When I nod, she says, "Paleolithic means 'old stone.' So the Paleolithic Era is the Old Stone Age, meaning that the people then used only stone tools. The Mesolithic and Neolithic came after that but before the invention of metalworking."

"Excellent, Rae. That's a perfect definition."

She sits up straighter, and her lips curl into a lovely little smile.

While I continue my lecture, the other students get more involved as they become more comfortable with me. I might be Scottish, and I might be wearing a kilt and a *sgian dubh*, but I am not a frightening man. I discuss the Paleolithic in Scotland, and my students actually take notes and ask questions. This is a good start. I had worried that the students might not accept me readily, but those fears have evaporated.

Especially when I look at Rae.

Christ, I should not be thinking about her this much. She's a student and far too young for me.

Rae stays behind after the other students have left the room. She approaches me as I'm putting all my notes and pictures into my attaché case. «Dr. MacTaggart?»

"Please call me Iain."

She hunches her shoulders and smiles shyly again, which makes me want to kiss her right now. "Okay, Iain."

"Did ye have a question, lass?"

Rae nods. "I wondered if today was the only time you'll talk about the Paleolithic. I'm really interested in that era."

"Aye, this was the only in-class lecture on that topic. But I'd be happy to discuss it with you outside of class."

"You mean like a tutoring type thing?"

No, because I hadn't thought that far ahead. The words poured out of me before I'd bothered to consider them. What's the harm in tutoring a student outside of class? Rae wants to know more about the Paleolithic, that's all. I won't get so randy that I'll seduce her. I might find her attractive, but I have self-control.

"Aye," I say. "A tutoring thing."

She grins. "That would be fantastic. Thank you, Iain."

"My pleasure, Rae. We could start at four o'clock today, if you're free."

"Yeah, I'm free."

"Let's meet at the campus museum. I can tutor you while we look at actual relics from that era."

Her grins gets even bigger. "I love museums."

A student who loves museums? I've never met anyone like her before. None of my pupils back in Scotland would've begged for extra work outside of class. But Rae honestly wants to learn more about my country's ancient past—and I honestly want to teach her about that.

We walk out of the classroom together, then go our separate ways. At four o'clock this afternoon, I will meet Rae for what might turn out to be the first of many tutoring sessions. She seems very keen on learning as much as possible. I don't even know what type of degree she's working to achieve, but I can tell she will excel at anything she tries.

For the rest of the day, until four p.m. arrives, I keep glancing at every clock I see. And I keep thinking about Rae Everhart.

Chapter Two

Rae

*I*ain MacTaggart is the hottest man on earth. Okay, maybe that's hyperbole, but I don't care. I love his pale blue eyes, his light brown hair, and that hook nose. He has the kind of rugged sex appeal that I never knew I'd love—but I do. I'd never met anyone like Iain until today. He's a real man, the kind every woman secretly dreams about but thinks she'll never find.

Oh God. I've turned into one of those girls I used to make fun of, the ones who drool over every guy they see.

Though I love my classes, my mind keeps wandering back to Dr. Iain MacTaggart. He's an amazing teacher, and I'm not just saying that because I have a crush on him. He makes ancient history exciting and entertaining, especially when he smiles with devilish humor right before he makes a joke. Yeah, Iain is electrifying.

My last class of the day ends at four o'clock, so I rush over to the museum and burst through the main doors before I realize I shouldn't be sprinting into the lobby. I probably shouldn't have sprinted all the way from the math building, either. Now I'm breathing hard and my cheeks feel warm, a sure sign of overexertion. So I guzzle water from the fountain in the lobby, splashing a little on my face to cool me down. Jeez, Iain will think I'm insane or asthmatic or something.

Once I feel capable of speech again, I shuffle backward, away from the fountain.

And bump into someone.

I whirl around—and my heart thuds. "Oh, Iain. God, I'm so sorry I crashed into you."

"No worries." He smiles and winks. "My kilt protected me."

I glance at his kilt with a touch of skepticism. "Plaid has some kind of magic powers to save you from falling down and cracking your skull?"

"Aye. I've cast a *sain* on my kilt, and my *sgian dubh* is also my *luirgean*."

I stare at him, blinking slowly. "Are you speaking another language?"

"Scots Gaelic. I said I've cast a charm on my kilt, and my knife is also my magic staff."

For some stupid reason, I glance down at his groin.

Iain hooks a finger under my chin and lifts until our gazes meet. "My magic staff is my knife, remember?"

He spoke those words in a sensual tone. Or maybe I imagined it was sexy because I'm so insanely attracted to him. Did he realize I was staring at his other 'magic staff'? Not that I can see it. Well, I did notice a slight bulge down there.

Snap out of it, girl.

Iain turns to the side and waves for me to go with him. "Let's start our tour of the Nackington Museum of History with the Paleolithic exhibits."

He leads the way until we enter the Hall of Prehistory, then he slows down just enough that we can walk side by side. People give us funny looks, but I think they're baffled by his clothing, not horrified that an undergraduate is hanging out with a professor. He doesn't look thirty-seven. But I have no idea what someone of that age is supposed to look like. Maybe everybody in their late thirties has the same youthfulness and virility as Iain.

I assumed tutoring would involve Iain talking and me listening. But no, we have conversations. He shares what he knows about each exhibit, then invites me to ask questions which in turn becomes a back and forth that's way more fun than sitting in class listening to a lecture. I love his voice. The man could recite the instructions for performing an appendectomy, and I'd still swoon.

Not that I have swooned. Maybe a little on the inside.

Once our tour has ended, Iain suggests we go to the museum's café to «have a piece.» Turns out that means to have a snack, preferably a sandwich. But when we get to the café, I want something sweet, and Iain goes along with that. We sit on either side of a round table and talk some more while we enjoy our cinnamon rolls. He tells me about Scotland and makes me laugh so hard that I accidentally spit out a glob of half-chewed pastry. It gets stuck on my chin.

Iain reaches over the table to wipe my chin off with a napkin.

None of the other guys I've known would do that. Iain is a gentleman on top of being hot and funny and surprisingly sweet. I've only slept with two boys in my life so far, and neither of them could hold a candle to the hot Scot. I'd love for him to kiss me, but he hasn't even tried to do that. Well, we are in a public place. I shouldn't want him to kiss me, but I can't help it. My body craves things I'd never even thought about until today. Naughty, dirty things.

Oh yeah, tonight I'll need to break out my vibrator and get off while fantasizing about Iain MacTaggart.

He insists on driving me to my apartment off-campus, since my old car died and I haven't bought a newer used vehicle yet, which means I've been taking the bus. But he says goodbye on the sidewalk just outside my building without touching me in any way, not even to shake my hand. I make my way up to the second floor of the complex and into the apartment I share with my roommate, Cecilia Bremner-Ashton aka Cece. I've only known her for a week, and I can't tell yet what kind of roomie she'll be. The girl seems kind of uptight and snobby. She's from a rich family, and her father is the university's largest donor. I learned that from Cece herself. She loves to brag about her family's wealth and status. I've heard rumors that the Bremner-Ashtons are powerful and almost like a Midwest mafia, but I've always dismissed that as gossip.

I do know, because Cece told me, that her parents insisted she should live on her own while attending Nackington University, rather than in their mansion. Maybe she annoys her family too.

I've just dropped my backpack on the living room table when Cece ambles out of her bedroom wearing her favorite silk teddy.

She yawns and stretches. "Where have you been? Thought your last class ended at four."

"I went to the campus museum."

Cece's lip curls. "Why would anybody do that? It's so…nerdy."

"That's me. I'm a nerd." I kick my shoes off and flop onto the sofa, resting my feet on the coffee table. "Did you eat yet? We could order pizza."

"Eat? It's only six thirty."

"Yeah, and I'm hungry. Aren't you?"

She rolls her eyes. "Nobody worth knowing eats dinner before eight o'clock."

I grew up in a completely different way than Cece did. My family ate breakfast at seven, lunch at noon, and dinner at six every day. I'm sure my snooty roommate thinks that schedule is hopelessly bourgeois. I mean, my family didn't even have a butler, much less a chef or a team of maids. Whether Cece's family is happy, I don't know. Mine isn't. Maybe my parents haven't been the happiest people, but I always believed they loved me and each other. Until this past summer. That's when I found out my parents had been separated for six months and had just filed for divorce. Mom didn't want to tell me what had happened, but I pushed until she confessed that Dad had been cheating on her for years. She finally couldn't take it anymore. I don't blame her. Dad hooked up with a slut two years older than I am, and now they're living together.

I know Mom loves me. But Dad… I don't want to think about him anymore, not today. I had a wonderful day at school and especially with Iain. So I'm going to focus on that and forget the bad stuff.

Grabbing the cordless phone off the end table, I start to dial a number. "I'm ordering pizza. Do you want some or not?"

Cece wrinkles her nose. "No thank you. I'm having dinner with a boy. At a restaurant. Five star."

Does Nackington, Wisconsin, have a five-star restaurant? I kind of doubt that. It's a small town, not a metropolis. If she wants to lie about where she's going and with whom, the girl can go for it. I don't care what she does. So I order a large ham pizza with extra cheese. Yeah, I'm going to eat the whole thing myself. I add a small dessert pizza to my order too. Pigging out sounds awesome right now. The time I spent with Iain today left me feeling invigorated and ravenous. Since I can't get it on with my professor, I'll stuff my face instead.

Cece and I lounge on the sofa to watch her favorite reality shows while I eat my meal. I can't stand these shows, but I'm trying to be a good roommate. If we're going to share an apartment for ten months, I need to learn the fine art of compromise.

My roomie doesn't seem to care about that.

During a commercial break, Cece turns toward me. Her smile seems kind of sneaky. "Soooo, I was looking out the window earlier, and I saw you and your new boy toy."

"Boy toy? I've never had one of those."

She leans toward me, seeming almost excited, and whispers, "The guy in plaid. Who is he?"

"One of my professors. He teaches Celtic history."

Her nose wrinkles. "Who wants to learn about that? Only dweebs like you."

"Uh-huh." Let her say what she wants. I don't care.

Cece seems even more excited now, like a dog that just found a juicy bone. "Are you screwing him? I mean, he's jalapeño hot. If you aren›t going to tap that, maybe I will.»

She is so not Iain's type. Right, like I know what kind of girls he prefers. But I just can't picture him screwing an uptight snob like Cece.

I roll my eyes to indicate the clock on the wall. "Shouldn't you get ready for your big five-star date?"

"Yep." She leaps off the sofa and trots toward the hallway. "Don't be jealous. I'm sure some pimply geek will snatch you up any day now."

Does she hate me? Or is she like this with everyone? I've never done anything to her, but I'm getting sick of her snide comments and nosiness.

Once my roomie leaves, I shut off the TV and go into my bedroom. I take care of my homework, then change into my nightie, intending to go to sleep. But I toss and turn, my mind racing with thoughts of Iain. When he had leaned in and said, in that rough and sexy voice, that his "magic staff" is his knife, I'd wanted to jump him right then. I swear I'm not that kind of girl. But Iain makes me feel so many things I've never experienced before. Maybe the reason I've only slept with two guys, and each time it was only once, is because I hadn't met a man like Iain MacTaggart.

I know I'll never get any sleep unless I can do something about the wet ache between my thighs. So I yank the nightstand drawer open and pull out my vibrator.

Shimmying under the sheets, I lift my nightie's hem up to my hips and spread my legs. Then I slide the vibrator between my folds and switch it on, using the lowest setting. I stroke it up and down my cleft while I grow slicker and my breaths quicken. I imagine Iain kneeling between my thighs, naked and aroused, whispering filthy things to me, and I can't stop myself from cranking the vibrator up a few notches.

Iain. Naked. Thrusting into me.

My back arches, and I thrust the vibrator into me, pushing it deep and hard while I fist my free hand in the sheets and start panting. But I need that finger, so I release the sheets and rub my clit furiously, fucking myself with the vibrator so hard that I hear a wet sucking sound every time I pull it out and plunge it back inside me. I can't breathe, can't stop, can't slow down, need to come so badly. The bed starts to creak, my body curls in on itself, and I'm teetering on the edge of an invisible cliff, about to tumble off it and free-fall into bliss. The climax hits me so hard that the breath I'd been holding explodes out of me, and strangled cries spill from my lips while wave after wave pulsates inside me. I pull out the vibrator and push my fingers inside to feel the contractions, which makes me come harder.

I lie here limp and tangled up in the sheets for I don't know how long. My chest heaves. My ears ring. Sweat drizzles down my temples. The vibrator still lies nestled between my thighs. Once I've caught my breath, I flip the sheets off me. Grabbing the vibrator, I go into the bathroom to wash it off and pee. I hadn't really needed to go until I started masturbating, then the urge to pee grew stronger in time with my escalating need to come. Once I've relieved myself, I crawl back into bed.

And fall asleep in seconds.

Yeah, Iain MacTaggart gives me fantastic orgasms—and he's not even in the room with me.

<h1>Chapter Three</h1>

Iain

Last night, I dreamed of Rae. I wish I could claim those dreams were sweet and involved nothing more erotic than hand-holding. But no, the fantasies that assailed me while I slept involved Rae naked and writhing beneath me. Bloody hell, I won't get a good night's sleep until the semester is over and I won't need to see the lass anymore. When we met yesterday morning, Rae had seemed almost shy and definitely uncomfortable with talking to me. By late afternoon, when I saw her again, she had recovered her self-confidence. I enjoyed giving her a tour of the museum's Paleolithic exhibits more than I should have.

Why had I suggested we do that? I need to avoid Rae, not spend more time with her.

Just as I'm finishing my breakfast, alone in my flat, my mobile phone rings. I answer without checking who might be calling.

"Iain, *gràidh*, how are ye settling in?" my mother asks. "America is so far from home."

"Aye, I know that. Donnae worry, Ma, I'm doing fine here." Meeting Rae has been a joy and a catastrophe. No, not a catastrophe. But being with her does test my willpower. "How are things at home? Is Da keeping out of trouble?"

"Oh, aye. Angus is well."

"What about you?"

"Nothing to complain about. Are ye sure nothing's fashing ye?"

I can't tell my mother the truth. She wouldn't understand why I'm "tutoring" a college senior, a beautiful one who makes me want to do things that would get me sacked. So I stick with banal subjects. "Nothing is fashing me, Ma. I taught my first classes yesterday, and everything went well. The students needed a wee bit of time to get used to me, but then they were highly engaged."

"Ye mean they liked ye."

"Aye, that's what I mean." I glance at the clock on the microwave oven. "I need to go. More classes to teach today."

We say goodbye, and I dress for my second day at Nackington. This time, I wear normal clothes that won't make my students ask why I'm wearing a plaid skirt. I don't care what they think, but I never intended to wear the kilt all the time. I walk out of my flat dressed in trousers and a button-down shirt, though I leave the top button undone to avoid seeming stuffy. As I stride across the campus to reach the humanities building, lasses whistle at me. Cannae help smirking at that. I was never this popular with women back in Loch Fairbairn, my hometown in Scotland. Aye, the lasses liked me. But they did not whistle and wink at me while smiling suggestively.

I don't remember university being like this when I'd been a student.

As I push through the doors into the humanities building, I bump into Rae. Literally.

She smiles and bites her lip. "Sorry, Iain. I didn't see you coming."

"The doors are tinted to reduce glare. So it's easy not to notice what's on the other side."

"You know the doors are tinted?" Her smile broadens. "You must be the only professor on campus who knows things like that."

"I'd wager the janitorial staff know. They clean the doors and windows, after all." Why the bloody hell am I havering about tinted glass? I've turned into an eejit, all because I bumped into Rae. "Well, I should get to class."

"Me too."

We brush past each other, then both glance back at the same time.

And I become worse than an eejit. I mutate into a dafty and ask, "Would you like to have another tutoring session at the museum? We could visit the Egyptian exhibits this time."

Her expression lights up. "Oh, I love ancient Egypt. Yeah, let's do that."

"Four o'clock again?"

"Sure." She grins. "Can't wait to see y—Um, see that exhibit."

Had she been about to say she can't wait to see me again? I'm a mature man, not a randy laddie, but I suddenly feel like a teenager again. Rae does this to me. And I can't wait to see that "exhibit" again too.

This morning, my first class is about archaeology in the UK. I love this topic, and I do my best to make it interesting and entertaining for my students, but thoughts of Rae keep slipping into my mind unbidden. Maybe I enjoy those thoughts a wee bit too much, but I've decided not to chastise myself for that. Thoughts can't be controlled. I learned that from a lass I dated during my doctoral program. She was training to be a school counselor, so she studied a lot about psychology.

Now that I've given myself permission to think of Rae, I feel more relaxed. The rest of the day seems to go by swiftly, and I'm glad for that. Not because I know I'll see Rae in forty-five minutes. Teaching can be tiring, and a museum visit will be relaxing.

I arrive at the museum to find Rae is already there, waiting in the lobby. She smiles when she sees me pushing through the doors. I smile and wave to her. She trots up to me, and I lay a hand on the small of her back as we meander through the museum to find the Egyptian gallery. Laying a hand on her was a reflex. I shouldn't have done that, I suppose, but it's a show of respect for women in general, not a suggestion that I want to shag her. Still, I pull my hand away as we enter the Hall of Egyptian History.

We amble through the exhibits, but I have trouble finding anything to say that she doesn't already know. Rae clearly has a deep interest in ancient Egypt. Since I can't impress her with my knowledge of the subject, I take a different tack.

"Do you know what the name Hatshepsut means?" I ask.

Rae angles her head to look at me. "No. Do you? I know she ascended the throne to become pharaoh in the Eighteenth Dynasty."

"Aye. But Hatshepsut means 'foremost of noble women.' She portrayed herself as a man in depictions on temple walls."

"It's cool that you know stuff like that."

"Name meanings are of great interest to me." I suddenly realize I've laid a hand on her back again and pull it away. "Sorry. I should've asked permission before doing that."

"Doing what?"

"Touching you."

She stares at me for a few seconds, her eyes wide and her expression blank. Then she laughs gently. "You mean when you put your hand on my back. I'm not annoyed about that. I think it's kind of sweet that you do that."

"Kind of sweet? You can tell me I'm a bloody erse for doing that. I won't be upset."

"What is an 'erse'?"

I exhale a long sigh. "An ass."

Rae shakes her head slowly while her lips curve into a soft smile. She places a hand on my cheek. "You are not an ass, Iain. I love that you're an old-fashioned gentleman. Most guys these days don't hold doors open for women, and they don't even bother to wait for a girl to catch up to them. They just hustle off."

"Are all American men such erseholes?"

"No. Just most of them." She pats my cheek. "But not you."

"Well, at least I've done better than most men in this country. It takes an old man like me to treat a woman like a lady."

"Old man?" She folds her arms over her chest and scans me up and down. "You don't look ancient. Mind if I ask how old you are? Since you mentioned age."

"Donnae mind at all. I'm thirty-seven."

"Really?" She feigns shock. "You *are* an old fogy. Should I get one of those electric buggies for you? The kind they have in grocery stores. Don't want you to have a stroke."

"Very funny, ye cheeky lass." I pretend to study her intently, tapping a finger on my chin. "How old are you? Maybe you're nothing but a bairn."

"A what?" she says with a laugh.

"It means a child. Scots call them bairns."

"You're in America now. Try using our words." She bumps her shoulder into me. "You might like it."

"Ah, perhaps." I glance at her sideways. "Since I'm a gentleman, I won't point out that you never told me your age."

"I'm not sensitive about that. I'm twenty-one, but I'll turn twenty-two in November."

Despite the fact I'd guessed as much, I still feel a chill rush over my skin when I hear her confirm it. I am flirting with a virtual bairn. Our fifteen-year age difference means I have become a dirty old man, the sort who seduces innocent young lasses and uses them for his own pleasure. Not that I've done anything of the sort with

Rae. Not yet. I want her, but I refuse to become just another pathetic sod who chases after young lasses.

Rae lifts her brows at me. "You seem shocked."

"No, I—It's not your age that fashes me. It's mine."

"Your age bothers you, but mine doesn't. That makes no sense."

"Aye." I wince and scratch my cheek. "But that's how I feel."

"So, you don't want to be my tutor anymore."

"I didn't say that." I should say it, but I can't make myself speak the words. Spending time with her feels like a breath of fresh air. After the troubles I'd endured back home, I need to breathe in every bit of warmth and sweetness she can give me. But… "We probably shouldn't see each other outside of class anymore."

"Why? It's not illegal to be friends with a student. Is it?"

"Not illegal, no. But I'm not sure about the university's code of ethics."

Her shoulders flag, and she looks down at the floor. "Okay. I understand."

But she sounds despondent. *Bod an Donais.* How am I meant to handle this situation? I suggested tutoring her, and now I've backed out and made the lass unhappy.

Rae lifts her gaze to mine, her eyes shining with the start of tears. "Guess I should go now. Sorry to have been so much trouble. It's just that I don't have any real friends and—Never mind."

The hitch in her voice makes my throat tighten.

She turns to walk away.

And I grasp her arm. "Donnae leave, Rae. I'm an erse for sure, and I overreacted to finding out how young you are. But I don't want to stop tutoring you."

She glances back at me with her glistening eyes. "Are you sure?"

"Yes, I'm sure. Let's enjoy the rest of the exhibits in this hall. If you still want to do that."

"Of course I do." She wipes at her eyes, and that lovely smile returns. "Let's go."

Maybe I've made a terrible mistake, but I don't care. How can I push away a sweet lass who only wants to spend time with me? I did suggest we do this. It's not her fault. No, I'm the dirty old man who lured an innocent young woman into my web. But I will behave like a professor and treat her like a student, no matter how much I want to kiss her and… No, I won't finish that thought.

Rae and I browse the rest of the Hall of Egyptian History, and she asks me what the names of pharaohs and officials mean. She thinks it's "adorable" that I'm fascinated by names and what they signify. Rae also announces that I am "so unbelievably sweet," though I don't understand why. She claims it's because I treat her with respect and haven't tried to "scam" my way into her "pants."

Do American college lads do things like that? They sound like bastards to me, and I can't imagine why any women want to sleep with them. I also can't believe she wants to tell me about those erses. I suppose it means she trusts me.

"Sometimes the bastards are the best at seducing a girl," Rae informs me when I voice my confusion over how American men behave. She hunches her shoulders and hugs herself. "I fell for it once. My sophomore year. I met this guy who seemed like he really wanted to get to know me better, and he was a pro at charming the pants off me. After we, you know, did the deed, he just vanished. A week later, I saw him making out with another girl. God, I was such an idiot."

"You are not stupid, Rae. Men like that deserve to be skelped. That means they should be smacked about."

She wraps her arms around herself more tightly. "Can't believe I told you all of that. You must be wishing you'd let me run away."

"No, I would never wish for that." We've stopped just outside the exit of the Egyptian exhibit hall. I brush a thumb over her chin. "Donnae waste any more time thinking about that wee shit. He's not worth your time."

"Thank you, Iain." She drops her arms and takes a deep breath, blowing it out. "I'm glad we're friends."

"So am I."

But for how long can I pretend I don't want more?

Chapter Four

Rae

Last night, I had a terrible dream that left me wondering if everything I've done recently had been a mistake. The things I'd done with Iain, that is. I dreamed that my father came for a visit and met Iain, and suddenly Iain realized I'm just a twenty-one-year-old student, and he told me I'm pathetic, then laughed at me. My dad made a joke about how young and stupid I am, believing that a grown man could want me. Iain laughed so hard at the joke that his eyes watered, and then both men pointed at me and laughed even harder.

Okay, it was a stress dream. I know that. But I can't shake the feeling that Iain really will realize I'm too young for a man like him to even hang out with me, much less…do things we can't do anyway. Because I'm a student. Because he's a professor.

All week long, I'd spent my late afternoons with Iain MacTaggart, perusing the campus museum and listening in rapt fascination while he explained the history and significance of every exhibit. Whenever I asked a question, he would smile and call me a "clever lass," then give me his answer. Twice he called me "sunshine," which made my cheeks feel as warm as the sun. I love that nickname. But why does he have to be so sexy? Why does his voice have to sound so rumbly and hot? I want to throw myself at him and crush my mouth to his.

But I can never do that. *Rats.*

At least I finally bought a car. No more bus rides that rattle my teeth. I hate that my mom paid for my new ride, but she insists I should not work while getting my degree. "Concentrate on your studies," she always tells me. I think she mostly feels bad that my father has zero interest in me.

Since it's the weekend now, I feel like doing something fun. By myself. I don't have any friends yet—unless I want to invite my roomie to go shopping with me. No, I don't think I'll do that. I doubt doing anything with Cece would qualify as a fun excursion. That means I'll explore the town of Nackington alone. Well, I've been alone here for three years. It's nothing new. Still, I miss my mom and the way we used to go on shopping trips together, though we rarely bought much. We just liked hanging out. But I won't see Mom again until Christmas break.

Cece is still asleep, so I leave a note telling her I'll be gone all day. I have no idea if she cares, but it seemed like the polite thing to do.

While I'm getting dressed for my day of solo shopping, my cell phone rings. I answer without glancing at the screen, engrossed in selecting the right pair of tennies. "Hello?"

"Guten Morgen, Rae."

My heart stutters. I swear it does. My pulse accelerates too, and for some reason, I lick my lips. "Good morning, Iain. How did you get my cell number?"

"You gave it to me yesterday. Remember?"

"Oh, yeah. I forgot."

He clears his throat, and his deep voice sounds a touch hesitant when he speaks again. "I was, ah, wondering if you have plans today."

"No, I don't." If he wants to take me somewhere, I will drop all my plans instantly, if I'd had any. Yeah, I'm pathetic. Especially since I want him to "take me" in the dirty sense of the phrase.

"Would you like to explore the town with me? I've only just moved here, but you must know the area."

"Actually, I don't. For the past three years, I've stuck to the places I needed to go—the campus, my apartment complex, the grocery store, stuff like that."

He says nothing for several seconds, then speaks in a deeper, sexier tone. "Then we can explore together."

Damn, Iain makes that statement sound so hot. But I doubt he meant it in a naughty way.

"Sure," I say. "Let's explore."

"I'll pick you up in an hour." He pauses. "But, ah, you'll need to give me your address. I forgot to write it down when I drove you home."

After I recite the address, we say goodbye—and I feel a ridiculous urge to change my clothes, the stuff I just put on five minutes ago. But I resist that impulse. I look fine. And if Iain doesn't like my outfit, that's tough.

Will he wear his kilt?

I roll my eyes at myself. Yeah, sure, because everybody dresses like a medieval Scot when they go sightseeing.

He picks me up in his car, and we spend several minutes just sitting in the parking lot while we discuss where we want to go. I had gotten online while I waited for him and looked up where the shops are in this town, as well as touristy sites. We finally agree on shopping first. Yeah, a man actually wants to do that. When I tease Iain about it, he smiles and calls me a "cheeky lass."

We visit several shops but don't buy anything, not until we walk into a novelty store that offers all kinds of silly gifts. Iain finds a T-shirt that he insists on buying for me. It features an ancient Egyptian design reminiscent of hieroglyphs with the words Nackington Museum of History printed on it.

"Thank you, Iain," I say while bouncing on my toes. "I love my new T-shirt."

His lips kink up at the corners. "I love how much you love that shirt."

I grin. "Maybe I should pick a T-shirt for you."

"Go on. I could use something new."

Wow. No other guy I've known would want a girl to pick out clothing for him. I hunt through the racks of T-shirts in search of one that seems appropriate for him. But I can't find anything that feels right. So I tell Iain to stay put while I scurry over to the checkout counter and ask the clerk if it's possible to get a custom-made shirt. He tells me, yeah, they can do it. I explain what I want, and the nice young man rushes into a back room to fulfill my order.

I can see Iain standing among the racks, watching me with a puzzled expression.

While I wait for my order, I trot back to Iain. We check out the racks of postcards, and he chooses a few to send home to his parents and some of his cousins.

"Are you an only child?" I ask.

"I am. But I have many cousins who are like brothers and sisters to me."

"Cool. I'm an only child too, but I don't have any cousins."

The store clerk has just emerged from the back room, and he waves for me to meet him at the checkout counter. Iain moves to follow me, but I slap a hand on his chest. "Wait here. It won't be a surprise if you see it before I'm ready to give it to you."

He smirks. "I've never seen you bossy before. It suits you."

I get a delicious glow in my chest when he says that, and when he smirks that way. I can feel the warmth and firmness of his chest too, thanks to my hand touching him. But I tear my hand away and jog over to the counter. The clerk has already put the gift into a bag, so I pay and take my surprise back to Iain.

He reaches for the bag.

I snatch it away. "Uh-uh-uh. Not until we're in the car."

The Scot makes a face that seems like a cross between annoyance and humor.

"Still like my bossiness?" I ask, bumping my shoulder into his.

"Aye, I still do."

We exit the shop and start down the sidewalk toward Iain's car, which is parked two blocks away on a cross street. As we pass another shop, Iain stops and moves to go inside, reaching for the door handle.

"Sure you want to do that?" I ask. Then I point to the sign above the door. "Did you read that?"

He glances up. His eyes go wide briefly, then he turns away and clears his throat. "Let's bypass this shop."

Yeah, I figured he hadn't noticed the sign. It says, "Adult Novelties."

We walk side-by-side back to his car, and he opens the passenger door for me like the gentleman he is. Once he's climbed into the driver's seat, he holds out his hand to me, palm up. "My gift now, please."

"Kinda anxious to find out what it is, huh?"

"Aye." He leans closer and speaks in a softer, deeper voice. "So give it to me now, Rae."

A thrill races over my skin whenever he uses that tone of voice. I hand him the bag.

He reaches inside to pull out his gift, unfolding the T-shirt so he can see the images and words printed on it. And he chuckles. "Real men wear plaid skirts? And there's a cartoon of a Scotsman dancing about in his kilt."

"Yeah. That seemed like the right gift for you."

"But you've never seen me dance."

"That was the best Scottish image the store clerk could find. I don't actually expect you to dance."

"Good. Because I have two left feet." He studies the shirt, and his lips curl up at the corners. "Thank you, Rae. It's a cheeky but thoughtful surprise."

"You're welcome."

He whips his shirt off.

And I gape at him. Shirtless Iain? I've never seen him do anything more salacious than exposing his calves when he wore his kilt. But now he sits there topless, and I get my first look at his muscular chest. Fine brown hairs pepper his skin. I want to trace the lines of his pecs and abs with my tongue, and the thought makes me suddenly feel warm and slick in places that are not appropriate right now.

Then Iain pulls on his new shirt, depriving me of the view of his gorgeous bod. But the fabric clings to his chest and biceps, which does not help me recover from seeing his naked torso.

"Fits just right," he says. "How did you know my size?"

"I guessed."

He glances at me sideways with a sneaky glint in his eyes. "Don't you want to try on your new shirt?"

A panicked laugh bursts out of me. "In your dreams, Dr. MacTaggart."

He wags his eyebrows, then winks. Starting up the engine, he pulls out onto the street. "Where should we go next?"

"I'm starving. Let's go eat."

"Aye, it is lunchtime."

We drive around for ten minutes until we spot a Mexican restaurant. Turns out we both love that kind of food. Who knew a small town in Wisconsin would have Mexican cuisine? But I'm glad we found this place. The food is amazing, and we have lots of fun talking while we share a bowl of queso. When the main course arrives, I devour my enchilada in a very unladylike fashion. Iain seems to think the way I eat is entertaining. Well, I am shoveling it in like I haven't tasted food in a month.

After devouring another loaded forkful, I wipe my mouth and give Iain a sheepish smile. "Sorry. I don't usually eat this way, but I am so hungry right now. Must be all that exercise we got while we were exploring the shops."

"Donnae care how you eat, sunshine. I like a woman who isn't afraid to show her passion for food."

Iain is the most unusual man of any age that I've ever met. I've never been the type to eat like a bird so I won't offend anyone, and I love that he appreciates my enthusiasm for food.

After lunch, we take a drive out of town to admire the scenery and the fields full of dairy cows. Iain teases me about my statement that cows are cute, and I respond by saying something that seems innocuous until the words come out. "Well, you and the cows have something in common. I think you're pretty cute too."

He jerks his head to look at me. Behind his sunglasses, I can't tell if his eyes are wide. But I think they must be. *Duh, Rae, you just flirted with him.* Accidentally, but yeah.

I swerve my attention to the windshield. "I just meant, um, that you, uh…"

"Relax, Rae. I know you didn't mean that the way it sounded."

Actually, I did. But I hadn't meant to say it out loud. "Maybe we should head back to town and my apartment. It's getting late, and I have homework to do."

"Let me buy you dinner first."

He's gazing out the windshield again, one hand on the steering wheel, seeming quite casual now. Guess the shock of my silly statement has worn off.

"I don't know, Iain."

"Please, Rae."

How can I say no to a sexy man who wants to buy me dinner? Other guys expect me to pay for my half of any meal. Of course, he might not have meant that he intends to pay for the whole thing.

"I want to treat you to dinner," he says. "You work hard, and you deserve it."

Wow. He does want to pay. "Okay. Thank you, Iain."

"My pleasure."

Oh, I wish he would never say that word again—unless he develops a squeaky voice. That smoky timbre coupled with his Scottish brogue makes me want to rip that T-shirt off his body.

How will I survive being friends with Iain?

Chapter Five

Iain

Two days ago, I treated Rae to dinner at an expensive restaurant. I hadn't known how pricey the food would be until I saw the menu, but I wasn't going to back out at the last minute. Rae deserves the best. She seems to take her studies too seriously, working harder than any student I've ever met. I have a feeling her home life might have something to do with that. But it's not my place to ask her about that, especially since I would feel obliged to explain what my life has been like.

I do not want to discuss that.

No, I would much rather enjoy spending as much time with her as I can. We're mates. Not…anything more. But I had noticed her expression when I removed my shirt in the car. She looked like a woman who wanted to do more than have a friendly conversation. *Bod an Donais*, I want to fuck her more than I've ever wanted to fuck any woman.

At least I won't see Rae as often this week. We finished her tutoring sessions at the museum, so I have no reasonable excuse for trying to see her again outside of class. All week, I avoid looking at her, though the fact she sits in the third row directly in front of my lectern doesn't help. Whenever she asks a question, I answer quickly and move on. I might be overcompensating. Never before have I become enamored of a student. But Rae is not an average undergraduate, and my feelings for her intensify every time I learn something new about the lass.

She eats with gusto. I love that. She gave me a silly T-shirt, and I love that too. Rae called me "pretty cute," and I even loved that. Aye, staying away from her seems like the safest option to prevent what I sense is coming.

If I keep seeing Rae, I will fall for her. Maybe I already have done.

After a week of trying to ignore the sweet lass, I go home and try to think of something, anything, I can do to take my mind off Rae. I could ring my parents, but I'm afraid of what I'll find out if I do. I love my father, but he has bad habits that I've had no luck talking him out of, no matter what I try. Bad habits? Aye, that's the polite term for it. He doesn't mean to do things he shouldn't, but he feels it's the only way to stay afloat.

So no, I won't ring my parents.

I can't do any work since I finalized all my lesson plans yesterday and graded all the papers then too. Maybe I could come up with some visual aids to accompany my lectures for next week. But making a slideshow doesn't take long, which leaves me with nothing to do but watch television. Cannae stand that for long. So I ring my cousin Lachlan, and we chat to each other for a while. He tells me humorous stories about what other MacTaggarts have done. Aye, we have an unusually large and unusually boisterous family. I miss them, but I love being here with Rae. *Mhac na galla.* I am not *with* Rae. Why can't I stop thinking about the lass?

By evening, I've had enough of struggling not to think about Rae. Maybe I can temper my desire for her in another way. Avoiding the lass hasn't worked. I need to take a radical approach. It's the only way I might get her out of my head. I will see Rae again on Monday, but by then, I'll have gotten this lust out of my system.

I step into the shower, turn on the water, and let the steam swirl around me. Then I shut my eyes and picture Rae. She's naked. Lying beneath me on a bed. I have no idea what her body looks like, but I have a vivid imagination when it comes to that bonnie, sexy lass. While I envision fucking her, complete with the sound effects of her moans and the wet slapping as our bodies collide, my cock begins to stiffen. I stroke it slowly while I switch my fantasy to something else. I imagine Rae kneeling before me, taking my length into her mouth, pumping me with one hand while she sucks and licks.

A deep groan rumbles out of me. I let my head fall back and keep one hand on the wall while I pump my iron-hard erection. Rae. Her mouth. My *slat*. Her soft lips enveloping me and her velvety tongue devouring me.

"Fuck," I groan while I pump faster.

Rae's mouth around me. Her erotic moans and grunts.

My body stiffens. I know I'll come soon, but I donnae want this fantasy to end yet. So I slap both palms on the wall and picture myself hoisting Rae off her knees to toss her onto the bed. She spreads her legs as if begging me to take her. I leap onto the bed and do what we both want, shagging the lass like a madman.

And my cock throbs.

I grasp my *slat* and pump it hard and fast, but I stop the second I feel like I might come. No, I'm still not ready for this to end yet. If I cannae shag Rae, I can at least pretend I've done it for as long as I can stand the pressure. It grows so intense that I cannae breathe, and my ears start to ring. I release my *slat* and slap my hands on the wall again, my fingers curling. My ears aren't ringing anymore, but I cannae catch my breath, and I feel like I my entire body might explode.

No more waiting.

While I picture myself fucking Rae so hard the mattress bounces, I grip my cock and pump it. The climax barrels down my spine so fast that I've barely finished my fantasy when I come, releasing everything I have while I shout and groan and finally sag against the wall.

Bloody hell. I've never experienced anything like that.

Have I slaked my lust for Rae? I sleep well that night. But my morning erection feels stiffer than usual, and I need to wank off again to relieve the pressure. Oh, aye, by the end of this semester, I will lose my mind for sure. Will I see Rae after the current class ends? She won't take another of my courses. Will she? If Rae does that, I might have a heart attack.

But I cannae stand the thought of not seeing her anymore.

I manage to arrive for my Friday morning classes without terrifying the students because my rock-hard *slat* finally cooperated with me, returning to a normal, family friendly state. I feel relatively normal as I set up the lectern and arrange my notes on it, then set up the projector and screen so I can share slides too.

Rae walks into the room and smiles at me. "Good morning, Iain."

And I drop the projector. It smacks down on the floor, scattering my slides. I hiss Gaelic curses under my breath as I struggle to reassemble things.

Rae kneels beside me to help.

I know she's trying to be helpful, but having her so close makes me flash back to what I did last night in the shower—while fantasizing about her. Now I'm staring at the lass as if she's just disrobed.

"Are you okay?" she asks as she hands me a disorganized pile of slides. "I can help you get the projector fixed."

"No, no, that's not necessary." I snatch the slides from her a wee bit too quickly, and her eyes flare wide. "Take your seat, Rae, please. I can deal with this."

"Well, if you're sure."

"Aye, I'm sure."

She rises but bends over to pick up a few slides that skidded under the lectern. And I'm staring at her erse which lies inches from my face. Just when I manage to tear my focus away from those cheeks, the lass turns toward me while still bent over and proffers the slides. "You missed these."

Now I'm staring at her tits, thanks to her blouse that sagged away from her chest.

I grab the slides. "Thank you. Now please go sit down."

Aye, I growled those words. Rae jerks her head back as if I surprised her, but then she rises and heads for her assigned seat. Thank the stars. If she had stayed in that position for much longer, I would've suffered a stroke.

The rest of the students begin to arrive, and I'm too busy fixing the slides to notice Rae anymore. I manage to teach the class without any further calamities and without gawping at Rae's body. I donnae know what's come over me. I never leer at women. I treat them with respect, which is what I need to do with Rae. She's no different from any other lass.

Of course she's different. I shouldn't deny that, but I also need to stop thinking of her in a sexual way. Aye, because it's so bloody easy to stop wanting a woman. We can be just mates, if I can get my lust under control. I had taught myself how to master my emotions and my desires, but moving to another country and starting a new job has thrown me off balance. Then I met Rae, and my Zen attitude flew out the windae.

All I need to do is recapture that state of mind.

That night, I meditate—my way. I don't do that "ohm" bollocks or try to turn my body into a pretzel. My version of Zen involves lying in bed, in the nude and with the sheets pulled back, while I shut my eyes and find my center. Maybe that is partially meditation. It's the Iain MacTaggart version. I often fall asleep while doing this, and tonight is no different.

I awaken in the morning feeling centered and calm, ready to face the day. But it's Saturday, so I have no classes to teach and no paperwork to tackle either. I feel bad about the way I snarled at Rae, so I decide to apologize to her. With my psyche centered and my cock once again cooperating, I dial Rae's number on my mobile.

She picks up on the second ring. "Iain?"

"Aye, it's me. How did you know?"

"I've got your number programmed into my phone, so it shows your name whenever you call."

"Oh, aye. That makes sense. I never think of doing that with my mobile."

She laughs, but it's affectionate and sweet. "You're kind of a Luddite, huh? It's cute."

"I'm not a Luddite. I just don't care about programming my mobile or playing games on it."

"Yeah, I'm not into games either. I get a headache from that stuff."

I clear my throat. "Rae, I'm sorry for the way I behaved yesterday."

"What did you do? I don't remember anything."

"Ye donnae remember me snarling at you?"

She hesitates, then laughs again. "Oh, that. I wasn't offended. You dropped all your slides, and anybody would get annoyed about that."

"Not me. I do not like feeling that way."

"Don't worry about it."

I shove my free hand into my hair and wince, though she can't see that. "Do you accept my apology, then?"

"Yes, Iain, I do. You are hereby forgiven."

"Thank you." I fidget in my chair, another thing she can't see. Thank heavens. "I wondered if you'd like to go sightseeing with me. I found something I think you'll appreciate since you love ancient history."

"Sure. Sounds like fun."

"I'll pick you up in an hour."

"Perfect." She hesitates again. "Um, how should I dress? Not knowing what kind of ancient thing it is, I'm not sure what clothes to wear."

"Dress for a casual walking hike."

She snorts as if she's trying not to laugh at me. "Casual walking hike? Is that a real thing? I thought people either walked or hiked. Never heard of doing both at once. Aren't those, like, the same thing?"

Fortunately, I had already reasserted my Zen attitude, so I'm not the least fashed by her teasing. "Dress for a walk, then."

"Gotcha. I'll be ready in an hour."

We say goodbye, and I change into appropriate clothes. As I head out the door, I realize I'm smiling. I always enjoy seeing Rae, but I am no longer in any danger of developing a problem that will expose my attraction to her. No, my *slat* will behave.

I whistle a tune as I climb into the car and keep on whistling during the drive to Rae's apartment building.

Chapter Six

Rae

"When are you planning to tell me where we're going?" I ask. "I've had this blindfold over my eyes for at least ten minutes, thanks to your bossy command that I wear it because you 'cannae' trust me not to peek. I so do not appreciate that, by the way. I thought we were friends."

"Aye, we are." He pats my knee. "But I want this to be a surprise. And you were peeking. That's why I brought a handkerchief—so I could blindfold you in case you couldn't stop yourself."

"Hmm. I think you're full of it. I mean, you seem so calm most of the time, almost like the Buddha, but then you order me to get in the car and obey your commands."

"I never said that. And it wasn't an order. It was a fervent suggestion."

"Uh-huh." I want to roll my eyes, but he wouldn't be able to see that, so I don't bother. The sarcasm in my voice will accomplish the same thing. "If it's a suggestion, then I can take this blindfold off now, hey?"

"No, ye cannae."

Maybe I secretly love it when he gets bossy, and maybe I also secretly love all his Scottishisms and his accent and basically everything about him. But a girl needs to assert herself sometimes, just so the man she's with knows she is not a pushover.

Am I with Iain? Only in the sense that we're in the same car at the same time. It's not like we're dating. Friendship only. But more and more lately, I have trouble remembering that. We've never kissed or embraced, never even held hands, much less had sex. I want all of that, but I understand we can't go there. Iain only ever touches me in casual, chaste ways, like when he lays a hand on my back as we walk through a door. Occasionally, he touches my chin. But that doesn't feel romantic or sexual either. It seems more like a friendly gesture of affection.

I have so much affection for him. The crush I've had since the day we met has grown into something more. I still can't figure out exactly what it is. I know only that I love spending time with him and I feel so good when we're together.

The car begins to slow down. I know this because I can feel the gradual deceleration.

"All right," Iain says. "You can look now."

I whip the blindfold off and blink rapidly until my eyes adjust to the brightness of the sun. As Iain steers the car off the road and onto a paved driveway, I see a sign that explains where we are.

And I hop up and down in my seat while softly clapping. "Aztalan? Wow, Iain, this is amazing. I've heard of this place, but I've never had the chance to come here." I plant quick kisses on his cheek in between saying, "Thank you, thank you, thank you."

He chuckles while pulling the car into a parking space. "Don't think I've ever met another woman who gets excited about Pre-Columbian monuments."

"You know history is my thing. Of course I'm excited." I throw my door open and leap out, then lean in to grin at him. "Hurry up, Dr. MacTaggart."

He smiles and shakes his head, but he gets out of the car.

I race over to the historical marker, a brown sign held up by worn wooden posts, while Iain hurries to catch up. He stops beside me. I bounce on my toes as I read the words on the sign. "Wow, people lived here way before the Pilgrims set foot on this continent. How amazing is that? I've been to Cahokia, but this is my first time at Aztalan."

"Cahokia? I haven't heard of that place."

"Oh, it's really cool. Cahokia is in Illinois, right next to St. Louis. In fact, you can see the Gateway Arch from the top of Monks Mound."

"So, it's a mound site just like Aztalan."

"Yep."

He studies the sign, but I can tell he's pretending to read it because he keeps glancing at me furtively without moving his head. "Maybe we can visit Cahokia together sometime."

"I would love that."

We walk side by side across the parking lot and make our way toward the monument we came here to see—the rounded, rectangular mound backed by a strange-looking wooden barricade. The mound has two levels, each with an essentially flat surface, and stairs that lead up to the summit. The steps were probably added later to make it easier for tourists to ascend the mound. Iain and I stand here enjoying the panoramic view of the surroundings and the blue sky.

Since it's October, we both wore light jackets. I still feel a slight chill, though, thanks to a cool breeze. Stuffing my hands under my armpits doesn't help much.

Iain removes his leather jacket and drapes it over my shoulders. "You seemed a wee bit chilled."

"Thank you." I snuggle into the jacket. "You really are a gentleman, Iain."

"It's good manners, that's all."

While we explore the site, we chat about what life might have been like for the ancient people who lived here, and Iain suggests I might want to visit Scotland sometime to see the ancient cairns and standing stones there. I've learned about them in his class, but seeing those monuments in person would be incredible.

Especially if Iain served as my tour guide.

By the time we return to Nackington, I'm wiped out. Iain drops me off at my apartment building, and though he wants to walk me to my door, I tell him not to bother. He looks as tired as I feel. When he says "good night, sunshine" in that Scottish brogue, I want to crawl onto his lap and curl up to sleep there. Instead, I go into my apartment and barely manage to change into my nightie before I pass out on the bed.

I don't mind being exhausted when it happens because I spent an entire day with Iain.

The next morning, I'm sitting on the sofa with my laptop computer browsing information about Aztalan when my roommate finally emerges from her cocoon. It's ten thirty. But Cece yawns and stretches like she just crawled out of bed. I guess I'm the only college student who gets up before eight on weekends. Jeez, most of my fellow students don't get up that early on weekdays either, unless they have an eight o'clock class. Cece complains about having to go to class at ten.

My roomie drops onto the armchair across from me, propping her feet on the coffee table. "You're such a geek. Nobody gets up as early as you do, not during the week and definitely not on a weekend. But you do it so you can study."

Her lip curls faintly when she says the word study.

I love to learn. Even when I'm done with college, I will continue investigating everything that fascinates me. Cece will probably toss her diploma into the garbage can, then head for the nearest bar to get drunk. I don't hate her, but I can't understand the girl. She looks down her nose at everybody and skates by with a C plus GPA. I know that because she likes to brag about her GPA by saying "C plus means cool to the extreme."

"Good morning to you too, Cece." I close my laptop's lid and set it on the cushion beside me. "I made French toast, and there are leftovers if you want to eat it."

"Okay." She pushes up out of her chair and sashays toward the kitchen. "French toast is better than what you usually eat. Just looking at oatmeal makes me want to barf. I mean, that crap even looks like vomit."

Whenever she says snooty things, I ignore her.

My roomie gets a sneaky look on her face that matches her sneaky tone. "Sooo, who's the hottie you've been hanging out with? I saw you two in the parking lot last night."

I wish that statement surprised me, but it doesn't. Cece has turned out to be a nosy little snoop. "He's a professor at Nackington. We're friends."

"Mm-hm." She squints her eyes as she examines me. "Guys don't do the 'just friends' thing. He wants in your pants, and as soon as he's had his fun, he'll move on to the next girl."

Iain isn't like that, but I refuse to participate in this conversation any longer. So I open up my laptop and get back to work.

But she won't shut up. "I could have your professor anytime I want. Maybe I'll go for it."

Yeah, whatever. She's delusional if she thinks Iain wants to get in *her* pants.

Fortunately, she changes the subject.

"Halloween is on Thursday," Cece declares from the kitchen. I hear the microwave door click shut, then the thing revs up—to reheat the French toast, I'm sure. "Are you planning to stay home and study? Or will the geek come out of her shell to tap some hot ass?"

God, I hate it when she talks that way. It's so crude. "Not interested in dating. But I might dress up for fun."

"*You* are going to wear a costume?"

Does she have to sound totally shocked? I dressed up for last Halloween too, but Cece wasn't my roommate then. My old roomie transferred to Texas A&M over the summer, and I got stuck with Cece. Can't afford this apartment on my own. The university has on-campus housing, but it was all full too by the time my old roomie announced she was leaving.

Yeah, I never would've chosen Cece. She drives me nuts.

A few minutes later, Cece returns to the armchair with a plate of French toast drizzled with a dainty amount of syrup. I drown mine in the sticky stuff.

She sets her feet on the coffee table again and picks at her breakfast. "You're seriously going to dress up."

"Yep. I already rented a costume."

"Rent? Ew." She fake shudders. "That is so gross. Who knows who wore it before you."

"The costume shop dry cleans all their stuff before they rent it out again." I tuck my feet under me cross-legged. "What are you dressing up as?"

She slides a tiny piece of French toast between her lips and chews it like a bunny rabbit gnawing on a carrot. "My costume is totally hot. I'm going as Xena the Warrior Princess."

"Oh. That sounds…cool." I can't picture prissy little Cece wearing skimpy leather gear and pretending to be a warrior, but whatever. "I picked a historical costume. I'm going as Nefertiti."

"Nefer-titty?" Cece says with a snort of derisive laughter. "Can't picture you going topless to show off your titties."

"It's Nefer-tee-tee. She was an ancient Egyptian queen and one of the most beautiful women in history."

She snort-laughs again. "That's really not you."

I decide to ignore her and go back to browsing the internet for "nerdy" stuff about Pre-Columbian cultures. While I explore that world virtually, my mind starts to wander to other topics—like what I want to do once I graduate. I haven't thought much about that. I'm getting a degree in general studies, but I still haven't decided what to do after that. Maybe the upheaval in my family life has kept me from considering the future. But I suddenly realize exactly what I want—to go to grad school and study to be a teacher, a professor of English. Why do I want that? Well, maybe I want to work side-by-side with Iain. Maybe I want us to become an academic power couple. Does he even feel that way about me? I'm too much of a chicken to ask him about that, and I definitely can't ask whether he wants to kiss me.

By the time Halloween comes around, I've let that silly fantasy drift away into the recesses of my mind. I've got more immediate issues to deal with, like what Iain will think of my costume. I invited him to go to a Halloween bash with me, though not one on campus. We're going to a neighboring town where nobody will know us. I didn't tell Iain that was the reason. He thinks I just wanted to go to a more refined event than the ones hosted at Nackington University. Frat parties are so immature.

I put on my costume and look at myself in the full-length mirror attached to the back of my bedroom door. Will Iain like this? I can't wait to see what outfit he chose.

The doorbell rings.

Cece had left for a frat party an hour ago, so I rush out to answer the door. The second I swing it open, my jaw drops. Iain stands there, tall and proud and sexy as hell. He wears a kilt in what he had had once told his students is the MacTaggart clan tartan. But unlike the kilt he wore on the first day of class, this one consists of a single huge length of plaid wrapped around his hips and draped over his shoulder to hang down past his buttocks. A leather belt holds the whole ensemble in place. His *sgian dubh* sticks up out of his knee-high black socks, and black shoes cover his feet.

And oh yeah, he wears no shirt.

Seriously, *no shirt*. I'm gazing at his muscular chest—okay, I'm ogling his muscular chest and probably drooling too. Holy shit, he looks so good that I want to drag him into my bedroom and rip that plaid off his body. But I can't do that. *Rats.*

"Iain, you look amazing," I say, trying my damnedest not to drool or gawk at him anymore. "I love kilts, especially when you wear one."

He chuckles. "Thank you, lass. I love your costume too."

I tear my focus away from his chest and realize he's raking his gaze over my body with a look of hunger that I've never seen before from any man. His voice sounds rougher and deeper when he says, "You look every bit the Egyptian queen."

"I'm Nefertiti."

"Aye, that you are." He rubs his jaw as he drags his attention away from my cleavage to look me in the eye. "You are the most beautiful woman in history, for dead certain."

I'm wearing a white kilt-like pleated skirt that hugs my hips and thighs along with a bra that reveals more cleavage than I've ever shown before in public. My hat is modeled after the famous statue of Nefertiti, and a pleated white cape drapes over my shoulders. My high-heel sandals aren't exactly period appropriate, but neither is most of my outfit. This is Halloween. Who cares about historical accuracy?

The way Iain is devouring me with his gaze, I know he doesn't care about accuracy either.

Since we can't do what we're both thinking about right now, I clear my throat. "Should we go? Don't want to miss the party."

"Aye, we should go." He turns to the side and offers me his arm. "Allow me to escort the queen."

I can't help grinning. Iain makes me feel like royalty every time he looks at me. Am I in love with him? If I hadn't been before, I'm completely in love with him tonight.

Chapter Seven

Iain

Bloody hell. Rae looks so bonnie in her costume that I felt my cock rousing the moment I saw her. I can't seduce her. No matter how badly I want to feel her body enveloping my *slat*, I need to keep my lust in check. Tonight is for Rae. She wanted to go to a party, and I cannae deny her anything she desires.

Unless she wants to shag.

I don't care for parties, especially ones that involve costumes, but I find myself enjoying this do. A ceilidh is more my style, but no one in America has those as far as I know. I watch in awe as Rae charms everyone she meets, from students who traveled three hours from their university to come to this event, to elderly people and everyone in between. She doesn't behave this way at Nackington. I suppose she feels constrained there, and I've wondered if other students harass her about the time she spends with me.

Should I end our friendship? I have no idea what's right in this situation, but I know I can't give up Rae just yet. When she graduates… Donnae want to think about that.

I glance around to see where the lass has gone this time. To watch her having so much fun makes me smile, but I came here to spend time with her, not stand in a corner alone. Then I finally catch sight of her. She's on the dance floor taking a spin with an elderly gent, though calling it a "spin" seems inaccurate. The gent shuffles along with Rae. They both smile and laugh, and Rae positively glows. I wave until I catch her attention.

She says something to the old man, then kisses his cheek and sashays toward me.

The swaying of her hips mesmerizes me. I know this because she snaps her fingers in front of my face.

"Wake up, Iain," she says. "Did you drink too much wine?"

"No, I—" Rubbing my neck, I grimace. "I was distracted, that's all. And I didn't drink wine. I sipped Scotch, though it wasn't the authentic Scottish variety."

"Poor Iain. You can't get Scottish liquor in America."

"Are you ready to leave yet?"

She glances around, then her attention settles on me again. "Yeah, I'm done. This was a hoot, but I've hit my limit on revelry for the month."

I offer her my arm. "Allow me to escort you home, Your Highness."

Rae slips her arm around mine. "I feel bad for Nefertiti. She never got to be escorted back to her palace by a brawny Scottish warrior."

"That was a wee bit before the age of the kilt."

We exit the building and go straight to my car, which I'd parked directly across the street. As I help Rae into the passenger seat, she gazes up at me with a sweet expression. "If I could go back in time, I'd want to wind up in medieval Scotland. Kilts are hot."

She pulls the door shut.

And I stand here for a moment, frozen by what she said. *Kilts are hot*. She wasn't referring to me specifically, but I can't help wondering if she does think I'm "hot." Not that it matters. I can never be anything more than a mate to her. I drop Rae off at her flat, and I insist on walking her to the door. Though I experience a powerful impulse to kiss her cheek, I fight it. Even kissing her hand seems like too much. So I say good night and leave.

After Halloween, we go back to our usual routine of "hanging out," as Rae calls it. Neither of us discusses the party and what we both wore on that night. We're back to behaving like a professor and a student who have become good mates. It's bloody awful in some respects, but I'll take whatever time I can have with Rae. If she ever finds a boyfriend, I don't know what I'll do.

She told me once that she would be twenty-two in November, but I have no idea when her birthday is. I vaguely remember my faculty orientation, during which someone mentioned something about a Student Information System that I would have access to, though at the time I didn't see why I would want that. Now I need to use that system. No bloody clue how to do it. At some point, I was given a password that would let me "log in," but I'm not good with computers.

Time to expand my skills.

I get on my computer in my office and hunt about on the university servers until I find a link to the Student Information System. It takes me several more minutes to figure out how to log in to that, and even longer until I find the information about Rae. I can't see her grades except in my class, but I have no doubt she's doing as well in her other courses as she does in mine.

At last, I locate her birth date. She will turn twenty-two in eight days.

That's not much time to organize a celebration for her, but I can at least buy her some sort of present. Should I get a cake for her too? I can't bake. My mother attempted to teach me how to cook, but I failed so miserably at it that she told me never to try to cook or bake anything again. I've heeded her advice. I would need to buy a cake for Rae. What sort does she like? I can't find that information on the university server.

Since I'm a bloody-minded eejit, I embark on a campaign to trick her into revealing what sort of cake she prefers. This involves me asking sideways questions in the hopes I'll stumble onto the fact I need to know. Aye, I am most definitely an eejit. No one would go about this task the way I'm doing it.

The next day, as we sit on a concrete bench in the middle of campus, I begin my secret campaign. "Rae, do you enjoy sweets?"

"Sure. Doesn't everybody?"

"Not diabetics." What a dead stupid thing to say.

Rae laughs in the soft way she often does when I say something that's inadvertently amusing. "No, I guess they wouldn't. But yes, I love sweets."

"Do you eat them often?"

Now she seems a wee bit suspicious. "Often? I'm not sure. I don't keep a candy diary."

Of course she doesn't. I'm the worst interrogator on earth. A spy would know exactly how to get information. That's one of many reasons I should never become a secret agent.

What else can I do? I resort to the bull in a china shop approach. "I love cakes. Do you enjoy them?"

Rae freezes with a half-eaten sandwich hovering near her lips. "Uh, what?"

"I, well, asked if, ah…" I bow my head and blow out a breath, then raise my face to hers again. "What sort of cake do you like?"

She stares at me for a moment. Then the lass grins and punches me in the arm—gently. "Are you planning to buy me a birthday cake? I didn't realize you knew when my birthday was."

"Well, I…looked it up on the Student Information System."

"Ohhh. That does explain your bizarre fixation with sweets." She chews another bite of her sandwich before speaking again. "You don't need to do anything for my birthday."

"But I want to. I had the impression your family lives far away."

"Not that far away, but I doubt they'll show up to give me presents. My mom will probably send me something, though."

"Good. But I'd still like you to have a cake and at least one present. I'm incapable of baking, so this would be store bought."

She bites into a potato chip, chewing it slowly. "I'm not picky. I'll love anything you give me. You're very thoughtful and sweet."

"I don't think you should be alone on your birthday, that's all."

"Okay, but no present. Cake is enough." She leans toward me to whisper, "My favorite is chocolate with vanilla frosting and vanilla ice cream."

"I can manage that."

A laddie who is obviously a student, judging by his rucksack, walks right up to Rae, ignoring me. "Hey, I've seen you around campus. Wanna go out sometime?"

Rae's brows lift. She glances at me, but I remain calm, like the Buddha she thinks I am. So Rae turns to the laddie and says, "No thank you. It's rude to interrupt people who are having a conversation."

"Yeah, well, everybody knows about you two." He jerks his head toward me. "You shouldn't hang out with the Notorious Dr. MacT if you don't want everybody to think you're easy."

The laddie walks away before I get the chance to do anything. I want to hunt him down and batter the scunner for suggesting Rae is "easy." But that wouldn't fit with my Zen attitude, which Rae seems to like. Besides, that *cacan* isn't worth the trouble. Wee shits like him rarely are.

"Can you believe that?" Rae asks. "What a moron."

"Aye, he is an eejit for sure."

She bites her lip, which I've come to know means she's feeling shy about asking me something.

"Go on," I tell her. "You know you can tell me anything."

"Did you already know what the campus asses call you?"

"No. I had never heard that before."

She chews the inside of her cheek for a moment, but then rolls her shoulders back and looks straight at me. "That was the polite version of the nickname obnoxious frat boys invented for you." She squeezes her eyes shut, which makes her whole face pinch up. Then she says in a rush of syllables, "The full version is the Notorious Dr. MacT, Professor of Fuckology."

I say nothing for a few seconds. They call me what? Well, I suppose I should applaud the fact they used their brains for once to invent that nickname. After the shock wears off, I can't help chuckling. "That's quite a moniker they've given me."

"You aren't royally ticked about it?"

"Ah, lass, ye know me better than that. I never waste time letting scunners fash me. They aren't worth the effort."

"Right. You don't get angry. I mean, even that time when you growled at me, it didn't seem like genuine anger."

I snatch a potato chip from her lunch plate and chew it up before I can summon the nerve to tell her the truth. "I wasn't growling at you, not for the reason you think. You were, ah, bending over and your blouse fell away from your chest."

She clamps her lips between her teeth, and her whole body quivers.

Is she about to cry? "Rae, I didn't mean to upset you. Should've kept that to myself. I didnae mean—"

Rae bursts out laughing. "Relax, Iain, it's fine. I can see why that would 'fash' you. Sorry I accidentally exposed myself. You must've been so embarrassed."

"No, I wasn't."

We finish our lunch and go our separate ways. She hurries toward the science building while I make my way to my office in the humanities building so I can prepare for my next class. In the late afternoon, I endure office hours, which means listening to students complain, beg for better grades, or tell me their personal problems. I don't mind giving advice, but I know nothing about how young lads and lasses live these days. I grew up in a small town in the Highlands where everyone knows everyone else and we all poke our noses into each other's business. Most of those people are my relatives.

Sometimes I miss my home. But every time I feel melancholy, I think of Rae. Being with her erases all my homesickness.

The week goes by faster than I expected, but I made time to get everything for Rae's birthday. Though she doesn't want a gift, I can still make the day special for her in other ways. Rae deserves the best of everything. Since I don't want those annoying laddies on campus to blether about the two of us, I invite Rae to my apartment for a private birthday celebration. She orders me to promise I won't go overboard. Aye, I agreed to that. Anything for her.

I have everything set up by the time the doorbell rings.

Chapter Eight

Rae

The door swings open, and Iain smiles at me. "Happy birthday, *gràidh*. You look as bonnie as a sunny day, and I hope you're ready for a feast to celebrate your twenty-second year of lighting up the world with your presence."

"I thought we agreed you wouldn't go overboard." I have no idea what that strange word he said means, but I don't feel like asking him about it right now. "Everything you just said is the definition of 'overboard,' Iain."

"No. Unless I bring out a three-foot high cake and puppies burst out of it, I haven't gone too far."

"Puppies? I think it's strippers who jump out of cakes."

"Aye. But you wouldn't want that."

Maybe I'd like it if he jumped out of a cake and stripped for me. He'd be wearing his kilt and nothing else, then he'd unhook his belt and let that plaid drop. I've seen the man's chest twice, up close, and his brawny arms too. I can extrapolate from that what the rest of him might look like. Muscular chest equals muscular everything.

Iain steps aside. "Come in, Rae."

As soon as I cross the threshold, I can see what he's organized for me. It's nothing outlandish, nothing inappropriate, just the sweetest thing anyone has ever done for me. While Iain shuts the door, I hurry into the living room. The coffee table has been covered up with a blue cloth, and it now serves as a makeshift dining table. A cardboard box sits there alongside two plates hidden under dome-shaped lids, while two champagne flutes sit empty beside an unopened bottle.

This kind of seems like going overboard, but I won't chastise Iain for doing that. He could've really gone crazy. Instead, he held back and only went slightly too far. Besides, I love that he cares enough to create a beautiful birthday surprise for me.

"Sit down," he says as he enters the living room. "And enjoy the view."

My gaze shifts to the picture windows that bookend the glass doors to the balcony. His apartment isn't super spiffy or huge. It feels comfortable and just right for a man like Iain. Through the windows, I can see the lights of Nackington and the ghostly shapes of the hills beyond the city limits.

I settle onto the sofa, then Iain sits down a couple of feet away. "Thank you for doing all this. It's the sweetest thing any-one has ever done for me."

"You deserve it, Rae. I know how hard you work to get excellent grades, and I also know you're away from home like me. Maybe that's why I want to ensure you celebrate the little things, like your birthday."

My throat goes thick, and I feel a hint of tears stinging in my eyes. "You have no idea how much this means to me."

"Donnae cry. This is a happy occasion. Aye?"

I nod.

"Then let's enjoy your birthday together." He pulls the lids off the plates. "All your favorites."

Can't help giggling when I see what his grand meal con-sists of—fried chicken, French fries, mozzarella sticks, and ribs. Yeah, it's a strange combination, but I love it. When he opens the champagne and pours it into our flutes, I don't care that nobody eats fried chicken with champagne. Iain went to so much trouble for me, and I love him even more for doing that.

Not that I can ever tell him how much he means to me.

The food is yummy, but Iain feels the need to tell me he got it all from restaurants. Like I care. I want to kiss his cheek for being so thoughtful and honorable. Can't do it, though. Even in private, we need to maintain those damn boundaries to prevent us from getting into trouble. Once I graduate… No, I don't dare finish that thought. False hope will only make things worse.

After dinner, Iain clears the plates off the table and slides the big cardboard box into the center. "Now, for the pièce de résistance."

"Thought you were Scottish, not French."

"I'm trying to bring an elegant, continental tone to this evening's festivities."

"Uh-huh." I poke his arm. "Hope you're not violating our agreement about not going overboard."

"Not at all." He plucks up the cardboard box, revealing a cake seated on a platter. "Happy birthday, *sunshine*."

The cake has four layers of fluffy dark chocolate goodness sandwiched between vanilla frosting. The words "Happy Birthday, Rae" are elegantly scrawled across the top. I get choked up again and hold my hand to my mouth while I struggle not to cry.

"What's wrong, *gràidh*?" Iain asks. "Ye look miserable, but the cake was meant to make you smile."

"I'm not miserable. I'm happy." I spot a box of tissues on the end table and snatch one out of it, then dab at my eyes while sniffling. "This is just the most wonderful thing anyone has ever done for me."

He reaches out as if to touch me, but pulls his hand away. "Crying means you like it?"

"No. It means I love all of this."

"Oh." He scratches under his shirt collar and avoids looking at me. "Glad to hear it."

Have I embarrassed him? I thought the Unflappable Iain MacTaggart didn't experience discomfort of any kind. Well, he did get slightly flustered when I accidentally flashed him a glimpse of my cleavage. Other than that, he's always calm and level-headed. I often want to ask him how he manages to do that, but I don't have his equanimity. I'd get nervous and wind up saying something stupid.

Yeah, like "I love you, Iain."

Since I've never been in love before, maybe I don't really know what it feels like. I might have mistaken infatuation for love. He must not feel the way I do, anyway. He would've said something if he did. Right? God, I have no idea.

And now I've invented my own nickname for him. But I don't think I'll share it with Iain. It's goofy to call him unflappable.

Iain offers me a knife. "The birthday girl should cut the cake."

Cutting slices off a four-layer cake isn't as easy as it sounds, but I manage to get two pieces for us. Then Iain retrieves a carton of ice cream and dishes it out for us. We talk while we stuff our faces, mostly joking about the stupid boys on campus and the moronic nickname they gave Iain. Professor of Fuckology? What does that even mean? And Iain is the opposite of notorious. In the time I've known him, he has avoided causing a scene, no matter how often annoying jerks hit on me right in front of him.

Just the other day, a persistent twerp kept trying to flirt with me while I was sitting right next to Iain in the campus cafeteria. I told the idiot no three times, but he kept harassing me. Iain simply aimed his neutral expression at the boy and said in a placid tone, "You're interrupting our lunch, laddie."

The twerp threw his hands up and made a disgusted noise. "She's not worth the trouble, anyway."

And he walked away.

Did Iain's Buddha attitude scare that guy? I don't know, but I appreciate that Iain never gets upset.

I eat two slices of cake and more ice cream than I should have. Then it's time to go home. Iain walks me to the door, and we say good night. As I'm getting into my car, I notice Iain watching from his balcony. Only when I've pulled out onto the road does he retreat into his apartment. How many men would keep an eye out to make sure his guest gets safely on her way? Iain isn't like anyone else. Maybe that's why I have these strong and confusing feelings for him.

The weeks fly by after my birthday. Iain is busy getting ready for final exams and making sure all his students are prepared too. In the Celtic history class, he gives us half a dozen pop quizzes in the two weeks leading up to finals. Christmas is coming soon, which means I'll fly home to Iowa in ten days, then spend two weeks with Mom, returning to Nackington the day after New Year's. Being away from Iain for two weeks feels like ripping my own heart out, but I know that's silly.

Still, what I feel for him is not a simple crush. I know I love him, though I don't think I'll ever be able to tell him so. My only hope is that after graduation, he will tell me how he feels. If he says I'm just a "mate," that would destroy me. But I won't give up the months I have left with him. However our story goes, I will see it through until the end.

A few days before final exams, I get a surprise phone call at seven a.m., just as I'm getting ready to leave for the campus.

"Hello, Rae," a familiar voice says when I answer the call. "It's your father."

"Oh, hi, Dad. What's up?" I haven't heard from him in months. Not so much as an email. He didn't even send me a birthday card.

"Look, here's the deal." He sighs heavily. "Brooke and I are moving to Hong Kong so I can take over as general manager of the company's resort there. It's a major promotion."

"Um, congratulations?" I sound uncertain because I am. Totally confused might be a better description.

"I'm starting a new life with Brooke. Can't let the shadows of my past ruin the best thing that's ever happened to me." He pauses, then adds, "Don't try to contact me ever again. I hope you have a good life, but I can't be a part of it anymore."

He hangs up.

I hold the phone in front of my face and stare at it for I don't know how long. My father just disowned me. A chill races over my skin, sinking deep under the surface. I stagger to the sofa and drop onto it while still holding my cell phone. I've started to shiver, though I don't think it's from the cold air outside. Can't really think at all, though, so maybe the temperature has plummeted below zero, inside and out.

Cece sashays out of her bedroom and barely glances at me. "Morning, roomie. I'm heading out early for a breakfast date with a real steamy piece of ass."

What did she say? It sounded like gibberish to me. I can't do anything except stare out the window, not seeing anything. My dad told me never to contact him. He has a new family. With a woman two years older than I am.

Peripherally, I notice when Cece grabs her backpack and purse and heads for the door. "See ya later, roomie."

I stare blankly at the window for several minutes after she leaves. Then I rouse from my stupor enough that I know I need to do something. I can't go to my classes today. No way. But I don't want Iain to worry if I'm not there. So I clumsily call up his number on my phone and dial it.

"Rae?" he says when he picks up.

"Hi, um, yeah, it's me." My voice sounds a little shaky, but I can't seem to make it stop doing that. "I can't come to class today. I'm… sick. Sorry. I just need to—Well, I should rest. Okay?"

"Of course. Maybe you should see a doctor. Ye donnae sound well at all."

"Just need rest. I'm sure I'll be fine tomorrow. Goodbye."

I hang up, but my hands are shaking so much that I drop the phone. All I can do is stumble into the bedroom and curl up in a ball on top of the covers. Tears dribble down my cheeks. I don't sob. And I only cry for ten minutes, then I make myself get up and go into the bathroom to take a shower. Just as I'm getting dressed, the doorbell rings.

Scuffling to the door, I peer through the peephole.

Iain stands there, tall and gorgeous and wearing a calmly determined expression.

Oh God, I can't see him now. But I can't just tell him to go away either. So I open the door a few inches to peek out at him. "What are you doing here? Shouldn't you be teaching a class?"

"Aye. But I called in my teaching assistant, and he's handling my classes for today."

I rub my eyes, still feeling kind of off-kilter. "Why would you do that?"

"For you." He leans against the jamb. "I'm worried about you, *gràidh*. Please let me in."

"Um, okay." I scuffle backward so he can walk inside. Then I wave toward the living room. "Sit wherever you want."

He pushes the door shut and studies me. "Have you eaten anything this morning?"

"No, I don't think so."

"Ye don't think so?" He grasps my arm to lead me toward the sofa. "Sit down. I'll find something to feed you for breakfast."

I huddle on the sofa with my knees tucked up to my chest and my arms wrapped around them. Iain grabs a fleece throw and drapes it over my shoulders. Then he disappears into the kitchen. I blow my nose and go back to staring at nothing.

A few minutes later, Iain sits down beside me, holding a bowl and a glass of milk, both of which he offers to me. "Oatmeal. It's the only thing I know how to make. Please eat it, Rae."

I never can resist him when he asks me to do anything. So I take the bowl and start picking at the oatmeal. Iain holds the glass of milk, handing it to me whenever I ask for it, then taking it back so I don't have to try to balance that and my bowl on my lap. The more I eat, the better I feel. Or maybe I feel that way because Iain is here taking care of me. By the time I've finished eating, I'm not shaking anymore.

"Feeling better?" Iain asks as he brushes damp hair away from my face.

"Yeah, I feel a lot better. Thank you."

"Anything for you, *gràidh*." He wriggles until he's half-turned toward me and stretches an arm across the sofa's back behind me. "You are coming with me. We will have a good time, and you'll forget all about whatever made you so miserable this morning."

How Iain can issue a command and make it sound so calm and reasonable, I don't know. But my mood improves even more when he tells me that. I started feeling better gradually after he arrived, but now I can't help smiling, though not as much as usual.

"Does your smile mean you'll come with me?" he asks.

"Uh-huh. Where are we going?"

"To a museum. You love Egyptian antiquities."

I set my oatmeal bowl on the table. "We've seen all the Egyptian exhibits at the Nackington Museum."

He shakes his head, his lips curling into a slightly devious expression. "I'm not taking you there. Ye need a break from this town and the university. We're going to Milwaukee, to a museum that has a limited engagement exhibition of Egyptian antiquities. You'll get to see the golden mask of Tutankhamen."

"Really?" Yeah, now I sound excited. I leap to my knees and simultaneously spin toward him. "Tutankhamen's mask? What else?"

"You'll see, lass. You'll see."

Chapter Nine

Iain

Rae loves ancient history more than any student I've ever met, possibly more than any human being I've ever met. The bonnie lass races into the museum the moment I shut off the car's engine, and I need to sprint to catch up to her. She'd been distraught when I arrived at her flat, but her mood improved after she ate—and particularly after I informed her of my grand plan for the day. She's adorable when she gets excited about history. When I told her the exhibition also includes one mummy, she squealed with delight like a wee bairn.

Aye, then I wanted to kiss her. But I didn't do it.

She hadn't been unwell, not physically. That's all I know. Though I want to ask what made her so miserable, I know it's not my place to question her. If she wants to tell me, I'll listen. Since I have no desire to explain my family life to her, I cannae expect the lass to share all her secrets with me.

A few days later, after Rae finishes all her final exams, she gets on a plane headed for Iowa to visit her mother. Though I wanted to drive her to the airport, I realized that wouldn't be appropriate. Too often I've skirted the line between friendship and something more, blurring the distinction between student and professor. Having Rae as a mate might be the best thing that's ever happened to me, but I never want to overstep. She might not feel for me the way I feel for her.

Two weeks without her, without even speaking to her on the phone, tests my Zen attitude more than anything ever has. I could fly home to Scotland, and my mother wants me to do that, but I make up excuses why I can't. If my father gets into trouble again, I don't know if I can rescue him. I know he means well, but nicking things from strangers doesn't help anyone.

Staying here in Nackington without Rae... I have no words for how empty the whole world feels without her in my life. I know she will fly home the day after New Year's, but classes won't start again until the following day. She isn't my student anymore, so I might not see her at all. She doesn't need me anymore. Maybe she found a laddie her own age to, ah, be her...friend.

I'm sitting behind my desk in my office on campus, poring over the lesson plans I'd made over the past two weeks, when Rae stumbles into the room. Literally. She stumbles into a chair, almost knocking it over, her expression full of excitement. Her grin melts the ball of ice that had formed in my chest on the day she left. My pulse beats so fast that I feel almost lightheaded.

Though I want to rush over there and pull her into my arms, I force myself to stay in my chair and gaze at her with a neutral expression. "Are you all right, Rae? Have you hurt yourself?"

"No, I'm fine." She straightens and grins. "I got my grades for last semester. Straight A's. My perfect four-point-oh GPA is intact."

I cannae help myself. I jump out of my chair and hurry around the desk, reaching out as if to...hug her. But I freeze a few feet away from the lass. My face must look blank. When I finally regain my equilibrium, I clear my throat and do a dead stupid thing. I shake her hand. "Congratulations. I knew you would do well. You're the cleverest person I've ever met."

"Thank you, Iain. I loved your class, and I was hoping I'd get to have you again this semester."

Have me? Aye, I'd love to have her for certain. But I know she didn't mean it that way.

Now her face goes blank, though her eyes flare wide too. Mine hadn't done that. I think. She must've realized her statement sounded slightly inappropriate.

Rae hunches her shoulders and gives me a bashful smile. "Anyway, I couldn't get into any of your classes. Since you won't be my teacher anymore, I understand if you don't want to hang out with me."

"Rae, I want to spend time with you even if I'm not your teacher." I touch her arm. "We're mates, aren't we?"

"Yeah, of course."

I withdraw my hand. "Then nothing will change, except that I won't get to see your bonnie face in the classroom anymore."

"Learning about Scotland from you was amazing."

"Teaching you has been a privilege and a pleasure." I wave toward the door. "If you have time before your next class, we could have a celebratory dessert in the cafeteria."

"Sure, I'd love that."

After our sweet snack, I walk Rae to the science building. I pat her arm as we say goodbye, though I want to do much more than that. She seems vaguely disappointed. Even if she feels the way I do, we can never act on those desires. I might be imagining that she wants more. I don't have time to worry about that, though, because I need to hurry to get to my next class. A teacher's job is never done. When I reach the sidewalk, I pause to glance back.

Rae has just pulled the door open. She waves and gives me the sweetest, most beautiful smile. My chest aches, and I suddenly can't catch my breath. Even after Rae walks into the building, I stand here for a moment reveling in the afterglow of that smile. Even the snow on the ground can't lessen its warmth.

Aye, I'm in love with Rae Everhart.

If I'd thought not being her teacher would mean I see less of Rae, I was wrong. She visits my office sometimes, but only to ask me questions about Scottish history. We spend the most time together away from the campus when we take trips to nearby sites that have some relation to history, the older the better. By early February, we've seen most of the historical sites in Wisconsin.

Since I still feel that I need an excuse to spend time with her, so no one will think we're romantically involved, I keep coming up with reasons to invite her to my flat. I've only been to her apartment once. Maybe she doesn't want me there because of her roommate, or maybe she's uncomfortable with the idea because the only time I was there happened to be the day I found her in a state of shock. I don't mind if I never visit her apartment again, as long as I can see her.

What will I do when the semester ends and Rae graduates?

Valentine's Day sneaks up on me, and though I shouldn't care about that, I experience an irresistible impulse to give Rae a gift. Valentine's isn't only for lovers. Children give their friends and family cards, after all. I'm no bairn, but I want Rae to have something special for the holiday. A friendly gift. Nothing romantic. Luckily, I had brought something with me to America that I think she'll like.

I start to wonder if Rae has psychic powers when she finds me in my office and invites me to come to her flat on Valentine's Day for "pizza and pop." She seems genuinely surprised when I say yes, but her shock soon changes to excitement. I love how exuberant she can be when I surprise her with a road trip or just agreeing to eat pizza and pop with her.

On the night, I arrive precisely at seven o'clock, as she dictated. Aye, the lass can be bossy. I love that about her too. She's very bonnie when she orders me to do things. I have her present wrapped up in pink paper that has red hearts on it and with a pink bow on top. I know she loves that color. I ring the doorbell and wait.

She yanks the door open almost instantly, as if she'd been waiting for me. Rae smiles, then her gaze falls to the package in my hand. "You didn't need to bring anything."

"It's Valentine's Day." I thrust the present at her. "Friends can give each other gifts for this day. Aye?"

"Sure, yeah." She hugs the gift-wrapped package to her chest. "Thank you, Iain. Nobody has ever given me anything for Valentine's Day."

"Never? I should've bought you flowers too, then."

"Whatever you give me is plenty. But I should've gotten you something."

"No need."

I follow her into the apartment, and we both sit on the sofa—at opposite ends. I sat down first, and Rae opted to settle onto the cushion furthest from me. So I move over to sit in the middle, much closer to her.

"Open your present," I say. "It will complement your eyes."

She turns the package over several times as she studies it with the most adorable look of concentration. Her tongue pokes out between her lips, and her eyes glitter with excitement. She seems to relish drawing out the suspense, but I get impatient.

"Are ye planning to open it this year?" I ask. "Or not until next Valentine's?"

She flashes me a sly grin. "Maybe I'll wait until later."

"You're teasing me, aren't you?"

"Of course." She grasps the package and rips it open with both hands. The bow springs free and lands on my chest, held there by the adhesive strip attached to it. Rae laughs. "Look, the bow is right over your heart."

The same place where a piece of her will always live.

She extricates her gift from the remnants of the wrapping paper. Her eyes go wide. She lifts the scarf and gazes at me with what I can only describe as awe. "Iain, is this—It looks like the same fabric as your kilt."

"It is the same." I rest my arm on the sofa's back, my fingers grazing her shoulder. "It's the MacTaggart clan tartan. My mother made that scarf for me, and now I want you to have it."

"Me? Why?" She sets the scarf on my lap. "Won't your mother be upset you gave it away?"

"No." I hand the scarf back to her, and she fingers the fringe at either end. When she tries to give it back to me, I drape it around her neck. "Please accept this as a token of… friendship."

She bites her lip while she runs her hands up and down the soft plaid fabric. "Okay. I accept and appreciate your thoughtful gift."

"Good."

We enjoy the pizza and pop, though I have to ask for clarification about what that term means. Rae laughs and says, "Soda pop. You know, carbonated beverages." Aye, I would've guessed that, but being a newcomer in this country, I needed to make sure.

A few weeks later, the dean of the humanities department calls me into his office for a "conference." As soon as I sit down opposite his desk, he begins to interrogate me. Not what I expected.

"I've been hearing things about you," Dean Milton says. "Not good things, Dr. MacTaggart. How many students have you slept with?"

"None." And I don't appreciate his tone or the baseless accusation.

The dean leans forward, his arms locked on the desktop. "I've heard what everyone calls you. The Notorious Dr. MacT, Professor of—Well, you know the rest, I'm sure."

"It's not my fault juvenile laddies have decided to call me a moronic name."

He sighs and leans back in his chair, rubbing a hand over his eyes. "In my experience, rumors that spread do so for a reason."

"Aye. The reason is boredom and jealousy."

"What about Rae Everhart?"

I set one ankle on the other knee. "Donnae understand the question."

"Of course you do. What have you been doing with an undergraduate?"

"We're mates."

He jerks his head as if I've struck him, though I haven't come within three feet of the eejit. "Did you just admit to having sex with her?"

"Sex?" I chuckle. "No, sir, I did not confess to anything. I said we're mates. That means we are friends."

"In what language?"

"Have you never been to the UK?"

The dean's brows draw together as he studies me. "Of course I have. But you are Scottish, not British. Only people from England refer to friends as mates."

I can't stop myself from sighing. "Scotland is part of the UK. If you've been to England, you must know that."

"My travel habits are not the issue." He leans forward again, almost hunching over his desk. "I want to know how many students you have seduced."

"For the second time, the answer is none. I do not sleep with students."

Dean Milton stares at me for a moment while his expression tightens into something almost like pain. Then his face relaxes. "All right. I will accept your response—for now. But I'll have my eye on you, Dr. MacTaggart."

I don't bother to respond or even say goodbye. I march out of his office and shut the door behind me. Though I've tried to like Dean Milton, I failed at that. The best I can do is tolerate the weaselly man, thanks to his lack of a spine and his filthy insinuations. Let him think what he wants. I have never violated the university's ethics code.

The months roll by, but I hardly notice the passage of time. Why? Because Rae and I spend most of our free time with each other, visiting places of less historical value like a dairy farm and a museum dedicated to the sport of fishing. Rae enjoys those destinations, but she doesn't get as excited about them as she had done with Aztalan or the campus museum.

Before I know it, the semester is ending.

I'm sitting in my office grading final exams when Rae rushes into the room. She stands there for a moment breathing hard, apparently waiting to catch her breath. Even while she does that, she grins at me. Her lopsided expression makes me smile too.

"You seem excited," I say. "Have you found another barmy roadside attraction to visit?"

She shakes her head. "I finished all my final exams."

"I see."

"That means I'm technically not a student anymore. Just thought you might want to know."

My mouth opens, but I snap my jaw shut. My mind cannae quite process what she just said. Not technically a student. She finished her exams. The reality of what that means at last penetrates my brain, and my pulse races, every beat thundering in my ears.

Oh, aye, I know what she meant.

"I have a few things to take care of here," I say summoning all my Zen-like calmness to keep from leaping across the desk to drag her into my arms. "Go home, wait for me."

Rae's grin broadens. Then she whirls around and hurries out of my office.

Forty-two minutes later, I knock on the door to her flat.

The second it swings open, I surge across the threshold, pushing Rae inside. Then I back her into the door and push it shut, pressing my body to hers.

And I kiss her.

She straps her arms around my neck while I thrust my tongue into her mouth, groaning with the deepest satisfaction I've ever felt. I'm kissing Rae. Finally. She moans and rocks her hips into me while I explore her mouth with all the subtlety of a starved man who at last found a meal. She tastes like heaven, like everything sweet and savory and perfect.

When we peel our lips apart, I gaze straight into her eyes. "I need to make love to ye, Rae. But first, I want to give you the all the dates we never had—today."

"All in one day?"

I brush my lips over hers. "Aye, all in one day."

Chapter Ten

Rae

Iain kissed me. Wow. That kiss had taken my breath away and made me tingle from head to toe, especially between my thighs. He wants to make love to me. God, I want that too, so much. But I also love the idea of spending the day with him, as a couple, enjoying all the stuff we couldn't do before. This day is heaven.

Suddenly, I'm glad I researched how to give a blow job. Yeah, okay, that's weird and slightly deranged. But I wanted to make sure I'd know what to do if Iain and I ever had sex.

He insists on taking me to a lovely little café for breakfast, one we had never visited before. The place just opened up a few weeks ago, but I'd heard the French ambiance and cuisine are exquisite. The word of mouth didn't lie. Iain and I share a meal—literally, as in sharing one plate and feeding each other. I've never loved eating more than I do today, especially when Iain slides a French toast roll-up into my mouth.

But even the most delicious delicacy of all can't compare to the taste of Iain's kisses.

After breakfast, he whisks me away to a shopping mall where he insists on buying me whatever I want. I tell him I don't need anything, only him. He hits me with the steamiest smile I've ever seen, then rushes me into a photo booth. Never in my life had I stepped into one of these contraptions. I never saw the appeal of hunching inside a booth to take cheesy pictures of yourself. But today, I get it. With Iain, this doesn't seem like a dumb thing to do. It feels romantic.

Once we've squeezed into the booth, he slings an arm around me to tug me into his side. As the camera snaps pictures of us, we both grin and laugh as we press our cheeks against each other. I can't believe the Unflappable Iain MacTaggart is behaving like a lovestruck teenager, or that I'm doing the same. Everything about him today makes me feel exhilarated and free and so damn happy.

Just in time for that last picture, he pulls me close and kisses me.

As we peel our lips apart, he gives me a different kind of smile. The sweet kind, imbued with tenderness and something much deeper. Even if he never says the words, in this moment, I know he loves me as much as I love him.

Iain grabs the photo strip, handing it to me. "You should keep this, love. I don't need mementos to remember this day forever."

We stroll along the streets of Nackington, stopping in to explore all the cute little shops. Though we don't buy anything, shopping with Iain is even more fun than I remember from that day when I'd given him a silly T-shirt. Oh yeah, real men definitely wear plaid skirts. I would've loved it if he'd worn his kilt today, but that would've caused a distraction for every person we passed on the street. I don't want anything to mess up our day together.

After lunch, we go to a movie theater. Neither of us watches the movie. We sit in the back row and make out. The way Iain kisses makes me melt from the inside out, and I can't give up his lips until the movie ends and I have no choice but to ooze out of my seat while he leads me back to the car. He reclaims my lips the second we're in the vehicle, breaking away only long enough to drive to a smokily lit restaurant and order a sensual meal consisting of oysters, figs, spicy and savory delicacies, and a dessert of strawberries drenched in warm chocolate sauce with a hint of vanilla flavor.

I had no idea food could be so erotic. Maybe it's the sizzling-hot man feeding me who creates that steamy atmosphere, not the meal itself.

When we settle into the car, Iain takes possession of my mouth yet again, devouring me with a kiss of such intensity and sensuality that my heart pounds and my sex throbs. I know we will make love tonight. It's inevitable.

He drives to his apartment, and it takes us fifteen minutes to reach the second floor. We can't stop kissing. Iain even punches the stop button in the elevator so we can devour each other for even longer. I can hardly stand the anticipation. Even as we stumble out of the elevator, our lips remain fused. We stumble through the door to his apartment, stumble across the living room, and fall onto the sofa without ever giving up each other's mouths. We make out there on the cushions for half an hour.

But he still hasn't touched me in any overtly sexual way. Doesn't seduction involve a lot of fondling and sexy talk? Since I've only been with two guys in my entire life, I have no idea what to expect. But I'm beginning to worry that kissing is all he wants to do tonight. After ten months of holding back, I want everything with him.

I'll die if he doesn't make love to me tonight.

He pulls his mouth away, depriving me of the taste of his lips, and a frustrated noise grunts out of me. When I open my eyes, the look of unadulterated hunger on his face steals my breath and weakens my knees. Good thing I'm sitting down. Otherwise, I'd dissolve into a pool of molten lust at his feet. But beneath that hunger I see a tenderness that makes my throat go thick.

Iain combs his fingers through my hair as he traces circles on my cheek with his thumb. "Stay with me, Rae."

The smoky timbre of his voice makes me feel weak in the best way. "I'd love to."

His lips quiver the slightest bit as he gives me a soft yet carnal smile. Then he pushes his arms under my bottom and hoists me up while he springs off the sofa. Cradled in his strong arms, I can only gaze adoringly at his face like the lovestruck fool I am. This almost feels like a wedding night, with the groom carrying his bride across the threshold, except he isn't crossing the doorway of our new home. He's whisking me away to his bedroom for what I pray will be hours of intensely romantic and outrageously hot sex.

Based on our kissing, I know I'll get exactly what I want.

Iain sets me down near the foot of the bed. My knees wobble a teeny bit, but I'm not about to collapse. Before I can move a single muscle or form even half of a coherent thought, he begins to undress me, taking his time as he unhooks buttons, unzips my jeans, and removes every last stitch of my clothing while keeping his hands on my skin the entire time. The sensation of his palms skimming over my body arouses me even more, almost to the point of pain, because I've waited so damn long for this moment. Once I'm naked, he pulls the covers back and lays me down on the bed.

Then he slowly removes all his clothes.

Watching him unveil that body little by little… Holy shit, I might pass out from the power of my lust for this man. I'd seen his muscular chest before, but now I get to drink in the sight of his narrow hips and powerful thighs, though I can't resist studying every inch of his chest and biceps too. But it's his glorious cock that captures my focus so thoroughly that I can't stop staring at it. He is fully aroused right now. The long, veined length of his erection proves that all my fantasies over the past ten months fell woefully short of the reality. I want him inside me this minute. This second. I *need* it.

But I have no voice to tell him that.

He lies down beside me, skating his hands over me from head to toe with such leisure that I clench my fingers and bite down on my lower lip. This feels incredible, like a dozen feathers dancing over my skin, but when he touches his lips to my flesh, I can't stifle the soft whimper that rushes out of me. He retraces the path he'd taken with his hands, exploring me with his mouth, nibbling and licking as he travels over my body. By the time he reaches my throat, I'm panting and wriggling and so fucking wet that my cream drenches my sex and the hairs on my mound.

My other lovers hadn't wanted to go slow. Wham, bam, let's have a beer. That had been their method. But Iain seems in no hurry to get to the main event, as calm in bed as he is in the rest of his life.

Zen sex rocks.

His hair tickles my cheek as he flicks his tongue out to tease the corner of my mouth. Then he pulls my earlobe between his lips and suckles it so gently that I close my eyes to revel in the sensations he evokes in me. But when he shimmies down the bed to swallow my nipple, I clutch his head and arch my back.

"Iain, oh God, yes," I whisper as I force my eyes to open. Don't want to miss one second of the look on his face.

He slides his body over mine, holding himself up with both arms, then gradually lowers his full weight onto me. But he still doesn't penetrate my body. Instead, Iain kisses me tenderly while he glides his hands down my sides and back again, his touch delicate and maddeningly sensual. My nipples rasp against his firm chest as he spreads my thighs with his knee and pushes his cock inside me oh-so-slowly, filling me up inch by inch until I feel light-headed from the pleasure and the swiftness of my pulse. He pulls his hips back and plunges into me over and over, always maintaining a measured, gentle pace.

A groan rumbles out of him, resonating in his chest and vibrating against my nipples.

With his mouth still fused to mine, he closes a hand around my breast and begins to knead it in a leisurely, sensuous rhythm that has me clinging to his biceps and wanting to cry out, but I can't do that. His lips and tongue won't let me.

His other hand drifts down to my knee, and he slips his fingers between my thighs, dragging them up until he finds the slickness that coats the hairs on my mound. He gives up my mouth so he can rise onto all fours, his dick now dangling between our bodies. He lunges his head down to capture my nipple and pluck at the stiff peak with his teeth while his erection brushes across my belly, spreading my own wetness across my skin.

Though his need to come tightens his features and tautens every muscle in his body, he doesn't let go and fuck me like crazy. I'd love that, but somehow, the slowness and aching tenderness of the way he makes love to me feels more intense and pleasurable than anything I've experienced before. Not even the orgasms I gave myself while thinking about him can compare to this moment.

He lowers onto his elbows and shimmies his hips until his cock lies nestled between my folds. As gently as he has done everything else, he glides his length up and down my cleft, and I lose all control of myself, bucking my hips up into his movements in a desperate attempt to take him inside me. I grasp his shoulders to get more leverage, but still, he doesn't take me, not the way I want—with his hard, hot dick buried inside me. I moan and whimper, my nails digging into his flesh.

With a husky groan, he sinks his length into my body.

My hands fall down to his biceps, gripping him hard. I feel like I have no control over my muscles, as if an outside force has seized me. Though he keeps thrusting in a steady, even rhythm, I thrash and moan and shout things that aren't quite words, suddenly incoherent because of what he's doing to me. A high-tension wire inside me stretches tauter every second, until it chokes off my voice and freezes the breath in my lungs. The velvety hardness of his cock glides in and out, inflaming my already wet and achy flesh, and the sound of our bodies merging fills the room, a slick sucking that counts out the rhythm of our lovemaking, while the scent of my cream wafts around us.

I open my mouth but can't produce anything except a sharp gasp.

Without leaving my body, he rises to his knees and shoves his hands under my ass to lift it off the mattress. Still, he continues at that insanely hot and maddening pace that makes me want to both pull my hair out and beg him never to stop. That electric tension intensifies, and I feel myself crawling up a cliff, clawing my way toward orgasm, as my entire body goes rigid and Iain keeps thrusting. I fling my hands out to clamp them around the headboard rails, my mouth open, unable to breathe until…

The climax hits me so hard that a half-strangled scream explodes out of me. My inner muscles pulsate around his cock, making him hiss in a sharp breath. Even while my orgasm goes on and on, he doesn't speed up at all, plunging inside me and pulling out again over and over and over until his face cinches up with the best kind of agony—and he comes.

"Fuck, Rae," he growls, thrusting a few more times. He holds the last thrust as if his body has turned to stone. Even his expression doesn't change. I swear he's not breathing either. Just as I'm about to smack his cheek to wake him up, he exhales a long, groaning sigh that relaxes every muscle. He pulls out and lies down beside me with that Buddha smile on his lips. "Worth the wait, aye?"

"Oh, yeah. So worth it." I reach for the covers, but he bats my hand away. "What are you doing?"

"We are not done yet." He lays a hand on my thigh and skims it up and down my skin. "But before we have another go, I need to feed you."

"Not hungry. We had dinner already."

He smiles with so much heat that the expression could melt an iceberg. "I want to feed ye sweet, sensual treats to bolster ye for another shag."

"Oh. Well, go ahead and do that."

I watch him slide off the bed and saunter out of the room, admiring his tight ass and those strong thighs until he moves out of sight. I felt all his muscles tonight. Sex with Iain MacTaggart blew away all my expectations. And now, we have the rest of our lives to revel in the afterglow together.

Chapter Eleven

Iain

I return to the bedroom holding a bowl of ice cream. Rae lifts her brows when she notices me, but she doesn't say anything. Her attention swiftly shifts to my body as she roves her gaze over me, and her lips curl into an expression of appreciation and hunger—not for food, though. I know she craves my body as much as I crave hers. After ten months of fighting my desire for Rae, I needed all my Zen willpower to keep from ravishing her like an animal.

Rae is beautiful after a shag. I love the way her cheeks and chest have been dappled with a rosy pink. Her lips still seem slightly swollen, but they've looked like that for most of the day. Neither of us wanted to stop kissing. We had to, of course, in order to eat and drink and use the bathroom. And while I was driving. But we are not in a car right now. And I've come up with a way to kiss her and feed her at the same time.

She licks her lips as I sit down on the bed beside her, but I can't decide if she hungers for the ice cream or me. I allow myself a moment to drink in the vision of her nude body one more time, then I slap her hip. "Sit up, *gràidh*. Cannae feed ye when you're lying down."

Rae shimmies backward while pushing up with her arms until she can lean against the headboard. "I'm ready. For anything."

"I already knew that." I slide closer to her and dive my spoon into the ice cream. "I brought you two sauces for this treat—hot fudge and caramel."

She rubs her palms together, and her tongue pokes out between her lips. "Yum. But there's only one spoon. Are we sharing?"

"The spoon? No."

I turn partway toward her and pull the spoon out while fudge and caramel drizzle over its edges to coat the ice cream. Then I slide the spoon into my mouth.

"Hey!" She kicks my foot. "Thought we were sharing."

Smiling with my lips sealed, I lean toward her and press my mouth to hers. She opens for me without hesitation, the way she's done all day, and I deepen the kiss to mingle the taste of her with the flavor of the ice cream, fudge, and caramel. *Bod an Donais*, those flavors drive me mad. I haven't tasted *her* cream yet, but I mean to do that soon.

We explore each other's mouths for several minutes while I keep slipping bigger and bigger spoonfuls of our dessert into my mouth before I dive in again to devour her. She moans and thrusts her tongue deep as if she means to take all her nourishment from me. I would love that, but this was only foreplay, or maybe intermission. I haven't fulfilled all my plans for her body yet.

Still, I need to tease her a wee bit more. "Lie down again, please."

The lass doesn't even ask why. She slides down the bed until her head rests on the pillow, then raises her arms to clasp her hands near the headboard. The sexy slant to her smile lets me know she wants another shag as much as I do.

I fill the spoon with the melted remnants of our ice cream and drizzle it over her belly. Then I scoop up the last of the thick liquid and drop it onto her stiff nipples.

"Whatever you're doing," she says in a breathless tone, "keep doing it. Please."

"Aye, love, I will."

I bend over to lick the melted ice cream off her belly, starting near her navel and working my way up toward her breasts. Rae arches her back as a wee moan escapes her lips. She has the most beautiful body on earth, and I love the way she responds to my touch. I mean to keep giving her pleasure for the rest of our lives because I plan on proposing to her tomorrow. I need a ring first.

But right now, I need to make her so desperate for me that she'll say "Iain, oh God, yes" again.

When I flick my tongue over her ice cream covered nipple, she lets out a sharp cry. I swirl my tongue around that peak, delicately, again and again until she starts clenching the pillow and making desperate noises. Once I've licked all the ice cream off that nipple, I move to the other one and repeat the process.

Rae thrashes beneath me. "Oh God, Iain, please."

That's not the exact phrase she said earlier, but I love this one just as much.

Now that we've finished off the ice cream, I crawl down the bed to kneel between her feet. "Time for *my* dessert. I've waited a long time to feast on you, Rae."

"I've dreamed about this. About you…"

"Going down on you and lapping up every last bit of your cream?"

"Yes, oh, yes. I've wanted this for so damn long."

I chuckle. "Relax, love, I'm about to make your dream come true." I wink. "Multiple times."

She spreads her legs, and her chest rises and falls as she struggles to keep breathing evenly. She cannae do it, though. The lass is a wee bit excited about this.

I lie down between her legs and crawl forward until my face hovers above her mound. The scent of her desire envelops me, sweet and musky, more addictive than any drug. I rest my hands on her hips and dive in, lapping at her flesh and groaning as I get my first taste of her. It's as sweet as her scent, but even more intoxicating, but with a hint of saltiness. She bends her knees slightly while I drag my tongue up and down her folds, forcing myself to go slow and make this last—not only for her, but for me too. How had I stayed sane for all those months when I couldn't let on how much I want her? For Rae, I would endure any hardship to get to this moment with her.

She moves her hips in a circular motion, her breaths growing shallower and shorter. Could she already be on the edge? Given her reactions when I took her body earlier, I doubt she'll last long now. I imagine college laddies don't know how to give a woman real pleasure. The ones I've met at Nackington seem like the sort who would go off prematurely and leave the lass unsatisfied.

Why am I thinking about those scunners?

I focus on Rae, plunging my tongue inside her entrance while I tease her clit with my fingers, making her gasp.

"Oh, Iain, you're so amazingly good at doing—oh—this kind of—" She lets out a whimpering cry. "You're a god, Iain."

Her statement makes me sputter because I'm trying not to laugh while I have my tongue inside her. But that results in Rae thrashing again. I guess she likes what I accidentally did. So I lift my head and smirk at her. "Did ye like my new and entirely original method for driving you wild?"

She nudges my cheek with her knee. "Are you going to make me come sometime this year?"

Her sly smile assures me she is not annoyed.

I move my mouth up her cleft, taking my time so I can torment her flesh with soft kisses and fast flicks of my tongue. She makes a noise that's somewhere between a moan and a whimper with a slight gasp underneath. Every little cry makes my cock throb, but I donnae care. Once my lips close around her clit, I reach down to push one finger inside her. My gaze remains focused on Rae, on her expression and the way she bites her lip every time I plunge my finger into her body. But when I slide two fingers into her slick heat while devouring her taut nub, she shouts my name and her entire body jerks.

Her breathing has turned into sharp gasps.

Bod an Donais. The look on her face does me in, and I plunge three fingers inside her, pumping hard and fast, while I scrape my teeth over her nub and suckle it fiercely. She thrashes even more wildly, then her body stiffens. The moment her orgasm strikes, her muscles begin milking my fingers and strangled cries erupt from her.

"Iain!" she shouts as the final spasms wane. Then she goes limp, her bonnie tits heaving. "Wow, oh God, wow."

Rising to my knees, I lean forward to kiss her. "Say 'wow' again. It's dead sexy."

"Mm, wow." She sounds almost dreamy now, and her expression matches her tone. "You really are a god, Iain."

"A god?" I say with a chuckle. "No. I'm only a man."

"Not to me. You're..." She fans her face with one hand. "I can't even describe how amazing you are."

"Let's find out together." I kneel between her legs again, and she spreads them for me. On hands and knees, I straddle her body. "One more time before we're both too jeeked to go again."

She seems puzzled, but she doesn't ask me what "jeeked" means. Tomorrow, I'll explain all the things I've said to her—and I'll start with *gràidh*. It means "darling." Then I'll call her *mo chridhe* and tell her that means "my heart." She is that for certain. Maybe I'm too old for her, but I don't care.

Soon, I'll need to tell her about my family—and my father. But not tonight.

I slide into her like I donnae care how long this takes, going slow so I can experience every sensation. The slickness of her cream. The satiny smoothness of her body molding to my cock. The way her hairs tickle my *bagais*. I lower onto my elbows and press my lips to hers while keeping my eyes open. She keeps hers open too, and we gaze into each other's eyes even as I plunge inside her again and again. She grips my biceps, her soft gasps in rhythm with my thrusts.

I love you, Rae, I want to say. But I cannae speak.

So I seal mouth over hers and let her blue eyes hypnotize me while I thrust faster and deeper, suddenly unable to catch my breath. The pressure builds inside me until I cannae breathe at all, cannae move except to keep punching into her. My ears ring, and I feel like I'll explode any second.

I throw my head back as my harsh yell echoes in the room and I come, spilling everything deep inside her body, the sweet pressure finally released. Nothing else has ever felt as satisfying as making love to Rae. I hold still for a moment, unable to move even to lie down beside her. The warmth of her sheath surrounds my cock, and I'm breathing so hard that I cannae speak.

Rae combs her fingers through my hair. Her loving smile gives me a pang in my chest.

When I finally pull out of her body, I lie on my side and cradle her to me. "Are ye happy, love?"

"Never been happier." She makes a pained face. "But I need to pee."

I slap her erse. "Go on. I think I can survive a few minutes without you. But no more than that."

She kisses me, then hops off the bed and trots into the bathroom.

Rolling onto my back, I gaze up at the ceiling and imagine what our life together will be like. Rae mentioned the other day that she wants to become a teacher and she's applied to graduate schools. Whatever she wants to do, I know she'll excel at it.

A yawn overtakes me, and I fold my hands over my belly, shutting my eyes. I imagine us going to work together, teaching together, doing everything together. We'll have bairns, and they will all be bonnie, clever lasses like their mother.

I drift off to sleep with that dream in my mind.

Chapter Twelve

Rae

Iain had fallen asleep by the time I got done in the bathroom last night. Well, we did have sex twice. I've never done that before, but I can believe it would make a man wiped out and in need of serious sleep. So I didn't disturb him. I crawled back into bed and pulled the covers over us both, then cuddled up to Iain. I fell asleep not long after that.

This morning, I wake up sprawled over Iain's body. My arm is draped across his torso, my leg is draped over his thigh, and my cheek rests on his chest. I can hear his heart going *thump-thump, thump-thump*. I rub my cheek over his skin, inhaling a deep draft of Iain-scented air because he smells unbelievably good. Like sweat and sex and pure man.

His hand rests on my bottom.

I never did get around to showing Iain what I'd learned about blow jobs, but I don't care. Last night was incredible.

Iain sighs and grasps my ass. "*Guten Morgen, mein Liebling.* About bloody time ye woke up."

He's speaking German again. I have no idea what the second part means, and right now, I don't care.

"Good morning, Iain." I can't resist gliding my hand down his chest to his groin and laying my hand over his slowly growing erection. "Could we, um, do it again right now?"

He chuckles. "Later, *gràidh*. First, we both need a good breakfast to fortify us." He squeezes my ass. "Donnae worry. We have all the time in the world, and we will shag again later."

"Promise?"

"Yes, love, I promise." He kisses my forehead. "Are ye sore at all?"

"Only a little."

"Well, then we definitely should wait until later to have another poke."

I roll onto my back and exhale a long, satisfied breath. Then I stretch and sit up, gazing down at the gorgeously nude Scotsman lying beside me. I want to do nothing but admire his body all day long.

But Iain sits up too. "Let's get dressed."

I make an annoyed noise. "Can't we stay in bed for a few more hours?"

He shakes his head, though he's smiling. "If we do that, I'll shag you again. Ye need time to recover first."

Reluctantly, I get out of bed and put on the clothes I'd worn yesterday. I don't have anything else to wear since this isn't my apartment. Will Iain want to move in together? God, I hope so. I want to spend the rest of my life with him.

Iain makes oatmeal for breakfast like he had on that day in December when I'd been miserable. Yeah, I don't mind at all that he sucks at cooking. He makes up for that one flaw with all his amazing strengths and talents. After we eat, he drives me back to my apartment. I open the door and turn to face him on the threshold.

"Wait for me here," he says. "I have a few last things to do at my office. Shouldn't take more than an hour or two. Then we're both free for the summer."

"Free to do any damn thing we want."

His smile warms me up from the inside out. "Aye, whatever we want."

Iain kisses me and walks away.

Shutting the door, I close my eyes and lean back against it. A smile tightens my lips. The man I love wants to be with me. Life is perfect.

"What do you think you're doing?"

The angry voice of my former roommate snaps me out of my reverie. I push away from the door. "Cece? You don't live here anymore. You left yesterday."

"Yeah, but I forgot my favorite pair of undies in the bathroom." She stalks up to me, her features twisted into the nastiest expression I've ever seen. Her voice is just as nasty when she shoves me into the door and says, "You fucking slut!"

"What's your problem?"

"You." She stabs her finger into my chest so hard that I wince. "What right do you have to screw a teacher? I knew your sweet little girl act was bullshit. You just couldn't wait to get your skanky hands all over him, could you?"

"My what?" I can't understand anything she's saying. Why should she care if I'm dating Iain? As far as I know, she's never met him.

Cece steps closer, leaving only a few inches between us, and spittle sprays onto my face when she starts ranting again. "You are the dumbest geek on the planet. Do you seriously think the hot professor wants to see you again?" She huffs and rolls her eyes. "News flash. He only wanted to have some fun and play out his sugar daddy fantasy."

Then she really goes off, cursing at me in the vilest, most infantile way imaginable. I barely pay attention to her tirade, so stunned that I can't move or speak. I've never done a thing to Cece, yet she has apparently despised me with a vengeance for the whole ten months I've known the girl.

"Of course the teacher wanted to get some," she snarls. "Guys will hump anything with a vagina. Only a stupid piece of shit like you would think it means something."

Cece glowers at me for a few seconds, then she whirls around and storms into the bedroom she used to sleep in.

I slump against the door and struggle to make sense of what just happened. She called me horrible names because I did what? She assumes I slept with Iain, which I absolutely did, but I have no idea why she's so enraged about that. Cece has a boyfriend. That girl definitely has loose screws inside her deceptively pretty head. Maybe an entire dump truck full of them.

I can hear Cece in her room shouting at someone—or maybe just railing at the injustice of me dating Iain. Who the hell knows? The girl is crazy. Ten minutes go by before she falls silent. A moment later, she stalks out of the apartment, never even glancing at me. She slams the door hard.

Ohhh-kay. I'm elated that I'll never need to see that nutjob again. After all, she mentioned several times over the past ten months that she's moving to New York City to study at a "prestigious school of design." At least Cece the nutjob is out of my life for good.

Hallelujah.

Since I have to wait for Iain, I go into my bedroom to pack up my stuff. In addition to my suitcases, I kept the cardboard boxes I'd used to mail my other belongings to this apartment. While I do that mindless task, I start to worry about what Mom might think about me and Iain. I mean, he's closer to her age than mine. Will she freak when she learns that her daughter is shacking up with a man fifteen years older? I shouldn't worry about that yet. Mom isn't expecting me to come home until the end of the week, which gives me time to figure out how to break the news. Today, I just want to enjoy the best thing that's ever happened to me. I love Iain MacTaggart. I know he loves me too, though neither of us has spoken those words. We will today. I'll say it first if he hesitates. Guys can be silly about emotional stuff.

Once I finish packing, I carry the suitcases and boxes into the living room, setting them down beside the door. Iain can help me carry them out to his car or my car when he gets back from the campus.

I feel different this morning. Not because of the hot sex we had last night. No, I feel different because I finally found something good. My dad might've destroyed my faith in men, but Iain has shown me that not all of them are jerks. He is wonderful.

With nothing else to do until Iain comes back, I watch TV and eat junk food.

Hours go by. At noon, I try to call Iain on his cell. No answer. When it goes to voice mail, I hang up. I try his office number too, but get no answer there either. What if he had a car accident? I pace the width of the living room for another ten minutes, then try both his numbers again. My heart is racing, I'm chewing on my lip, and I feel nauseous. So this time when his voice mail picks up, I leave a message.

"Iain? It's Rae. Um, you said you'd be back in an hour or two, but it's been four hours. Are you okay? Please call me. I'm really starting to freak out. I know I'm probably being silly, but please, just call me back? Okay?"

After hanging up, I realize how stupid and desperate that sounded. I can't help that. Iain always does what he says he'll do. If he promised to come back in an hour or two, he would do that. So I call every hospital within sixty miles of Nackington. But I still can't find him. I want to call my mom, but what could she do? Nothing. I'm an adult, and I can handle this on my own.

Five minutes after twelve noon, I jump into my car and race to Iain's apartment. My pulse pounds so hard and fast that I feel almost faint. But I will not pass out. Iain must be in some kind of trouble, and I will not stop until I find him. I trip when I burst out of the elevator, catching myself just shy of hitting the floor, and sprint to the door of his apartment. I ring the bell over and over, then give up and start pounding my fists on the door.

"Iain! Are you in there? Iain!"

A door across the hall opens. "Is something wrong, dear?"

Whirling around, I see an elderly woman gazing at me with concern. Tears burn in my eyes, ready to pour down my cheeks any second. I swallow hard, but my lip trembles and my voice comes out shaky. "Um, yeah, something is wrong. Do you know the man who lives in this apartment? His name is Iain MacTaggart. I was supposed to meet him today, but I can't find him anywhere."

"Oh, you poor dear." The woman walks over to pat my arm. "Are you his girl? Iain is such a nice man. He always carries my groceries for me."

"Have you seen him today?" I choked on the last word, and the first tears trickle down my cheeks. I sniffle and say, "I'm so worried about him."

"I can see that. Have you called the police?"

"N-no. But I think I should check his office before I do that."

The sweet woman pats my arm again. "You do that, dear. I'm sure you'll find him and realize everything is fine."

"Uh-huh. Thank you. I'm so sorry for bothering you."

I sprint to the elevator and tap my toes on the floor while the car descends, though it feels like it takes an hour to reach the ground floor. Ten minutes later, I'm sprinting across the campus and into the humanities building. The door to Iain's office hangs open. He must be in there, right? He locks the door every day when he leaves.

But I stumble to a halt when I reach the threshold. The desk is empty. Like no one has ever used it. I stand here breathing so hard that my ears ring.

Footsteps approach in the hallway, stopping just behind me. "Uh, miss?"

I spin around, almost falling over in the process, and gape at the janitor standing on the threshold. "Where is Iain MacTaggart? This is his office."

"Not anymore." He winces. "Sorry. I heard he quit or got fired or something. Anyway, they told me he's gone. I was supposed to clear out this office and then lock up. Just finished cleaning, then I almost forgot the locking-up part."

My brain can't form words. My voice won't function either. All I can do is shuffle past the janitor and shuffle down the hallway. I push the doors open and walk back to the student parking lot in a haze of confusion and numbness. Everything from my skin down to my bones seems to have turned to ice.

Back in my apartment, I sit on the sofa staring at the wall. After a while, I pick up the phone, intending to call the airline and move my flight up to tomorrow. But I stop myself before I even finish dialing the number. I need to get away from here, but I can't leave yet. When my mom calls to get the details about my upcoming flight, I recite the information in a voice that sounds eerily calm, even to me. Mom doesn't seem to notice. After we say goodbye, I go into my room and curl up on the bed, on my side, hugging my knees. And I let the tears flow.

Iain, where are you?

Chapter Thirteen

Iain

Leaving Rae feels like cutting my own heart out. But that's rubbish. I'll see her in a few hours, once I've done what I need to do and closed out my office for the summer. I'm not teaching again until the fall. If Rae gets accepted to a graduate school somewhere else, I'll go with her and find another position for myself. All I care about is being with her. The rest we can work out together, as a couple.

My first task takes me to a jewelry store.

Aye, I mean to make Rae my wife. Donnae care about our age difference. I've never loved anyone else and I never will. As I browse the glass cases, hunting for the perfect ring, I can't help imagining what our life together will be like. Will Rae's mother accept me? She might think I'm too old for her daughter, but I will do whatever it takes to ease her worries and prove that I will care for her daughter and cherish Rae forever.

I've become a lovestruck fool, and I donnae give a damn.

"This one," I tell the store clerk, pointing at the ring I want.

It isn't large, but it's not too small either. I doubt Rae would want an enormous stone since she doesn't like me to "go overboard." The clerk rings up the purchase and puts the ring in a velvet box. Though he offers to give me a bag for it, I decide to keep the box in my pocket instead. On my way back to the campus, I stop at a flower shop to buy a bouquet for Rae. White roses. I think she'll like that. Red seemed too severe for a lass who exudes light and life from every pore on her body. Aye, I'm completely off my head, but in a good way. The final tasks I need to complete shouldn't take long, which means I can rush back to Rae soon and ask that all-important question.

As I approach my office, I have my head down, gazing at the flowers in my hand. Though I hear scuffling sounds up ahead, the fact they're coming from my office doesn't register in my mind until I walk through the door and nearly crash into someone.

Raising my head, I freeze.

Three security guards are inside the room. Two of them seem to have just finished dumping all my files and everything on my desk into bin bags. I see my name plate sticking out of one bag.

"What's this?" I ask.

The men turn toward me, all of them looking stern. One bloke aims a flinty glare at me, while the other keeps his hand on his holstered gun and taps one finger on it. The third seems more relaxed, at least in his posture, and he gazes at me with a faintly pinched expression.

"Come with us, please," the guard with the flinty glare says. "The president wants to see you."

I doubt he means the President of the United States. "Why? I was just about to leave for summer break."

The gun-tapping guard twists one side of his mouth into a sneer. "You aren't going anywhere except to the president's office."

I glance at my empty desk, and a prickly sensation rushes over my skin, raising the hairs on my arms.

A guard snatches the bouquet from my hand, flinging it into a rubbish bin.

The other two guards each seize one of my arms and force me to walk with them down the hall. The third guard follows, maintaining a short distance behind us as if they think I might try to escape. Am I a prisoner? It certainly seems that way. But why? I have no idea.

We march outside and straight across the quad to another building, the one that houses various offices, including that of the university president. I'm so dangerous that I require three guards to control me? *Mhac na galla.* Even as we walk into the building and step into an elevator, the two guards maintain their grip on my arms. The third stands in front of us now. Everything becomes a blur while we trudge out of the elevator and down the fourth floor hall to a doorway identified as the "Office of the President."

But when we enter the room, President Schaech isn't the only person there. Dean Milton from the humanities department also waits inside, as does Conrad Bremner-Ashton, the university's single largest donor and the father of Rae's roommate. All I know about Conrad is the rumors that have percolated through the campus, most thanks to the wagging tongues of students. The gossip suggests the Bremner-Ashtons have been a sort of mini mafia that controls the town of Nackington and the university that bears its name.

I never believed that rubbish. But faced with the three powerful men in this office, I begin to wonder. Still, I shouldn't jump to conclusions since I don't know why I've been summoned here.

President Schaech sits behind his large desk, of course, while Conrad and Dean Milton relax in chairs on this side of the desk. An empty seat lies between them.

Schaech waves toward that seat. "Have a seat, Dr. MacTaggart."

I do what he suggested, and now I'm sandwiched between the dean and Conrad Bremner-Ashton. "What is this about? My office has been cleaned out with everything tossed into bin bags."

"Bin bags?" Schaech's brows draw together. "I guess you mean garbage bags. Yes, I ordered your office to be cleaned out since you are no longer an employee of Nackington University."

"What? I know the school year ended, but I have until July to decide if I want to extend my contract for another year."

"Request denied."

"I still don't understand what's happening. Just last month, you told me how pleased you've been with the success of my Celtic history course."

Schaech's expression has hardened, and he stares at me with a strange coldness in his gaze. "Conrad has told me what you've done, what sort of reprobate you are. I had no choice but to terminate your employment immediately."

"What do you claim I've done?" He can't know I slept with Rae last night. Besides, that's not illegal or an ethics violation.

The president looks at Conrad. "Why don't you do the honors? Explain the situation to this miscreant."

Conrad Bremner-Ashton turns slightly in his chair to face me. A smug smile tugs at his lips. "You seduced one student and sexually harassed another. That is a clear violation of the university ethics code."

"Bollocks. I never did any of that. Who told you those lies?"

He nods to one of the guards, who steps out into the hall. When he returns a moment later, Cecelia Bremner-Ashton shuffles over to her father and feigns being terrified as she glances at me. Her act is far from convincing. Cece should never try to become an actress because she's ruddy awful at it. No tears accompany her hiccuping wee sobs, and her eyes do not glisten with unshed tears. They aren't red either, as they would be if she had cried earlier. No, her eyes are clear and bright and glittering with excitement. Even her quivering lip is sheer artifice. Her mouth keeps shifting into a smile as smug as her father's, though she tries her best to hide it.

"Ye cannae believe this one-woman show," I say to Schaech. "She is lying."

He ignores me and stares down at his lap, clearly waiting for the real man in charge to speak.

"My daughter does not lie," Conrad says. "She can provide details concerning how you sexually harassed her in an attempt to seduce her into your bed."

"I donnae even like the cow. Why on earth would I want to shag her? This is pure rubbish."

Conrad lifts one brow. "Students call you the Notorious Dr. MacT, Professor of Fuckology. No one receives a nickname like that without just cause."

"You're using a moronic nickname as an excuse to sack me? College laddies make up things like that. It's how they entertain themselves."

"Stop talking, Dr. MacTaggart." Conrad leans toward me, his expression so full of hatred that I know he will never see reason. "You didn't only harass my daughter. You lured another student into becoming your illicit lover."

"I never touched your daughter, Conrad."

His lips curl into a sneer. "I'm talking about Rae Everhart."

All I can do is gawp at the man. How does he know I slept with Rae? My gaze gravitates to Cece, who has now given up her pathetic act and smiles with a smugness that tells me everything I need to know. She and her father have conspired to rob me of my position at Nackington. I don't give a toss about that. But if they do anything to hurt Rae...

"She's not a student," I say. "Anything I might have done with Rae happened after the semester ended. Ask her."

"We don't need to," Conrad says. "We have an eyewitness."

He looks up at Cece.

She lifts her chin and gazes down at me with supreme satisfaction. "I saw the two of you kissing this morning. I saw Rae go into your apartment last night too."

"You followed me?"

"I was worried about my roomie," she says in a tone of mock sincerity. "A lech was putting the moves on sweet little Rae, so I had to do something." She folds her arms over her chest. "Neither of you left that apartment until morning."

"So what? We are adults."

Every rumor I'd ever heard about the Bremner-Ashtons floods into my mind, and I realize how foolish I've been. The signs were there. Cece disliked Rae and was clearly jealous of her. Being a kind-hearted lass, Rae assumed the girl meant no harm. But the witch knew exactly what she was doing. Her obsession with the relationship between me and Rae had become far more intense than either of us realized. Now we are both in the crosshairs of a powerful family.

Conrad jabs a finger into the air near my face, almost grazing my nose. "You have two choices. Stay and fight, knowing you will be destroyed in the process. Or leave the country now."

"Leave the country? You're off yer head."

"Go willingly, or you will be deported by force. Unless you get on a plane today, we will punish your lover."

Bile surges into my throat, but I gulp it down. "Punish her in what way?"

"Any way we want."

I know from his tone and his expression that he means it. He will do who knows what to Rae, just to punish me for loving her and refusing to abandon the lass. I never even told her I love her. My mind races, but I cannae catch even a single thought, much less devise a plan in the next thirty seconds that might save me and Rae.

"You have until the count of five," Conrad says, "to agree to leave the country. Five, four—"

What else can I do? Rae's safety means more to me than my own life.

"Three, two—"

"I'll go," I say. Honestly, I have no bloody clue if they can have me deported, but I can't take that risk. "You've won, Conrad. I will leave the country."

Maybe I'm a sodding coward. I can't think clearly enough to know what the right thing is in this situation. *Protect Rae.* That's my only coherent thought.

Conrad straightens, his lips forming a nasty smile. "I'm glad you've seen reason. Your possessions will be shipped to you."

As I let the guards herd me out of the building and to a police car parked along the curb, I feel like I must've fallen asleep and this is all a terrible nightmare. Any moment, I'll wake up to find Rae lying beside me, her soft, warm body snuggled up to mine. But I will never see her again. She will never know how I feel about her. Conrad Bremner-Ashton has wielded all his power to rip us apart.

Two officers from the Nackington Campus Police Department escort me to my apartment so I can pack two small bags. They won't let me use the landline phone, and they confiscate my mobile, all so I can't contact Rae. Then they take me to the nearest international airport. I briefly consider running away, since the guards can't follow me into the terminal, but that would be a futile effort. As the wheels lift off the runway, I sag in my uncomfortable airline seat and cover my eyes with my hands. Cannae breathe. Cannae think. Donnae know what the fuck I'll do now.

But the memory of that beautiful night with Rae will stay with me for the rest of my life.

Chapter Fourteen

Rae

For three days, I scour the university and the whole town of Nack-Fington in search of any sign of Iain. No one knows where he went, when he left, or why he disappeared. My tears have dried, and I've developed a strangely determined attitude that must come across as tough, because everybody seems kind of uncomfortable talking to me.

After days of searching, I'm exhausted. So I sleep for twelve hours, then I gather my bags and get ready for my departure later today. I'd already shipped all the boxes of my stuff to Iowa. My few bags look so lonely in the empty apartment.

I'm about to call a taxi to go to a restaurant for breakfast, since I sold my car yesterday, when the dean of the humanities department calls me. He says he urgently needs to see me in his office. My flight doesn't leave until this afternoon, so I have time to find out what Dean Milton wants. When I walk into his office, he tells me to shut the door and have a seat. Yeah, that doesn't sound ominous at all. His somber tone does nothing to quell the acid roiling in my gut.

I settle into a hard wooden chair.

"You must be wondering why I summoned you," he says. "I'm afraid it's not good news."

A chill shivers through me. Bad news? Is it about Iain?

Dean Milton clasps his hands on his desk and frowns down at them. "I've received disturbing information about you and Iain MacTaggart."

"What do you mean?"

He sighs heavily, then lifts his head to aim a stony expression at me. "I know you had a sexual relationship with Dr. MacTaggart while you were a student in his class on Celtic history."

"No, that's not true." I didn't sleep with him until after the semester ended. "Who told you that?"

"Cecelia Bremner-Ashton."

Oh, that goddamn bitch. Spreading lies? I knew she was a jerk, but this...

"The trustees met to discuss the issue this week, and they've reached a decision." He stares straight into my eyes, his gaze cold and unforgiving. "Your grade for that course has been changed to an F. This means you are one credit short of graduating. Since you're also being expelled, you will not have the opportunity to make up that credit. Your degree is null and void."

"What?" I almost whisper that single syllable, too stunned to say anything else. Expelled? That can't be. "But you're doing this based on a lie. Cece has been jealous of me, and she—"

"Stop right there. Blaming Cece will not spare you. The decision has been made, and no appeal is possible." He rises from his chair to peer down at me. "Goodbye, Miss Everhart."

I'd heard rumors over the past four years, gossip about the Bremner-Ashton family being like a Midwest mafia, controlling this town and the university. I hadn't believed it. The stories sounded too outlandish. But here, today, in the dean's office, I suddenly realize it was all true.

"You could hire a lawyer," Dean Milton says. "But I don't imagine someone like you could afford the fees. The Bremner-Ashtons will sue if you make any public comment about Cece or your expulsion."

He's right. I can't afford a lawyer, and even if I sold everything I own, I would never win the battle. When a powerful family wants you dead, metaphorically, they will get their way at any cost.

Dean Milton waves toward the door. "Leave now, please. By the way, you are also barred from setting foot on campus ever again."

Like I would ever want to come back here. Everything I dreamed of has been shattered into a million pieces.

As I'm walking out the door, Dean Milton tells me, "You should know the truth. Iain MacTaggart left the country of his own volition. He won't come back."

I swallow hard, but the constriction in my throat refuses to let up. Iain abandoned me. Maybe I shouldn't believe everything the dean told me, since he thinks my former roommate is a reliable source. But I can't imagine why Iain would have left of his own volition. He could've fought—for us, for me, for what I believed we had together. But maybe it was all a lie.

With no other options, I fly home to Iowa.

My mom picks me up at the curb just outside the airport terminal. I still feel weirdly calm and determined to do…something. Mom tries to engage me in conversation during the drive to our house, but I just stare out the window. Why did Iain leave? Did he do it voluntarily? The only involuntary way I can think of would be kidnapping. But that doesn't seem plausible. I mean, no one could have a reason to abduct a Scottish college teacher.

Who is Iain MacTaggart? Did I ever really know him? We never talked about our families. I know his full name is Iain Malcolm MacTaggart and that he grew up in Scotland, but that's about it. Maybe the fact that he never shared more about his past should've been a warning sign, but then, I'd never told him much about my past. Would we have shared everything on that fateful morning after he finished closing up his office? I never even got to tell him how I feel, how much I love him.

And I have no clue if he felt the same way.

We have all the time in the world, Iain had told me on the morning after our one and only night together. But we didn't have even the whole day. He walked out of my apartment and out of my life with no explanations.

Now I sit in the kitchen with my mom, staring down into a cup of tea while absently stirring it with a spoon and watching the milk swirl round and round. Just days ago, I was lying in bed with Iain. We were making love and sharing ice cream. Now he's gone.

Mom curls her hand around mine to stop my incessant stirring. "Please talk to me, Rae. What happened? Why are you so distraught?"

"Doesn't matter anymore."

"Of course it does."

I push the tea mug away, having drunk exactly none of it, and lean back in my chair to hug myself.

Mom watches me with a worried expression. "I wish you would tell me what happened, sweetie."

"Not today, Mom, please." Tears pool in my eyes, and try as I might, I can't stop them from spilling down my cheeks. "I don't know what happened, anyway. My life is over, that's all I know."

I drop my arms onto the tabletop and let my head fall down too as the tears become sobs.

Mom lays a hand on my back, rubbing it in gentle circles.

When I finally stop crying, she doesn't quiz me about what happened. She just leads me upstairs to the bedroom where I'd slept for my entire life, except for the time I was at Nackington. Over the summers, I slept here too. This is my home, but it doesn't feel that way anymore. No, I found a new home with a wonderful man.

And then it all came crashing down.

The next morning, I tell my mother everything. Well, almost everything. I can't bring myself to relate the events of that night with Iain. But I won't lie about the rest. "I fell in love, Mom. I met an amazing man who made me feel like we could conquer the world together. Iain MacTaggart is from Scotland, but he came to Nackington University last fall. I took one of his classes, and we became friends."

She doesn't speak. Mom just listens and watches me.

"We couldn't date because he was my teacher. But we both knew what we felt was more than friendship. Still, Iain behaved like a gentleman the whole time. Then my roommate got jealous and…" I squeeze my eyes shut for a moment. "She started a chain reaction that destroyed my life. I didn't just lose Iain. I lost everything I'd worked for, and I can't get it back. I was expelled."

"Oh, honey." She clasps my hand. "I know it seems like the world has ended, but you'll recover from this. One thing I know about my daughter is that she never gives up."

"I loved him, Mom." I tiny sob hiccups out of me as tears flow again. "I loved him so much."

"Oh, baby, I know."

"Maybe I misunderstood, and he didn't feel that way about me. I mean, why would a thirty-seven-year-old professor want to date a college senior?"

"He's how old?" Surprise flashes on her face, but only for a second. Then she regains her calm demeanor. "This man, this Iain MacTaggart, is fifteen years older than you."

I nod.

She puckers her lips, but she doesn't say anything. I can tell she doesn't approve of our age difference. It hardly matters now. Unless I can find Iain, I will never know how he really felt about me.

For weeks and weeks, I do nothing but wallow in my shock and grief. I'd never been in love until I met Iain, so I have no idea how to deal with the loss. Mom wants to help, but I just can't make myself talk about it anymore. Though I feel like I should get a job or something, every time I suggest that, Mom tells me not to worry about it. I have the rest of my life to figure things out, she says. Since I was expelled from Nackington, I don't know if I can get into another school to finish my degree. Do I even want that anymore?

Soon, two months have gone by—and I come to a realization that changes everything.

I've been feeling off for a while, but I assumed the tiredness and intermittent nausea was a side effect of grief. Then one day, I realize I haven't had my period since I left Nackington. No, I can't be—No. I rack my brain for information about that night with Iain and struggle to remember whether we used protection. I have no idea. The only thing I can recall for certain is the way Iain made love to me.

Later that day, I go grocery shopping with Mom. While she heads for the meat section, I tell her I need to go to the restroom, but what I really do is hurry to the pharmacy inside the grocery store and buy a pregnancy test. I stuff it into my purse to make sure Mom won't see. Until I know for sure, I don't want to worry her.

The next morning, I finally work up the nerve to take the test. The stick turns blue.

I'm still sitting on the toilet, with the lid down, and I let the test stick tumble from my fingers. Then I drop my head into my raised hands. I'm pregnant. In seven months, I will have Iain's child. *Oh God.* How can I do this without him?

The time for wallowing is over. I need to think about my child now. And that means I need to tell my mom the news. I find her in the kitchen making pancakes for breakfast. "Uh, Mom, can we talk?"

"Sure, honey." She slides the last pancake off the griddle and sets it on the plate with the others. Then she settles onto a chair at the table. "The look on your face tells me we should sit down for this."

"Yeah." I perch on the chair beside hers and just say it. "I'm pregnant, Mom."

Her face goes blank. She doesn't even blink. After a moment, she finally speaks. "Pregnant?"

"Yes."

She clears her throat and shakes off her shock. "The father is Iain MacTaggart."

I nod.

"But you have no idea where he is."

"No. Even if I never find him, I want this baby."

She grasps my hand firmly. "Of course you do. And I will help in whatever way I can. Have you been to a doctor to confirm it?"

"I did a home test. But I'll make an appointment today."

"Don't worry, baby. You can do this. Everhart woman always rise to a challenge and overcome adversity."

Mom has definitely done that. Despite Dad's cheating, despite the impending divorce, despite Dad running away to Hong Kong, she persevered. I couldn't ask for a better role model. So I lay my palm over hers, where she still grasps my other hand. "You're amazing, Mom."

In the afternoon, I go to my doctor's appointment and get confirmation. Yes, I'm pregnant. I don't need a doctor to tell me who the father is. The news spurs me to embark on a mission to find Iain, though I have no idea where to start. I try everything I can think of to track him down. Mom lets me do that and doesn't tell me I'm wasting my time, though she gets a disapproving look on her face whenever she catches me scouring the internet for men called Iain MacTaggart. Who knew there would be so many of those in Scotland? Iain never told me exactly where he lived, not even the general region. Scotland might be way smaller than the United States, but hunting for a specific Scotsman turns into the most grueling task I've ever undertaken.

But I will not wipe myself out in the process. I have someone else's life to worry about, and my child matters more to me than anything else. I'm not even showing yet, but I already love this baby more than I ever could have imagined I might. I can't resist closing my eyes every night before I go to sleep just to lie here and imagine what my son or daughter will be like. Iain is in those fantasies too, right there by my side.

As my search continues, I consider hiring a private investigator, but I don't have enough money for that. I can't ask my mom. She's been my rock ever since I came home and fell into a puddle of misery, despite the fact that she clearly disapproves of my relationship with Iain and the way I'm desperately searching for him. I tried to call his cell phone again the day after he disappeared, but I got a message that the number is no longer in service. Probably because it was a US number. When he went back to Scotland, he must've gotten a new one. When I resort to calling Iain MacTaggarts in the desperate hope I'll find the one I need, my mom puts her foot down. Yeah, the international phone charges might bankrupt me if I keep going.

"Stop this, Rae," my mom tells me. She's leaning over the back of my chair, where I sit with my computer on the desk in front of me. "You can't live like this anymore. I know you loved that man, but it's time to move on—for the sake of your child, if not for yourself. It isn't healthy to cling to something you can never get back."

I tip my head back to look at her upside-down face. "Sorry. I know I've gotten kind of obsessed. But you're right, it's time to lay that ghost to rest."

A few days later, when I finally unpack all my boxes that I'd shipped home from Nackington, I discover something that nearly does me in. I find the scarf Iain gave me, the one made from the MacTaggart clan tartan. My hands start to shake as I hold the fabric to my cheek, and tears dribble down to drip off my chin. I want to wrap that scarf around me and never take it off, but I can't dwell on the past anymore. I have a future to write for myself and my baby.

So I tuck the scarf into the back of a dresser drawer and get on with my life.

Will I ever forget about Iain? As much as I want to banish the ghost of him, I know our child will bind me to him forever, whether or not he ever learns the truth.

Chapter Fifteen

Iain

A mature man should know how to handle losing a lass, but I've lost more than Rae. I have no job and no prospects for finding another one because that bastard Conrad Bremner-Ashton has made certain of that. I am, for all intents and purposes, universally blacklisted. Dean Milton and President Schaech must have helped Conrad do that by spreading lies about me. I doubt he has the international connections to manage it on his own. What can I do now? Nothing. What will I do? Well, that's another question, one I can answer. As much as I wish I could say I've behaved like a mature man in the aftermath of the worst disaster I've ever experienced, I won't lie to myself. Certainly can't lie to anyone else either. Everyone witnesses my downfall.

Maybe if shagging half the women in the village of Loch Fairbairn had been my only mistake, I could've recovered from it better. But no, I doubt anything would've stopped me from sliding down that slippery slope into self-destruction. I never knew I had it in me. I wish I still didn't know. Learning the dark truths about myself does nothing to stave off the grief and shame of what I did to Rae, abandoning her because I was too cowardly to defy the Nackington mafia. Why didn't I fight for Rae? After I came home, I could have rung her to explain and to beg her to move to Scotland to marry me. I have no bloody clue if she would've done that. But I didn't even try.

The day after I returned to my homeland, I finally think to check the voice mail on my mobile. I can't do that, though, because the Nackington mafia had confiscated it, and now my service has been disconnected. It was a mobile I'd bought in America, anyway, so it might not even work over here.

Then I receive an email from Conrad Bremner-Ashton. The bastard has sent me an audio file with no text to explain what it might be. Maybe I shouldn't do it, but I open the audio file anyway.

"Iain? It's Rae. Um, you said you'd be back in an hour or two, but it's been four hours. Are you okay? Please call me. I'm really starting to freak out. I know I'm probably being silly, but please, just call me back? Okay?"

The fear and pain in her voice wrecks me, and I do something I haven't done since I was a wee laddie. I slump to the floor, bury my face in my hands, and cry.

After an hour, I wipe my eyes and get up. For three weeks after that, I try to pretend I'm fine, though I know I'm nothing close to it. Channeling my Zen side works for a while and convinces everyone except me. But not for long. I try drinking to numb the pain, but after a string of incidents at local pubs in which I behave like a *tolla-thon* and start brawls with laddies I don't even know, I realize I don't want to make a name for myself as a drunken ersehole. Then I turn to sex for pain relief. Shagging women in pub hallways and the backs of cars does little to alleviate the ache in my chest, though. No one else can fill the hole carved out of my heart. Only Rae can do that, but I've given her up.

Fate has a wicked sense of humor, as it turns out. Or maybe I'm just cursed.

I'm sitting in the living room of the house I rented last week since I didn't want to burden my parents anymore with my behavior. I've just turned on the television to watch a rugby match when my landline rings. The second I say hello, my mother sobs, "Iain, please come home now."

"What is it, Ma?"

"Your da, he—" She lets out another, harder sob. "Angus has been arrested again."

I jerk forward. "Arrested? For what?"

"The usual. We donnae have much in the bank account, and you know how Angus gets when the purse strings are tight. I know he does it because he loves me and wants to protect me, but I cannae go through this again. What if he's sent back to prison?"

Bloody hell. I thought we'd gotten past all that. "What has he stolen this time?"

"Donnae be angry, Iain. Your da doesnae mean to get into trouble."

Aye, he never does mean to do these things. I love my father, but I can't handle this right now. Doesn't matter if I can or not, though. I must deal with it. "Who did he burgle?"

"Rhys Kendrick."

"Who? I've never heard of the bloke."

"He's a Welshman who moved to Loch Fairbairn while you were away in America. Kendrick is very wealthy, apparently from mines that he owned and then sold." Ma pauses, and I can hear her sniffling. "Everyone knows Kendrick has a collection of... What do you call them? Some sort of trinkets."

"It must be worth a great deal for him to be arrested, which means it's no trinket."

"Aye, but I donnae know what it is. Something made of gold, I think. It's all so confusing."

"Relax, Ma. I'll take care of things."

Ten minutes later, I jump into the old Land Rover I'd bought recently and race to the police station in Loch Fairbairn. My father has indeed been arrested and charged with theft by housebreaking for stealing a solid gold bowl. Aye, that qualifies as a "trinket." Who the bloody hell needs a thing like that? The officers let me speak to my father, and he tells me what happened, which gives me the information I need to understand the situation. I leave him and head for the home of Rhys Kendrick.

A woman in a maid's uniform answers the door. "May I help you?"

"My name is Iain MacTaggart. I need to speak to Rhys Kendrick."

Her expression turns puzzled. "MacTaggart? You can't be the man who broke in and stole Mr. Kendrick's bowl."

"That was my father."

"Oh, I see." The woman steps aside. "Please come in. I'll let Mr. Kendrick know you're here."

I walk inside, and she closes the door. Then the woman leaves me in the entryway of this mansion while she wanders off—to find her employer, presumably.

Footfalls clap from elsewhere in the house. A large brute of a man veers into the entryway, his expression fierce and sullen. He halts an arm's length from me. "You dare to set foot in my house? The son of the bastard who invaded my home and stole from me."

"Aye, I dare to set foot. I'd like to discuss the matter with you, Mr. Kendrick."

"Discuss?" His lip curls into a nasty slant. "I don't invite criminals into my home—or their spawn, either."

"My father didn't mean to upset anyone. You see, my parents have suffered financial setbacks lately and—"

"Shut up!" His shout echoes off the walls of the entryway. "I do not care about your setbacks. Angus MacTaggart stole from me, and I will have him prosecuted to the fullest extent of the law."

"I'll make sure he never bothers you again. Please, don't send him to prison. I will make restitution in whatever way you feel is appropriate."

Kendrick smacks both palms onto my chest and shoves so hard that I stumble backward into the door. "Take yourself away from me. I have nothing else to say. Leave before I decide to shatter your jaw with my fist."

He won't relent. I might be stubborn and desperate, but I know when I'm fighting a losing battle. The *tolla-thon* wants to punish my father. I suspect he's the sort who enjoys punishing everyone he deems to be weaker than himself. Can anyone change his mind? I drive back to my house and ring my cousin Rory, who recently finished his traineeship and became a solicitor. He's one of the cleverest and most determined people I know, so I hope he can help my family and talk Kendrick out of imprisoning my father. Rory offers to represent Da—and to speak to Rhys Kendrick.

But Rory has no better luck. From what he tells me, I think my cousin just avoided getting into a barnie with the *tolla-thon* that would've sent him to jail too. I appreciate that he tried. Mac-Taggarts always help each other, no matter what. The fact that sometimes our efforts fail doesn't diminish our commitment to each other.

The next day, Rhys Kendrick invites me to his house. He says he wants to offer me "an alternative solution" to the problem of my father and the item he stole. Since even a solicitor couldn't do much, I feel I have to meet with Kendrick and hear his offer. Even if Da can handle prison, Ma might not survive being separated from him again and suffering the shame of what he's done.

When I arrive at Kendrick's mansion, the man himself opens the door and ushers me inside. We go into a study where he takes the big leather chair behind the desk and I sit on a much smaller chair across from him. I see gold and silver items on shelves, decorative pieces that must've cost a ruddy fortune but that serve no useful purpose other than to make a rich scunner feel important.

Kendrick leans back in his chair, hooking one ankle over the other knee, and nails his gaze to mine. "Here's my offer. I will rescind my complaint against your father and make sure the charges are dropped—if you do a favor for me."

No, I don't like the sound of that. A favor? For a *bod ceann* like him? But I need to save my father. Maybe if I hadn't spent weeks drowning my misery in alcohol and women, I could've stopped my father from taking such drastic action to protect his family. This is my fault, and I will make it right.

"What sort of favor?" I ask.

"I want you to authenticate an artifact for me."

Oh no, that's not suspicious at all. "What sort of artifact is it?"

"Agree to do this, and I will show it to you."

For a moment, I stare at him and consider my options. I have none. "All right. I'll do it."

Kendrick smirks. "Come with me, then."

He reaches under the lip of his desk, presumably to flick a switch since a section of wall to my left slides open. I follow Kendrick into the space revealed by the hidden door. Ancient artifacts rest on shelves.

Rhys Kendrick approaches an artifact that lies atop a pedestal, sets his hand on the edge, and turns toward me. "Here it is."

I amble up to the pedestal and study the object. It's a marble statue carved in the style of similar examples I'd seen in museums and in the field years ago. "This looks like a Neolithic idol, most likely from Greece."

And it looks like a fake to me. I'm hardly an expert on the Neolithic in Greece, but during my years in the field I'd learned how to spot a forgery.

Kendrick smirks again.

But that expression crumbles when I say, "The statue is a forgery. I can't authenticate it."

The brute's eyes narrow, his nostrils flare, and he slams his fist down on the pedestal so hard that the statue wobbles and nearly tumbles off. I catch it before that happens and set the item back where it belongs.

Kendrick glowers at me. "I know the fucking thing is a forgery. But you will authenticate it if you want to free your father. Who knows what might happen to him in prison? Accidents, brawls, or worse."

It doesn't take a genius to figure out he means to guarantee those "accidents" happen if I refuse his demand. His tone makes that clear.

"Here's what you need to know," he says, "to ensure your continued cooperation. I own the original artifact that is identical to the forgery. But I need you to authenticate the fake so I can pay someone to steal it and then file an insurance claim for the full value of the genuine version—over fifty thousand pounds, according to my estimates."

"Why not just pretend the original was stolen? Why create a fake?"

"Because I want to bilk the insurance company. It's the thrill of getting away with something, don't you see?"

Kendrick's plan is nonsense, but I won't point that out. If he plans to claim the forgery was stolen, he doesn't need the fake at all. He could use a picture of the genuine artifact to commit his insurance fraud. This man is more than off his head. He's a bloody stupid ersehole of the most dangerous kind. I can't risk my family's well-being. I must do what Kendrick wants. His eyes have lit up with a perverse glee that suggests nothing will dissuade him. This man takes pleasure from cheating despite the fact he clearly doesn't need the money.

"You're in too deep to back out now, MacTaggart," he snarls.

Maybe I am. He seems like the sort who would batter me bloody if I tried to end this charade right now. Ever since I came home from America, I've made dreadful decisions. This is just one more. Might as well take my self-destruction to the final level and commit a crime myself. Like father, like son. Kendrick brings out a document that I sign. I've confirmed, in writing, that the forgery is the genuine artifact. Rhys Kendrick has won. I'm an accessory to a crime or something like that. I don't know the official terminology.

Instead of dropping the charges, though, Kendrick urges the police to move forward with them. And at the trial, he convinces the judge that a repeat offender deserves harsher punishment.

My father is sentenced to three years in prison.

All I can do is take care of my mother until Da is released. No one knows what I'd done for Kendrick, and they never will. But I'll have to live with the knowledge for the rest of my life. It's just as well that I lost Rae. She deserves a man who can take care of her and who would never debase himself the way I have—and I did it all for nothing.

From this moment forward, I will do everything possible to make up for my mistakes and become a better man.

Chapter Sixteen

Nine months after Iain vanished, on the day after Valentine's, our daughter is born. When my mom drove me to the hospital, I made her promise to go home and retrieve the scarf Iain had given me. I had planned never to look at the thing again, but when I realized I was about to give birth, I suddenly needed to have that scarf with me. Mom didn't complain. She rushed home to get it.

Now I lie in a hospital bed with my daughter in my arms and Iain's scarf wrapped around her tiny body. I just hold her for a while—a long while, actually—while tears stream down my cheeks and I gaze at her sweet face. These tears represent the joy of meeting my child at last and the grief of realizing her father will never know her.

"Look," I tell my mom. "She has pale blue eyes like Iain."

"A lot of babies are born with blue eyes, but the color might change later."

"No, her eyes will stay like this." Maybe I want that because it means a sliver of Iain will always be with me. Yeah, it's pathetic. But I can't help that I still love him. "I already know what I want to call her."

"I've seen you poring over books of baby names. You didn't know I saw, but I did." My mother moves over to sit on the bed's edge right beside me. She gazes down at my daughter and smiles. "Whatever name you've chosen will be the right one. And I know this girl will be as good and strong as her mother."

And she will be like Iain too. I believe that, though I can't explain why. So I kiss my daughter's forehead and say, "Her name is Malina."

"That's beautiful, Rae."

I won't confess that I chose that name because it's the feminine form of Malcolm, Iain's middle name. Choosing the feminine version of his first name seemed too obvious. Once I found the name Malina, I knew that's what I would call my child if I had a daughter. I hadn't wanted to know the baby's sex beforehand, but I hoped for a little girl.

My parents' divorce had been finalized last year, four months after Iain vanished, and Mom used the settlement to buy us a house in Texas—a new home for me, Mom, and Malina, in a place far from where all those bad things happened. We now live in the Hill Country, where wildflowers bloom in the rolling green fields every spring, heralding a new beginning. We need that. Mom is divorced, and I lost the love of my life, so starting over here feels like the best thing that's ever happened to us.

Though Mom says she doesn't care how long I take to decide what I want to do with my life, I realize I need to come up with a plan soon. I have a child to take care of, after all. Our new house came with plenty of acreage, so I could do something with that. But it takes me a few weeks to settle on a plan. Then I sit down with Mom to explain it all.

"I want to raise sheep," I tell her. "For the wool. I did a lot of research, and there's a big market for wool these days. Lots of shops sell genuine wool yarn for people who want to ditch the synthetics and go natural."

"You really have researched this, haven't you?"

"Want me to recite all the statistics I've learned about the wool industry in the US?"

Mom laughs. "No, sweetie, I believe you. One thing I know about my daughter is that she's smart enough to do anything she sets her mind to."

"Starting an at-home business will also give me the chance to spend as much as time as I can with Malina."

"You're a wonderful mother, Rae." Mom clasps my hand. "I'll help you however I can. Anything you need, just ask. And it goes without saying that I'm your on-call, in-house babysitter."

"Thanks, Mom."

Will my plan work? I'm about to learn the answer. My mother provides the working capital to get started, but she sank most of her divorce settlement into buying this property. I don't want to empty her savings account, but she insists on giving me whatever I need. I can't secure a loan on my own, so to get the rest of the capital, I create an LLC with Mom as my partner. With her on board, our local bank agrees to loan us what we need. I can't believe I'm doing this. But like Mom often reminds me, Everhart women never give up. We strap on our mud boots and our overalls and climb into the muck.

Maybe I lost the only man I ever loved, but I've found my true love at last. She's six months old and the sweetest little girl in the world. Every time I feel like I can't make the business work, I look at my daughter—and then I know I can and I will succeed.

Though Mom offered to babysit, right now I prefer to keep Malina with me as much as possible. I get a baby carrier thingy that straps onto my chest like a reverse backpack. That way, I can survey the property with my daughter and my mom too. We figure out where the property line is and devise a plan for the sheep pasture and the paddocks we'll need too. We hire some guys to put up the fencing and to build an addition to the existing barn.

Months roll by, and finally, it's time for the sheep to arrive.

Sometimes I think about Iain and wonder how he would feel about my new life. But it's only a fleeting thought. I'm too busy to worry about the past.

On the day the sheep arrive, Malina has just turned ten months old. She walks like a pro now, and she gets so excited about the sheep. Mom keeps hold of Malina while I oversee the unloading of the sheep. They arrived in a huge trailer pulled by a massive pickup truck, much bigger than the one I've got. But I won't need to transport the sheep, so I don't need a heavy-duty vehicle.

After the big day, it's back to the grindstone.

Two months later, we celebrate Malina's first birthday. Later, on the day that marks exactly two years since Iain disappeared from my life, I allow myself to wallow a little bit.

Mom has taken Malina outside to visit the sheep, which the kiddo always loves to do. While they have fun, I go inside to dig out the scarf Iain had given me on Valentine's Day back in Nackington. I also find the photo strip from that booth in the mall. Wrapping the scarf around me, I gaze at the pictures. Tears dribble down my cheeks, but I'm not in any danger of sobbing. These are goodbye tears. The time has come to lay the memories to rest and enjoy the rest of my life with only the occasional thoughts of Iain MacTaggart. I feel freer afterward, and I stuff the scarf into the back of a drawer. But I put the photo strip into a little photo album I've been making that documents important moments in Malina's life. Then I shove that into the drawer too.

Why? Because that album isn't for me and Mom and Malina. It's for Iain. Not that I think he'll ever see it, but I've given up on fighting the impulse to save something for him, just in case. I take a lot of pictures of our daughter. Some go into the family album, while a select few make it into the one for Iain. Will I ever use this album? It's doubtful. Moving on doesn't mean I can't save a few memories for the man who gave me the most incredible gift I've ever received—our daughter, who will always remind me of her father.

As the years pass, I occasionally date, though nothing much comes of it. I never bring men to the house, and my daughter will never meet or even know about them. Even my mom doesn't know the details. Of course, for safety's sake, I tell her when and where I'm going when I have a date. If I sleep with a guy, though, I keep that to myself. After a while, I give up on romance. It just doesn't interest me anymore.

Seven years after we moved to Texas, Mom meets a wonderful man. Soon, they're married—and I have a stepfather, a stepbrother, and a stepsister. Malina adores them all, and so do I. At least one of the Everhart women managed to find Prince Charming and get that happily ever after. Mom now lives in California, but we see each other several times a year, either with me and Malina flying to California, or Mom and her new family coming here. Greg, my stepfather, is such a good man that I never even think about my real dad anymore.

Yeah, life is looking pretty damn wonderful these days.

When Malina turns ten, I let Mom talk me into "getting out there" again. A few more bad dates later, I'm ready to throw in the towel. Then I meet a man who seems like a nice guy and says all the right things—when we're in bed. I hired him as my ranch hand, but we sneak away to motels to have sex. My time with Grayson Parker is the closest I've come to having a relationship since that Scottish man whose name I've completely forgotten. Okay, even I know that's not true. I only think of Iain now because Grayson just dumped me. The second I suggested he could come to my house to meet my daughter, he scrammed at sixty miles an hour. The jerk actually told me he didn't want to play daddy to some other guy's castoff.

Nobody refers to my daughter that way.

I hear the loser now drives a taxi. The nearest town isn't large, which means he probably doesn't get much work. Is it wrong to feel a tiny flush of triumph about that? The ass did call my daughter a "castoff." Oh yeah, I'm better off without that moron in my life. I still see him occasionally, but we ignore each other as much as possible. My latest mistake will be my last. No more men. Who needs them? In the romantic sense, I mean. I don't hate all members of the opposite sex.

The new ranch hand I hire does not want to date me. Ben has a girlfriend. He's also incredibly kind and sweet, not to mention a hard worker. We've become good friends. Mom loves Ben, and so does Malina.

Can't believe my little girl will turn twelve next year.

Greg and Mom invite me and Malina to go to Bermuda with their gang. Malina is so excited she actually jumps up and down while clapping her hands and grinning. How can I say no? We get passports and pack our bags, ready to go in two days.

But Ben breaks his arm.

That means Malina and I have to skip the big trip. I know she's disappointed, but being an Everhart girl, she doesn't let it keep her down. Besides, I buy her an iPod to make up for it. After that, she doesn't care about Bermuda anymore.

On the day after Valentine's, Malina turns twelve. Since our California family couldn't make it here to celebrate with us, I make sure my baby gets all the presents she wanted and her favorite cake—chocolate with vanilla frosting and vanilla ice cream. She inherited that preference from me. But after the party is over and the presents are all unwrapped, after Malina has gone to bed too, I allow myself to wallow just a teeny bit.

That means I excavate from the depths of my dresser two items, the photo album and the scarf made from the MacTaggart clan tartan. I add a new photo to the album, one that shows Malina blowing out the twelve candles on her birthday cake. I pull out the photo strip that had been tucked inside the album and gaze into the pale blue eyes of the man who changed my life in ways he will never know about, though I've made peace with that fact.

I will always love Iain. I've made peace with that too.

Done reminiscing, I hide those items once again. Then I head into the living room for the last itty-bitty bit of wallowing. I approach the shelves that hold numerous books about topics that hold a special meaning for me, though no one except my mom understands why. They're books about Scotland. History. Architecture. Folk beliefs. Whatever I could find, I bought it. I even own a primer on the Gaelic language, though I haven't worked my way through the whole thing yet. Most of the words Iain had used are not in that book. I couldn't remember those terms he'd used on the day we met—something about his magic staff, but in Gaelic—so I had no way to look those up. Kinda doubt they're in the book, anyway.

Oh well. The thing he used to call me that I loved the best had nothing to do with Gaelic. Now I close my eyes and let my mind travel back to those days, and I hear Iain's voice, smoky and irresistible, as he calls me "sunshine." Though I will never forget him, I've made a new life for myself.

But now that life is threatened. The wool market has been on a downward turn lately, which cuts into my profits. I could let Ben go, but I don't want to do that. I know the economy goes through ups and downs, but the slump in the wool market shows no sign of easing up. What will I do? I don't know. My income has decreased over the past three years. I've started selling some of my lambs, but only to people who want them as pets, since I can't stomach the idea of selling them for food. I eat meat, so I know I'm a hypocrite. But I see their cute little sheep faces every day. That's why I can't send them to the slaughterhouse. The money I get from selling them as pets hasn't made much of a dent in my financial problems.

I need to plan for Malina's future too, to save in case she wants to go to college. Right now, she thinks she wants to become a sheep rancher like me. But she's twelve. She'll change her mind a hundred times before she graduates from high school. I want her to have options.

Done browsing those books about Scotland, I go to bed and try not to worry about money. After an hour of tossing and turning, I realize only one thing will help me sleep. So I sink into the memories of Iain and our time at Nackington, of his smile and those blue eyes, the ones that mirror our daughter's. I remember his kisses too, the sexy way he smiled when he fed me ice cream with his mouth. But mostly, I fantasize about Iain holding me and calling me "sunshine" as well as that Scottish word he never explained—*gràidh*.

Soon, I fall asleep.

But in the morning, I realize I need to give up that crutch. I will give it up. Iain is my past.

No, I will never fantasize about him again.

Chapter Seventeen

Iain

What have I done with my life? Well, I've made a fair amount of money, enough to support my parents and ensure Da never burgles anyone ever again. Finding artifacts that had been lost to history earns me a reward every time. Rhys Kendrick does not harass me anymore. He got what he wanted, so he ought to be happy. The bastard has celebrated his victory by buying up half the village of Loch Fairbairn. Everyone knows the *bod ceann* takes advantage of store owners who have fallen on hard times, offering to buy them out with a significant settlement. I don't blame them for giving in. But whatever Rhys Kendrick means to do with those buildings, I doubt it involves improving the village.

My father spends eighteen months in prison. Well, at least he's home now. Ma took his absence better than I'd expected. Better than I did, for sure.

I wish I could say I've become a better man, but that would be a lie. I've shagged more women than I care to count, though most of those encounters were brief and happened in the early years after I came home from America. Still, I've made even worse mistakes.

First, I marry a woman I don't love and expect to feel satisfied with the situation. Julia is a sweet lass, but I have no right to use her to fill up the gaping hole in my heart. It doesn't work, anyway. After seven months of marriage, she can't take it anymore—and I don't blame her. My marriage is over.

My second mistake might be even worse.

One day, I bump into a bonnie woman in a café in Inverness. She'd been visiting the local shops to find items she could use to re-decorate her home. I went there to visit the Highland Archive Centre in hopes of uncovering information about a potential new discovery in the Loch Fairbairn area. The woman I meet has a familiar name—Delyth Kendrick. We share a table and get to know each other a wee bit, but that's not the problem.

Delyth seems like a lonely woman, and living with a man like Rhys can't be good for her. She won't leave him, but that's all I know. Maybe I feel sorry for her, or maybe I've reverted to my old ways, because I accept Delyth's offer to become her secret lover. Her husband often takes business trips, so Delyth and I meet at the Kendrick mansion whenever Rhys is away. I suspect he shags other women during his absences. Is that an excuse for my behavior? No. But I honestly like Delyth, though I know I will never develop deeper feelings for her. I've told her about my lost love, leaving out Rae's name and the details of our relationship, to make sure Delyth understands my limitations.

I can never love anyone else, not after Rae.

During the fifth year of our affair, I begin to pull away from Delyth. We don't see each other as often, and I don't feel any real satisfaction from our encounters, except for the sexual kind. Even that isn't as good anymore.

But one day, my life changes. My cousins have asked me to take in Gavin Douglas, the boyfriend of our cousin Jamie, and let him live in my house while he sorts out the mess he made with the love of his life. I know exactly why my cousins chose me for this task. Gavin and I have taken similar paths down the wrong road, for similar reasons. I let go of Rae out of shame, because of our age difference and my father's larcenous escapades, while Gavin threw Jamie over out of shame related to his disastrous marriage to a narcissistic woman. He doesn't take more than a decade to realize he made a mistake, though. Gavin recognized that five minutes after he broke Jamie's heart.

So aye, I let him stay with me. We have serious discussions about his relationship with Jamie, talks that do more than help my new mate. They also make me realize that I should never have given up on Rae so easily. The years have taught me many lessons, but I didn't know until recently that the Bremner-Ashton mafia couldn't have gotten me deported. I abandoned Rae for no reason.

Jamie and Gavin reconcile, but my mate has a few choice words of wisdom for me. "It's never too late to rectify the mistakes you made. I strung Jamie along for eighteen months while I lived in America and she stayed here in Scotland. Having a relationship across an ocean could never work. Jamie didn't want to trust me again, but I never gave up—not even after I dumped her."

"Aye, but I did give up on the lass I loved. The situations aren't the same."

"Not on every point. But we're both stubborn morons. Don't give up on your girl until you're one hundred percent sure there's no chance."

I exhale a long sigh. "It's been almost thirteen years. Ahmno likely to find her now."

"Have you tried? I mean, like, really tried?" He lays a hand on my shoulder. "Listen, I know it's a damn scary thing to do, trying to reconnect after all these years. But if there's one lesson you can learn from me, it's that you have to let go of the fear and shame. Just do it, Iain. If I could let Jamie's brothers hound me for two months to prove I was serious about their sister, you can bite that bullet and look for Rae."

"You're right, I know." I rub my jaw. "Let me think on it."

"Okay. But don't think too much."

With Gavin's experience as a guide, I should begin my quest. But I waste two months worrying about it before I finally I realize what I need to do. Finding Rae had felt like a goal I could never achieve, until I remembered what I have on my side. The MacTaggart clan, that's what. Not only my blood relatives, but the Americans they've married as well. The lasses who tied the knot with my cousins Lachlan, Aidan, and Rory started an official organization to meddle in other people's lives. They call it the American Wives Club. Those lasses took matters into their own hands with Jamie and Gavin, rallying anyone and everyone in the MacTaggart family to get it done.

Can they help me find Rae? I decide to ask Rory about that.

"You don't need the American Wives Club," he says when I ring him. "Whatever it is you think you need, discuss it with me first. I have connections at the Home Office and in America too."

He invites me to his office to discuss the matter. On the following day, February fifteenth, I walk into his office. The room is a mess, which would never have happened before Rory married Emery. The bonnie American lass has cured my cousin of his uptight tendencies.

Rory invites me to sit down and takes a seat in the big chair behind the desk, then the discussion begins. When I admit that I've been slightly jealous of Rory and the other men in the clan who have found their soul mates, he gives me a strange look.

"Jealous of what?" he asks. "You have more than enough money, you do what you want when you want, and you can have any woman you want."

"Aye, any woman I want. Except the only one who matters."

The more we talk, the more I realize Rory is trying to wheedle the truth out of me delicately, the way I imagine a solicitor often needs to do.

"We all know something happened to you in America, but you've never wanted to talk about it," he finally says. "Is this about a woman? The MacTaggart grapevine has embellished the story over the years, but it all began with what Kevin Lister claimed he heard you say at a pub one night."

"Yes," I say, trying to sound calm despite the acid boiling in my gut. "I lost a woman. No, that's not quite right. I gave her up without a fight, and I've regretted it ever since."

Rory raises a Valentine's card and turns it so I can see the words his wife scrawled inside it. *Love is a journey from pain to redemption. Never forget how far we've come.*

My throat grows tight and thick, but I manage an even tone. "What am I meant to take away from your wife's effusive love for you? It's charming but—"

"Never give up. That's the lesson." Rory sets down the card. "Tell me more about your woman."

Rory goes on trying to convince me that I need to try to find Rae, and that I deserve a second chance. But why would a vital young woman want me? I'm fifty years old. She must be thirty-five now. For all I know, she already has a husband and children. But Rory doesn't give up. He keeps pushing me to admit what we both know I want—to see Rae again.

When he asks for the name of the woman, I hesitate for only a moment before I take a deep breath and tell him. "Rae Everhart."

Then he instructs me to write down everything I can remember about her. While I do that, a sort of excitement I've never experienced in my entire life electrifies me because, for the first time in thirteen years, I have a chance to see Rae and at least apologize to her. I leave Rory's office with his assurances he will contact whoever he must in order to track down the lass.

After four months, I've ignored Rory's advice and given up. Rory's investigator had called yesterday to tell me he's had no luck tracking down Rae. Though I'd stopped sleeping with Delyth after my cousin convinced me he could find my lost love, now I crawl back to my former lover and try to lose myself inside her body, but it doesn't work. I still think about Rae.

Eight days later, I receive the news I've dreamed of hearing. The investigator Rory hired has found Rae at last.

A weight has lifted off me, and I feel almost lightheaded from the knowledge that I can see her again, speak to her again, find out if she thought of me every day for the past thirteen years just the way I'd thought of her. Rory lends me his private jet so I can get to America faster. My journey doesn't end there, though. Since the car hire agency at the airport had no vehicles available, I jump into a taxi and ask to be taken to the address Rory had found for Rae, though he couldn't swear she still lives there or that it's the right Rae Everhart. Her driver's license gave this as her address, but the property is owned by Cheryl Raines. The taxi driver takes me from Austin to Llano, the farthest he can go. Then I find a second taxi for the next part of my journey, which ends at a small town called Ricksville. For the third and final leg of my quest, I ride in a rickety taxi with a surly driver. But he boots me out of the car at the end of Rae's driveway.

"Hope you're in better shape than you look," he says in a snide tone. "You've got a half-mile walk to get to the house, and ambulances don't come out this far."

I throw my large bag over my shoulder, pay the driver, and start down the half-mile-long gravel drive. My felt fedora shields my eyes, but it makes my head sweat too. Maybe I'm no young laddie, but I can handle the walk. For the chance to see Rae again, I will endure any hardship.

Finally, I reach a metal gate that has a latch holding it shut. After crossing through the gate and shutting it behind me, I notice a figure up ahead. A woman. My pulse accelerates, and I suddenly have trouble pulling in a full breath. It's not exhaustion, though. I swear that's Rae waiting for me, though I cannae even see her face yet. I keep my head down as I traipse across the last stretch of the drive. Though I notice a house and a barn, nothing else catches my attention once I lay eyes on Rae.

"Hey!" she shouts. "Stop! This is private property."

I pause to remove my hat so I can swipe a hand over my forehead. Sweat has dribbled down my temples. I continue striding toward Rae until I stand an arm's length from the lass, then I drop my bag on the ground and smile. "Rae Everhart. It's been a long time, but I found you."

The lass just stares at me slack-jawed.

Well, I have arrived with no warning after thirteen years away from her.

She swallows hard enough that I can see the movement. "Iain?"

"I've waited thirteen years for this. Can't wait a second longer."

I close the distance between us, sling an arm around her waist, and drag her into my body.

"Whuh—"

I silence whatever she'd been about to say with my lips. She has stronger muscles than before, and I love the feel of them against me. Her lips are soft and warm, and the slightest flavor of her teases me, though I don't even try to deepen the kiss. Not yet. I've only just found her again, and we'll need time to get reacquainted. Even after I peel my lips away from hers, she keeps her eyes closed. Aye, Rae did that often on the day when I'd finally kissed her after ten months of waiting. I couldn't stop then, and I donnae want to stop now. But we need to talk.

Still holding her close, I murmur, "You have no idea how happy I am to see you, Rae. You're even more beautiful than the last time I saw you."

The lass shoves me away. "What on earth do you think you're doing? You can't waltz up my driveway, invite yourself through the gate, and then kiss me."

"But I did, and you let me." I grab my hat off the ground, though I don't remember dropping it. Kissing Rae distracted me. I dust my hat off. "I came a long way to see you."

"And that gives you the right to barge into my life?"

She tugs her shirt down and squares her shoulders, giving me the stubborn look I remember well. "Iain, go home. Turn around and walk back the way you came."

"Afraid I can't." I slap the fedora back onto my head. "I'm not leaving until you've heard me out."

She stares at me for a long moment. Then she spins around and stalks over to the house and up the steps onto the porch. She shuts the front door behind her.

Does she honestly think that will stop me? I jog over there and spring over the steps to land on the porch floor. Then I approach the door and shout, "I'll wait out here until you change your mind."

I receive no response.

"Rae," I shout at the door. "I'm asking for a few minutes, that's all."

The door swings open, and Rae steps aside, waving an arm. "Get in here and say whatever it is you think you need to say. I'll listen, but you will leave once you're done. No arguments. When I say go, you go."

I tip my hat to her. "Whatever you say."

Hat in hand, I follow her into the house and cannae resist admiring her bonnie erse along the way. When she closes the door, I drop my bag on the floor with a rather loud thunk. Maybe I had over-packed slightly. The only thing of any real value inside that bag is the diamond engagement ring I'd bought for her thirteen years ago.

Rae faces me, her brows raised and her arms crossed.

Bod an Donais, I want to ravish her with a kiss hotter than the Texas sun. I'll do that in a few minutes. First, I need to tell her the truth. "What I have to say is simple. I never should've let you go without a fight, and I won't make that mistake again. I've come to win you back, Rae."

No matter what I must do, no matter how long this takes, I will win back the heart of the only woman I've ever loved. The journey that brought me here began thirteen years ago, but it ends today. I will fight for our second chance the way I should've fought for Rae more than a decade ago. Whatever it takes, however long I need to struggle to convince Rae she can trust me, I will succeed.

Aye, we will have our fairy-tale ending.

**Find out how Iain helped Gavin win back Jamie
in *Gift-Wrapped in a Kilt* (Hot Scots, Book Four),
then experience Iain and Rae's story
in *Notorious in a Kilt* (Hot Scots, Book Five).**

THE British BASTARD

Chapter One

Alex

I lie here in this bed, in a posh hotel suite in a strange town, and wonder why I keep seducing women whose names I don't care to learn and who I never intend to see again. Oh, I know why. It's because I'm a bastard. I can't risk getting to know anyone too well, which means I will never allow myself to become embroiled in any sort of romantic relationship, whether I want that or not. My desires are irrelevant. So I roll onto my side and slap the hip of the anonymous American woman lying naked beside me. "Time for me to go, pet."

She pouts. "Stay a little longer, or even for the night. This was so much fun."

"Yes, but I'm tired of you now. Sorry, darling, it's time to say good night."

This woman has a fantastic body and an insatiable hunger for sex, but I do not want to fuck her again. She kept shouting, "I love your dick, I love your dick!" What a bloody stupid phrase to repeat over and over during sex. I realized the moment I saw her in the hotel bar that she has the IQ and temperament of a chihuahua, but I hadn't chosen her for my fling because I wanted to plumb the depths of her soul. I needed a good shag, that's all. I wish I could meet an intelligent, beautiful, sweet woman who arouses not only my lust, but also my curiosity. I can't search for a soul mate, though, if that sort of thing even exists. I cannot get involved with anyone. No girlfriends, no mates, no ties whatsoever. Only two people in all the world know the real me—not Dr. Alex Thorne, professor of archaeology, but the lost boy who still hides inside that persona.

"You're gorgeous," my bedmate purrs. "But why does a hot British guy live in New Mexico?"

"None of your business, pet." I slide off the bed and start reassembling my clothes. "You don't need to know anything about me, and vice versa."

She crawls across the bed toward me, apparently assuming I can't resist her naked body. She's wrong.

I pull my shoes on, check that my wallet is still inside my trouser pocket, and march out the door without glancing back. Why did I choose that woman for tonight's lover? Because I know I can never care for a pouting sex kitten like her. She's probably married to a geriatric multimillionaire. I walk at a brisk pace as I head for my car, which I'd parked two blocks from the hotel. Yes, I might also have hired a car for this occasion, strictly to make it harder for anyone to track me. Privacy matters to me, more so than for most people.

I return the car to the rental agency and drive my personal vehicle for the rest of the two-hour trip to my home.

Do I sleep well? No. But that's a frequent problem for me. I awaken in the morning feeling less than enthused about the day ahead, because classes begin this morning. I'm destined to spend the day lecturing to students who would rather be playing video games or shagging in their dorm rooms. As much as I look forward to my new job as an associate professor of archaeology and ancient history at Ballesteros University, I always feel a bit exposed whenever I need to speak in public. I'm not shy, but I have reasons for this anxiety. It's only a twinge, anyway. Hardly anything at all.

I go to my office to get situated, but once I've finished, I realize I still have thirty minutes before my first class begins. What should I do? Sit here in my office fiddling with pens and pencils? My gaze shifts to the window and the sunshine outside. Fresh air sounds good.

So I grab a book—the text I'll be teaching from today—and make my way to the quad and one of the benches I find there, under a tree that shades me from the heat of the sun. Sitting down, I lay the textbook on my lap and begin to browse the chapters. Yes, all right, maybe I should have read the text before today, but honestly, I know more about archaeology than the stuffed shirts who wrote this book. Still, I dutifully skim the pages. And I groan. I could've written a better book than this when I was a teenager.

Movement peripherally catches my attention, and I glance up.

A beautiful girl hovers a few yards away, clutching a spiral-bound notebook to her chest. A rucksack hangs over one shoulder, but it's not her academic paraphernalia that seizes my attention. She has the loveliest face I've ever seen, with blue eyes as pale as glacial ice and cinnamon hair that complements her creamy complexion. I love the faint pinkness of her cheeks, which seems natural rather than cosmetic. Her thick hair tumbles over her shoulders and nearly reaches her full breasts. I can't see those mounds, but I can imagine what they might look like.

She's a student. I should not be fantasizing about her naked body.

I can't help it. My lips curve up a touch, and like a moron, I wave at her. "Hello there."

The girl smiles shyly.

"You must be new here," I say. "You have that slightly dazed look about you."

She nods.

Her shyness makes me want to pull her into my arms and kiss her. Unlike the woman I'd shagged last night, this girl does not shamelessly flirt with me or devour my body with her gaze. She just stands there, seeming uncomfortable yet curious. She is a breath of fresh air, and I want to inhale every bit of her sweetness.

I close my book and shimmy sideways to make room. Then I pat the bench beside me. "Have a seat. Maybe I can help you with that confusion."

She bites her lip.

Can't stop myself. I grin at the adorable girl.

And she finally shambles over to the bench to sit down beside me.

I offer her my hand. "I'm Alex Thorne."

The girl slips her hand into mine. "Catriona MacTaggart. I just moved here from Scotland. To get my PhD."

"Ah, a grad student." I can't make myself release her hand because I love the feel of her soft, warm palm clasped to mine. "What department are you in?"

Catriona hesitates. "Archaeology."

Did she think I'd be disappointed by that fact? I can't resist moving my thumb over her skin in slow circles. "Me too. But I'm not your adviser, that I'm sure of. I'd remember being assigned a Scots student."

"No, you're not my adviser. I haven't met her yet."

"Just set foot on campus, have you?"

"Aye."

I smile again, enchanted by the angel beside me. "I do love the way Scots speak. Your accent is lovely."

"I like yours too."

Her eyes widen briefly, as if she thinks she's made an egregious error in etiquette. If she knew me, she wouldn't worry about rubbish like propriety. Not sure I want her to experience my world, though. She's perfect, just as she is.

And I am toxic.

"Thank you," I say in response to her statement. Then I tip my head to the side to study her and imagine what it would feel like to kiss her sensuous lips. "I hope we'll see each other again sometime. Even though I'm not your adviser, feel free to stop by my office anytime."

"I appreciate that." She pulls her hand free of mine and gets up. "I need to go, or I'll be late for my first meeting with my adviser."

"Good luck, Catriona."

She gives me another sweet little smile, then walks away.

But she glances back at me several times before she disappears from view.

That lass wants me. I want her too, but getting involved with any woman is too dangerous. Dating a student probably wouldn't violate the university's ethics rules, since Catriona is a graduate student. So I could ask her out, strictly to discover if we have as much chemistry as I think we do. No, I cannot do that. *Stay away from the bonnie Scots lass, you sodding arse.*

Being with me would stain her sweet soul.

My morning goes the way I'd thought. I attempt to force-feed education to students who can't stop chatting to each other. I resign myself to having only half the class, at most, listening to my lecture. At lunch, I grab food from the cafeteria and eat in my office with the door closed and locked. If students want to confer with me, they'll have to wait until another day. In the afternoon, I make my way to a different lecture hall to give another lesson, but this time, I have a room full of fourth-year students who seem more inclined to pay attention.

A miracle, for sure.

In the middle of my lecture about ancient Rome, I glance around the cavernous hall to make eye contact with some of the students. Most of them I can't see because they're in the back, too far away from me. I'm surprised I have a full house for this lecture. But I only consider that thought for half a second. Then my attention veers to a familiar face.

Catriona MacTaggart stands near the open door, at the top of the sloping floor.

Our gazes collide. I can't look away from her, and I realize I've stopped speaking. Even when I return to my lecture, I can't look away from Catriona, and she gazes right back at me as if she can't look away either. The lass who loves my accent seems entranced, but I don't think it's because of the subject matter. She has hypnotized me, and I know I will need to speak to her again, soon, if only to hear her lovely voice again.

No, I will not do that. Never again will I speak to her.

My resolve lasts only until the students vacate the hall. I see Catriona lingering by the open door as if she's waiting for me. I could exit via the other set of doors on the opposite side of the hall, but that would make me a bleeding coward. Walking past the Scots lass won't be difficult at all. If she tries to grab me, I will overpower her.

Oh, bloody hell. Now I'm afraid a woman will assault me because she's so desperately attracted to me. Even I'm not that arrogant.

I nod to Catriona as I pass her. She says nothing. But just as I turn to head down the corridor, I hear her voice.

"Dr. Thorne?"

I haltingly turn toward her and affect an air of casual interest. "Yes, Ms. MacTaggart?"

"Please call me Catriona." She squares her shoulders and lifts her chin. "You said I could come to your office anytime."

Oh, fuck. I'd also said I hoped I would see her again. When did I develop loose lips? Mine have always been tightly sealed. But if I tell her to go away… Nothing bad will happen. Yes, I should tell her to bugger off. Those aren't the words that come out of my mouth, though.

"My office is on the second floor," I tell her. "We can talk while we walk."

Catriona smiles. "Thank you, Dr. Thorne."

I start down the corridor with Catriona beside me, and she keeps smiling in the sweetest way.

Oh yes, I am doomed.

Chapter Two

Catriona

Alex Thorne is the most beautiful man I've ever seen, and I get a flutter in my tummy every time I see him. I've only seen him twice, but the fluttering happened on both occasions. He makes me feel like a teenage virgin, which inspires my mouth to say silly things and my body to behave like a shy schoolgirl. What must Alex think of me? I've acted like an eejit. Maybe he wears pheromone cologne so he can seduce lasses more easily.

As we walk up the stairs toward the second floor, I can't help noticing his body. He clearly has muscles under his dress shirt and trousers. Since I'd gazed into his eyes while we had our wee conversation on that bench in the quad, I know he has gorgeous brown eyes that seem almost the same shade as his hair. Whenever he smiles, a tingly sensation sweeps over my skin, and I suddenly can't piece together a single word. How could any woman stay coherent in his presence? Alex reminds me of a Michelangelo statue, the picture of masculine beauty and angelic grace.

I wonder if his, um, private parts resemble the statue of David.

Oh, for heaven's sake. I am a grown woman, not a bairn, and a PhD student too. It's time I stop gawping at Alex.

He leads me into his office and sits down behind the desk, then gestures for me to take one of the chairs in front of him. The sunlight streaming through the windows paints his features in shades of gold, accentuating his full lips. What would it feel like if he kissed me? I'd wager he knows how to kiss a woman, not like the lads back home who can't figure out what to do with their tongues.

I'm sure Alex knows exactly what to do with his tongue.

"Catriona?" he says. "Are you all right?"

"What? Oh, aye." Settling onto my chair, I set my rucksack on the floor and fold my hands on my lap. "This is a nice office."

Maybe if I'd tried harder, I could've said something even stupider.

"Thank you." His lips kink up at one corner. "I've never been complimented on my office before."

"Well, I, um—" *Haud yer wheesht, ye eejit.*

Alex relaxes against his chair and raises his brows. "What did you want to discuss with me?"

"I'm bothering you. Aren't I, Dr. Thorne?"

"Not at all. And please call me Alex." He gives me a wry smile. "Dr. Thorne sounds like the name of a Victorian arse."

"I think it's a sexy name." Why the bloody hell did I say that? Maybe I should ask him for a roll of tape so I can seal my stupid lips.

"Sexy?" he says while smiling even more. His eyes twinkle in the sunlight. "Well, that name is beginning to grow on me. But I'd still rather you called me Alex. All right?"

"Aye."

He studies me for a moment while gently rocking his chair. "You still haven't told me what I can do for you, Catriona. I'm not your adviser, so…"

I have no idea what I wanted him to do for me. All I thought about was how much I wanted to see him again. "You teach archaeology. That's what I'm studying in my PhD program, so I hoped you might have advice or suggestions."

"For what? Those would be questions for your adviser."

"Oh. Aye, of course."

He tips his head to the side, gazing at me with curiosity. "How long have been in America?"

"Eight days."

"No wonder you seem ill at ease here. Do you have any mates in this country?"

I shake my head. "Donnae know anyone. Well, except for you."

"And your adviser."

Does he keep mentioning that because he wants me to go away and leave him alone? Maybe I do feel a wee bit out of place here in another country, far from my home. But I cannae tell Alex that.

"I've been in America for a few years," he says. "So I can under-stand what you might be feeling right now. Perhaps I could be your adviser on how to acclimate to a new and very different environ-ment. It might be more accurate to say we could be mates."

He wants to be my friend? My pulse accelerates, and that fluttery sensation returns. Aye, I want to be Alex's mate a bit too much.

"What do you say?" he asks. "Will you be my mate, Catriona?"

"Aye. That would be, um, lovely."

His mouth slides into a sexy grin. "Brilliant."

I pick up my rucksack. "You must have work to do, so I'll leave you to that."

"Yes, I do have lessons to plan. However, I'm free this eve-ning." He eyes me up and down, and his tongue flicks out to moisten his lips. "Would you have dinner with me, Catriona? As a mate."

Will dinner with him be a platonic event? I'm not sure. My at-traction to him could have influenced how I interpret his actions and words. Maybe he isn't attracted to me. He might only want to help a newcomer to this country.

But I need him to want me the way I want him.

"That would be lovely," I say. "Thank you, Alex."

"Where are you staying?"

"Graduate student housing. I have my own flat."

His lips twitch, though it's not quite a smile. "I know where that is. May I pick you up at eight?"

"Yes. I'll be ready."

"Excellent." He stands and escorts me to the open doorway. "I look forward to seeing you again, Catriona."

"I look forward to seeing you too, Alex."

As I walk down the corridor, I can't help glancing back. Alex is still standing on the threshold of his office, watching me. I wave to him, and he waves back. This time, though, I do not look back four more times. No, I restrain that impulse and keep moving at a brisk pace while I exit the building, cross the quad, and find my vehicle in the car park. I think Americans call it a parking lot. Tonight, Alex can help me get used to the way people in this country speak and teach me their idioms. I do know some of them from watching American television.

I shut the car door and sag into my seat. Cannae stop my lips from forming a smile or my body from tingling yet again. Alex Thorne wants to have dinner with me. Aye, with *me.*

Since I have no more classes today, I drive back to my flat in the graduate housing complex. I've just walked into the bedroom and kicked off my shoes when the phone on the bedside table rings. I snatch it up. "Hello?"

"Cat, how are you settling in?"

"Lachlan?"

"Aye, it's me. I asked how—"

"I'm settling in fine." Should I tell my oldest brother about Alex? No, not yet. We're just friends, anyway. "It's only my first day on campus, so ye donnae need to check up on me yet."

"Of course I do. My wee sister is on another continent, and you've been there for eight days."

"Ahmno 'wee,' and I can take care of myself."

"I know that." Lachlan pauses as someone in the background speaks, but I can't tell who it is or what that person says. "Rory wants to say hello."

Honestly, my brothers are so overprotective.

Rory comes on the line. "Are you sure you're all right, Cat? America is nothing like Scotland."

"How would you know? You've never been here."

"No, but Iain told me what it's like."

I can't help making a derisive noise. "He lived in this country for one year."

"Which means he has one year's more experience than you."

All I can do is sigh. "I'm fine, Rory. And I'm a grown woman who can take care of herself."

"Fair enough. Do you like it over there?"

At first, I felt homesick. But since I met Alex… Aye, things are looking up. "Yes, I do like it here. Satisfied, Rory?"

"We are your brothers. That means we have the right and the responsibility to check on you."

"Fine, aye, you do."

I chat to my brothers for a while, then we say goodbye. It must be the middle of the night in Scotland, yet my brothers rang me just to make sure I'm all right. Aye, I love them. And aye, I miss my family. But I don't regret moving to America.

For the next few hours, I debate what I should wear for my dinner with Alex. It's not a date. But I don't want to dress like a student. I want to present myself as a woman. How do I do that? Why do I want to do it? The how part is fairly simple, but I can't explain why I care if Alex views me as a woman instead of a student. Oh, aye, it's a mystery. That desire has nothing to do with how attracted I am to Alex.

I eventually decide on a pale-blue dress with a hem just above my knees and matching shoes. Then I realize I should really shave my legs, and after that, I spend twenty minutes putting on makeup and fixing my hair. I decide to leave my hair loose because I like the way it feels brushing against my bare shoulders. No, I don't care what Alex thinks of the way I'm dressed. I wanted to feel feminine for me, not for him.

Someone knocks on my door at precisely eight o'clock.

I rush to pull the door open and smile when I see Alex standing there.

"Are you ready?" he asks. "I've reserved a table at a restaurant that sounds quite nice."

"Yes, I'm ready."

He offers me his arm. "You look stunning, Catriona."

"Thank you." I hook my arm around his and take note of his charcoal suit and golden tan dress shirt that has two buttons undone. "You look very handsome yourself."

But he looks more than handsome. The color of his shirt complements the warm brown of his eyes, and the suit makes him look so dapper and sexy that I experience the strongest wave of tingly anticipation that I've ever felt in my life.

Alex leads me down the concrete steps and across the concrete walkway, guiding me straight to his car. It's a Mercedes convertible, though he hasn't rolled the top down. Is Alex rich? I didn't think associate professors made that much money. Not that I will ever ask him about that.

He opens the passenger door for me and offers me his hand as I climb into the car. Then he hurries to the driver's side and settles into his seat.

We glance at each other at the same time and smile at each other too. Gooseflesh pebbles my arms. I have never been this excited to spend time with any man, even one who only wants to be my mate.

As Alex drives the Mercedes down the streets of Ballesteros, I gaze at his profile and wonder what will happen next.

Chapter Three

Alex

*D*inner with a student? I've lost my mind. The fact that she's a grad student and that I am not her adviser doesn't make me feel any less uncomfortable with what I've done. The university ethics code does not bar professors from dating students, and honestly, I never used to worry about that sort of thing. My conscience seems to have decided now is the right time to wake up from its long slumber.

Yes, all right, I want Catriona. As more than a mate. I want to strip her naked and do very unprofessional things to that body.

But I won't do it.

When we reach the restaurant, a waiter leads us to our table. It's a corner booth in a secluded area, just as I'd requested. I might not have ever visited this establishment before, but when I requested a table with a romantic atmosphere, the gent on the phone had assured me he would arrange that. I'm certain it helped that I offered him a large monetary inducement. Why I've gone to this much trouble, I can't explain. I shag women and don't ask for their names or give them mine. Yet with Catriona, I needed to…impress her.

It's bollocks. But here I am, placing a hand on her back as we wend our way through the tables to our booth.

Catriona slides into the semicircular booth first, then smiles at me.

I'm sure she expects me to sit right beside her, but I maintain an arm's length of distance instead. The waiter hands us menus and then leaves us alone. In this booth. Where no one else can see us. I've never taken a woman to a restaurant before, so this is new territory—and I haven't the slightest idea how to handle it.

The Scots lass pats the bench between us. "You can sit closer to me, Alex. I don't mind."

"Well, I, ah, don't want to crowd you." What a twat I've become since this morning. I don't want to crowd her? It's ridiculous.

Catriona smiles again. "It's all right. Please come closer. It's hard to talk to each other when you're so far away."

She makes it sound as if a continent separates us.

But I can't seem to control my own body, and I find myself sliding across the bench until I sit no more than a foot away from her. "Happy now?"

"Aye."

I flip open my menu and study my options while I take a sip of water.

Catriona leans in, her breasts brushing against my arm. "I see oysters on the menu. Have you ever eaten those?"

I choke on my water and barely avoid spewing it across the table. "What? No, I've never had those."

"Are you all right, Alex?"

She just asked if I want to eat an aphrodisiac, so no, I am not all right. Her nearness doesn't help matters. So I do what I'm best at—avoiding the truth by deflecting the question. "Tell me, Catriona, do you have any siblings?"

"Oh, aye." She straightens and aims those stunning blue eyes at me. "I have three brothers and two sisters."

"Five siblings? Blimey. Do you get on with all of them?"

"We get on very well. Lachlan and Rory, my oldest brothers, can be overprotective, but they mean well. I'm the fourth oldest, after my sister Fiona. Aidan and Jamie are the youngest."

"Fascinating." I tear my focus away from her eyes and force myself to study the menu again.

"Do you have brothers or sisters?"

Every ounce of blood in my body freezes. My fingers curl, the nails scraping the vinyl cover of the menu. I never react this way when someone asks me that question, but I think I...don't want to lie to Catriona. It's an unprecedented feeling. Since I can't tell her the truth, I resort to a little more deflection. "Do you have any other family? Parents? Aunts? Cousins?"

"Yes, I have many of those."

"Tell me about them. I'm fascinated by your family dynamic."

She says nothing for several seconds. When I glance at her, expecting to find the lass browsing the menu, instead I catch her staring intently at me. I recognize that look. It means the person I'm with wants to understand me, but no one can accomplish that feat.

"My cousin Logan is in the army," she says. "And my cousin Iain is an archaeologist. Watching him work inspired me to take a similar path."

"You're studying archaeology, correct?"

"Aye. I told you that in your office earlier."

"Did you? My brain is a bit muddled, apparently." Because she's so beautiful that I can't think.

Catriona laughs, the sound so delicate and sweet that I want to kiss her. "I asked you for advice."

"Oh. Well, I assumed you picked me at random because we met on that park bench."

"I chose you because—" She bites her lip. "Because you seemed so nice, and you were reading an archaeology textbook."

"Ah, I see." At least now I understand her reasons for insisting on getting to know me. Yes, I can be mates with Catriona Mac-Taggart. That won't result in a catastrophe.

Probably not.

I listen while Catriona tells me more about her siblings and cousins, and she grows more animated with every passing moment. Her smile is bright, her eyes sparkle, and her voice entrances me. Have I ever been as cheerful as she is? Of course I haven't. I am not the sort who gets a happily ever after ending. My story will conclude in a far darker manner. But the lovely lass beside me never needs to know who I really am or why I'm hiding in America, much less what I've done.

Neither of us order oysters, though we do both choose seafood entrées. Considering everything she shared with me, I feel uneasy about not telling her anything about myself. But I stay away from the issues of family and my background, instead relating humorous stories from my adventures as a PhD candidate and an associate professor. She loves the tale of the only time I participated in a field expedition and wound up falling into a river while trying to rescue what I thought was an artifact. It turned out to be a plastic hair clip.

"At least you didn't drown," Catriona says. "That would've been a right shame."

"Would it? I am an arse of the first order, so perhaps I deserved to drown."

Her smile disintegrates. "Why do you call yourself an arse of the first order?"

Oh, bollocks. I've committed the one error I never make. I let my guard down. "It was a joke, darling, that's all."

Her lips curl up at the corners, dimpling her cheeks. "I like that."

"What? That my jokes are bloody awful?"

"No. That you called me darling."

I can't come up with even one syllable in response. Maybe I call my anonymous lovers that, but I don't mean it in a romantic way. How did I mean it when I referred to Catriona that way? I have no fucking idea. "I'm glad you liked it, but I call every woman 'darling.' It's a British thing."

"Hmm." She eyes me with the most adorably fake expression of disapproval. "I donnae think I believe you, Alex. You're full of rubbish, aren't you?"

"Often and unrepentantly. You'd be better off finding someone else to take as your friend."

"No, I'm happy with you." She spears her fork into the last bite of her fish. "I like being with you. Haven't laughed this much in a long time."

"Neither have I." Maybe I've never enjoyed myself this much before. The thought is…unsettling. "I should take you home. It's getting late, and we both have classes in the morning."

I pay the bill, and we make our way out of the dining room into the entryway with its twilight ambiance. Catriona needs to use the ladies room, so I wait for her in a secluded space, leaning against the wall while I wonder what has happened to me. Dating a grad student? Dating, full stop? I never do that. Can't risk it. But since the moment I first saw Catriona, I've had no willpower to stay away from her.

She emerges from the loo and slips her hand into mine, smiling with what seems for all the world like affection.

I can't make myself shake her hand off. I push away from the wall, meaning to walk out the door, but then I stop and turn toward her. She is so bloody beautiful, and a need to taste her lips just once before I cut her out of my life grips me so hard that I can't breathe.

"What's wrong, Alex?" she asks.

The words she spoke barely penetrate my brain, and I can't stop myself. I back her up to the wall, cover her body with mine, and lift her hands to press them to the wall at either side of her shoulders. Her eyes flare wide, then drift half-closed. The sensual curve of her lips shatters my self-control. I crush my mouth to hers and plunge my tongue between her lips, diving deep to devour the flavor of her. Her breathy moan makes my cock jerk, and the feel of her breasts mounded against my chest makes me groan. I rock my hips to rub my growing erection into her belly even while I consume her mouth as if she is the only nourishment that can sustain me.

When I finally relinquish her lips, I can do nothing except stare at her.

She stares right back at me, but then her mouth curls into a sexy smile.

"Catriona, I—" What can I say? I'd meant to go out to my car and drop her off at her apartment, not molest the woman in the restaurant entryway. "I'm sorry."

"For what? I loved that kiss."

So did I. But I can't admit to that. "I need to take you home."

I lay a palm on her back to guide her out of the building and to my car. Neither of us speak on the ride to her flat, and though I walk her to her door, I do not kiss her good night. She seems confused when I don't even look her in the eye. I've just turned away, about to start back down the walkway, when she grasps my arm.

"Alex, wait."

Don't look at her. The only response I can safely give her is to revert to my old cavalier persona in a desperate attempt to escape. I do not glance at her even when I say, "If you were expecting me to fall madly in love with you after one mediocre kiss, I'm afraid you will be disappointed."

"If you want to chase me away, you'll at least have to look at me first."

Of course she insists I look at her. The Scots lass I'd taken for a shy girl has turned out to be the opposite. When I turn to face her, she gazes at me with nothing like shyness. A fire burns in her gaze, and I swear I can feel the heat penetrating my soul. That makes me want her even more.

"Happy now?" I say. "You wanted me to look at you before I tell you to bugger off, and I've done it. Dinner with you was a pleasant distraction, but I'm tired of you now."

I just stop myself from wincing when I speak those words. I'd meant it when I told my anonymous bedmate I was tired of her, but I'm lying to Catriona.

"*Mhac na galla*," she hisses. "You are the most obstinate man on earth. I donnae believe you, Alex, and I am going to figure out why you're so afraid to be with me."

"What was that phrase you spoke? It sounded like gibberish."

She bars her arms over her chest. "Never mind what it means. That was a curse, aimed at you because you're an eejit if you think I'll believe your insulting claim that kissing me was mediocre."

"Afraid it was, darling. Ta-ta."

I walk away, rather too swiftly, and trip over a seam in the concrete walkway. By the time I reach my car, my hands are shaking. It's ridiculous. By tomorrow, I will have forgotten about Catriona MacTaggart.

She will never haunt me again.

Chapter Four

Catriona

I attend class the next day, but I don't hear the lecture despite the fact the subject matter is of interest to me. Why can't I concentrate? Because of that *bod ceann*, Alex Thorne. Aye, he is a dickhead. Why else would he try to chase me away with insulting sarcasm? Something about kissing me terrified him. I've seen other men respond that way to intimacy, but I have never known anyone to say he's "tired" of me afterward. Is it any wonder why I cursed at him in Gaelic, calling the erse a son of a bitch?

That kiss had been bloody amazing.

Yet Alex wants me to believe it meant nothing to him. The way his left eyelid twitched when he said that convinced me that he didn't mean a word of it.

Why is Alex afraid to like me?

After class, I go to his office. But he isn't there. I check the schedule of classes on the university website and learn the *bod ceann* is teaching a class on British archaeology right now. So I head for Alex's classroom, though I don't go inside. I peer through the small window on the door which lets me see Alex where he stands at the front of the medium-size room. It's not as enormous as the lecture hall he'd used yesterday, but I assume British archaeology isn't as popular as his world history class. After all, that course is aimed at undergraduates, but the one today is for grad students.

While I watch secretly, Alex grows more animated as he lectures to his captive audience. He even grins when a student asks him a question. I wonder what the lass asked, because he clearly loves answering her question. The entire class laughs at something he said.

Alex Thorne might be a *bod ceann*, but he's also the most captivating teacher I've ever seen. Maybe I can't hear his lecture right now, but I sat in during his entire presentation yesterday. Alex is magnetic, electric, and completely mesmerizing.

But he pushed me away.

When did I become a coward? I have three large brothers, and I handle them quite well. I might have been nervous around Alex at first, but only because I have never been as attracted to any man as I am with Alex. Now that I've seen other sides of him, thanks to our intimate dinner last night, I no longer feel shy in his presence.

I watch Alex for a moment longer, then I hurry back to his office to wait for him. I sit down in the chair in front of his desk and watch the clock on the wall opposite me. His class should be ending in a few minutes. I resist the impulse to snoop in his office. I desperately want to do that because I need to understand why he behaves the way he does. But I'll need every ounce of patience I possess to solve the mystery of Alex Thorne.

Footsteps draw closer, and I glimpse the figure of Alex reflected in the window. He turns to the side as if he's thinking about sneaking away.

I crane my neck to glance back at him and smile. "Hello, Alex."

"Catriona." He speaks my name haltingly, as if he can't believe it's actually me. "Why are you here?"

"It's wonderful to see you too." I stand and face him. "I thought we should talk about last night."

"Whatever for? It was a pleasant distract—"

"No, Alex. I want to talk about *us*."

He scratches under his shirt collar. "There is no 'us.' There's me, there's you, and nothing between us."

"You kissed me."

"Do you stalk every bloke who kisses you?"

"Alex, please—"

He spreads an arm as if encouraging me to walk out the door. "I have a job to do. Goodbye, Catriona."

Alex won't talk to me. I have no choice but to leave.

Maybe I'm better off forgetting about Alex Thorne. Whatever his problems are, I need to focus on my studies and not the infernal man who kissed me, then called it mediocre and implied the experience was meaningless.

So that's what I do all week long. Occasionally, I pass by Alex's office and see him hunched over his desk studying papers. That posture doesn't seem like a sign of relaxation or happiness. He looks miserable. But I make some friends, and one lad even flirts with me. But I donnae feel anything for him other than platonic friendship. He seems fine with that, though the lad still flirts. Maybe "friends" isn't the right word to describe the other students I meet. They don't invite me to go anywhere with them, but we chat to each other in class. The lad who wants to date me sometimes approaches me on the quad when I'm reading or writing papers. Sooner or later, he will give up.

One day, I'm eating my lunch on the same bench where I'd met Alex when that boy, Aaron, sits down beside me.

"Hey, Catriona," he says. "You look really pretty today."

"Thank you." I don't even lift my head to look at him since I don't want to encourage the lad.

"What do I have to do to get you to go out with me?"

Morph into Alex Thorne, that's what. It's pathetic, but I can't stop thinking about that infuriating man. "I'm too busy to date, Aaron."

"Are you, like, a lesbian? I'm cool with that if you are. My half-sister is gay."

"No, I'm not a lesbian." I just don't want *him*.

I notice movement out of the corner of my eye, but it's not Aaron. The flash originated from the other direction. When I swivel my eyes toward the movement, I glimpse Alex spinning around to rush away.

What is he doing now?

I sling my rucksack over one shoulder and stand up. "It was nice to see you again, Aaron. Goodbye."

Though I would rather turn left, away from where I'd seen Alex, the classroom where I need to be in fifteen minutes is to my right. I won't see Alex. He ran away when he spotted me on the bench with Aaron. So I forget about him and walk down the concrete path. Halfway to my destination, I stop.

Because Alex is leaning against a tree, staring down at the ground with his hands jammed in his trouser pockets.

He looks so forlorn that I want to hug him. But he threw me over the other night, which means I owe him nothing. He'd been so sweet and charming during our dinner, and I'd loved that side of him. Do I want to get involved with a man who is clearly damaged by things he refuses to talk about? If I want a boyfriend, I can find someone less complicated.

Alex lifts his head and sees me. His head jerks back, and his eyes widen.

I have two choices—continue past him as if he doesn't exist, or stop and speak to him. Since I've never been good at shunning people, I approach the pitiful man. "Hello, Alex. How are you today?"

"Are you dating that child?" He doesn't sound angry. No, his voice is rife with pain.

"Do you mean Aaron? He's not a child. We're both working on our PhDs."

"You *are* dating him, then."

"No."

"But you've shagged him."

I shake my head. "Stop it, Alex. If you don't want to be with me, then you have no right to interrogate me about who I spend time with."

He bows his head and grips his nape. "I'm sorry. This is none of my concern."

Walk away, my logical brain tells me. But my heart urges me to find out what's fashing him. I inch closer. "Look at me, Alex, please."

He sighs, straightens, and clears his throat as he meets my gaze. "You're better off without me."

"Isn't that my decision?"

"You have no idea what you'd be letting yourself in for if you get involved with me."

"What have you done that's so awful?"

"It's complicated." He raises a hand as if to touch me but yanks it away. "I want you, Catriona. But I can't—You shouldn't want me."

"Alex—"

He takes off across the grass, making a beeline for the humanities building at the opposite end of the quad from where I need to go. Why do I care if Alex feels bad? He treated me wonderfully at first, then turned around and tossed me away like so much rubbish. I wish I hadn't seen the pain in his eyes when he'd done that or heard the tension in his voice when he told me our kiss had meant nothing. But I did see and hear that. And I can't help that I want to know more about him, to find out what has made him so afraid to get close to me.

I should forget about him. I *will* forget about him.

That evening, I'm sitting in my living room watching a bad television show when the doorbell rings. I yawn and stretch, then pad over to the door. Who would want to see me at nine o'clock? I don't really know anyone in this country, not anyone who would stop by at such a late hour. But I peek through the peephole—and freeze.

It's Alex.

Maybe I shouldn't do it, but I cannae stop myself from opening the door. "What are you doing here?"

Alex leans against the jamb, giving me that sexy half smile I'd seen often during our one and only date. "I wanted to apologize. In person. May I come in?"

I chew on my lip for a moment while I consider how to respond. He looks delicious in casual clothes—jeans and a polo shirt—but I cannae let my hormones make this decision. My heart does that instead. "Aye, you can come in."

Stepping aside, I wait until he's crossed the threshold, then shut the door. I'm completely alone with him. A man I barely know. Yet I trust him. Why? Not a bloody clue. He hesitates halfway to the sofa, seeming unsure of what to do now.

"Go on, sit down," I say as I wave toward the sofa and the armchair. "Wherever you like."

He drops onto the nearest end of the sofa.

I sit at the other end. "Did you have a reason for coming here?"

"Yes, of course." He sets his hands on his knees and curls his fingers over them. "I've behaved horribly. You have every right to tell me to sod off, but I hope you won't."

"Why would I tell you to do that?"

He glances at me sideways, almost smirking but not quite. "You wouldn't, naturally. I'm the arse would say something like that. I did say something similar to you after our date. I want to apologize for that, Catriona. I loved spending time with you—and kissing you."

"So it wasn't mediocre after all."

"No." He turns his face toward me. "It was the most incredible kiss I've ever experienced. I'm sorry for everything I said after I drove you home."

"Apology accepted."

His brows cinch up, and his lips fall open. "Why are you forgiving me?"

"Because I believe you're sincere, and everyone deserves a second chance."

"Everyone? Not sure that's true."

I'm about to ask why he thinks that, but then he yawns and sags into the sofa, letting his head fall back against it as he shuts his eyes. He looks so exhausted that I donnae have the heart to question him anymore tonight.

"You seem too jeeked to drive home," I say.

He peels one eye open to look at me. "Jeeked?"

"It means you're exhausted."

"Oh. Yes, I am that." He blows out a sigh and closes both eyes again. "This sofa is so comfortable that I think I could sleep for a thousand years."

"Why don't you sleep on the sofa tonight?" Did I just invite him to spend the night? Aye, and I meant it. Maybe being away from my entire family and living in another country has driven me off my head, because I don't regret making that offer.

Alex rotates his head toward me, and his caramel eyes zero in on me. "Are you sure you want me to do that? Stay the night, I mean."

"Yes, Alex, I'm sure. Cannae have you careening off the road on your way home."

He stares at me. "Thank you, Catriona."

"You can call me Cat if you like. It's my nickname."

"Thank you, Cat."

His eyes drift shut again, though his head stays turned to the side. I crawl on my knees until I'm right beside him, then raise my hand as if to caress his face, but I stop. Maybe I shouldn't touch him. Maybe I ought to ring for a taxi to take him home. But he looks so innocent and sweet right now, not at all like the way he'd behaved after our date. So I give in and spread my palm over his cheek, sliding it across his skin and into his hair.

One of his eyes opens partway. "What are you doing?"

"Hush." I begin combing my fingers through his hair in a gentle rhythm. "I'm trying to help you relax."

"Mm." His lid falls shut. "It's working."

He sounds very sleepy, but I keep brushing his hair with my fingertips until his breathing grows shallow and regular. I think he's asleep, or at least almost there. I carefully slide off the sofa and tiptoe into my bedroom to retrieve a blanket, then I return to the sofa.

Alex now lies stretched along the sofa's length, his shoes on the floor and his eyes closed.

I drape the blanket over him and grab a throw pillow which I gently tuck under his head. He doesn't even stir. I gaze down at him for a moment, then I lean in to kiss his cheek. He seems almost angelic in sleep, as if all his worries have evaporated.

Back in my bedroom, I change into a nightie and crawl under the covers. But I can't stop thinking about one question.

What will I do with Alex Thorne?

Chapter Five

Alex

I wake in the morning feeling rather good. Much better than yesterday, for sure. Catriona has forgiven me for my abominable behavior, and for some reason, that makes me feel bloody fantastic. She tucked me in last night too. I doubt she realized I was only half-asleep, but I'd been just awake enough to feel it when she kissed my cheek.

Only one other woman has ever done that, and she wasn't even my lover. Catriona isn't either, though I want her to be that and so much more. I don't deserve this kind of chance with this kind of woman, but I will take whatever she offers me.

The past be damned.

I suddenly realize today is Saturday, which means I have the entire weekend with Catriona, if she wants me to stay for that long.

Since her bedroom door is closed, I decide she must be sleeping. In the kitchen, I find all the ingredients I need to cook a decent breakfast for her. I'm hardly a gourmet chef, but I know how to make edible food. I've just gathered everything I need when Catriona sashays out of her bedroom wearing nothing but a blue nightie. Its spaghetti straps and short hemline give me a tantalizing view of her thighs and the slopes of her breasts.

"Good morning, darling," I say, with no sarcasm at all when I speak that word. "Are you hungry?"

Catriona halts mid-step. She lifts her head to gawp at me. "Alex? Why are you—" She winces. "I invited you to stay."

"And you clearly forgot about that when you woke up this morning." I rove my gaze over her from head to toe and back again. "You should dress this way more often."

"It's a nightie, Alex. I only dress this way at night."

"That's a shame, love. You are even more stunning barely clothed and mussed from sleep."

"Mussed?" She pats her hair and winces again. "I forgot to brush my hair."

"I know, and I like it. Nothing is sexier than a tousled woman in a skimpy negligee." I can't resist smirking. "Well, except for a nude woman."

"Donnae get ahead of yourself, Alex."

"Why not? It's my default position."

Catriona ambles up to the kitchen bar and perches on a stool. "What are you cooking?"

"I was planning to make you a decadent feast." I survey the ingredients I'd laid out. "But now I'm getting a different idea."

"You don't need to make a fuss. Honestly, scrambled eggs are fine with me."

"That's not what I meant." My focus gravitates to her chest and the tantalizing slopes of those generous breasts. "It's your choice, darling. Would you rather eat breakfast or make love?"

She stares blankly at me.

Well, I did warn her that going too far is my default position. I've wanted her since the moment we met, and now we're alone in her flat. We've already kissed once, and she invited me to spend the night on her sofa. So I'm hoping she wants what I want.

I raise my brows at her. "Is the decision that difficult?"

"No." She hops off her stool and sashays around to my side of the counter, stopping an arm's length away. "Let's make love, Alex."

For two seconds, I assume I've misheard her. Then she drags her tongue across her lips and moves her fingers over her chest in slow circles. Oh no, I did not misunderstand her.

I grasp her hips and tug her closer. "I'm glad you said that, because I need to fuck you right now."

"What happened to making love?"

"Don't worry, we'll do that too. I mean to give us both a workout before breakfast."

"I'd love that." She cocks her head as if she wants to study me. "Were you lying when you said calling me 'darling' meant nothing?"

"Yes, I was. I am a bloody liar, sometimes. So before we do this, you should understand a few things about me."

Catriona slips her arms around my waist and snuggles up to me. "I'm listening."

"In all my life, I have never made love to a woman. I only shag them."

"Am I meant to be shocked? I can handle that, Alex."

Maybe she can, and I hope I won't need to test that faith. "I will never tell you about my past or my family."

"Why not?"

"Because I won't. If that's a deal breaker for you, then I will walk out the door and never bother you again."

She chews on her upper lip while scrutinizing me again. Just when I think she'll tell me to bugger off, she kisses me instead. Sweetly. On the lips only. Then she smiles. "I agree to your terms."

"They're not terms. They're facts of life with me."

"And I agree to your facts."

Why on earth she wants to live with my limitations, I cannot fathom. But she knows what I can't give her, and she still said yes.

Catriona wriggles against me. "I've never slept with a man I met less than a week ago."

"You still haven't. I slept on the sofa, and you slept in the bedroom." I lay my palms on her arse. "And if I have my way, we won't be sleeping this morning, either."

"You know what I meant."

Oh yes, I know. "Last chance to change your mind."

"Are we going to have a poke today? Or will ye keep trying to change my mind until next Wednesday?"

I sweep her up in my arms. "Does this answer your question?"

She laughs.

God, she's beautiful. And so sweet that I want to hold her in my arms forever. But my cock disapproves of that idea, so I carry her into the bedroom and set her down at the foot of the bed. "Shall I undress you? Or would you rather strip for me?"

Catriona bites her lip in that shy yet sexy way I've seen before. Does she realize how desirable she is? I doubt that. She's probably dated men her own age, which means twats who have no idea what to do with a real woman.

"How old are you?" I ask.

"Twenty-four. How old are you?"

"I'm twenty-nine."

She leans into me. "Were you worried I'm not legal?"

"No, darling. You're a grad student, so I was reasonably sure I wouldn't get arrested for shagging you. I was curious, that's all."

The lovely lass takes hold of the hem of her flimsy nightie. "I'll undress myself."

I take a few steps backward. "Go on, Cat. Strip for me. Though it won't take long considering how little you're wearing."

She pulls the nightie over her head and tosses it away, which leaves her standing completely nude. I couldn't look away from her if I tried, not that I want to do that. Her full breasts capture all of my attention, and I can't help fantasizing about touching and tasting them. Fuck, she's perfect. Her creamy skin is sprinkled with the faintest freckles, including one on her left nipple. She has the best combination of muscle tone and womanly softness, from her slender waist to her wide hips and down to her thighs that seem strong enough to grip me while I fuck her.

"Cat, you are exquisite."

She smiles shyly.

And that makes me want her even more. But it's my turn now, and I get rid of my clothes as fast as possible because I feel like I might explode if I don't start touching her right now. I yank the covers off the bed. "Lie down, love. On your back."

She obeys, and I crawl up the bed on my hands and knees until my face hovers directly over hers. She reaches up to touch her fingertips to my mouth. I kiss her fingers one by one, then lunge my head down to claim her lips, kissing her with a sort of abandon I've never experienced before. I don't generally kiss the women I shag, but with Cat, I need to taste her mouth and explore every silky corner of it before I devour the rest of her.

I pull my mouth away, now breathing harder. "When was the last time a man went down on you?"

She hunches her shoulders. "Never."

"Never? What sort of arses do you date?"

"Boys don't like to do that."

"Are these American arses or Scottish ones?"

She lays a hand on my cheek while smiling at me like I'm the daftest man on earth. "Scottish ones. I only moved to America two weeks ago. You're the first not-Scottish man I've been with."

"I see. Scotsmen don't know how to pleasure women. Can't say that surprises me. After all, they do wear plaid obsessively, and they love those horrid bagpipes."

"Oh, one day you will regret saying that. My three large brothers love to wear kilts—and toss cabers."

"Could we not discuss your brothers while we're naked in bed?"

"Aye." She makes a zipper motion across her lips.

"Feel free to speak. Just not about your brothers. I will be very disappointed if you don't at least scream my name."

She giggles. If any other woman did that, I would've thought it was moronic. But when Cat giggles, it's the most charming thing in the world. "I donnae even scream on roller coasters, Alex."

"Oh, but I'm going to give you pleasure beyond your wildest dreams." When she starts to speak, I seal her lips with one finger. "Wait and see."

I crawl backward until my head is aligned with her hips, then I lower myself onto my belly. My face lies just over the soft, curly hairs of her mound. "Spread your legs and bend your knees, pet."

She does that without any hesitation. Cat trusts me. She must, otherwise she wouldn't have let me stay the night, much less let me make love to her. Do I trust her? I suppose I must. Never have I let anyone get as close to me as Catriona has done. Well, no one except for the only two people in the world who really know me.

I nuzzle her mound. "You smell so fucking good, Cat. I can't wait to taste you."

She's breathing harder, her breasts rising and falling.

With two fingers, I separate her folds to expose the rigid nub of her clitoris, surrounded by the glistening evidence of her lust for me. "I'm going to lick up every last drop of your cream."

I push my face between her thighs and devour her with quick swipes of my tongue, though I avoid her clit for now. Instead, I lick my way down one side of her folds and flick my tongue into her opening before I lick my way up the other side. Cat gasps and writhes beneath me, fisting her hands in the pillow while her neck arches. My breathing has accelerated too, along with my pulse. My cock had been marginally firm when we lay down on the bed, but now it feels like it might explode if I don't shag her in the next thirty seconds.

I never rush, though—especially not with Cat.

"Alex," she moans as I latch on to her clit and suckle it. "Oh God, yes."

The flavor of her suffuses my mouth and makes me feel almost drunk. I need to push her over the edge now, before I come all over her flower-print sheets. So I plunge two fingers inside her and pump while ravishing her nub.

Her body goes rigid an instant before the first spasms grip my fingers. She cries out just as her body bows inward, and she squeezes her eyes shut while I keep finger-fucking her until she collapses onto the mattress. "Alex…"

I rise to my knees. "We aren't done yet."

She gives me a smile so charming and sexy that my cock throbs. "You are as good as you think."

"Am I? Perhaps you should wait until I'm done before making a pronouncement like that." I glance around to look for my trousers, but then I realize we have a problem. My head falls forward as I groan. "I don't have a condom."

"Donnae worry. I have one." She twists her upper body to reach the nightstand and pull the drawer open. Then she tosses me a condom packet. "See? No problem."

"Why do you have condoms? I thought you hadn't been with anyone since you moved here."

"I haven't. But I believe in being prepared. I have packets in my purse too."

"You are wonderful, Cat."

She laughs.

And I get the condom on as quickly as I can. Then I plant my hands on the mattress at either side of her shoulders and thrust inside her lush body. She feels even better than I'd imagined, despite the condom. Her heat surrounds me, and her hairs tickle my skin as I begin a measured pace. We gaze into each other's eyes the entire time, and the glacial blue of her irises seems darker and more intense thanks to the dilation of her pupils. Understanding the physiology of that does nothing to diminish the beauty of her eyes. Faint pinkness dapples her cheeks as her lips fall open and her breaths quicken.

I'm breathing harder and faster too. Though I'd love to stay nestled inside her forever, the pressure inside me grows with every thrust, and I know I won't last much longer. So I reach down to rub her clit, pistoning my hips faster, plunging deeper with every inward lunge.

Cat gasps and grips the headboard rails. "Yes, Alex, yes. Donnae stop."

With a strangled cry, she comes.

Even as her body milks me with pulsating spasms, I keep punching into her, knowing I'll explode any second. The bed creaks and thumps as I thrust wildly with both palms flat on the mattress. Everything inside me feels like I'm on a roller coaster that's crawling up the highest hill and I'm about to crest it. I can't stop myself from pounding into Cat while the tension escalates so much that the breath freezes in my lungs.

Then I hit that peak and roar down the slope in free-fall.

I come so hard I can't even shout. But my body takes over since my brain has shut down, and it forces me to pump into her a few more times as sweat dribbles down my temples. When I finally collapse onto the bed next to Cat, making the mattress bounce, I'm fighting to catch my breath.

The lovely lass beside me is struggling to breathe too.

Once I've recovered my wits, I roll onto my side to drape an arm over her belly. "That was incredible, Cat."

"Aye, it was." She rolls over too, her delectable body rubbing against mine. "How soon can we do that again?"

I chuckle.

Chapter Six

Catriona

Why are you laughing?" I ask. When Alex only smirks at me, I flip onto my back and fold my arms over my breasts. "You said it was incredible, but now you're acting like you think sex with me is hilarious. I donnae understand men at all."

"No, you clearly don't." He slings an arm over my belly and kisses me. "I gather the blokes you shagged didn't stay for round two. Did they at least spend the night with you?"

I shrug. "They usually said they had to get up early for work and didn't want to bother with setting an alarm for an earlier time just so they could go home and change clothes."

"Bother? Sleeping with a woman is not a nuisance. Waking up with one isn't either."

"You said you only shag women. You don't sleep with them."

"Well, yes…" He bows his head and scratches the back of it. Then he peeks up at me through his thick lashes. "But now I want to do that—with you. And I want to make love to you over and over too."

"Then why did ye laugh when I asked if we could do it again?

"Men aren't machines, love. We need time to recover before we can have another go."

"How long does that take?"

Alex seals his open mouth over my belly button and blows out a breath. His lips vibrate my skin, and I start to giggle. Honestly, I never do that. But Alex knows exactly how to make me do silly things and love every minute of it. He also knows how to give me intense pleasure.

Alex kisses a path up my belly and straight to my throat, where he feathers his lips over my skin. "Why don't we have a light breakfast first? I'm sure I'll be up for it after that."

"I could eat a whole haggis by myself."

He feigns disgust. "I hope you don't expect me to kiss you after that. And I said light breakfast. We don't want to gorge ourselves right before sex."

"Men are finicky about this, aren't you?"

"It's biology, darling. I can't change that."

"All right. Breakfast first." I try to sit up, but he gently pushes me back down. "Stay here. I will bring you breakfast in bed."

"What should I do while I wait for you?"

"Anything you like." He pecks a kiss on my lips. "It will be worth the wait, I promise."

I watch Alex climb off the bed. Then he walks out the door, giving me a perfect view of his arse until he moves out of my sight. That man has a beautiful body and the face of an angel. But when he makes love to me, his expression turns into fierce hunger. I've never seen a man look like that during sex. I love it, and I cannae wait until we have another poke.

What should I do now? Alex suggested I should lie about in bed, but that's dead boring. I count the balls on the ceiling until I start to go cross-eyed, then I play thumb war with my own hands, which isn't very satisfying. The scent of food wafts into the bedroom, making my tummy rumble. Aye, I'm fair starved. Sex with Alex turned into an aerobic workout.

A sensuous warmth rushes through me as I flash back to a little while ago when Alex had been inside me. Poised over me. Thrusting and gasping, his expression the picture of intense need. He's always gorgeous, but in the throes, he becomes a god. I'm growing slick between my thighs again just from remembering what we did. My favorite bit was when he said in that rough, rumbly voice, "I'm going to lick up every last drop of your cream."

Now a tingling erupts between my thighs too.

I need him to fuck me again right now, but Alex insisted he cannae do that yet. Though I try not to, I cannae help fantasizing about those moments in this bed. The more I think about that, and him, the more I need to come. My clit throbs as I wriggle uncomfortably, afflicted with a growing need to relieve the pressure.

How long will it take Alex to make breakfast? I glance at the clock on the nightstand and realize it's only been ten minutes since he left the room. Cannae wait that long.

So I close my eyes and slip a finger between my folds to stroke myself while I imagine Alex licking me the way had earlier. Oh, his tongue. It had felt like velvet on my flesh. I move my finger in a rhythm that matches how he had devoured me, and excitement rises inside me. My back arches. I moan his name and rub faster.

"Bloody hell, Cat. Don't get started without me."

My eyes fly open. I stare at Alex, feeling strangely embarrassed that he caught me. After what we did earlier, I donnae know how I can feel that way, but I do. "Alex. What are you doing?"

He's not holding a tray of food. He just stands in the doorway gawping at me.

Alex clears his throat. "I, ah, wanted to know if you prefer your eggs fried or scrambled."

"Oh. Scrambled." Just like my brain.

"Good. I'll, ah, go finish cooking everything." He turns away, then glances over his shoulder at me. And he smirks. "No cheating, love. You are not to come until I say so."

Normally, I don't like bossy men. But when Alex commands me not to come, I obey because I love everything he does to me. Still, I'm a wee bit fashed that I need to wait for my next orgasm. At least with Alex, I know it will be worth the wait.

I'm having sex with a man I barely know. My family would be horrified if they found out, but I donnae need to tell them everything. I'm a grown woman who can make her own decisions. And I've decided to be with Alex Thorne.

He returns a few minutes later carrying a tray of food. "Sit up, darling. You can't eat lying down."

I push up into a sitting position and grab the top sheet to pull it over me.

Alex sets the tray on my lap. "Go ahead and start eating. I'll join you momentarily."

Before I have the chance to ask where he's going, he strides around to the other side of the bed and climbs in beside me.

"I thought you meant you were leaving the room," I say. "But you're still here."

"Did you want me to leave?"

"No. I like having you here."

He picks up a cherry tomato and slips it between my lips. "I assumed we would share the food."

I eat the tomato and kiss him. "I'd love to do that."

We enjoy our shared meal, feeding each other bits of food and making jokes so often that it takes us an hour to finish. It's hard to chew while laughing. I've never had this much fun with a man before. Well, my brothers are entertaining too, and so are my male cousins. But the fun Alex and I have together is different. None of the other men I dated wanted to enjoy this kind of intimacy with me. Sharing a meal while naked? No, they wanted to leave as soon as we had a poke. They didn't even stay a few minutes to cuddle.

But Alex, the man who confounded me all week long with his strange behavior, seems to be in no hurry to leave this bed.

After setting the tray on the floor, Alex whips the sheet off to expose our naked bodies—and his growing erection. "Shall we have another poke, my bonnie Scots lass?"

I laugh. "Aye, we should."

He called me his lass. I like that.

We spend the rest of the morning in bed, though not asleep. Alex knows how to turn sex into a workout, but then he'll turn around and make love to me with such tenderness that I get a strange pang in my chest. It's not a bad feeling.

In the afternoon, we go sightseeing since neither of us know the city well. Ballesteros lies in the mountains rather than the desert, so it has grass and conifer forests. When I decided to do my PhD program here, I'd expected that all of New Mexico must be flat and dry, but I was wrong. I'd looked up pictures of the area on the internet while planning my move, and the landscape had intrigued me.

When I tell Alex that, as we're driving down the road, he chuckles. "You moved to another country for the trees. Cat, you are adorable."

"Not only for the trees. I liked the mountains too."

"Well, that makes sense, of course."

He's teasing me, but I love that. Since Alex is driving, I decide to tease him in return.

I lay a hand on his thigh and slide it up toward his groin. "Why did you move to New Mexico?"

"Not for the ruddy trees, that's for sure." He grimaces when I move my hand a wee bit higher, grazing his cock. "But I'd be happy to fuck you in the woods if that's what turns you on."

"What turns me on is you."

He glances at me and smirks, though I can't see his eyes because he's wearing sunglasses. "Better remove your charming little hand from my leg, darling. If I develop an erection, I won't bother pulling over to the side of the road to shag you. I'll do it while the car is moving, and I can't swear we won't cause a mile-long pileup."

I pull my hand away and laugh. "Eyes on the road, Alex."

"You are so provincial."

We stay in town for our first joint sightseeing trip, but Ballesteros has plenty of fun ways to spend an afternoon. We visit a wee museum dedicated to the town's history. I love history, of course, since I'm a student of archaeology. But I have trouble focusing on the displays. My attention keeps drifting back to Alex. He's so animated while he talks about the artifacts in glass cases, waving his hands and making the cutest expressions. I have trouble reconciling this Alex with the man who had told me our first kiss was "mediocre" and who had seemed so melancholy when he saw me speaking to another man.

Aye, he's complicated. One day I will ask him to explain his behavior, but I don't want to do that just yet. I'm loving this version of him, and asking questions might send him into another downward spiral.

I shouldn't care for him, not yet, but I do.

We spend the entire weekend together, both of us sleeping in my bed at night. On Monday morning, I wake up before Alex does and just lie here watching him sleep. Does he dream about me? I dream about him, but not in the way I'd expected. Instead of having steamy dreams about him, my nighttime fantasies involve Alex enfolding me in his arms, smiling at me, holding my hand as we take a walk together. Those dreams might be more dangerous than the erotic sort.

Alex rouses and yawns, stretching his arms above his head. "Good morning, love. Did you sleep well?"

"Very well, thank you."

He lifts an arm as an invitation to cuddle up to him, and I happily accept that offer. "I'm afraid it's back to the grindstone today. But maybe we could have lunch together."

"I have a free hour at noon."

"So do I." He kisses the top of my head. "Meet me on our bench at twelve o'clock. I'll bring the food."

We lounge in bed for a few more minutes, but then it's time to start the day. After having a shower with Alex, one that does not involve sex, I make breakfast while he teases me about feeding him pancakes instead of something Scottish. When I suggest I could make him haggis for lunch, he pretends to gag, then grins at me in the way that always makes my pulse beat faster.

We take Alex's car, which means we can park in the faculty lot instead of in the boondocks where students are allowed to park. Before he gets out of the car, we kiss. It's not a sweet kiss either, but a steamy one that leaves me feeling wonderfully warm and tingly.

Hand in hand, we amble down the concrete paths until we reach the intersection where he needs to turn left and I need to turn right. Even after we go our separate ways, we keep glancing back at each other and grinning. What is this tingly sensation I'm feeling? Why does his smile make warmth blossom in my chest? The answer is dead obvious, and it doesn't frighten me the way I'd expected it should.

Oh, aye. I'm falling for Alex Thorne.

Chapter Seven

Alex

Catriona MacTaggart has cast a spell over me. I have no other explanation for what I've done or what I plan to do moving forward. I mean to go on behaving in a ridiculous manner, which means tickling her belly until she's laughing so hard that tears roll down her cheeks, teasing her about haggis, and making love to her as often as possible for as long as possible.

I didn't only spend the night with her. I stayed for the entire weekend. Even worse, I did nothing except play silly buggers with her. Can't remember the last time I took time off simply to…have fun. I work, I shag anonymous women, I eat, I sleep, and I go back to work. Christ, what a dull existence I've carved out for myself.

Not anymore. A single weekend with Cat has given me something I never thought I wanted—happiness.

It will all go pear-shaped, eventually. It must. Someone like me does not deserve this kind of joy. Is that what I'm experiencing? Joy? I can honestly say it has never happened to me before. Maybe that explains why I suddenly find myself almost dancing down the path to the humanities building this morning, and worse, realize I'm whistling a cheerful tune. *Bloody hell.* I've become the sort of bloke I used to scoff at, one of those poor sods who loses his head over a pretty girl.

As I enter the building, I wonder what Cat is doing right now. She's taking a statistics course, which means she must be inside the mathematics building right now, listening to a boring lecture about percentages and calculations or whatever. I probably won't see her again until noon, when we have our lunch date.

"Good morning, Dr. Thorne."

I stop and turn around to face the man who spoke. The dean of my department gives me a pleasant smile, and I can't help smiling at him with genuine happiness for the first time in…ever. Well, I grinned at Cat all weekend, so it's not the actual first time.

"Good morning, Dean Wells," I say. "It's a lovely morning, isn't it?"

"Yes, it is." He studies me for a moment. "Don't think I've ever seen anybody look so happy on a Monday morning. What's your secret?"

Catriona is my secret elixir of happiness. But I tell the dean, "I had a wonderful weekend, that's all. I feel refreshed."

"Good for you." He pats my shoulder as he walks past me. "Whatever her name is, you're one lucky guy."

As the dean wanders off down the corridor, I stand immobilized. I am a lucky man. My life has changed in the space of a week, and I never want to go back to the way things were.

Though I teach my classes and grade papers the way I'm meant to do, my thoughts keep rewinding to the weekend and Cat and all the things we did together. Noon finally arrives, and I sit on the bench I've come to think of as ours, waiting for Catriona to stroll up the path. When I finally see her, I swear my heart skips a beat.

She smiles and waves at me.

And I get an odd twinge in my chest.

"What did you bring for lunch?" Cat asks as she sits down beside me. "I'm fair starved."

"Must be the aftereffects of two days of sex and sightseeing."

"I think so." She bumps her shoulder into mine. "I loved our weekend together."

"So did I." Reaching under the bench, I pull out the picnic basket I'd hidden under there. "Sorry. I didn't have time to cook for you, so I ordered a picnic for us from a restaurant."

Catriona rubs her palms together and licks her lips.

I chuckle. "You are adorably ravenous."

We enjoy our picnic while talking about nothing of consequence, unless secretly joking about what other people are wearing counts as an important discussion. On our way to the humanities building, I guide her off the path and into a secluded spot surrounded by bushes and trees, where no one will see us.

And then I kiss her.

She wraps her arms around my neck and moans. I need to kiss her all the time, to taste her and feel her body pressed to mine every moment of every day. But I can't do that. I'll have to resign myself to taking whatever I can get and making love to her every night.

For the next three weeks, we ignore the rest of the world as much as possible and just enjoy being together. The longer I'm with Cat, the more I want to keep her with me forever. Do I have the right to do that? Should I do it? She has no idea about my past, and I never want to explain that to her.

This weekend, I've invited Cat to stay in my loft. For me, that's a huge step and a huge risk, though it doesn't terrify me as much as what I mean to do next.

I drive Catriona to the outskirts of town where my apartment complex lies on a quiet street, surrounded by trees and set back off the road just enough that I can't see the street or the neighboring buildings. Yes, I cherish privacy. Cat's eyes widen as we walk through the entryway of my second-floor loft and continue into the living room.

"Are you rich, Alex?" she asks. "I've never seen a loft like this before."

She's referring to the posh furniture and the expensive lithographic prints on the walls, not to mention the Persian rugs on the floor. If she thinks I must be wealthy based on the living room decor, she will probably pass out when she sees the kitchen. Maybe one man doesn't need all these things. I can't explain why I felt an impulse to turn my apartment into something out of a model home show. I suppose it makes me feel safe.

"Well, Alex," she says, "are you rich?"

"Perhaps I have more money than some people. Does that matter to you?"

"No. But I'm curious about how you got so much money. Archaeology professors aren't usually millionaires."

"You could call it family money."

"I *could* call it that?" She turns to face me, raising her brows. "What does that mean?"

Rubbing my jaw, I try to think of a way to explain this without actually explaining it. "Family money means…family money. I inherited most of it and invested the rest to grow my assets."

"You inherited money from your parents?"

"Does it matter? I told you I won't discuss my past. It wouldn't be illuminating for you, anyway." I can tell she wants to interrogate me more, so I distract her by clasping her hand and guiding her into the kitchen. "I think you'll enjoy cooking in here, especially since you can see into the living room."

The open kitchen features a bar that sits just behind the living room, as well as every sort of kitchen gadget anyone could want but no one really needs. Cat ambles over to the large stand mixer on the counter and runs her fingers over the rim of its bowl. Then she glances at me sideways while smiling slightly in the manner I've realized means she thinks I'm being an "eejit." Yes, I am an idiot in many ways, particularly when it comes to stocking my kitchen with useless contraptions.

"Do you invite the entire faculty of Ballesteros University to dinner parties here?" she asks.

"No. I've never invited anyone to my home. I don't even let the FedEx man come inside."

"Then why do you need all these things?" She spreads an arm to indicate my outrageous collection of gadgets. "Ye donnae seem like the sort who loves technology."

"I have a mobile phone and a wide-screen TV."

She laughs in the soft and affectionate way I've heard often lately, the way I adore. "You are so cute when you're full of rubbish, Alex."

I pull her into me. "I also own an electric shiatsu massager. Care to try out that device?"

"Only if you're using it on me while we're naked."

"Naturally." I take her hand, leading her through the living and down a hallway to an open door. "This is my bedroom."

"May I go in there?"

"Have at it, love."

She races into the room and belly flops onto the bed, then flips over to move her arms and legs as if she's creating a snow angel on the comforter without any snow. My God, she is enchanting. I love every ridiculous thing she does, and watching her writhe around on the bed while grinning makes me want to tear her clothes off and fuck her.

But I have something to discuss with her first.

I sit down on the bed near her. "Could we talk for a moment?"

Catriona springs up into a sitting position and wriggles her lovely arse to get closer to me. "What did you want to talk about?"

"Well, ah…" I suddenly can't speak the words. That's bollocks. I always know what to say to a woman, how to maneuver anyone into my bed, but this is different. I don't want to seduce Cat. All right, I mean to do that too. But first, I need to tell her something I've never told anyone. I scratch my arms and feel my face pinching up. "Catriona, I—Uh, it's—"

She grasps my face and urges me to look at her. "Whatever it is, Alex, you can tell me. I won't run away."

Maybe she should run. But I can't bear the thought of losing her. So I suck in a breath and do it. "I'd like you to move in with me."

"Oh." She stares at me for a moment, then breaks into a grin. "Yes, Alex, I'd love to live with you."

Why? That's what I want to ask, but I won't cock this up by acting like an arse. I need her with me all the time, and she just agreed to share my home—and my bed. "There are a few things you need to know first. I've told you I won't talk about my past or my family."

"Aye, and I said that's all right."

"From this moment forward, I don't want to even think about the past. All that matters is us, our present and our future together."

"I agree."

Part of me still can't accept that she understands my rules and agrees to abide by them. If one day she grows tired of my limitations and leaves me… I won't think about that today. Or tomorrow. Or next month. I will relish having her with me for as long as I can.

"Are you hungry yet?" I ask. "Or should we delay dinner and shag instead?"

Her sexy smile melts my heart. "Sex first. And get the shiatsu massager."

"Anything for you, love."

For the next hour, I use that massager, as well as my mouth and hands, to drive Cat to multiple orgasms. Then she uses the device on me, but I can't resist flipping her over so I can shag her the right way—with my cock buried inside her.

After our exercise routine, we make dinner together.

Yes, I'm calling sex an exercise routine. It was very athletic, after all.

In the morning, we go to Cat's flat to retrieve her belongings. Then I take her to lunch at a nice restaurant. She plans to give up her flat so another student can have it since she doesn't need her own place anymore. We're living together. We are a couple. I expect to experience a twinge of panic whenever I think about what I've done, but I feel only good things.

Cat and I develop a routine of going to the grocery store on Saturday mornings and then having lunch at our favorite café. On this day, having just left the restaurant, we stroll down the sidewalk hand in hand, in no hurry to reach our car. Well, technically it›s my car since my name is on the registration. But I›ve come to think of it as ours. Catriona had hired a car when she first moved to Ballesteros, and though she›d intended to buy one eventually, she never got round to it.

She stops me half a block from where we parked our car. "I need to use the restroom. In that shop behind us."

"You don't need my permission."

"Would you rather I ran off without explaining?"

"I see your point." Kissing her cheek, I release her hand. "Go on. I'll wait here."

The woman I adore hurries into the shop, and I shove my hands in my trouser pockets while I wait for her to return.

"I don't believe it," a feminine voice declares from behind me. "It's actually you."

That voice…I recognize it. Turning toward the woman, I can't help grimacing. If fate exists, it clearly despises me. Because the woman I shagged the night before I met Cat, the "I love your dick" idiot, is standing there grinning at me.

She sashays closer and speaks in a sultrier tone. "Imagine my luck bumping into you again. I'm staying in the big hotel near the freeway on-ramp."

Am I meant to give a toss where she's staying? I never knew her name and never wanted to see her again. Cat will come out of the shop at any moment, which means I need to shake this woman off quickly. "Sorry, I think you have me confused with someone else."

She wags a finger at me. "No, no, baby. I could never forget that face and those lips."

"Please bugger off," I say as if the woman means nothing to me, which is true. "I have no desire to speak to you and certainly no inclination to go anywhere with you."

The bloody woman pouts, though it's sheer artifice. "Come on, baby. We had so much fun together."

"I enjoyed the orgasms, not you." Yes, I feel like a wanker for saying that, though it wouldn't have bothered me before I met Cat. I have no choice right now. The tart won't leave unless I berate her. Then again, she might like that. "I said go away, darling. You can bat your eyelashes for the next hour, but it won't make me want you."

The bloody woman huffs and throws her hands up. "Fine. It's your loss."

At last, she ambles off down the sidewalk.

I rub my eyes with the heels of my hands and exhale a long sigh.

"Alex, who was that?"

When I remove my hands from my face, I can do nothing except stare at Cat. She's just walked out of the shop and seems rightfully baffled. I consider lying to her, but I don't want to do that. Instead, I approach her and clasp her hands. "That was a woman I shagged the night before I met you. It was just sex, and I spent only a couple of hours with her. It meant nothing."

"I understand. You have a past, and I can handle it." Her lips curl into a sweet little smile that dimples her cheeks. "Even if a horde of your former bedmates swarm me, I'll be fine."

"Why? I can't imagine any other woman would accept the way I used to be."

"I do, Alex. Because I'm in love with you."

She must expect me to tell her the same thing, but I can't do it. In my entire life, I have never spoken those three words to anyone. She said she's in love with me, not "I love you," but it feels the same to me. Am I in love with her? Just considering what the answer might be makes me itchy from head to toe.

Maybe she accepts me as-is for now, but sooner or later she will want more from me. And that will be the day I lose her.

Chapter Eight

Catriona

Living with Alex is the best thing that has ever happened to me. I don't even mind that he hasn't said he loves me, though I told him how I feel. Men don't like to deal with feelings, a fact I learned from watching my two older brothers deal with the lasses in their lives, beginning when they were teenagers. Aye, men have no clue how to handle romance. That's all right. I can wait for Alex to say those words because he shows me every day that he does love me.

Actions speak louder than words. That's how the saying goes, and I've decided to live by it.

When I ring my brother Lachlan six weeks after I moved in with Alex, I don't mention the man in my life. I've spoken to my sister Fiona in the meantime, but I didn't tell her either. I do let my family know I've changed addresses, and they don't ask why. They trust me. Sometimes I do feel guilty for keeping my relationship with Alex a secret, but I'm an adult, not a bairn. If I want to have this one thing for me and only me, without my family interfering or judging, then that's what I'll do. None of them suggest they might visit me in America. It's too far away and too expensive to fly here, and besides, they have their own lives. Moving here was always meant to be temporary, just until I get my PhD. My cousin Evan, who's almost done with his university studies, already knows more about computers than anyone I've ever met. So he helps us set up our computers to do video conferencing, which lets us see and hear each other.

Time flies by, but I love every minute of it. Sometimes I wish I could slow down the clock, just to have more time with Alex. But we have the rest of our lives. I won't get greedy and hope for more. I never ask him about his past. Am I a fool? Donnae care if I am. For the first time in my life, I have everything I need.

Six months after we moved in together, I get an offer I want to accept—but only if Alex doesn't mind. I'm excited to share the news with him, but I wait until we get home before I tell him. Alex had insisted on driving, and he might've crashed the car if I surprised him with my announcement. The second we walk into the loft and shut the door, I turn to stand in front of him, barring his way.

"What are you doing?" he asks. "If you want to shag before dinner, we should at least go into the living room to make use of the sofa. The entryway floor is marble, you know."

"I have something to tell you."

"Are you up the duff?"

Cannae help rolling my eyes at him. "No, I'm not pregnant."

He grasps my shoulders. "What is it, then?"

"I've been offered the chance to go on an excavation in Nevada."

"That's brilliant, Cat. Why do you look so stricken?"

"Because it means I'll be away for six weeks."

Alex pulls me into his arms and kisses my forehead. "I will miss you terribly, but I know how much this chance means to you. Go for it, love."

"I'll miss you too, Alex. Are you sure you don't mind?"

"You've wanted an opportunity like this for a long time, haven't you?" When I nod, he taps the tip of my nose. "I want you to do it. And maybe I could sneak onto the dig site in the dead of night to make love to you in your tent."

"We're staying in a motel."

"Even better. I can steal into your room."

"I'll have two roommates."

He tips his head back and makes a sarcastically pathetic noise. "I'll never survive."

I know he's joking, but I also know he will miss me—and I will miss him. Six weeks might pass quickly. Still, I'll think of him at least ten times a day. Leaving my home in Scotland hadn't been as difficult as spending six weeks away from Alex will be.

He drives me to the airport two weeks later, and he kisses me goodbye at the doors to the terminal.

As the plane takes off, I peer out the window as if I think I'll see Alex waving goodbye to me. Of course I can't spot him. But my heart hurts a wee bit when I realize I won't see him again for six weeks. The excavation takes my mind off Alex during the day, though not completely, and our nightly phone calls don't ease the stress of being away from home, away from him. Aye, the loft we share has become my home. I get every Sunday off, but that doesn't give me enough time to go back to Ballesteros and see Alex, though he offers to pay for my airline tickets. I know he has plenty of money. That's not the issue. I don't want to race back to Ballesteros just to spend a few hours with him. It wouldn't be relaxing, and I've got enough stress with the ongoing excavation.

But on my third Sunday in Nevada, Alex rings me on my mobile phone.

"What are you wearing, darling?" he asks instead of saying hello. "Please tell me you're having a naked pillow fight with your roommates."

"Afraid not, *gràidh*. They're both sleeping."

"But it's ten o'clock in the morning."

"You know how grueling an excavation can be."

He sighs. "Yes, but I never had a lie-in on my days off. And I had enough of field work while working on my PhD. That's why I became a professor."

"You are an amazing teacher. It's what you were meant to do."

"What I'm meant to do right now is shag you."

I stifle my laugh so I won't wake my roommates. "Are you suggesting phone sex?"

"No. I'm suggesting you get your arse to the Presidential Suite so I can make love to you in person."

"Presidential Suite? Where are you, Alex? I'm at an old motel on the outskirts of nowhere."

"That's where I am too, but I found better accommodations. Give me your address, and I shall pick you up in my chariot forthwith."

"Chariot? Your bum's oot the windae."

I recite the motel's address to him, and we say goodbye. How long will it take him to get here? I have no idea where his "presidential suite" is. This wee town has no luxury accommodations, which means Alex must be exaggerating. He likes to do that.

Ten minutes after our call ended, someone knocks on the door to my room. The two lasses I've been rooming with finally woke up and got dressed a wee while ago, though they keep yawning. I feel wide awake, not only because I got up early, but because I knew I'd see Alex any minute.

I swing the door open and smile. "Alex."

"Were you expecting some other bloke? I wouldn't mind your roommates joining us, but I won't share you with any other man."

From behind me, one of those roommates shouts, "Ooh! I'm in for a threesome with your super-hot boyfriend, Cat."

I glance over my shoulder at her. "No one shares Alex. He's mine."

The Brit in question smirks. "Rather possessive of me, aren't you?"

"Aye." Grabbing my purse, I push Alex backward with my body and shut the door. "You're mine, Dr. Thorne."

He slings an arm around my waist. "And you are mine, Catriona. By the way, I love it when you call me Dr. Thorne. It makes me very randy."

"Better get me to your 'presidential suite' fast, then."

"Not sure I can stand to wait that long."

When we reach his car, the one he hired at the airport, I realize I cannae wait either. So aye, we have a quick poke in the car. I straddle his lap and unzip his trousers, suddenly glad that I decided to wear a skirt and no knickers. After our quickie, Alex drives out to his "palatial accommodations" on the opposite side of town. Aye, he actually called this place palatial. I suppose it qualifies, if a body likes a worn-out mobile home with a creaky twin bed.

"This is your 'presidential suite'?" I ask.

"Yes. Nothing is too good for my girl. Shall I ring for room service?"

I pat his cheek. "You are the most adorable liar I've ever met."

He lifts my hand to his lips and kisses it. "I'm sorry I couldn't find better accommodations."

"Donnae worry, *gràidh*. I'm not a snob."

"You've called me that twice today. What does it mean?"

"Snob? It means—"

"The other word, love. The one that sounds like a different language."

"Oh, that." I lean in to whisper into his ear, "It means 'darling' in Gaelic. Does that fash you?"

"Well, I call you 'darling' in English, so I can't be annoyed because you say the same thing to me."

He doesn't mind what I said. Since he has never told me he loves me, I wondered if he might feel uncomfortable with endearments, especially since he knows I'm in love with him.

"I have champagne," he whispers into my ear. "Shall I pop the cork?"

"Yes."

He reaches under the bed and pulls out a bottle of sparkling white grape juice.

I laugh. "That's not champagne, Alex."

"Let's pretend it is. I couldn't find genuine bubbly anywhere in this charming hamlet, and I couldn't get real alcohol either. Apparently, this is a dry town."

"Donnae care. Let's pretend it is champagne."

He nuzzles my neck. "I'd love to pour this all over your body so I can lick it off."

"Only if I get to do the same thing to you."

For the rest of the day, we hide out in Alex's "presidential suite" and make believe the sparkling white grape juice we pour onto each other's bodies is really the most expensive champagne on earth. We laugh almost as often as we moan and gasp, and I lose count of how many times he makes me come. Sex with Alex is always more than just a path to orgasms. It's an experience.

Alex wants to throw out the empty bottle of sparkling grape juice. But I snatch it away. He tries to steal it from me while I dig in my purse to find my lipstick. It's a bonnie pink. I apply a thick coating to my mouth, then kiss the bottle's label, leaving my lip print.

"What's this?" he asks.

"A memento of our time in a luxurious hotel."

He smirks, then kisses me. And he takes the empty bottle with him when we leave.

Alex drives me back to the motel and kisses me again at the door to my room. He promises to come back every Sunday since he claims I'm the only thing that will sustain him and he will "die of starvation" if he can't devour me every weekend. I want to see him too, so I don't complain about his overblown claims.

During my last week in Nevada, I volunteer to drive to the nearby town of Fernley to get supplies—food and tools, not booze. As I'm walking out of the hardware store holding bags in each hand, I notice a man across the street just exiting a grocery store. His head is down, so I can't see his face, but something about his posture and gait seems familiar.

Then he lifts his head, revealing his profile, though it's partly in shadow.

Alex? No, it cannae be him. He's in New Mexico. My brief glimpse of the man as he climbs into a car parked along the street doesn't provide conclusive evidence. It can't be him. But a tingle swept down my spine when I saw that face. I rush across the street, but the man has driven away before I get there.

Was it Alex? Why would he keep it a secret that he came to Nevada? Maybe he means to surprise me.

I hurry back to the dig site and get to work, but I keep thinking about what I saw in Fernley. I glance at the road repeatedly during the rest of the day, hoping to see Alex driving up to surprise me. He doesn't. After a long day of work, we all head back to our motel. I ring Alex, but he doesn't answer. I take a shower, then try again. This time, he picks up.

"Good evening, Cat," he says. "Did you dig up any thrilling new finds?"

"No." I hesitate, afraid to hear his answer to the question I need to ask. But then I just do it. "Were you in Fernley, Nevada, today?"

"Fernley where? What are you on about?"

He sounds sincere in his confusion. As far as I know, Alex has never lied to me. He invents grandiose tales to entertain me, like when he called a dilapidated mobile home the "presidential suite." But he wouldn't outright lie. Would he? Of course not. I know Alex, and he's a good man.

"Why would you think I'm in Nevada?" he asks.

"I saw—I'm an eejit, that's all. Seeing mirages in the desert, I suppose."

"Your mirage was of me? I'm flattered."

We chat for a bit longer, then say goodbye so I can go to bed. A long day at the excavation site has left me jeeked. But as I'm falling asleep, one thought haunts me.

Did I imagine seeing a man who resembled Alex? Or is he hiding something from me?

Chapter Nine

Alex

Last night, I lied to Catriona. Well, it was more like I sort of obfuscated the truth. She must've suspected I had done that, though she held back from questioning me about it. I don't like keeping anything from Cat, but I cannot tell her the truth. Too much is at risk if I share everything with her. Maybe I should end our relationship and move away to a place where she can't find me.

Christ, what am I doing? Running away is not the answer. I haven't done anything illegal by taking a trip to Fernley without notifying Cat of my plans. Lying to her about it… That makes me feel like insects have burrowed deep under my skin. She isn't sure of what she saw. All I can do is hope the incident has faded from her memory by the time I fly to Nevada this weekend to see her.

If she remembers, she doesn't say anything. We enjoy a lovely Sunday together before I leave her.

When she finally comes home, everything goes back to normal. I've escaped by a hair this time, but I know one day she will realize the truth about me. This year, next year, or not until we're in our sixties. However long it takes, I know I can't avoid my past forever. Yes, I am a coward. A better man would tell her everything now.

It's too dangerous.

The months roll by, and soon even I've forgotten about that day in Fernley. All right, maybe I sort of think about it once in a while, but that doesn't mean I feel guilty. An important date arrives, taking my mind off whatever things I might have possibly worried about briefly now and then. I make plans to celebrate the occasion with Cat. I track her down in the university library. How do I know exactly where she is in this enormous building? I rang her mobile to find out. She didn't even ask why I wanted to know, or why I asked her to stay right where she is. She trusts me. I try not to consider the implications of that as I wend my way through the library to a corner on the lowest level which lies half underground. When I catch sight of her, I stop to admire the view.

Catriona stands on a wheeled ladder in an aisle between freestanding shelving units, stretching her body up in an attempt to reach the top shelf. She balances on her tiptoes with one arm outstretched. Her posture makes her shirt ride up, exposing her lower belly.

I come up behind her and palm her arse with both hands. "Careful, darling. You might fall."

Cat glances down at me and smiles. "Alex. What are you doing here?"

"Surprising you. Though I would've thought you'd guess my intentions when I rang to ask where precisely you were."

"I did wonder." She gives up on reaching whatever book she wanted and shimmies around to face me, leaning against the ladder. "Give me a hand?"

"Of course." I grasp her around the waist and pluck her off the ladder, setting her down on the carpeted floor. "No book is worth breaking your neck for."

She touches her lips to mine. "I wasn't going to break my neck. But you're so sweet to worry."

I slide an arm around her waist, pulling her snugly against me. "Do you know what today is?"

"Tuesday."

"Yes, but what else?"

She shrugs.

I cup her cheek in my hand. "It's our anniversary."

"Anniversary? Donnae understand."

"We met one year ago today." I reach behind my back to pluck an item out of my waistband. I hold up a single yellow rose for Cat to see. "This is for you, love. I've had you in my life for one full year, and I mean to demonstrate my gratitude for that fact."

"It's really been a year? Seems like just a few days ago when I saw you on that bench." She teases the hairs at my nape with her fingers. "I'm grateful for you too."

"We need to celebrate our anniversary. And I know exactly how to do that."

"Do you want to go back to the restaurant where we had our first date?"

"No." I back her up to the shelves, then place my mouth over her ear. "I mean to fuck you right here."

"In the library? We cannae do that, Alex."

"Of course we can." I reach into my trouser pocket and bring out a condom packet. "I'm fully prepared."

She glances side to side without moving her head. "We cannae."

I slide a hand down her thigh until I feel the hem of her skirt. "We can, and we will. Right now. Can you honestly tell me you don't want this as much as I do?"

Her breasts rise and fall as her breathing grows heavier. "I want this, but—"

"No thinking, Cat. Just give in to your desire." I push my hand under her skirt, gliding it up until I reach her knickers. Then I slip my fingers under the silky fabric to feel the hairs there. "Say yes, darling. Say it now."

She gasps when I tease her mound with my fingertips. "Yes, Alex, yes."

I grasp her knickers, tear them off, and lift them to my face to inhale the scent of her cream.

Cat starts breathing even harder, and she curls her fingers over the lip of one shelf.

"No more talking." I stuff her knickers in my pocket. She watches with rapt attention as I open the condom packet, unzip my trousers, and cover myself. "Time to make you come for me, love."

I lift her skirt up to her waist and grasp her thigh to hook it around my hip. She lashes her arms around my neck.

And I thrust into her.

Her eyes drift half-closed while I take her body in a slow and steady rhythm, the heat of her enveloping my cock. She lets her head fall back against the shelves even as she digs her fingers into my shoulders and wraps her thigh around me even more tightly. I take care not to push too hard. Why am I holding back? She loves it when I fuck her hard and fast and make her come so fiercely that she can't even shout my name. So what if the shelves might topple backward and spill books everywhere? I won't stop until she screams my name so loudly that even the patrons on the top floor can hear it.

I grip the shelf above her head with both hands and pound into her over and over, barely aware of the shelving unit creaking and the slapping of our bodies crashing together. Cat lashes both legs around me now, and her mouth falls open as if she's struggling not to cry out. I seal my mouth over hers, then shove a hand under her top and inside her bra to flick my thumb over the nipple, swallowing her cry.

Several books tumble off the shelves.

What if a book hits Cat on the head? Even while I keep thrusting into her wildly, I summon enough mental acuity to notice a table nearby. I pause in my thrusting only long enough to stagger to that table and lay her down on it. Since my cock is still nestled inside her, I need only start pumping again. She wraps her entire body around me, her face mashed to my neck, and I pummel her so powerfully that my ears ring and breaths bluster out of me in time with my movements.

The table wobbles. Something cracks, but my brain barely registers the sound.

Her inner muscles contract around me in strong, sensuous waves, and her body curls inward. Though her mouth gapes open, she can't make any sound except for a tiny, strangled gasp. I grip the table's edge above her head and slam into her a few more times. Then I collapse on top of her, almost wheezing while I try to regain control of my lungs. "Bloody hell, Cat. That was—"

The table tips sideways, then collapses.

Luckily, I had pulled my hands away from the table's edge before the thing crumpled to the floor. But I spring to my knees and frantically scan Cat's body. "Are you hurt?"

She seems a bit dazed, but she pushes up on her elbows and blinks up at me. "No, I'm fine. Did we actually break the table?"

"It must have been fragile to start with. But yes, I, ah, think we did break it." I survey her again. "Are you sure you haven't injured yourself?"

"Yes, Alex, I'm positive."

Offering her my hands, I help her up while I get to my feet too. She glances down at my groin, and her lips kink into a sexy expression that makes my cock twitch. "We knocked down books and destroyed a table. I can honestly say no other man has ever shagged me like that."

"Good. I never want to be boring."

"Might want to zip up your trousers before someone shows up to find out what happened down here."

Oh, that's why she stared at my cock. I zip up, then toss the condom into a nearby rubbish bin. "I might have just given you false expectations. I can't reasonably fuck you this way all the time, though I'd love to try."

She glances back at the table. "Aye, ye might have trouble topping this."

"Next time, I suppose I'll need to knock down an entire building to impress you."

Cat grasps my shirt and pulls me close. "Thank you for my anniversary gift."

I glance at the shelves and realize the rose I'd given her lies crushed under a large book. "Afraid your gift is now headed for the compost heap."

"That's not the gift I meant." She rubs her nose against mine. "You are the best thing that's ever happened to me. Thank you for being you, Alex."

What am I meant to say in response? She thinks I'm a gift. Catriona has given me more than I could ever explain, though I know I will never tell her that. I can't. Well, that's not quite true. I could, but I won't. Speaking the words feels like the most dangerous thing I could ever do. But in my thoughts, I can admit to the truth.

I am in love with Catriona MacTaggart.

Footsteps echo from elsewhere on this floor as someone rushes in our direction. A moment later, a young bloke comes around a corner and halts, gawping at the broken table. "What happened? I was in the microfiche room when I heard a crash."

The microfiche room is on the other side of this floor. Still, I'm surprised he could hear the crash. All these shelves seem like they would muffle that noise, but apparently not.

Cat stares at me, her eyes wide.

Time to do the one thing at which I never fail. I affect an air of cavalier disinterest as I wave a hand toward the table. "It must have been suffering from intense dry rot. The university really should take better care of its furniture."

"Dry rot?" the bloke says, his brows knitting together.

"Yes, that's right." I pull out my wallet and select several bills, then hand them to the confused young man. "This should cover the cost of replacing the table."

He flips through the bills, and his eyes bulge. "This is a thousand dollars."

"Take a bit for yourself, but save most of it for the library."

The young man bites his upper lip. "I'd better give it all to the library. I don't work here."

I pat his shoulder. "You are a rare upstanding citizen."

Then I clasp Cat's hand, leading her away.

Once we've exited the building, Cat halts and turns toward me. "You gave that boy a thousand dollars. For a table that probably cost fifty at most."

I shrug. "Money is not a problem for me. But you know that."

"Aye." She squints at me for a moment. That expression always means she's trying to figure me out. "I love you, Alex, but I don't think I'll ever understand you."

A wave of cold rushes through me. She had told me once that she's *in* love with me, but now she has proclaimed outright that she loves me. I know it's essentially the same thing. Still, I can't deny that her statement makes me uneasy. Things might be wonderful now, but eventually, my house of cards will fall.

But I won't think about that today.

I throw an arm around her shoulders and start walking. "Let's have lunch at our favorite restaurant. It is our anniversary, after all."

Cat grins—and my chest aches.

Chapter Ten

Catriona

For days after the library incident, I obsess over what happened and how Alex reacted when I said I love him. Aye, I'd told him almost a year ago that I'm in love with him, and I let him get away with not telling me how he feels. But now that I've said those three words, I thought he might say them back to me.

Why did I think that? Alex is Alex. He hasn't changed, and I need to accept that he might never express his feelings in words. He loves me, I know that. He proves that to me every day with his actions and the way he looks at me. Will I actually leave him if he never verbalizes his emotions? I've never met a man who wanted to do that. Maybe it doesn't matter what he says, only how he treats me.

No one has ever taken care of me the way Alex does. He always knows how to make me smile when I'm feeling anxious or stressed. And he remembered the one-year anniversary of the day we met. So I resolve to move on and enjoy my life with him, regardless of what he hasn't said.

I continue my studies in the meantime and secure a position as a teaching assistant for my second year at Ballesteros. Sometimes I even get to teach a class. Whenever that happens, I always notice a familiar face at the back of the room. Aye, Alex likes to sneak in to watch me. At first, that makes me feel nervous, but I get over that soon enough and begin to enjoy knowing he's there, supporting me just by observing. I peek into his classes too, though not as often as I'd like. My studies take up a lot of my time, especially since I've decided to begin mapping out what I'd like my dissertation to be, though I still have awhile to go before I reach that point in my doctoral program. Sneaking into Alex's classes helps me relax. He is mesmerizing, and I think every lass in the room has at least a wee crush on him.

Donnae blame them. I fell for him the day we met.

The months roll by, but I hardly notice the passing of time. My life is too full to worry about that. When I'm not on campus, I'm at home studying or having fun with Alex. When one of my professors asks if I'd like to do more field work at the site of newly discovered petroglyphs, I jump at the chance. An opportunity to study ancient rock art? Aye, that's a chance I can't pass up.

We're sitting on the sofa in our living room when I share the news. Alex clutches his chest and feigns having a heart attack, even falling over onto my lap.

"Are you done with your outlandish display?" I ask.

He doesn't sit up, not even when he smirks at me. "I think I'm paralyzed from the neck down. You'll need to stay home to care for me."

"I'll hire a nurse for you." I shake my head and pretend that I'm severely disappointed. "It's too bad you won't be able to have sex anymore. I'll have to find another man to satisfy my needs."

He springs upright, drags me into his body, and gazes straight into my eyes from inches away. "You don't need anyone else. No other man on earth could make love to you so thoroughly that the table you're shagging on breaks."

I brush my lips over his. "Are you sure you don't mind me leaving for two weeks?"

"Yes, darling, I'm sure. I'll miss you, but I never want to stop you from doing what makes you happy."

"I love archaeology, but you make me happier than anything else in the world."

He lifts my hand and kisses it. "It's the same for me, love."

I won't leave for Utah for another week, which gives me time to sit in on one of his classes the next afternoon. The subject for today is sexual imagery in the ancient world. He keeps the discussion academic and rather dry, probably because he worries he might get in trouble if he unleashes his naughty nature in a room full of fresh-faced undergraduates. I'd love to hear him give a real, no-holds-barred lecture on sexuality in the ancient world. But even this watered-down version is electrifying, thanks to the man giving the lecture. Alex Thorne is always a force to be reckoned with and the most unashamed person I've ever met. I think he would strip naked on the quad if he thought that would entertain his students and engage their minds.

Once all the students have filed out of the room, Alex approaches me. "Did you enjoy the show, Cat?"

"Aye, it was wonderful. I think you made all the female students blush. I'm dead sure they all want to shag you."

"The only woman I want is you."

I might be blushing now too. Donnae know why, but every time Alex says something like that, I feel like a silly schoolgirl again.

We walk out of the building while holding hands, then find our favorite bench on the quad so we can discuss my upcoming trip. We agree that while I'm away in Utah, Alex and I will talk on the phone at least three times a day. He suggests we could try phone sex to avoid "the tragedy of not actually fucking each other for two weeks." I feel strange about the prospect of doing that. It's not real sex. We would masturbate while listening to each other over the phone. Besides, I'll be sharing a room with another student, so we wouldn't have privacy.

Alex expresses his disappointment with sarcasm, of course, but I know he doesn't really mind. That's one of his best qualities—his desire to make me happy, even if that means he doesn't get exactly what he wants. I wish I could make him happy too. And aye, I've been thinking of ways I can make it up to him once I get home. My plans involve lots of sex, of course, but also plenty of kissing and cuddling. Alex loves to make cheeky comments about snuggling, but I know he secretly loves it.

On the last day before I fly to Utah, I'm sitting on our bench waiting for Alex. He often gets waylaid by students after class, most of whom want to talk about their studies. A few of the lasses just like to bat their eyelashes at him. I've never been jealous. I know he loves me, and he has no interest in other women. He doesn't even glance at buxom blondes who wear skimpy clothes.

While I wait, I admire the clear blue sky and the birds flying past overhead.

A group of students wander over to my bench—three lads and two lasses. One lad steps closer to me and leans in to study my face. "You're Dr. Thorne's girl, aren't you? Everybody knows about you two."

"If you know who I am, why did you ask?"

He shrugs and sits down at the opposite end of the bench, draping an arm over its back. His fingers are inches away from my shoulder. "I love Irish chicks."

"I'm Scottish."

"Same diff." He smiles in a way he probably thinks is charming, but I think he looks like a moron. "Why do you want to date a British guy? He's a dick, that's what I hear. Let me take you out tonight, and I'll show you what a red-blooded American can do."

"Thank you for the offer, but my social calendar is full."

"Social calendar?" he says with a laugh. "Damn, the way you say that makes me so hot for you."

"I feel chilly for you."

"Catriona, darling, you should've told me you invited your harem." Alex walks up to the bench and offers me his hand. He holds a picnic basket in his other hand. "I would've brought more food. Group sex always leaves me famished."

I accept Alex's hand, rising from the bench.

The American scunner stands up too and sneers at Alex. "Dude, I don't get naked with other guys."

"Neither do I, so we're even." Alex waves a hand in a negligent gesture. "Toddle off to your nursery. I'm sure it's time for your next bottle feeding."

"You really think you're hot shit, don't you? Nobody here is impressed, sissy boy."

Alex chuckles. "I've been called much worse than that."

"I bet you have." The scunner moves closer, and his friends edge nearer too. "I can take you anytime, anywhere."

"Can you?" Alex sets down the picnic basket and steps to the side, drawing out a distance between us. "Let's make a wager on that."

"You're on. What are the stakes?"

Alex pulls a quarter out of his pocket and holds it up between his thumb and forefinger. "If you can take this coin from me, I'll let you have Catriona."

He won't actually give me to the eejit. Whatever Alex means to do, he's dead sure he can pull it off. And I trust him. Besides, I never agreed to this wager, so I can skelp the laddie if he wins. Aye, that means I'll slug him. It helps to grow up with three brothers. They taught me how to throw a punch.

"On the count of three," Alex tells the scunner, "you grab the coin. One, two, three."

The laddie lunges for Alex, but the Brit dodges the American deftly. The eejit tries three times, but he can't catch Alex. So he tries to ram his head into Alex's gut, but the Brit sidesteps him again. The lad trips and falls down on the concrete path.

"I'll report you to the campus police," the scunner snarls as he struggles to his feet. "That's assault."

"No, it's not," Alex says while tossing the coin and catching it in his palm. "I never laid a finger on you. Your clumsiness is hardly my fault."

"I want a rematch."

"Well, if you insist." Alex tucks the coin into his trouser pocket. "Try to get that quarter now."

The laddie runs toward the Brit and shoves his hand into Alex's pocket, clearly trying to retrieve the coin. He digs around in there as if he can't quite find the quarter. Finally, the laddie gives up, throws his arms in the air, and lets out a frustrated noise. "You cheated somehow. It's not in your pocket."

"I never said it was." Alex opens his hand, palm up, revealing the coin. "You assumed that's what I meant when I told you to try to get that quarter."

The scunner bares his gritted teeth. "You slimy—"

"Uh-uh-uh. I never assaulted you. But I'm afraid all these witnesses watched you assault me and sexually harass me."

"I never touched your dick."

"You were rooting about in my trousers."

"Because you said—Gah! You're one sick, twisted piece of work."

Alex tosses the coin to the laddie. "Here's your consolation prize. Now toddle back to your wet nurse. A twat like you shouldn't try it on with a sophisticated woman."

Did he just call me sophisticated? No one has ever referred to me that way before. I like it.

The "twat" makes a petulant face, then stalks away with his mates trailing after him. The crowd disperses quickly now that the excitement has ended.

Alex takes my hand, holding it more firmly than usual. "Are you all right, love?"

"I'm fine. You know how to handle a scunner. I'm impressed."

He winces the slightest bit. "It's a skill I learned out of necessity."

I want to ask him what that means, but he doesn't like to discuss his past. Am I a fool for not demanding he tell me everything? Maybe that's why I've never told my family about

Alex. Sometimes I wonder if, deep down, I know our relationship won't last forever.

The next day, Alex drives me to the airport and kisses me goodbye. Aye, I'll miss him.

As for how long we might last… I'll think about that another time.

Chapter Eleven

Alex

Catriona flew to Utah six days ago, and I've spent the entire week teaching classes while on autopilot and making appropriate noises while students tell me their problems during my office hours. I barely notice anything they say. I can't remember what topics I discussed in my lectures. All my mind will let me think about is Cat. Friday evening, I can't take it anymore. I get on a plane and fly to Salt Lake City, Utah. Luckily, I manage to secure a suite at the most expensive hotel in the city, which isn't expensive by my standards. Catriona will think it is. But she deserves a plush mattress—to sleep on and to shag on.

I ring her from the suite.

She answers with a sleepy hello.

"Been working hard?" I say. "Well, it's a good thing I've come to whisk you away to my palace. Your servant shall attend to your every need and desire."

"Alex? What are you talking about?"

"I'm here in Salt Lake City."

"Here?" She sounds more awake now. "Where? We're staying at a tiny motel on the south side of town."

"Give me the motel's name, and I'll find it. Don't eat anything because I mean to spoil you with five-star room service."

"You don't need to do that."

"Of course I do. Now give me that address."

She recites it for me, and we say goodbye. Half an hour later, I pull into the car park at the rundown little establishment where the archaeology team has taken up residence. If I'd known what sort of hovel she'd been staying at, I would've insisted on booking her a suite for the duration. She wouldn't have let me, though. Cat is bloody-minded when it comes to letting me spoil her.

Tonight, she will be treated like a princess—whether she likes it or not.

When I knock on the door to her room, a blonde with spiky hair and a nose ring opens it. Her eyes widen, and she peruses my entire body before speaking. "Who are you? And how can I get some of what you're selling?"

"I'm here for Catriona."

The girl sighs. "Oh well. It figures a hot guy wouldn't knock on the door for me." She twists her head around to shout, "Cat! Your boyfriend is here."

Catriona appears behind the spiky-haired girl and tells her, "I'll be gone until Monday morning."

"Have fun." The girl winks at me. "Don't work her too hard, hon."

Since I have no response to that, I clasp Catriona's hand and lead her to the car I hired at the airport. It's a BMW sports car, but Cat doesn't comment on my choice of vehicle. She lifts her brows a touch, that's all. During the drive back to my hotel, she fills me in on what happened today during the team's investigation of the newly found petroglyphs. I always love listening to her talk, mostly because she has the sexiest voice, but also because I enjoy her enthusiasm. I don't think I've ever gotten as excited about archaeology as she does.

Every time she smiles, I smile too. And every time she laughs, I do the same.

When we arrive at the hotel, I park the car and rush to get to the passenger door before she can open it herself. Cat always kisses my cheek when I do that. She brought a small bag, so I carry that for her. She kisses my cheek again. But when we reach my suite, all she seems capable of doing is gawping and turning in circles.

"Is something wrong?" I ask.

She stops twirling and stares at me blankly for a moment. Then she blinks rapidly. At last, she looks at me and shakes her head. "You weren't joking when you called this your palace."

"It's a hotel suite, not the residence of a king."

"Might as well be that. This is even more posh and expensive than our loft. It might be bigger too."

"Try the bed. You'll love it."

She lies down atop the covers and links her hands above her head. Her eyes drift shut, and a sensual smile curves her lips. "You need to shag me on this bed right now, Alex."

"What about dinner?"

"Sex first." She opens her eyes and stretches her entire body, sighing with contentment. "Undress me, Alex. You know I love it when you do that."

I tug my shirt out of my waistband and begin unbuttoning it. "Writhe around a bit more, darling. I love watching you move."

She stretches her arms above her head and wriggles her hips.

By the time I've shed my clothes, my cock is hard as steel. Maybe I shouldn't have encouraged her to writhe about like an erotic serpent, because I don't know if I can wait more than thirty seconds to fuck her. Self-control is my forte, though, and I strip her swiftly. Then I take my time getting her ready for me, gorging myself on her cream until she comes for me like a dew-drenched flower blooming in my hands. We make love until we're too knackered to have another go, then we order room service. Cat informs she is "fair starved," so I choose a wide selection of dishes and desserts for us. After that, we can't shag again. Our bellies are too full. Instead, we crawl under the covers and sleep.

The next day, we stay in the suite to talk and shag. I won't see Cat again for another week, when she will finally come home. I'd survived six weeks away from her last year, so two weeks shouldn't seem like a terrible trial, but it does. Though I don't tell Catriona, on my way home I make a detour to Fernley to visit the only two people in the world who know all the things Cat wants me to tell her. She accepted not knowing, but I doubt she will go on accepting the secrecy forever.

Maybe that's why I need to be with her as much as possible.

A week later, I pick her up at the airport. Then I do something I've never done before, though I can't explain why I need to do it. I wait at the curb, leaning against the car, and the instant she walks out of the terminal, I pull her close for a deep, hot kiss. I don't give a stuff that everyone must be staring at us. When I pull away, Cat seems dazed.

I brush stray hairs away from her cheek. "Welcome home, love."

"Alex, I…" She glances around with a guilty expression. "You shouldn't do that in public."

"Why not? I missed you."

Her lips curl into an adorable smile. "I missed you too."

"I've decided you are forbidden from going anywhere without me ever again, not even to the grocery store." I open the passenger door and hold her hand while she climbs inside. "I won't survive another separation."

Can't believe I said that. Cat seems shocked too.

I pretend I haven't just confessed in the most embarrassing way and hurry to the driver's door. As I navigate the airport road, I avoid glancing at Catriona. Well, I try to do that. But my eyes insist on glancing her way.

She's smiling.

"We've reached another milestone," I say. "Today it's been exactly one year and ten months since we moved in together."

"That long? It feels like yesterday."

"How should we celebrate? I vote for sex."

She laughs. "You always vote for sex. If I asked what you want to eat for dinner, you'd say let's have a poke instead."

"Oh no, I would never say 'have a poke.' I would've told you let's shag, or possibly let's get a leg over."

"A man who's an expert on ancient sexual practices can do better than that."

"Is that a challenge?" I throw her a sideways smirk. "When we get home, I'll read you excerpts from a medieval collection called *The Decameron*. One of my favorite stories concerns randy nuns who each have their way with one young bloke. He must've been completely knackered but very happy after that."

"You should read me those stories. After dinner."

I sigh with no small amount of sarcasm. "Yes, I will feed you first."

"Thank you, Alex."

"But I will need to feast on you after."

She throws her head back and laughs so boisterously that, whilst admiring her joyful expression, I take my eyes off the road for a moment too long. A horn blares. I veer the car back into our lane just in time.

And Cat laughs again.

We do eat first, then shag between my recitations of bawdy medieval literature. By the time we finish, it's after midnight. We both need to get up early in the morning, but neither of us minds the lack of sufficient sleep. Memories of last night keep me awake all day.

Later in the week, I run a secret errand. Catriona has gone to the library to do research for the potential topic of her dissertation, so I seize the chance to do a bit of shopping on my own. Impulsive purchases are not my strong suit, but I felt inspired this afternoon, and since I had no classes after four o'clock, I decided to just do it.

I visit a jewelry store.

The clerk helps me choose two items. The first is a pair of sapphire earrings that will complement Cat's eyes. I couldn't find a pair with stones as pale as her irises, but I chose the lightest blue available. The stones are surrounded by white gold. She will look lovely in these earrings, but that isn't the most important thing I wanted to buy today. I keep the second item in its box and slip it into my trouser pocket as I walk out of the store—until I realize the box creates a visible shape in my pocket. So I pull it out and remove the ring, stashing that in my pocket instead. Yes, it's a diamond ring. The glittering stone rests in a cradle of much smaller stones, all of them surrounded by white gold.

Tonight, I am going to propose to Cat.

I ring Cat on her mobile to ask when she might be home. She assures me she'll be done at the library in an hour, then she will come straight home. That leaves me with enough time to do what I need to do. She will say yes. Won't she? Of course she will. I set about making our lavish meal and creating the proper atmosphere for a proposal, which means candlelight and soft, sensual music, as well as roses in a glass vase and a lace tablecloth that I bought on my way back from the jewelry store. I also change my clothes. A suit without the tie seems more appropriate than the T-shirt and khaki trousers I'd been wearing.

Catriona arrives moments after I've finished the preparation. She hurries into the house while staring down into her purse as if she's hunting for something.

I clear my throat.

She freezes and glances up. "Alex, what is all this?"

"Dinner. It's a special occasion."

"What sort of occasion?"

I pull out a chair and gesture toward it. "Have a seat, and you'll find out."

Ringing emanates from her purse. She digs her mobile out and answers it. "Lachlan?"

Her brother isn't supposed to know about me, but I can't help wondering if fate has given him a nudge. Either that or I'm cursed. Why else would her brother call tonight? She doesn't speak to her family every day.

"Oh, aye," she says to Lachlan. "Well, I should speak to Jamie first. She's a teenager, and everything seems like a catastrophe at that age."

This does not sound promising, not for my proposal plans.

Cat disconnects the call and gives me a sheepish look. "I'm sorry, Alex. The dinner you've made looks wonderful, but I need to ring my sister Jamie. Her boyfriend just broke up with her. Threw her over for another girl. She won't stop crying, and she won't speak to anyone, not even our sister Fiona. Lachlan wants me to try to calm Jamie down."

"You should do that, then. I'll keep the food warm."

"This might take hours, Alex. Go ahead and eat."

Whilst she heads into the bedroom, I make a plate of food for her and deliver it to her. She gives me a grateful smile. I eat alone in the living room. By the time her call to Jamie ends, we both want nothing more than to go to sleep. I don't ask her to marry me. I don't even tell her about the ring. I do give her the earrings, which she loves, but I've apparently lost my nerve when it comes to popping that question. Maybe her sister's romantic problems are a sign that I shouldn't propose to Cat. I don't do it the next day or the day after that, not a week later either. I have lost my nerve, haven't I? That has never happened to me before. But then, I've never loved any woman except for Catriona MacTaggart.

And I still haven't told her that either.

Chapter Twelve

Alex has been behaving strangely ever since last night, when I came home to find he had cooked a big dinner for us. He said he understood why I needed to talk to my sister, and he gave me the beautiful earrings he'd bought as a not-quite anniversary gift. When I opened the box and saw the light-blue sapphire stones, I couldn't believe what he'd done. Expensive earrings? There's no such thing as a year and ten months anniversary, but I didn't tell Alex that. For some reason, he wanted to turn a pseudo-event into a real one, and he was clearly disappointed when that didn't happen.

This morning, I wake up alone in our bed. After quickly dressing, I rush into the living room to look for Alex. He's in the kitchen making tea, it looks like, staring down at two cups as he fills them.

He lifts his head when I approach the island and smiles tightly. "Good morning, Catriona."

"Aye, good morning, Alex. I'm sorry about last night."

"You have already apologized several times. There's no need for more." He hands me a cup. "I ate earlier, but I'd be happy to make something for you."

"I can do that myself." Alex always waits to have breakfast with me. The fact that he didn't today, coupled with his tight expression, proves that he's not himself this morning. "Are you sure you aren't upset about last night? I know you had a gourmet meal planned for us—"

"Not gourmet. Just food."

"But Alex—"

"I am fine, Cat. Stop worrying." He strides over to the sofa and sits down, taking a sip of his tea. "I let you have a bit of a lie-in, but you should eat quickly or you'll miss your nine o'clock class."

My gaze darts to the clock on the microwave oven. *"Mhac na galla.* I didn't realize how late it was."

After a quick breakfast, I gulp down the last of my tea and grab my rucksack, then race out to the car. Alex is already in the driver's seat with his hands firmly gripping the wheel. He stares straight ahead, only glancing at me sideways. The second I've got my seat-belt done up, he backs out of the driveway and onto the road. We don't speak in the car. And when we arrive at the campus, Alex gives me a quick peck on the cheek before he marches off to his office.

I go to class, but I have trouble concentrating. Why is Alex in such a mood? He doesn't seem angry. I almost think he's embar-rassed or ashamed. Alex is the most confident man I've ever met, so I cannae imagine what might upset him this way. We have lunch together, and he seems more relaxed then. I hesitate to ask him about last night and this morning, but by the time we're done eat-ing, I can't wait any longer.

So I set down my water bottle and face him. "I know you said you didn't mind that I talked to Jamie instead of having dinner with you last night. But I feel like I have hurt you by doing that."

"Not hurt." He wriggles on the bench and avoids looking at me. "I was disappointed. You see, I had planned—Well, it was nothing, really."

"Please tell me, Alex."

His fingers curl into his thighs. He still won't look at me. "I had an idea, but I realized later that it was just as well my plans didn't work out."

"What plans? Dinner? I donnae understand why it was just as well that didn't happen."

"Not dinner." He shoves a hand into his hair and sighs. "Can we forget about last night? I'd rather move on."

I've lived with Alex for almost two years, and I know that once he decides a topic is closed, I can't convince him to reopen it. Aye, I knew when I started dating him that he had secrets he would never share with me. I accepted that because I believed the present and future mattered more than the past. Was I an eejit to believe that?

Alex rises and tosses the remnants of his lunch into a nearby trash bin. "I'll meet you at the car after your last class."

He doesn't even kiss me goodbye. He just walks away.

In a situation like this, I would normally ring one of my sisters to talk about it. I can't do that. Once I resolved to keep our relationship a secret, at least from my family, I shut that door for good.

After my last class, I step out into the corridor, prepared to head for the faculty car park. But Alex is there in the hall, leaning against the wall.

He smiles and takes my hand. "Shall we go, darling? I'm famished, so I thought we might stop at our favorite bakery for a decadent snack."

Aye, he has suddenly reverted to his usual self. And I feel like a crash test dummy that just got flung through a windshield.

"I'm glad you're in a better mood," I say as we walk down the corridor. "But it seems to have happened very fast."

"Never mind last night or this morning." He slings an arm around my shoulders and aims his patented charming smile at me, the one that always makes me forget everything except how much I love him. "I prefer to focus on right now, with you."

Maybe I should question him, but he starts telling me humorous stories about his students, and I love listening to him describe those incidents. Alex is a consummate storyteller—and a consummate seducer. Whether he uses his charms to enthrall students during a lecture or to make love to me, I've never been able to resist him when he's like this.

We visit the bakery and enjoy a selection of pastries chosen by Alex. When I bite into a raspberry Danish, and a bit of the filling sticks on my lips, Alex leans over to drag his tongue across my mouth and remove the jam. Then he leans in more to whisper into my ear, "We have caramel syrup at home. I'd love to drizzle that over your skin and lick it off slowly."

Aye, we hurry home to do that.

Though I've mostly set my worries aside, in the back of my mind, a question niggles at me. How much do I really know about Alex? Until recently, I would've answered that question with another one. How much can anyone really know about their partner? But now... I don't know what to think about anything.

A few days later, I manage to surprise Alex. He would never tell me when his birthday was, but this year, I resolve to find out. If he won't tell me, I will discover the truth on my own. But I'm not a private investigator. I don't need to be, since Alex leaves his wallet on the nightstand when we go to bed. When I wake in the middle of night, I take his wallet and tiptoe into the living room so I can turn on a lamp. Then I find his driving license.

His birthday was three weeks ago.

It might be a wee bit late, but I mean to celebrate that occasion. In the morning, I get up before Alex and start baking. By the time he walks into the living room, I've completed my mission.

Alex stops halfway to the kitchen island. "What are you doing over there? It doesn't smell like breakfast."

"Oh, I made that too. But I also baked something just for you." I raise the plate that holds the layer cake I made. "Happy birthday, Alex."

"Today is not my birthday."

"I know. But I missed the actual day because you would never tell me when it was."

"That's because I don't celebrate it."

I set the cake down and light the candles, then carry it over to him. "Make a wish and blow out your candles."

He eyes the cake with suspicion while the flames flicker and wax dribbles down toward the icing. "This is important to you."

"Aye. And to you, whether you realize it or not. You insisted on celebrating my birthdays, and you gave me presents too." I hold the cake closer to him. "The candles will melt if you don't blow them out."

He sucks in a breath and puckers his lips.

"Make a wish too, Alex. Please, for me."

He rolls his eyes and blows out the candles. "Aren't you going to ask what I wished for?"

"No, of course not. That's private. I never told you what I wished for either." I place the cake on the island. "Time to cut a slice and eat it. Sorry I don't have a gift for you."

"No need for trinkets. You are the only gift I need."

Alex cuts two slices of cake, and we eat that before we have breakfast. While we're cleaning up after our impromptu celebration, I get curious. "You say you don't like birthday parties and presents, but you gave me both of those last year and this year."

"That's different. You should celebrate your birthday. It's a happy occasion for you and your family."

"But not for you."

"No." He finishes putting the last of the plates into the dishwasher. "Besides, I only gave you a bottle of Scottish whisky. It wasn't even an expensive brand."

"It was Talisker, my brother Lachlan's favorite. I mentioned that to you, but I never expected you'd buy me a bottle of single-malt Scotch whisky direct from the Isle of Skye."

"Well, I thought it might make you feel less homesick."

"You are my home, Alex. I never feel sad about leaving Scotland."

He stares at me for a moment, then clears his throat. "We should get going or you'll be late for class."

We don't discuss birthdays or gifts anymore. Everything goes back to normal, though we do have cake for dessert three evenings in a row.

One day, Alex and I are browsing the shops in downtown Ballesteros when a strange thing happens. He has just ducked into a novelty store after announcing he needs to take care of a "secret errand." Those were his exact words. He might not like birthdays, but he loves surprising me with wee gifts. So I sit down on a bench near the curb and watch the traffic go by while I wait for Alex.

A woman sits down at the opposite end of the bench. I recognize her, though I only saw her once before. This is the woman Alex had a poke with on the night before he met me. What does she want now?

"Hey, Catriona," she says, though she seems unsure of how to pronounce my name. "Glad we bumped into each other again."

"I have nothing to say to you."

"Oh, I don't want to have a conversation. Where is Alex, anyway?"

"How do you know our names? We never told you."

She smiles. "I have connections, hon. That time when I saw Alex on the street, he turned me down when I offered him another chance to screw me. But I bumped into another guy, somebody who was more than happy to get tangled in the sheets with me, no strings attached."

"Is there a point to your story? I donnae care if you shag every man in the city."

"Here comes the point, hon." She sidles a wee bit closer. "The man I screwed in my hotel room that day turned out to be powerful. He hooked me up with a sweet bachelorette pad, and we've been doing the nasty twice a week ever since."

I've had enough of this. I rise and smooth my blouse.

"Oh, you can't go yet," she says. "Sit down, Catriona. My name is Gloria Harris, by the way. We should be on a first-name basis considering what I want from you."

"Which is what?"

"Alex. I want to fuck him again, on a regular basis. My new lover is good, but Alex was better."

"You are off your head."

Just as she opens her mouth to speak again, Alex strides out of the shop carrying a small bag. He halts beside me and narrows his gaze on Gloria. "What are you doing here?"

"Having a girl chat with Catriona."

"Bugger off. Neither of us has anything to say to you."

"Come on, baby—"

"Leave now," he says in the nastiest tone I've ever heard. "Go, or I will force you to do it."

Gloria raises her hands. "Okay, okay. I'll go. But we'll be seeing each other again."

She ambles down the pavement and eventually disappears from our view.

"What did that slag say to you?" Alex asks.

"That she lives here now, and she has a powerful lover. Oh, and she wants to shag you."

He grunts. "Don't worry about her. She is clearly a very unhappy woman." He offers me the bag he'd been carrying. "Here's your surprise."

I pull out the items inside the bag—two teddy bears, a boy and a girl. The girl is dressed in a white T-shirt that has the Scottish flag printed on it while the boy's shirt features the British flag. I can't help laughing. "Thank you, Alex. You are so sweet."

He hooks an arm around my waist. "If ever I'm not here to cuddle with you, these bears will fill in for me."

I kiss his cheek. "This was very thoughtful."

As we head for home, I wonder about his statement. Why wouldn't he always be here with me? He must've meant that if I go on another excavation, or if he goes on a trip, I can use the bears as a fuzzy surrogate.

Aye, that must be what he meant. Isn't it?

Chapter Thirteen

Alex

Catriona seemed puzzled when I gave her two teddy bears, and I can't blame her for that reaction. Why did I do it? Stuffed animals to stand in for me. It's ridiculous. Yet lately, I keep feeling like my time with her is limited and I need to appreciate every moment. Seeing that stupid woman again did not help matters. Cat is even more confused by her encounter with the tart I fucked once than she is by the gift of stuffed animals. I have no clue what that woman wants, though I'm positive it isn't just another shag with me.

On the way home, Cat told me the woman calls herself Gloria Harris. Well, if that's her real name, I can find her—and find out what the bloody hell she wants. I need to know more about the woman who seems determined to cock up my life.

After Catriona falls asleep that night, I sneak into the living room to search the internet for some clue about who Gloria Harris is. The woman claims to have a powerful new lover, but that might be bollocks. I refuse to believe Gloria simply wants my body. She is up to something, and I doubt it's a good thing. So I use my admittedly mediocre internet skills to hunt for answers. My first search nets me thousands of women with the same name. *Bugger me.* This will take years. I can't risk hiring a private investigator. If Cat found out, she would want to know why I'm paranoid about a virtual stranger harassing us. I told her after the most recent encounter that I'm sure it's nothing and she shouldn't worry.

Cat believed me. She trusts me. Whether she should… Well, I'll worry about that later.

I trust no one, with only three exceptions including Catriona.

Since I must do this alone and in secret, I go back to bed and pretend to sleep. Maybe I do catch a bit of sleep, but not enough. I put on a good show for Cat, pretending that I'm well-rested and carefree. I even suggest we eat lunch at a restaurant instead of bringing our own food and having our meal on our favorite bench. After that, I drop Catriona off on campus, telling her I need to run a few errands. It's to do with my classes, of course. Now I'm outright lying to her. I swore to myself I would never do that, but I have no choice. If Gloria turns out to be just a woman who has a crush on me, I'll never need to tell Cat about any of this. It won't matter that I lied. The untruths will evaporate.

Yes, I've spent a lifetime learning how to con other people. Now I'm doing it to myself.

Catriona told me yesterday that Gloria claimed to have a "bachelorette pad" paid for by her new lover. She was wearing what looked like designer clothing, as well as large diamond earrings and a large emerald ring. If her lover paid for those items too, which seems likely, then I should be able to figure out where she lives. It would be a posh flat or a house. Any man who gives a woman designer clothes wouldn't set her up in a tenement. This town doesn't have many clothing stores, which means it shouldn't take me long to figure out where she bought her wardrobe and where she lives. I remember what Gloria was wearing yesterday, which gives me enough information to get started on my search.

I visit several shops, asking similar questions about the items they sell, taking care not to sound too interested. I tell the store clerks that my girlfriend loved an outfit that one of her mates bought and she wants to find something by the same designer. Then I describe Gloria's ensemble. After striking out four times, I finally hit a home run.

And I don't even like baseball.

The clerk in the fifth shop remembers Gloria's outfit and the woman herself. Apparently, she loves a particular designer, Amadeo Gaspari, whose clothing is only sold in this store. The bloke lives in a nearby town and attended Ballesteros University. I learn the name of the clerk, Angelina, and chat her up—though I'm careful not to give her the impression I have any sexual interest in her. I walk a very fine line with sweet little Angelina. Maybe that's why I feel slightly nauseous after my conversation with her.

But I get the information I need.

No, Angelina does not provide that information. Not directly. After browsing the items designed by Amadeo Gaspari, I ask Angelina if the shop has any more of his creations that haven't been brought out for display yet. She disappears into a back room to check.

I take the opportunity to investigate. Leaning over the counter, I snatch up what looks like a logbook of customers and purchases. While I keep half an eye on the door to the back room, I skim the logbook in hopes of discovering the information I need. Just when I think I've struck out—and yes, I need to give up on the ruddy baseball metaphor—I finally see a name I recognize.

Gloria Harris.

The logbook includes her home address and phone number. I grab a flyer from a stack on the counter, flip it over to the blank backside, and scrawl Gloria's contact information on it. Just as I tuck the folded paper into my pocket, Angelina returns. She couldn't find anything in the back room. I thank her and leave.

Now that I have Gloria's address, I have no idea what I meant to do with it. Spy on her? Confront the woman? For the moment, I can't do anything. I need to go back to the campus to pick up Catriona and go home. My investigation will need to wait until tomorrow.

That night, as we're settling in for bed, Cat snuggles up to me and traces circles on my bare chest with her delicate fingertips. "Let's make love, Alex."

Considering what I've been doing today—deceiving her, spying on a stranger, playing detective—I know I can't get aroused, not even for Cat. I'm tired and on edge.

"What's wrong?" she asks. "You seem anxious."

"No, I'm tired after grading papers all afternoon."

Another deception. Never before have I wished I weren't so good at conning people. If she caught me in a lie, at least my secret mission would be out in the open, and I wouldn't need to obfuscate the truth anymore. But I can't make myself confess, and she trusts me too much to suspect anything.

Cat crawls under the covers and closes her eyes. "Good night, Alex."

"Good night, love."

Another night with little sleep leaves me even more on edge in the morning. But I do what I must, relying on skills I thought I'd left in the past, and convince her I feel right as rain today. I want to ask my teaching assistant to handle my classes, but Catriona might stop in at my office to see me. She likes to do that whenever she has time. So I slog my way through topics I normally love to discuss, biding my time until I can sneak away to continue my espionage mission.

Lunch with Cat tests my acting skills, but I don't think she noticed anything amiss. Christ, she really does trust me without reservations. I don't deserve her faith, but I can't make myself push her away.

At least I get one bit of luck. Gloria's house lies on the outskirts of town, and trees screen it from the view of nearby homes. The lot has a large yard which provides even more camouflage thanks to more trees lining either side of the property. All of that means I can easily spy on her. I park my car a block away, on a side street, and skulk onto Gloria's property. I'd worn dark clothes today, knowing I would be doing this.

Catriona complimented me on my clothing. She thinks it's "dead sexy." And her statement made me feel like even more of a bastard.

But I'm doing this for her.

No, I'm not sure even I believe that anymore. I don't want Gloria anywhere near Cat ever again, partly because the woman upsets her, but mostly because I don't want her telling my girlfriend about all the things I did with her. Gloria's vague threats might mean nothing. She could simply enjoy causing trouble.

Just as I'm skulking around the house from behind, approaching the front corner, a nondescript four-door car pulls into the driveway. The visitor parks right behind what I take for Gloria's vehicle. The cherry-red convertible looks like a luxury model, though I know little about cars other than how to buy and drive one.

A man steps out of the other car.

I pull out my mobile phone and take a picture of the gent as he saunters up to the front door, then brings out a key to let himself in. I approach the living room window and peer inside, hoping for a glimpse of the man and Gloria. I don't need to wait long. The couple walks into the living room and sits down on the sofa. The house appears to be furnished in style, probably with designer furniture to match Gloria's designer clothes and her expensive car.

The man pulls Gloria into his arms and kisses her passionately.

He is definitely her new lover. I snap a few pictures of them snogging, then sneak around the front of the house to capture an image of the license plate on the man's car. I also photograph Gloria's license plate. With this information, maybe I can figure out who the geezer is.

I mean to head back to my car, but I need to pass by Gloria's house to do that. As I slink away, movement catches my eye in a different room, and I sidle up to the window. Gloria and her lover are in bed. Naked. Fucking on top of the sheets as if they couldn't wait even to pull the covers back before they started shagging. Though I feel like a ruddy voyeur, I take several pictures of the couple in flagrante. They go at it like animals. Gloria hadn't been quite that passionate with me, a fact for which I am grateful. Behaving like a rutting stag does not appeal to me.

Now that I have some evidence, I return to my car and drive back to the campus to pick up Cat. After dinner, I tell her I need to work on lesson plans for next week, which is true, but that's not the main reason I need time alone. I don't get my wish, though. Cat insists on watching the telly while I sit on the sofa with my computer on my lap. I glance up and find her smiling at me, the expression soft and affectionate.

Bile rises into my throat. I grab my water glass from the table and guzzle the entire contents.

With the woman I love nearby, I plug my mobile into the computer and download the pictures I took today. Then I find a website that will let me search for public information easily, just by paying a fee. My search gives me what I wanted to know—the name of the man who owns Gloria's house. He is Darnell Miller, and he serves as the chief of police in Ballesteros. That means he does have influence in the community, though I doubt he's as powerful as she wants me to believe.

Miller also owns Gloria's car. I'm certain he paid for all her designer clothes too, and her jewelry. Where does a police chief get that kind of money? Darnell Miller must be bent. I suppose he could have inherited money, but to afford all the luxuries he lavishes on Gloria, the man would've had to come from the Rockefeller lineage. I doubt that. I've come across bent coppers before, and I can sniff them out from a mile away. Miller smells as dirty as a heap of rotting rubbish.

Now that I know who Gloria's lover is, I have no idea what to do next. Confront Gloria? That would be risky. If her lover is corrupt, he won't hesitate to use every method at his disposal to cover up his misdeeds. I'd hoped gaining more information would help somehow. But now I realize that I need to give up on this quest. To keep going might bring trouble, and I can't risk Catriona getting caught in the middle.

So I shut down my computer and crawl into bed with Cat.

I will only use the information I've gathered if Gloria or Darnell Miller forces me to do it. Neither of them can know about my past.

Unless the chief of police has connections I don't know about yet.

Chapter Fourteen

Catriona

On this Monday morning, I'm in the university library scouring books for information that will help me with my dissertation. I've settled on a topic, and soon I will graduate from doctoral student to PhD candidate. That means I need to get a head start on my dissertation. Alex offered to help me, as my unofficial adviser, but he needed to do some paperwork first.

For the past week, Alex has not behaved strangely or gone on secret missions that he calls "work-related research." I let him get away with that because I know he wouldn't keep anything important from me. Whatever he needed to do, it must be exactly what he said.

Hands cover my eyes. "Guess who, darling."

I smile and peel his hands away, then glance up at Alex and pretend to be surprised. "Oh, I thought you were my other boyfriend."

"Hmm. I think I'll take these back." He thrusts a bouquet of daisies in front of me. "Unless you care to apologize."

I grasp the back of his neck and pull his head down so I can press my lips to his. "I'll give you my full apology tonight."

"When we're naked, I hope."

"Aye, of course."

He rests his erse on the table's edge beside me. Glancing around, he sighs with mock disappointment. "I was hoping you'd be in the basement again so we could ruin another flimsy table. But you're on the first floor within sight of the circulation desk."

"And a number of other students."

He picks up my hand, kissing it. "What are the chances I can talk you into doing something very naughty with me?"

"Your chances are excellent—when we're at home."

"What if I can't wait that long?"

I rise and pick up my rucksack. "Let's go home now."

"What about your afternoon classes?"

"*Mhac na galla.* I forgot about that."

Alex's mouth quirks into an amused expression. "I do love it when you curse in Gaelic. Did your brothers teach you to do that?"

"No. My sister Fiona did."

He raises his brows. "The MacTaggart women are a foul-mouthed bunch, eh? I need to meet your family."

Does he want that? I doubt he was being serious, but I wonder if he might actually like to meet my family someday. I've mentioned many of my cousins to him, and he didn't seem shocked by how large the MacTaggart clan is.

I sniff the flowers and smile again. "Thank you for these. They're lovely. But is there a special occasion I forgot about?"

"Do I need a reason to spoil you?"

"Of course not. I love it when you surprise me like this."

He slings an arm around my shoulders as we walk out of the library. "I'll walk you to the humanities building, then run a few errands. I grabbed your list off the refrigerator door this morning."

How many men would volunteer to go grocery shopping? Well, my brothers would. And some of my male cousins too. But I haven't met many other lads who would. Alex is an unusual man, but I love that about him.

We part ways outside the humanities building, and I go to my classes. Both lectures are interesting, but I can't wait for these two hours to be over with so I can go home with Alex. The moment class ends, I snatch up my rucksack and hurry outside to find him, knowing he won't be far away. I see him, but he is not alone. Gloria Harris is talking to him, and while she seems quite pleased with herself, Alex looks the opposite. He isn't angry, not exactly. But he does appear tense and uncomfortable.

"Alex, there you are," I say, trying to sound casual as I approach him. I hook my arm around his and aim a polite smile at Gloria. "How nice to see you again."

The woman smiles in a way that does not seem friendly. "Catriona. Isn't it a coincidence that we all bumped into each other here? I've never been to the campus before."

"Why are you here?" Alex asks. "You still haven't explained that."

Gloria grins, but again, it doesn't seem like a pleasant expression. "I'm here to see you, of course. Have you considered my offer?"

Alex huffs. "Offer? You demanded I shag you."

She laughs. "Honestly, Alex, you're being melodramatic. Yes, I want to have sex with you. But I don't mind at all if you still want to screw Catriona. We could even have a threesome."

"Nothing that you just suggested will ever happen."

"Really?" Gloria moves closer to him. "I have friends in high places, hon. Might not be the smartest idea to tick me off."

"Please. As if I'm frightened of you, the twenty-six-year-old slag who offers herself to any stranger who happens along."

Gloria snaps ramrod straight and puckers her lips. "You'll regret this."

Then she whirls around and stomps away from us.

I look up at Alex. "How did that woman ever find you in the first place? Do you believe the story she told us before about how she accidentally wound up in this town and saw us?"

"Yes, I think I do believe that. Or maybe it's fate punishing me for being a chancer."

"Alex, you are a good man who made mistakes. Donnae take all the blame. Gloria wanted to sleep with you."

"I know. But... Well, let's just forget we ever saw her."

"What if she comes back again?"

He lays a hand over mine on his arm. "Don't worry about Gloria. She likes to stir up trouble, that's all. She will give up once she realizes it's no fun harassing us when we don't give her what she wants."

If Alex believes Gloria will give up soon, then I believe it too.

Once we get home, Alex starts doing things on his laptop computer again, like he's done often lately. I guess his lesson plans have become more of a burden, which makes me wonder if his TA is doing anything at all to help him. Cannae see any other reason why he would need to work so hard every evening.

I go into the bedroom and ring my sister Fiona. We talk for a while and laugh quite a bit because she tells me all the barmy things our siblings and cousins have done lately. Our conversation turns more serious when she tells me that our cousin Logan has been deployed to Iraq in his capacity as a military intelligence officer. That means he might go on dangerous missions, though neither Fiona nor I fully understand what his job entails. I hope he doesn't get deployed for more tours after this, like other people I know back home.

Alex ambles into the bedroom just as I'm saying goodbye to Fiona. I hang up, but I stay in the same position—knees drawn up to my chest, one arm around them.

He sits down beside me on the bed's edge. "What's wrong, love? You look worried."

"I am worried. My cousin Logan, the one who's in the army, has been sent to Iraq."

Alex pulls me against his side and holds me. "I'm sorry, Cat. Can't imagine how stressful that must be, for your cousin or for you. I imagine your whole clan is anxious about it."

"We are. My cousin Magnus is in the army too, but he hasn't been deployed to a war zone yet. That might happen any day, though."

He strokes my hair, which always soothes me. "From the way you described those two blokes, I think they can handle themselves. Try not to worry overmuch."

I wrap my arms around him, snuggling my cheek into the hollow of his shoulder. "As long as I'm with you, I know everything will be all right."

Alex picks me up and cradles me with one arm while he pulls the covers back. Then he lays me down gently and crawls over me to lie down too. I cuddle up to him. He tugs the covers over us both, and soon, I drift off to sleep.

When I wake in the morning, Alex has already made breakfast for us. We don't discuss last night, but instead focus on today and what we plan to do since it's Saturday. Alex wants to go for a drive to explore the areas around Ballesteros that we haven't seen yet. We enjoy our day trip so much that I almost don't want to go home, but I know we have to do that. Though Alex might have a lot of money, I don't want to waste it all today. Could I do that in one day? He never has told me exactly how big his bank account is, only that he's wealthier than most people and that it's family money.

I don't need to know more. Not unless we get married.

But he hasn't asked me that question—or said he loves me.

"What's wrong?" Alex asks. "You look melancholy, which isn't like you. Are you still worried about your cousin?"

"No, it's not that. I just feel… I don't know. That woman Gloria fashes me, that's all."

"Do not let that woman ruin a beautiful day. She won't 'fash' you anymore."

"How can you know that?"

Alex pats my thigh and gives me a reassuring smile. "Because I won't let her harass you anymore. If she tries it, I will report her to the police for stalking."

I don't know if that would work, but Alex is right. I can't let one woman ruin a perfectly beautiful day.

He pats my thigh again. "Feeling better? You're not biting your lip anymore."

"Aye, I feel better. You always know what to say to cheer me up." I lean over to kiss his cheek. "I love you, Alex."

"Yes, I know."

That's all he says. What else can I do? I've never been good at making anyone confide in me, and I donnae like to force the issue. But the longer he avoids telling me how he feels, the more I realize I shouldn't let him sidestep his feelings. But for today, I will enjoy the time I have with him. Tomorrow…

He'd better start talking.

Chapter Fifteen

Alex

Catriona wants me to say I love her. Even I am not blind and deaf enough to have missed the signs. Back when she'd told me she's in love with me, I could dismiss that as… ah… nothing I need to worry about. I know I'm a bloody stupid arse and a bastard. Cat should have left me ages ago. Instead, she stayed and loved me and forgave me for not sharing my past with her. And now she has said those four words.

I love you, Alex.

So what if she said that? I didn't ask her to do it, which means I don't need to say it in return. Or maybe it means I should have said it yesterday when she spoke the words. It's too late now. Maybe I might possibly have wanted to… I don't know what I wanted.

Today, the morning after Catriona dropped her word bomb on me, she has gone to the campus to do more research in the library. That leaves me with nothing to do since this is Sunday. I have no classes to teach and no lesson plans to, ah, plan. I sit in our living room, watching ruddy awful television shows. And all the while, I keep slipping my hand into my trouser pocket to finger the diamond ring I'd meant to give to Cat on that cursed night. Do I still want to give it to her? What if I do? Maybe I don't. The fact that I carry it around in my pocket every day could mean nothing.

Have I lost my mind? I should probably have myself committed.

The doorbell rings while I'm still obsessing over what I should or should not have told Catriona and when or when not I should have done that. I mute the telly and shuffle to the door, swinging it open.

And I freeze.

The bloke staring back at me… I recognize him. I took photographs of this man and Gloria Harris going at it like chimpanzees on acid. Yes, the chief of police stands on my doorstep, glowering at me.

"Yes?" I say, as if I don't give a toss. "If you're selling band candy, I've already bought several cartons of that."

"Band candy?" Darnell Miller shakes his head. "Do I look like a high school nerd?"

"No, but you do seem like the sort who would play the oboe."

"Don't get cute with me, dirtbag."

"Why not? I am very cute, according to women." I casually slide my hands into my trouser pockets. "Just ask Gloria Harris."

"That's why I'm here. You upset her, and I'm gonna make it right."

"Are you?" I lean against the doorjamb, affecting an air of disinterest. "Go on, make it right."

Miller lifts his chin and smiles with smug self-assurance. "You think you're so damn smart, don't you? Well, I know who you really are."

"How nice for you."

"Cut the crap." Miller jabs a finger into my chest. "When Gloria told me what you did to her, I contacted my buddy at the Metropolitan Police in London."

"Interesting. You're quite an enterprising chap, aren't you?"

He stabs that finger into my chest again. "You won't be so full of piss and vinegar after you hear what I found out."

"I don't think you understand the phrase. Piss and vinegar means I have energy and enthusiasm." I give him my best sarcastic smile. "Thank you for the compliment, Chief Miller."

"Stop trying to distract me. You're an arrogant jackass, and I'm going to take you down so many pegs that you won't know what hit you."

This man is a moron. But sometimes that sort can become the most dangerous enemies. They take irrational risks because they are imbeciles.

"Tell me what you want," I say. "This conversation is growing tiresome."

"Fine by me." He reaches inside his jacket and pulls out a sheaf of rolled-up papers. Then he thrusts them at me. "Look at this."

Naturally, he sounds pleased with himself. Very pleased.

I pluck the papers from his hand, unrolling the pages. Then I stare at the words printed on the top sheet. Stare at them for so long that my eyes begin to burn because I've stopped blinking. How in the world? He can't—This is not possible, yet the evidence stares right back at me from the page I'm holding. But I will not give this cretin the pleasure of making me angry. That's what he wants, I'm sure. Probably so he can arrest me for assaulting a police officer.

I roll up the papers and offer them to him. "That's an interesting story, but I prefer fiction."

Miller sneers at me. "I've got you dead to rights, and we both know it."

"Things that happened in another lifetime have no bearing on the present. Why don't you distract yourself by fucking Gloria?" I feign surprise. "Oh, that's right. She prefers me. Bad luck, mate."

His face turns crimson, and he snarls words through his clenched teeth. "Wait'll I show this to your cute little girlfriend."

"Go on, show it to her." I slap his arm. "She loves a good comedy."

"Maybe I can do better than showing her your record." He twists his mouth into a nasty expression. "I'll make sure she has a record too."

"Oh, yes, I'm so bloody terrified."

I managed to speak those words in my best sarcastic tone, but I wonder. Can he do what he suggested? He is the chief of police, and I'm not at all sure that I can leverage those photos to get him off my back. I need more than pictures of him shagging Gloria. Am I prepared to become a blackmailer? For Catriona, I will do anything. This cretin doesn't understand what I've been through, the things I've done, or how far I'll go to protect the people who matter to me.

"Good night, Chief Miller," I say as I step back and start to close the door.

"Wait up, wiseass. Do you want your girlfriend to go to prison?"

I stop with the door halfway closed. "What are you talking about?"

"Here's the deal." He pushes past me to enter the house, and I'm too stunned to stop him. Miller slams the door shut. "If you don't do what I say, I'll invent some charges for your girl. She'll spend a good long while in the pokey. That means prison. Hard time."

I seize his shirt collar and smack him into the wall. "Careful, Chief. I'm not a mild-mannered professor who will crumble under pressure. If you try to take me down, I will make sure you go with me."

And if he hurts Catriona, even makes her shed one tear, I will snap his fucking neck.

"What I want shouldn't be hard for you to do," he says. "Nothing you haven't done before. Just get something for me."

"Such as?"

He digs a folded-up sheet of paper out of his trouser pocket and raises it for me to see. "Get me this, and I'll forget about your girl and your record. You have twenty-four hours."

Miller tucks the folded paper into the breast pocket of my shirt.

I back away from him and watch as the wanker saunters out of the house. Maybe I should've stopped the blighter and beaten him until blood covered his face. But violence has never been my strong suit, and assaulting Miller won't solve my problem. It would give him cause to arrest me and probably Cat too.

She won't be home for a while yet, which gives me time to search for a solution. I grab my handheld video camera and get in my car to follow Darnell Miller. I would've thought a police chief would spot me tailing him, but Miller spends the entire drive back to his house talking on his mobile—angrily, based on his gesticulating hands and the way he shakes his head. He swerves into the other lane three times. Luckily, there are no other cars near enough for him to cause an accident.

Police are meant to care about public safety. But no, I am not surprised that Miller only cares about himself.

Though I'm not adept at tailing someone, I've watched enough television shows to understand the basics. Picking someone's pocket? I could do that blindfolded. But surveillance is outside of my wheelhouse. I slow down as Miller turns onto a quiet street on the outskirts of town, on the opposite side of Ballesteros from where Gloria lives. He must be going home. I've slowed down enough that I'm still two blocks away when Miller pulls into the driveway of a small house. I turn down a side street and park along the curb, then walk to the house I assume Miller owns. His car still sits in the driveway, but I don't see the man himself. He must have gone inside already.

I head down another side street and find that I can access his unfenced backyard quite easily. Employing my less than prodigious surveillance skills, I creep up to the house and peek into the windows as I make my way toward the front. I've just reached the kitchen when Miller stomps into that room, snarling at whoever he's talking to on his mobile. Miller moves closer, and I can finally hear what he says.

"Gimme a break, Gloria." He grasps the nape of his neck. "I'm trying to get it for you. Maybe if you hadn't bled me dry buying that house and your goddamn car, I'd be able to give you what you want."

Miller snaps his flip phone shut, scowling at the floor, and shoves the mobile into his pocket.

Gloria bled him dry? I wonder if she's the one demanding that he steal a diamond necklace for her.

The police chief shoves both hands into his hair, his shoulders sagging. Then he brings out his mobile and makes a call. "Hey, baby, it's me. Need to see you now, please." His frown mutates into a sly smile. "Oh, yeah, you know exactly what I need. Let me tell you all the things I'll do to you."

I try not to listen while he describes in graphic detail what he wants to do with whatever woman is on the other end of that call. Did Gloria ring him to apologize?

Miller chuckles. "Don't worry about Gloria. She's a conniving little snake, but I'll be free of her soon. Then we can go away together like we planned because I'll sell that damn house and the car to finance our getaway." He listens, and his smile broadens into a grin. "Oh, yeah. My money and yours, that's all we need."

He disconnects the call and sets about gathering food items—champagne, strawberries, chocolates, whipped cream, and other sensual delicacies. He means to seduce the woman he was talking to on the phone. It's not Gloria, which means this man has two mistresses. *Blimey.* Where does he find the energy to please two women?

When Miller leaves the kitchen, carrying his romantic supplies, I sneak around to the living room windows. The police chief walks into that room a moment later. He turns on a stereo system, and music full of bass beats and lingering saxophone notes emanates from it. Sounds like a sodding porno film in there. Miller sets up his mini buffet of treats and puts the champagne inside a bucket of ice. Then he sits down on a recliner and shuts his eyes.

And I wait. Five minutes. Ten minutes. I lean against the house and slump onto the grass. Fifteen minutes. Twenty minutes. Just as I'm about to give up and go home, a car pulls into the driveway. From my position at the corner of the house, I can see into the living room and the porch.

A beautiful redhead emerges from the luxury vehicle and sashays up to the door, ringing the bell.

I hop up just in time to see Miller race out of the living room, heading toward the front door. The second he pulls it open, the woman flies into his arms and kisses him. Miller picks her up and carries her into the living room while they keep kissing with so much passion that I wonder if they can still breathe.

Grabbing my video camera, I start recording. Maybe what I film will never be useful, but I need to do something.

The lovers begin to remove their clothes, though they pause now and then to shove food into each other's mouths. Once they're naked, Miller pops the champagne cork and hands the bottle to his lover. He lies down on the sofa. The redhead straddles him and pours the bubbly onto his chest, then licks it off.

I think I'm going to be sick.

But I keep recording as she mounts his cock and the fucking begins in earnest.

While I watch—strictly to make sure I keep them in the frame—I realize I've seen this woman before. I'd met her briefly a few weeks before my first day at Ballesteros, at the mixer for new professors, which was hosted by the university trustees. I'd seen her again a few months ago at a fundraiser for the humanities department.

That woman is married to one of the trustees.

Oh, this is perfect. I have proof that the chief of police is shagging a trustee's wife. All I need to do is send a copy of this video to her husband. I've met the man, and he is a toerag, definitely the jealous type.

I've recorded enough of Miller and his lover's antics. To spare myself from vomiting on the hydrangea bush beside me, I turn off my video camera and hurry back to my car. Cat will be home soon, so I drive a bit faster than I should to make sure I arrive before she does.

Maybe I have a chance to save us both after all.

Chapter Sixteen

Catriona

I come home to find Alex busily cooking dinner. He seems more relaxed than I've seen him in quite a while, and he even hums while he works. As much as I love his new attitude, I can't help wondering what inspired it. Alex can be hard to pin down. Even after almost two years of living with him, I often feel like I'll never fully understand him.

"Welcome home," he says with a grin. "Dinner will be served in ten minutes."

I set down my rucksack and kick off my shoes. "Whatever you're cooking smells wonderful. What are we celebrating?"

"Nothing. Do I need a reason to treat you to a homemade meal?"

"We eat at home most of the time, but you don't go all out for an average dinner."

"I love to spoil you, darling. You know that."

Aye, Alex does enjoy doing that. I love letting him do it.

We share a wonderful meal, then relax on the sofa to watch television for a while. "Just until our food settles," he says. I know we will make love tonight. I can see that twinkle in his eyes, the one that means he wants a feast of sex too. We haven't had a poke in almost a week, and I've wondered why. The answer doesn't matter anymore. Alex is here with me, and he's his old self again. That's all I need to know.

Alex shuts off the television and leads me into the bedroom, then strips the covers off the bed. He sits down at the foot and leans back to rest his elbows on the mattress. "Strip for me, love. Please. Go slowly so I can relish every moment."

I unzip my jeans and push them down over my hips, taking my time and letting them fall to my ankles. Then I kick them away and unhook the buttons on my blouse one by one.

Alex is breathing harder now, and I can see the bulge growing inside his trousers.

Freeing the last button, I slide my hand inside my blouse and slowly push it off one shoulder, then the other. The shirt flutters to the floor.

"You are so beautiful," he says, his voice a husky murmur. "I love your body, Cat. It's a work of art."

I remove my socks next. While I reach behind me to unhook my bra, Alex licks his lips and tracks every movement I make. Since he wanted me to take my time, I release every tiny clasp slowly, pausing between each one and rolling my hips too because I love the way his gaze is glued to my body. By the time I slide the bra off my shoulders and toss it away, Alex is rubbing his cock through his jeans.

The hunger on his face makes my sex throb.

I slide a finger inside the waistband of my knickers.

Alex leaps off the bed and rushes toward me, yanking my knickers off with a single rough jerk of his fingers. The fabric rips apart. He snatches the ruined underwear off my body and flings it aside. Then he sweeps me up in his arms and drops me onto the bed.

While I bounce, laughter bubbles out of me. "I love it when ye get so randy ye cannae wait another second."

He tears off his clothes faster than I've ever seen him do that before. "Your striptease drove me mad. You are the sexiest woman on the face of the earth."

I glance at his erection and cannae help licking my lips. "I want to taste you tonight, Alex."

"All right. But don't make me come."

"I won't. Need you inside me right after this."

I rise to my knees and wave a hand in a come-hither gesture. He approaches the bed, halting right in front of me. I waddle closer, then rest my erse on the mattress with my legs hanging over the edge. His cock hovers right in front of my face, its sleek length curving upward slightly and the glistening tip now a rosy red. I clasp the base of his erection and slide my lips over his crown, taking him all the way into my mouth. The flavor and feel of his skin on my tongue makes me moan. I place my free hand on his inner thigh and begin massaging my way up toward his *bagais* until I can palm his sac.

Alex groans deeply.

Giving his sac a swift tug, I shift my hand down to his thigh and resume massaging his flesh. All the while, I lick and suck his hard length, devouring him while soft grunting noises emerge from my throat. Cannae help it. I always love tasting Alex and driving him barmy with the need to come. When I glance up at him, he has his eyes half-closed and wears an expression of pure pleasure.

I pull my mouth away from his *slat*. "Mm, Alex, I could you feast on you for hours. You taste so good, and you have the most beautiful cock in the world."

"You're full of rubbish," he says, his voice strained. "But I like it."

Taking him into my mouth again, I begin pumping his length with one hand while I work him with my mouth too. I watch his expression as it morphs from sheer pleasure to a sort of pain that I know means he will come soon.

So I release him and crawl backward on the bed. "Time to shag, Alex."

"Oh, yes, it is time."

Alex grabs a condom from the nightstand drawer, rolling it on quickly. Then he kneels between my legs and runs his hands up and down them, his touch so delicate that a warm tingle sweeps over me from head to toe. He slides his hands under my knees and lifts until I bend them, planting my heels on the bed. When he urges me to spread my thighs for him, I do it without hesitation. As he lowers onto his hands and knees, his cock grazes my cleft, and I instinctively arch my back. That warm tingle spreads into my folds and deeper to penetrate my sex, while Alex bends his head to kiss me tenderly.

"I'd love to taste you," he murmurs, "but I might come too soon if I do that. The way you look and sound when you climax drives me mad."

"Just take me, Alex." I clench the sheets in my fingers. "Now. Please."

He pushes inside me with such delicacy that my heart pounds, and I fist my hands even harder until my fingers start to ache, but I donnae care. His length fills me up, and when he lays his body on top of mine, his chest rubs on my hard nipples.

"Oh, Alex," I moan. "You feel so good inside me."

"I love the feel of your body wrapped around me." He begins a measured pace of thrusting while he frames my head with his hands, and our gazes align as if an invisible thread binds us. "Catriona, my darling, my love."

My heart skips a beat. Did he say… I cannae think about that anymore because he's kissing me now, delicately, sweetly, while he keeps thrusting and the sensation of his hardness inside me steals every other thought I might've had. I grip his biceps as his tongue coils around mine in a slow and sensual dance, teasing me and loving me at the same time.

The climax sweeps through me in slow motion, my inner muscles gripping him in softly rolling waves as a gasping cry tumbles from my lips. Alex rises onto his straight arms and thrusts harder and faster until he comes with a strangled shout. Our lovemaking might not have been earth-shattering, but it was more intimate than anything we've shared before.

Alex collapses onto me, his head nestled against my throat and his cock still inside me.

I comb my fingers through his hair. "Alex, I love you so much."

"Cat, I—"

The phone rings.

He pulls away from me and snatches the handset off the nightstand. "Hello?"

While he listens to the caller, his expression shifts from relaxed to almost stony, as if he doesn't like whatever the caller has told him. He hangs up without saying goodbye.

I push up onto my elbows. "What was that about?"

"Nothing, love." He gets rid of the condom and kneels between my thighs again. "It's time for me to feast on you, darling. Your sweet cream is the most delicious dessert any man could enjoy."

"But Alex—"

He shoves his face between my thighs and latches on to my nub, then begins suckling it while he teases my folds with his fingers. I meant to ask him something, but suddenly, I cannae remember what it was. He drives me toward the heights of ecstasy again so swiftly that the power of it robs me of breath and scatters my wits. I come harder this time, my body bowing inward while my feet lift off the mattress and cries erupt out of me. He keeps tormenting my clit until my voice goes hoarse and I'm sobbing from the intensity of what he's done to me.

Alex lies down beside me, facing me, and tugs my body against him. "I'll give you a few minutes to recover before I do that again. And after the second time, I'll have recovered enough to sink my cock into your sweet flesh again."

"We've never done it more than twice."

"Tonight is special." He circles his finger around my nipple, his touch so delicate that it makes my heart thud. "I mean to show you everything I can't say."

"Donnae understand."

"Hush, love. Let me demonstrate for you."

I don't get the chance to say anything else. Whenever Alex touches me, I lose my mind. But when he makes love to me the way he's done tonight, I know he must feel what I do. He must love me as much as I love him. Why he can't say it, I don't know. But for this one night, I will let him show me however he wants and I won't question him.

Not tonight. But soon, he will tell me. I'll make sure of it.

Alex makes love to me for hours, with breaks to eat savory snacks and drink Talisker from the bottle. I've never been with any other man who would treat me the way Alex does, as if I'm the only woman in the world who matters, as if he never wants to be with anyone else. He whispers the sweetest words to me throughout our marathon in bed, and I've never felt closer to him than I do now.

We fall asleep tangled up in each other, and in the sheets. I sink into a deep slumber spiced up by sensual dreams of Alex. I wake in the morning feeling so good that I think I must still be asleep. But I'm not. Alex gave me this feeling. Now he lies beside me with one arm draped over my hip. Since I'm facing him, I decide to just lie here watching him sleep, loving his relaxed and almost innocent expression, as if all the things he's been afraid to tell me no longer fash him.

I could watch him sleep for hours. The masculine beauty of his body takes my breath away, and so does the idea of rousing him so we can have another poke before breakfast. But instead of doing that, I leave him sleeping and slip into a dressing gown. Then I slink out of the bedroom to make breakfast for us. Alex often rises first, which means he usually cooks for us both. Today, I want to surprise him with a good meal full of protein that will give us both plenty of energy for the day ahead. We expended a lot of calories last night.

On my way to the kitchen, I take a moment to gaze out the picture windows and appreciate the view. Everything seems more beautiful and more meaningful today. I know Alex loves me, even though he has never spoken the words, because he proved that to me last night with his expressions and his body. As I trot into the kitchen, I already have a menu in mind for our post-sex meal.

Will Alex propose to me someday? I have an intuition that he will. Maybe I'll become Catriona Thorne soon. Of course, he'll need to meet my family first. I know they will love him almost as much as I do.

As I whip up our breakfast, I can't help dancing and humming along to the songs on the radio. Since I know how to cook these dishes from memory, I allow myself to fantasize about what our wedding might be like, how handsome Alex will look in a tuxedo, and how happy we will be.

Someone knocks on the front door so loudly that it rattles.

I race to the door and swing it open. All the blood in body seems to have turned to ice, and I stare numbly at the two men standing before me.

The police officers stare at me with stony expressions. One of them speaks. "Catriona MacTaggart?"

"Aye, that's me."

He brings out a pair of handcuffs. "You're under arrest for suspicion of smuggling antiquities."

Chapter Seventeen

Alex

I'd been lying in bed, enjoying the aromas of whatever food Cat had prepared for breakfast, when I heard someone banging on the front door. I pulled on my jeans and a T-shirt, then ran into the living room, meaning to reach the door before Cat. But she got there first. Two police officers stood just outside the threshold, each wearing a stern expression and carrying a firearm strapped to his hip.

"You've got it wrong," I say as I come up beside Catriona. "You don't want to arrest her."

"Stay out of this, Dr. Thorne. We have our orders."

He knows my name, which might give Catriona the idea that I know this wanker. I've never seen him before. But I do know his boss, Chief of Police Darnell Miller, and I have no doubts he sent these men. Whether they realize the charges are trumped up, I have no idea. Would they care if they did know? My only concern right now is to stop them from taking Cat.

I squint at the bloke who had spoken and repeat the words I'd said a moment ago, this time with more menace in my voice. "You've got it wrong."

The officers eye me with their lantern jaws tightly set and their gazes narrowed on me. Do they really think that will intimidate me? They're fools if they do.

"She's coming with us," the officer who'd spoken a moment ago says. "You can visit her in county lockup."

"At least let her get dressed," I snarl.

"Can't. Got orders." The other officer, the one who had handcuffed Cat, spears me with a knife-sharp glare that does not frighten me. "Orders from the top."

"You are making a mistake that you will regret."

"Doubt it, pal. You're not as smart as you think."

The officers drag her out of the apartment, despite the fact she's wearing only a dressing gown and not even a pair of slippers. Though I want to beat those men senseless for treating her like a criminal, I know that will do no good. If I'm arrested, I can't fight to get her released. We don't need lawyers. All I need is the video I recorded yesterday.

I want to follow those bastards to the jail, but I know that's the wrong thing to do right now. Instead, I finish getting dressed and grab the videotape, then climb into my car and drive too fast and too recklessly on my way to the home of Darnell Miller. I have a hunch he will be there. The man is not a hard-working professional, but a chancer who will do anything to get what he wants. That suggests to me that he will still be at home. I would bet all the money I have that he never shows up to work before ten o'clock.

And it's barely seven right now.

Since I no longer need to be stealthy, I slam my foot down on the brake pedal, screeching to a halt along the curb in front of Miller's house. I don't give a fuck that everyone in the vicinity might have heard that noise. By the time I stomp up the steps onto the porch, Miller has swung his front door open.

When he sees me, he scuffles backward and tries to close the door in my face.

I kick it open before the latch clicks into place and stalk into the house. Miller keeps backing up, apparently aiming for the living room behind him. Kicking the door shut, I seize Miller's shirt and drag him closer.

Spittle sprays from my lips as I snarl, "Call off your dogs. Do it right now. Release Catriona immediately, or I will make sure Raymond Anderson knows you've been fucking his wife, thanks to the video I took of you two going at it. I doubt Connie will want to shag you ever again once her husband knows about the two of you."

"You don't know the Andersons. You're lying."

"Am I? Raymond Anderson is a trustee of Ballesteros University, where I work. I've met him and his wife more than once." I shake Miller hard. "You have no idea who you're dealing with. You claim to know who I am and what I've done, but that is clearly a lie. If you knew the whole truth, you wouldn't have tried this blackmail scheme."

Miller's face has turned a few shades paler. His expression has gone slack too, a clear indication that he thought I'd be an easy mark for his blackmail-slash-burglary scheme.

"Release Catriona," I hiss. "And make certain there are no blemishes on her record. If I find out you've so much as mentioned her name in any reports, I will hunt you down and punish you."

"Okay, okay," Miller says, holding his hands up in surrender. "Relax, she won't have any record. Forget about that diamond necklace. Gloria said she'd tell Connie Anderson I was sleeping with her too. She knows I swore to Connie she was the only one."

"I don't give a toss about your infidelity problems."

"What I'm saying is please don't send the video to Raymond. He'll murder me—professionally, at least."

A harsh laugh bursts out of me. "Am I meant to feel sorry for you? I hope Anderson ruins your life." I let go of Miller and move toward the door. "Do what you promised. I think even your minuscule brain can comprehend the consequences if you renege."

"Yeah, I get it. Your girl will be released within the hour." When I keep glaring flaming daggers at him, he picks up the phone and dials. "Ronnie? Yeah, let the girl go, free and clear."

I walk out the door and slam it shut behind me.

By the time I arrive at the county jail, most of my fury has settled down to a low simmer. Every time I think of Darnell Miller, though, I wind up strangling the steering wheel and gritting my teeth. He deserves to be arrested and charged with some sort of crime, any sort, just to make sure he can't do this to anyone else. But I can't go to any type of authority to report him.

I had made one stop on my way to the county jail. Raymond Anderson lives in a mansion on the wealthiest street in town, which only has half a dozen homes. I have no trouble finding the right one. Parking on an adjacent street, I jog to Anderson's home and set my package on the doorstep, then ring the bell. I return to my car and drive past the Anderson home just in time to see the man himself pick up the package. Since I had included a note that said "Darnell Miller is not your friend and your wife knows why," I feel confident Anderson will watch the video.

I race to the county jail, which seems to be run by the sheriff's department, and I see blokes wearing those uniforms when I walk inside the building. But I also meet one of the toerags who had dragged Cat away.

He smirks at me. "I'll go get your girl. Maybe she won't be your girl anymore, though, huh? Probably realizes what a prick you are now that she got thrown in the clink."

Though I want to snarl at him, and possibly throttle the knob, I maintain a neutral expression and relaxed demeanor. And I wait. Minutes tick by on the clock on the wall. What is taking so bloody long? My neutral expression might be transforming into a stony look, but I can't help that. I refuse to let anyone see my anger.

The officer and Catriona emerge from the cell block or whatever they call it. The officer says, "Here she is."

My fingers curl into my palms, then tighten into fists. Cat looks bedraggled and frightened, still wearing nothing but her dressing gown.

The officer gives her a shove, pushing her toward me while he looks at her. "Alex Thorne is seriously bad news. You'd be better off running as fast as you can from him, before he drags you down into the quicksand, for good next time."

"Shut up," I hiss as I throw an arm around Cat's shoulders and guide her toward the exit. Darnell Miller must have shared what he knows about my past with this twat and probably his twat partner too. "You'll regret this, the lot of you."

Yes, I will find a way to make sure Miller's henchmen suffer too.

At the car, I stop to ensure Cat's dressing gown is securely tied, then whisk my hands up and down her arms. "Christ, you're barely dressed. You must be freezing."

I wrap my arms around her, and for a moment, I just hold her. What might've happened… It doesn't matter. It's over now. I kiss her forehead and help her into the car, then snatch a fleece throw from the backseat and drape it over her. Then I drive us home. I don't speak, and neither does Cat. But I know my reckoning has arrived.

Once we get home, I order her to have a shower and get dressed. While she does that, I slump onto an armchair, lodge my elbows on my thighs, and stare down at the floor. Though I hear Cat's footsteps as she enters the living room and the slight thump as she drops onto the sofa, it takes me a moment before I can raise my head to look at her.

"Bloody hell, Cat." I knife my hands through my hair and hurl myself backward against the chair. "I'm sorry. This is all my fault."

"How?"

I'm still gazing at her, but my voice refuses to work. She looks so young and innocent and sad, not to mention thoroughly confused. I want to hold her, swear to her everything is fine, but that would be a lie. Staying with me will destroy her.

The words I want to say get stuck in my throat. *I love you, Cat, please marry me.* She shouldn't do that. I can't let her do it, and I can't let her go on loving me.

"How is it your fault?" she asks.

"It's complicated," I say carefully. "The details aren't important right now. Just know that you are not going to jail. I will not allow that to happen. And your arrest record will be expunged."

She goes perfectly still, her unblinking gaze nailed to mine. "You know why I was arrested."

"It doesn't matter now." I rise and shut my eyes, frozen in place while I struggle to figure out what to tell her. Not the truth. Which leaves me with one agonizing choice. I marshal all my willpower to do what must be done. Then I kneel in front of her and meet her gaze. "I'm not going to explain any of this. You'll either trust me to take care of things, or you won't."

Is that my voice? I sound so cool and unaffected, but I suppose that's how I need to be right now.

"That's not good enough, Alex. I deserve the truth. I demand it."

"I can't do that, Catriona."

"Yes, you can." She slants toward me until our noses almost touch and aims her fiery gaze straight into mine. "Either tell me what is going on, or I will walk out that door and never come back."

Coldness floods through me, chilling me down to the core of my soul. If I even have one of those. "Do what you need to do."

"Dammit, Alex." She slaps her hands on my chest and pushes with all her strength, but she can't move me. "Why won't you talk to me? All I want is the truth."

"And that's the one thing I can't give you. Not today. Maybe never."

Cat gawps at me, searching my gaze for something that she clearly can't find. That would be my nonexistent soul, I imagine. I see it in her eyes the second she makes her decision. "Then there's only one thing left to say. Goodbye, Alex."

A pang stabs into my chest, as sharp and cold as a knife's blade. But I rise and take a step backward, giving a bang-on impression of a heartless bastard. I don't even move when she pushes past me to go into the bedroom and gather her possessions. I stand here frozen in place, feeling numb and yet relieved at the same time. I'd always known I couldn't have her forever.

Catriona hauls a suitcase to the doorway and rests her hand on the knob, glancing back at me. "I'll come back for the rest of my things while you're at work. This is the last time you'll see me, Alex."

I swear she's pleading with me to beg her to stay, in her eyes if not her expression. But I'm an arrogant arsehole, so she probably isn't doing that. "Goodbye, Catriona."

She walks out the door.

For several minutes, I don't move, rooted to the spot where I'd stood when Catriona MacTaggart severed our relationship. I made her do it. I needed her to do it. Maybe I had the strength to stand up to Darnell Miller, but when it comes to the woman I love, I am a coward through and through. So yes, I make sure to be elsewhere when Cat returns for the rest of her belongings.

No, I can't watch her leave me.

I do tail Catriona to the airport, though, and watch as she shuffles into the terminal. Then I wait in the car park so I can watch her plane take off, ferrying her back to Scotland. Maybe I should be happy. I got what I wanted. The only woman I will ever love has left me, and I can go back to being a loner with a dodgy background.

But I can't go back. My life will never be the same again.

Chapter Eighteen

Catriona

My family meets me at the Inverness airport. I'd rung my sister Fiona to tell her I was coming home, and I couldn't stop myself from crying while I talked to her. So naturally, she told everyone, and I wind up being greeted by not just my five siblings and my parents, but also a number of my cousins and aunts and uncles. Even my grandparents show up.

By the time the plane landed, I'd recovered my composure. No, I will not let Alex Thorne ruin my life. I love him, but I will get over that one day soon. Aye, my heart will ache for him, but not forever. I mean to move on.

How long will that take?

My family waits for me just outside the terminal doors, and the second I step out there, my mother drags me into a suffocating hug. She kisses my cheek and babbles things I can't understand. Though I receive similar treatment from my sisters, I don't expect that from my brothers. But they each hug me fiercely and vow to "skelp" the "*bod ceann*" who hurt me. I'd rather beat Alex with my own fists because the dickhead deserves it, but I appreciate the sentiment from my brothers.

I love Alex Thorne. Only time will ease the pain.

For the next week, I mostly hide in my bedroom, in the house where I'd grown up, and try to forget about that man. Aye, the betrayal is still too fresh for me to move past it yet. So I lie in bed, hugging the bears Alex had given me, and I cry.

On the seventh day of my self-imposed isolation, I force myself to go out into the world. I start by having breakfast with my family instead of sneaking into the kitchen to steal a snack. Then I accept Fiona and Jamie's invitation to go for a walk and get some fresh air. My sisters use that time to blether about our clan's antics, and aye, hearing all the good gossip does cheer me up a wee bit. My brothers do their part too—by recommending lads I might want to date. I'm not ready for that. I slept with the same man for the better part of two years, and I cannae sweep that all aside, not just yet. But I love them all the more for trying.

Though I've stopped hiding in my room, I still hug those bears every night while I fall asleep.

After a month of missing that man and sometimes crying over the loss, I decide enough is enough. Why should I let Alex Thorne make the rest of my life miserable? I'm young and bonnie and clever, three things any worthwhile man should appreciate. Since I'll be leaving for Edinburgh soon, to continue my doctoral studies, I'll have a much larger pool of lads to choose from which means I will definitely forget about *that* man. I still haven't told anyone the name of the *bod ceann* who broke my heart. But I need to call him something since everyone keeps mentioning him, and their nicknames for him are ridiculous. Lachlan calls him "the wee shit I'm going to batter one day." If I invent my own nickname for Alex, maybe everyone will stop talking about him.

Three weeks before I'm meant to leave for Edinburgh, I announce my new name for Alex. My family is having a barbecue, and my youngest sister, Jamie, gives me an opening.

"When will ye ever tell us that British scunner's name?" she asks. "We have a right to know."

"No, you don't," I say. "The British Bastard doesnae deserve to have his name spoken."

I think my relatives have decided the Limey Louse drove me off my head, and they mean to humor me whenever I mention him. Aye, I just created another nickname for him. A few days later, I invent yet another one when my cousin Iain asks how I'm recovering from my heartbreak. I tell him, "The Soulless Sassenach will never fash me again. I'm getting on with my life."

The move to Edinburgh is temporary, only until I finish my dissertation and earn my PhD. Then I will find a job as an archaeologist, either in the field or as a teacher, and my life will go on in spite of what the British Bastard did to me. During my first week on campus, I meet my two supervisors who will guide me through the rest of my program. Luckily, they've arranged it so I won't need to start over and all the work I'd done in America will count toward my doctorate. That means the Soulless Sassenach has not destroyed my professional dreams, even if he did shatter my heart.

But no, I don't cry anymore when I think of him. Anger has replaced the heartbreak.

That's why I decide to exorcise the demon once and for all. My sisters reluctantly help me gather what I need, and they watch me perform the ritual. I've acquired a small pile of twigs and a bottle of kerosene. Now I light the twigs with the flammable liquid, and once the flames have grown to a good height, I bring out the teddy bears Alex had given me. Then I douse them with kerosene and drop them onto the fire.

Yes, Alex no longer exists in my world.

As the months go by, I do date, though not often. That has nothing to do with the Limey Louse. I'm so busy with my dissertation and field work that I have little time leftover for personal matters. Who needs romance? It's a waste of time. I want to spend my life researching and preserving the past as well as teaching others about the rich and exciting history of our country. That's all the satisfaction I need. The fact that I occasionally dream of Alex, and those dreams are intensely erotic, does not mean I pine for him. The lads I date might not be as good in bed, but at least they don't hide their pasts from me or get me arrested.

Never will I tell anyone that every night as I'm falling asleep, I pray I'll dream of Alex Thorne, or that when I'm alone in my room, I often push myself to orgasm while fantasizing about him. Fantasies donnae mean I still have feelings for him. I absolutely do not.

But sometimes I remember our last night together, and I wonder. When he had whispered "Catriona, my darling, my love," it hadn't felt like an offhanded statement. I believed he had meant that he loved me, though he couldn't say it outright. Whatever Alex felt or almost said doesn't matter anymore.

The British Bastard will never again darken my doorstep.

Chapter Nineteen

Alex

What did I do when Catriona MacTaggart left me? I erased her from my mind and went back to the way I'd been before the lass with the fire in her eyes and in her soul wrecked my perfectly arranged life. I've got it all rearranged, back to the way I want it. So what if I didn't leave my loft for three days after that and rang the dean to tell him I have the flu and I can't teach my classes or deal with office hours for the rest of the week? I do feel a touch feverish. The sodding thermometer is wrong.

I love Cat, but I let her believe the opposite. Now I need to deal with the consequences of my actions. Maybe I should have explained everything to her, even my past, and let her decide whether she wanted to stay with me. No, that would've exacerbated the disaster I had already caused. Do I actually love her? Not sure I'm capable of that depth of feeling, so I probably imagined I felt that way because she insisted on telling me she loved me. Yes, that's what happened.

While I pretend—ah, recuperate from the flu, I receive good news. The local newspaper announces that the chief of police has tendered his resignation and has not announced yet where he will go next. To the nick, I hope. But I rather doubt the blighter will ever be arrested for his crimes. At the very least, I hope Raymond Anderson has gotten that wanker blacklisted so he can never work in law enforcement again. As for Miller's henchmen, I might have sort of planted a few incriminating items in their lockers at the police station, items that might have led to the new interim chief terminating their employment. I doubt either of them will get another job in law enforcement.

So what if that was a dirty trick? Those toerags conspired with their boss to frame an innocent woman for antiquities smuggling. They deserve to suffer for that. A darker and much less forgiving part of me wishes I'd strangled the lot of them. Whatever faults I might have, which are admittedly many and varied, I am not a killer.

A con artist, yes. But not a murderer. Well, former con artist. My days of picking pockets and swindling wealthy individuals have been over for a long time.

The week after Cat—ah, a certain person left the country, I realize I need a change of location too. I will never go back to the UK. I'm not wanted by the Met, never even served time, but I don't feel comfortable returning to the scene of my past crimes. I could go to Canada, or even Europe, but that doesn't appeal to me either. I quit my job at Ballesteros University and seek a new position at a different American institution. It's a college that doesn't even offer graduate programs, but I don't give a toss about that. Living in a small town where no one knows me seems like the safest course right now.

How do I spend the years after I lost the love of my life? By becoming the bastard Catriona thinks I am. I pawn the engagement ring and ignore the pang in my chest when I do that. Then I proceed to cultivate a persona that seems most likely to protect me from ever suffering that sort of pain ever again. I adopt an attitude of breezy sarcasm, as if I don't give a fuck about anything or anyone other than myself. Oddly, college girls love that. The silly birds try to seduce me by batting their lashes and speaking in a huskier tone while they ask if I want to "get busy" or "hook up." I decline their advances in my breezily sarcastic way. And those moronic females adore me even more after I rebuff them. Women are insane, and I will never date any of them ever again. I certainly will not marry one.

But I do occasionally find an anonymous partner for a few hours. We always go to a hotel far from where I live. Whether or not I enjoy those encounters is irrelevant. Perhaps I occasionally consider the possibility that I'm punishing myself with meaningless shags. Every time I come inside a stranger's body, I recognize that sex never feels as good as it did with...someone else.

Maybe I perform the occasional internet search to look for anyone called Catriona MacTaggart. I don't want to see her. It's curiosity, that's all. By the time the seventh year has elapsed, I force myself to give up on my obsess—make that my casual habit of searching for women with a certain name. Torturing myself had become a longtime habit before I ever met Cat. Now that torture is well and truly over.

At least that's what I think—until fate intervenes.

I never believed in that rot, and I especially did not believe it after Catriona walked out of my life. But I can't deny the event that occurs now seems far too serendipitous for my taste. I'm now living in Montana and working at Thensmore University as a professor of archaeology and ancient history. I've settled in enough over the past two years that I built a house, the sort that is, admittedly, too bloody enormous for one person and rather gloomy, with its crimson walls and dark trim fashioned from Indian rosewood. The paintings in the entryway feature various deities from mythology. A large portrait of the Fates, the Greek goddesses, occupies the entryway wall. Maybe this house is depressing, but I don't care.

One day, some twat who's probably a student at Thensmore decides to steal a priceless object from my private collection. Whoever the twat was, he destroyed the lock on the front door and the one that secures my personal collection of objet d'art. The particular item the knob stole has...special meaning for me. I want it back.

So I ring someone I haven't spoken to in years and ask for help. The gent is a social worker, but he has connections at the Met in London. I assume he won't remember me, but he does—and he wants to help. I suppose he empathizes when I tell him what the object means to me, though I do that only out of desperation. What if I am desperate? It's a temporary condition.

My old mate rings me a few days later with the name of a person who might be able to help me. He's an army veteran and a former MI6 agent, fresh out of his tenure as a spy. If anyone can help me and keep it confidential, this is the man for the job. So says my old mate. He gives me a phone number for the bloke. When I ask for his name, I get a shock.

Logan MacTaggart.

I pay for Logan's flight from Scotland to Montana, and my right-hand man picks Logan up at the airport. I wait in my study while Reginald escorts the Scot through the house.

And I finally lay eyes on Logan, Catriona's cousin, the one she had worried about deeply when he was first deployed to Iraq. I rise and offer him my hand. "I'm Alex Thorne. Welcome to Moirai House."

Logan shakes my hand. "Tell me what you want me to do."

"I see you're not a fan of pleasantries."

"No. What do you want me to do?"

Sitting down again, I gesture for him to do the same. "Someone has nicked an item from my personal collection, and I want it back."

"Do ye have any idea who stole it?"

"No. But I suspect it was a student at Thensmore University. I work there."

"Hmm. Why did you contact me and not the police? Or a private investigator?"

I consider Logan for a moment, wondering if he was always this suspicious or if his time with MI6 changed him. Catriona had called him "a sweet boy," but the man sitting across me is not sweet or a boy, not anymore. I've changed too, so perhaps Logan and I share more in common than I thought. "A mate recommended you. That was all I needed to know. Will you take the job?"

"Aye, I'll do it. Do ye have a picture of the item?"

"Yes." I pull a photograph out of my desk drawer and offer it to him. "This is the item in question."

Logan holds the photo and studies it. His brows hike up. He lifts his gaze to me. "If this is a joke, I donnae appreciate a scunner wasting my time."

"This is not a joke, though I freely admit I am a bloody annoying prat."

His brows rise even higher. "Ye know what 'scunner' means?"

"Yes." How much should I confess? I need his help, so I must make a few concessions to satisfy him. "I learned that word from Catriona."

Logan stares at me without any discernible expression. "Catriona who?"

"MacTaggart. Your cousin." I shift in my seat as if I'm uncomfortable, but that's rubbish. Nothing unsettles me, which means there must be needles under my arse. "I knew Cat a long time ago. We, ah, lived together."

The Scot keeps staring at me. Just when I think he must have suffered an aneurysm, Logan erupts in laughter. "You're the British erse who broke her heart. Every time someone mentions you, she spits on the ground and curses in Gaelic."

Well, at least she hasn't forgotten about me. Not that I care either way.

"So, Logan," I say as if I don't give a stuff what his answer might be, "are you still willing to take the job?"

"Aye." He stands and sets the photograph on my desk. "Donnae need this."

"Don't you want to know how much I'll pay you?"

He shrugs. "We can discuss that later."

I suggest we have a drink, but he declines my offer. Logan also says no to dinner. The Scot examines the two crime scenes, then leaves.

Two days later, he returns with my precious treasure. The former spy strides into my study one evening and sets the package on my desk, wrapped in a brown paper sack. "Ye didnae mention the laddie is a bodybuilder and the star of the university wrestling team."

I point at his face. "He gave you a black eye?"

"That's right. You said this would be simple, but ye lied. No wonder Catriona hates you."

"I apologize, Logan. I had no idea who had stolen the item, so I couldn't have guessed the job would be such a bother." I unlock a drawer on my desk and bring out several bound stacks of hundred-dollar bills, then hand them to Logan. "Here. It's the fee I had planned on giving you plus a bit extra for the trouble."

Logan fans the bills with his thumb. His brows lift the slightest bit.

I unwrap the package and gaze at the object he had retrieved for me—an empty bottle of sparkling white grape juice that bears the lip print of Catriona MacTaggart.

Logan eyes the bottle. "The laddie must've drunk the contents."

"No. It was already empty."

This time when I invite him to dinner, he accepts. We have a good chat, and Logan shares a few stories from his time with MI6—the stories he can tell without committing treason. I'm sure he wants to know more about me and Cat, but I can't talk about that. So I share stories about the moronic things college students do.

A few days after I reclaimed my precious treasure, I realize I need to stop obsessing over the past. So I run my thumb over the bottle to erase the lip print, then I toss the thing into the rubbish bin. I'd gotten rid of the engagement ring years ago. Why cherish a ruddy bottle? Throwing out the last remnant of my relationship with Cat will cleanse me of her forever.

Yes, I excel at self-delusion.

Three years later, I ask for Logan's help again. I've gotten myself into a bit of a mess, a habit I seem to have developed lately. Logan comes to my rescue again, but this time he brings his new love interest, Serena Carpenter. They convince me to fly to Scotland with them and face up to my past, though even they don't know the whole truth about me. But they're right that I do need to confront my worst mistake.

Logan cheerfully informs me that Cat has devised nicknames for me over the years, and that she only ever refers to me by those names. The British Bastard. The Limey Louse. The Soulless Sassenach. Maybe I am a soulless Brit and a bastard. But it's time I stopped hiding from what I'd done to the only woman I ever loved.

I'm about to see Catriona.

Maybe I should buy a suit of armor.

Chapter Twenty

Catriona

I stand on the green behind Dùndubhan, the castle owned by my brother Rory. He hadn't owned a castle back when I became involved with that British Bastard. In the past few years, Dùndubhan has become a hub for MacTaggart family gatherings of all sorts, including shinty and Highland games. I now wait among a crowd of MacTaggarts, as well as the Americans that some of them have married, waiting for the Soulless Sassenach to walk onto the green.

I can't see what's happening, but I hear a chorus of murmurs that suggests Logan and Serena have emerged from the doorway in the castle wall that serves as the entrance to the walled garden. Alex must have followed them out, based on the murmuring around me. I can hear Rory's voice echoing off the walls, though I can't see him or make out his words. He sounds angry, though, and that suggests he's giving Alex a tongue lashing.

Good. The Limey Louse deserves it.

But I can't let my brothers fight my battle for me, so I push through the crowd. Everyone begins to move out of the way, opening a path for me, and even my brothers step aside. I stop a few yards away from Alex. The fire of fury erupts inside me as I skim my gaze over him from head to toe. Aye, he looks as good as ever—better even than he had the last time I saw him. But I donnae care how attractive and sexy he is. The British Bastard needs to pay for stealing my happiness.

Everyone on the green has fallen silent.

The fury rises even higher inside me, too hot and caustic to hold back.

"You bastard!" I scream as I barrel toward Alex.

Only his eyes move—to widen in shock, of course—and he just stands there as if he's waiting for me to assault him. I swing my fist back and slug him in the gut.

Alex gasps and doubles over, stumbling backward. But then he straightens and clears his throat as if he wants me to punch him again. Aye, I'll give him what he wants. I pull my arm back, preparing for another strike.

But Alex catches my fist in his hand.

Maybe I haven't behaved in the most adult manner, but Alex Thorne tore my heart out and didn't seem to care at all about what he'd done. We exchange a few words, and Alex acts like an arrogant erse who doesn't give a damn about anything or anyone. Then I drag him into the garden, slamming the door behind us. What happens next leaves me shaken and confused—because Alex does something I never could have anticipated.

He seems genuinely upset.

Our argument provokes a depth of emotion that stuns me. Not just my emotions. Alex's too. Does he care more than he lets on? Did our breakup all those years ago destroy him too? Long after I walk out the garden door, leaving Alex alone in there, I keep thinking about our encounter at Dùndubhan.

After that day, I see Alex often at family events like Logan and Serena's wedding, and my brother Aidan's birthday party. On every one of those occasions, I snap at Alex and berate him with the nicknames I invented long ago. Alex knows exactly how to provoke me into lashing out at him, and I'm beginning to think he wants me to do that. Maybe he feels guilty and letting me verbally assault him—and sometimes physically assault him—makes him feel like less of a *bod ceann*.

Since Alex lives in America, I don't see him every day. I don't even know where in America he lives.

After months of occasionally bumping into him, I get a surprise job offer from Thensmore University in Montana. It's a tenure-track position, and the pay is good. I need to shake up my life, so I accept the job. A month later, I arrive for my first day as a professor of archaeology and ancient history, and I meet a very nice woman called Lydia, who is in charge of the human resources office. I go there first to fill out paperwork and receive a brief introduction to the campus. But Lydia tells me something that sets my blood to boiling.

"We're so happy to have you here, Catriona," she says. "Alex Thorne's recommendation tipped the scales in your favor. He swears you're the smartest, most capable archaeologist he's ever known."

My fingers curl into my palms, as stiff as talons. "Alex recommended me?"

"Oh, yes. He gushed about you."

Though I want to grit my teeth and snarl, I force myself to stay calm. It's not Lydia's fault that Alex is a lying, conniving *bod ceann*. So I thank her for all her help and for letting me leave my bags in her office until I can pick them up after work. I had flown in early this morning and haven't even seen the house on campus that the university is providing for me.

As soon as the door to Lydia's office clicks shut behind me, I clench my fists and my teeth. Then I stalk through the building until I find Alex's office, thrust the door open, and march up to his desk. I stab a finger toward him. "Alex Thorne, you slimy, conniving bastard. What the bloody hell do you think you're doing?"

He gestures at his desktop. "Grading papers."

"Donnae be cute with me. How dare you interfere in my life."

Our argument goes on for several more minutes, but I get nothing from Alex except his favorite air of amused disinterest, as my cousin Logan calls it. He and Alex have become mates, but I've chosen not to criticize Logan for his lapse in judgment. My encounter with Alex leaves me feeling strangely invigorated. It doesn't help that age has made Alex even more appealing, almost irresistible. But I will never have a poke with him again. Never.

Still, I can't help wondering if his nonchalance is a cover for pain that he hides deep inside himself. His behavior nine months ago in the garden at Dùndubhan suggests I'm right about that. Maybe I shouldn't want to dig underneath Alex's skin and unearth the truth about him, but I need answers. Why did he push me away all those years ago? Why has he become so closed off? If I dig deep enough, will I find the passionate, sweet man I'd lived with for two years?

One way or another, I will find out. Our story isn't over yet. And Alex Thorne will not slither away from me again.

Get the full details of Alex and Cat's reunion in
***Lethal in a Kilt* (Hot Scots, Book Seven),**
then experience their own story in
***Irresistible in a Kilt* (Hot Scots, Book Eight).**

HOW TO
Lose A Lass

Chapter One

Gavin

The line rings through my headset eight times before someone picks up the call. I immediately start talking. "Good afternoon, this is Gavin from Rapid React Emergency Restoration Services, the premier service provider in Minnesota. If you have a moment, I'd love to talk to you about what we can offer. If you've ever experienced an overflowing septic system or a leaking gas line, we're here to help. Whatever you need to get you back on track, we have all the options. Rapid React offers twenty-four seven, on-call packages to get you back to normal. Why don't I send you a brochure about our—"

"No, thank you," the woman on the other end of the call says curtly. "I don't need or want your services. Don't ever call me again."

She hangs up. And naturally, she slams the phone down.

I don't blame her. Cold calling must be one of the sins mentioned in the Ten Commandments, but God wrote it in invisible ink by accident. I can't believe this is what I do for a living—harass decent people. Maybe the services this company sells are useful, but the way we attract new clients just sucks. In the Marines, at least I felt like I had a purpose and a calling. Now, I'm nothing but an annoying telemarketer.

"Having a bad day, Gav?"

I lift my head to gaze at my coworker, who had spoken those strangely cheerful words. No one should be happy while working in the ninth level of hell. "Yeah, I'm not having the best day so far."

"Can't snag any new customers?"

"Nope. Everybody hangs up on me."

"Sorry, dude. That sucks." My coworker, Phil, has risen halfway out of his chair to look at me over the top of his cubicle. "But I'm sure things will get better tomorrow or the next day."

I manage only a tight smile. "Thanks for the encouragement, Phil. You're always upbeat, and I admire that."

Phil's eyes widen. "You admire *me*? I never fought in a war zone. You are a grade-A hero, Gav."

Hero? No, I don't qualify for that title. I did my duty, nothing more, nothing less. Maybe I saw things that I never want to think about again, but that doesn't make me a hero.

Phil sits back down in his cubicle, and I can just barely see the top of his bald head.

I sink back in my chair and gaze at the photo on my desk, positioned alongside my computer screen. The picture was taken years ago, and it shows my family in the last happy moments we ever had. My baby sister, Calli, grins at the camera. My parents have their arms around each other as they smile. And I stand there beside Calli, smiling just like they do.

Our happy family. It's all gone now.

Since I have nothing else to do with my life, I go back to cold calling people who mostly don't want what I'm selling. I do snag a couple new customers, though. At the end of the day, I say good night to my coworkers and head back to my tiny apartment that features inspiring decor—cement block walls, a rusty metal door, and an open design that somehow manages to still feel cramped. It would make a mole feel right at home.

After eating a so-so frozen dinner, I flop onto my worn recliner and reach for the phone, intending to call my sister, but I change my mind. It's an hour later in Michigan. She might be asleep already. Right, Calli goes to bed at seven o'clock in the evening. Duh, of course not.

I'm just about to fall asleep in my recliner when the phone rings again. I crack one eye open to see the caller ID. Then I snatch up the receiver. "Calli? Is everything okay?"

"Yeah, of course. Why do you sound panicked?"

"Uh… I don't know."

She snorts, clearly trying not to laugh at me. "That's the lamest response ever."

"Cut me some slack, C. I had a crappy day at the office, also known as the ninth level of hell."

"If you hate your job, look for something different."

I groan. "Considering how much trouble you've had finding another librarian job, you ought to know better than to tell me to just up and find something different."

"Yeah, I know. Sorry, Gav. I just want you to be happy. That's an order."

"Yes, ma'am. You can't see it, but I'm saluting."

"Ha-ha." Calli hesitates, then her tone turns sneaky. "You know, if you came to Tara's wedding, you might meet someone."

I throw my head back and groan again. "I don't want to troll for dates at our cousin's wedding. Besides, you hate it when I say things like that to you."

"Fine, I give up. Hide out in your little apartment and be miserable."

Tara had invited me to the wedding too, but my boss is sending me to Florida this weekend for a conference about how to respond to and help customers recover from home emergencies. I'd love to watch my sweet little cousin tie the knot for the second time. Blake is a good guy, unlike Tara's first husband. At least Calli hasn't married a louse like me and Tara had both done, accidentally. We're bad role models for marriage, and maybe that's why Calli has been hesitant to date, much less get into a serious relationship.

I yawn loudly.

"Fine, Gav, I get the point," Calli says with a laugh. "Go to bed. And have fun at that conference."

"Oh, yeah. Seminars about septic system restoration are always a hoot."

"Maybe you should have a one-night stand, just to get some action."

I swing the phone away from me, staring at it like the thing sprouted a set of devil horns. Yeah, I'm kind of obsessed with hell references today. "Calli Bethany Douglas, what in the world has gotten into you? My sweet baby sister would never suggest I should have a fling with a stranger."

"Sorry. I'm just worried about you."

"And I'm worried about *you*, C."

My sister sighs. "Quite a pair, aren't we?"

"Yep. Mom and Dad must be rolling over in their graves." I rub my eyes and yawn. "Better get some sleep, Calli. You've got the big wedding tomorrow."

"Good night, Gavin."

We hang up, and I drag my body over to the bed, collapsing onto it without bothering to pull the covers back or undress. Okay, I might be slightly depressed. I'll get over it. If I could recover from the shock of our parents dying in a car accident, then I can shake off this malaise too.

The next day, I fly to Florida. My sister is in Chicago this week, for Tara's wedding, but she finds time to call me and pester me about "getting back out there" so I can find my "soul mate." I tell her, "I'll do it when you do." She laughs, and that's how I know she'll be fine. Maybe Calli really will meet a guy at the wedding. Tara and Blake know lots of people, so it isn't out of the realm of possibility. Our cousin would love to find a boyfriend for Calli.

And I want both of them to be happy. They're all the family I've got.

In the evening, I enjoy dinner alone in my little hotel room. Then I try to call my sister, but she doesn't answer. Probably still hung over from the wedding reception. Nah, Calli doesn't like to drink. Maybe she spent the night with some guy. That thought does not make me feel any better. I wanted her to date, not sleep around.

After watching a bad movie on TV, I try again to get hold of Calli, but her phone goes straight to voice mail. So, I give in and leave a message. "Hey, Calli, it's me. How was the wedding bash? Tara texted me some pictures from the big event, so I know she looked gorgeous in her wedding dress. But she didn't send any pictures of you. Send some, hey? Then I'll feel like I kind of was there after all. Talk to ya later, C."

On the last day of the conference, I skip all the events and take a walk along the beach instead. The warmth of the sun feels good on my face, and I tip my head back to enjoy it. Maybe life isn't so bad after all. Three hot girls stroll past me, all wearing tiny string bikinis. They give me appreciative looks.

Yeah, I've still got it.

A few minutes later, those ladies invite me to join them at the bonfire they and their male friends had set up on the beach. They turn out to be a bunch of really nice people, and hanging out with them reminds me how good life is. I'm lucky to have a sister I love, a cousin I love, and good friends too.

But I'm still slightly worried about my sister.

When I head home in the evening, I try again to get hold of Calli. She lives in Michigan these days, which means we don't see each other as often as we'd like. I get her voicemail. Again. Well, she might still be tired from the wedding. I'm sure she'll call sooner or later. Tara is on her honeymoon, and I don't want to bother her. But after ten days of not hearing from Calli, I know something is up. Since I won't be able to relax until I banish this bad feeling, I break my vow not to bother Tara and call her. She and Blake are on Hawaii time, which must be about five hours earlier. Yeah, she won't be mad that I'm harassing her.

I *will* find out what my sister is hiding.

"Gavin? Why are you calling? Blake and I are on the beach toasting our naked bodies in the sun."

I wince hard enough that I might've popped a few veins. "Jeez, Tara, ever hear of too much information?"

"That's what you get when you interrupt my steamy honeymoon."

"Listen, I'm seriously worried about Calli. Haven't heard from her in almost two weeks, and she doesn't answer when I call."

Tara laughs in a way that she must hope will convince me that nothing's wrong.

Instead, it pricks my intuition big time. "Tell the truth, Tara. I know you know something. So, start talking."

"Well, um…" She shifts around on whatever chair she's lying on. "I suppose it's okay to tell you, since Calli never swore me to secrecy."

"Spill your guts, Tara. Now."

"Calli is shacking up with a Scottish hottie she met in Chicago."

"What?!" Yeah, I definitely shouted that loudly enough to make the entire hotel room quake. "And you weren't going to tell me about that? What if the guy's a predator?"

"Come on, Gav. You're overreacting. Calli is too smart to fall for a creep."

I think I just growled. Literally. "Where are they?"

"Well, um…at Calli's house in Michigan."

"Good girl. Now, go enjoy the rest of your honeymoon."

My sister is shacking up with some Scottish guy she just met. I still can't believe it, even while I'm flying across the Midwest to get to Calli and…save her, I guess. I didn't take the time to formulate a battle plan. I'd love to sucker punch the dirtbag, then drag him to the nearest cliff and chuck him off it. The waters of Lake Superior are very, very cold. Even if he didn't die from the fall, maybe at least his dick would get frostbite and fall off.

How could Calli not even mention that she had a boyfriend? We used to be so close, especially after our parents died. Now, she's keeping a secret from me.

Time to surprise Calli with a visit from her big brother.

I jump on an airliner and fly straight to the Houghton County Memorial Airport in the Upper Peninsula of Michigan. Then I grab a rental car and violate the speed laws to get to Calli's house in the woods.

Finally, I step onto the porch and ring the bell.

The door swings open.

Calli's eyes go wide.

I frown at her. "Why aren't you answering your phone?"

"My phone?" She stares at me blankly like she can't remember who I am or what a phone is. Then she abruptly straightens and rolls her shoulders back, meeting my gaze directly. "I've been busy."

She probably meant to say "getting busy." Christ, I never imagined my sister would ever behave this way. Calli doesn't offer any further explanation, and she doesn't move aside to let me into the house either.

I squint at her. "Are you going to tell me, or do I have to tell you?"

"Tell you what?"

I slant toward her. "I talked to Tara."

My sister does her damnedest to seem clueless, but I've known Calli all her life. She can't snow me that easily. But she tries anyway, blinking swiftly like she's confused. "What did Tara say?"

I can't help it. My fury boils up, and I flatten my lips right before I hiss, "You're living with some foreign guy."

"I'm not living with him. His motel room was damaged by a burst pipe, and he couldn't find anywhere else to stay."

"You've got a strange man in your house, not a stray puppy."

Though she clearly doesn't want me to go inside the house, I barge in anyway. No time for civility. I'm on a mission to smack down the jackass who has seduced my sister. Calli keeps behaving strangely, like when she uses her body to block my view of the hallway—not to mention her totally fake innocent expression.

My sister's crazy-but-cute puppies barrel into the house, then swiftly race down the hall with their ears pricked and their tails wagging. I have a strong suspicion about the cause of their sudden flight.

It came from Scotland and is probably screwing my sister.

Then I know for sure. How? Because a shirtless guy with wet hair, who wears only a pair of low-slung jeans, just sauntered out of the hallway.

I clench my fists so hard that my nails dig into my palms. My eyes narrow to slits, and I think my nostrils actually flare like a bull about to charge a matador.

"Hello," the Scottish asshole says in a cheerful tone. He has the gall to grin at me too.

I grit my teeth and fold my arms over my chest. "Who the hell are you?"

"Aidan MacTaggart." The bastard holds his hand out like he expects me to shake it. "And you are?"

I glare at him and curl my lip just enough to convey my feelings about this guy. "I'm the Marine who's about to kick your ass from here to Mexico."

Aidan MacTaggart seems completely unfazed by my threat. That makes me grudgingly respect him a little bit.

"Should I leave?" the guy who seduced my sister asks while running a hand through his hair. "Seems like the two of you have things to discuss."

Calli glances at him over her shoulder. "You don't have to leave. This is my brother Gavin."

Aidan smiles again, his curious gaze aimed at me. "Your brother? That does explain it."

I squint at him. "Explain what?"

"Why you're concerned about her welfare. I have three sisters, and I wouldn't like to find a man I'd never met staying in any of their homes. Especially not my younger sister."

I freeze, experiencing a sudden epiphany. One side of my mouth kinks upward. "Maybe I should go move in with your little sister."

"You could try, but Jamie lives with my older brother Rory at the moment. He's not as friendly as I am."

For some very annoying reason, hearing about the asshat's family makes me feel less…homicidal about Aidan MacTaggart. I grasp the back of my neck and frown. "I still don't like this, but…Calli's an adult. She can do what she wants."

But oh, yeah, the Scot is going down.

Chapter Two

Jamie

Och, Rory, you and Lachlan are treating me like I'm a wee bairn." I set my hands on my hips and lift my chin just enough to get the point across to my overbearing older brothers. "I am twenty-six years old, which means I'm an adult. So please, dinnae act like I can't handle myself."

Lachlan straps his arms over his chest. "You might be twenty-six, but I am forty-two. That means you should respect my authority."

"You are not in charge of me. If I want to go to America like Aidan did, I will do it—with or without your permission."

"But Jamie—"

I hold up a hand. "Please, Lachlan, show me a wee bit of respect. I'm not a moron, and I have never done anything rash. I worked full-time at the Loch Fairbairn Library for five years, before I was made redundant, so dinnae make it sound like I'm an impulsive teenager."

Aye, I'd loved working at the library. But they simply couldn't afford to keep me on anymore.

Rory glances at Lachlan. "She's right. And if she goes to America, Aidan will make certain she doesn't get into any trouble, accidentally."

Aidan is only two years older than I am, but I understand why Lachlan and Rory believe I need my youngest brother to watch over me. In a family of six children, the eldest ones feel a responsibility to care for the rest of us. Lachlan especially feels that burden.

And maybe I am being rather pigheaded about this, but I've never left Scotland, not even to visit England. It's time I saw another part of the world.

Lachlan and Rory exchange glances, though I can't figure out what those looks mean. Until Lachie says, "I'd be more inclined to trust your judgment if you hadn't sent that text message to Aidan."

Oh, aye, he had to bring that up. When Aidan had gone to Chicago to find an American wife, no one tried to stop him. I might have sent Aidan a cheeky text shortly after his arrival in America, but only because MacTaggarts love to harass each other. I had asked him, "Have you found your quarry, Don Juan? Expect details about American fling." That's nothing compared to what Lachlan did when he was in Chicago.

I cannae let him get away with implying that I'm the irresponsible one. "The man who had a four-week fling with an American woman and then ripped her heart to shreds has no grounds for chastising me for teasing Aidan."

Lachlan winces. "Aye, ye have a point."

Rory shakes his head at Lachie. "You caved without a fight. It's a sad state of affairs when a Scotsman lets his wee sister cow him. She's right, though. You treated Erica badly, yet she married you anyway. I will never marry again, so none of my siblings will have any fodder to use against me."

That sounds like a vow destined to be broken. I know Rory has terrible luck with women, and his three ex-wives clearly did more damage to his psyche than any of us know. But I believe with all my heart that he will find the right lass eventually. I want him to be happy.

Now that the family conference about how poor wee Jamie needs her brothers to run her life is over, I go for a walk to clear my head. My brothers can't stop me if I want to fly to America to visit Aidan and possibly meet a man. I've saved up enough money to pay for an airline ticket—economy class, of course. I don't relish a long flight in a cramped seat, but I'll do whatever it takes. I need to see more of the world than just Loch Fairbairn and my hometown of Ballachulish.

On my stroll down the streets of Loch Fairbairn, I bump into a few people I know. We say hello and smile at each other. Aye, I do love my home. But that doesn't change the fact that I need to expand my horizons. An entire world full of new places and new people awaits me out there.

I've just passed by my cousin Kirsty's metaphysical shop, which isn't open right now. It's after five o'clock. I would've liked to get her opinion on my plans to visit America, but that will have to wait. Kirsty went to university in England, so she might be able to help me convince my brothers to let me go on holiday alone.

The following day, Lachlan and Rory try one more time to talk me out of going to America. I understand their concerns, and I even appreciate that they want to look out for me. But I am a grown woman. And my one serious relationship crashed and burned, leaving me confused and saddened by the loss of someone I had thought I would spend the rest of my life with. Trevor wasn't the right one after all. So, I will go elsewhere to hunt—um, *look* for a different sort of man. No, I shouldn't use the word hunt if I mean to get my brothers on my side in this matter. That sounds like I'll be scouring seedy clubs for a "hook-up," as my new sister-in-law Erica would say. I'm looking for a good man, not a one-night lover.

Thinking about Erica spurs me to pay her a visit. I arrive at the farmhouse to find Lachlan putting up fencing for the chickens I can see waddling about in a temporary fenced enclosure.

He waves to me and calls out, "*Madainn mhath*, Jamie. We weren't expecting to see you today."

"I came to see Erica."

He sets down the implements he'd been using and saunters over to me, where I've just stepped out of my car. "You want my wife? If you're planning to get her on your side with the barmy American man-hunt idea—"

"Och, Lachie, ye make it sound like I mean to brainwash her. Erica is very clever, and I need some advice from a woman."

"Dinnae expect Erica to condone your plan, just because of, ah…" Lachie winces and scratches his cheek. "How we met."

I roll my eyes. "Honestly, everyone knows the story of how you met Erica when you were trolling underground clubs for an anonymous shag. But that's not what I want her advice about."

Lachlan twists his mouth into a disapproving expression. But then he sighs, and his shoulders flag. "All right, go on."

Though I didn't need or want his permission, I decide not to harass him anymore. When I walk into the house, I find Erica in the kitchen with their wee bairn, my nephew Nicholas.

She notices me and smiles. "Hi, Jamie. What can I do for you?"

"I was hoping for a bit of advice. I'm sure Lachlan told you about my plan."

"Yep. My husband isn't too happy about that, but I told him he needs to stop treating you like a child just because you're the youngest sibling."

For a couple of seconds, I can't speak. "You don't think I'm insane?"

She laughs softly. "No, sweetie, I don't. You are a very smart cookie, and besides, you'll be with Aidan when you go to America. Probably won't meet a lot of single men in the wilds of Michigan, but who knows. I never thought I'd meet the love of my life in an underground club in Chicago."

"Thank you, Erica. Can I help you with your cooking?"

"Why don't you hang out with Nicky in the living room while I whip up lunch?"

"Aye, I'd love to spend time with my nephew."

My lunch with Erica and Lachlan is lovely, but I never imagined it would result in me getting what I wanted. But that very evening, that's what happens. I've been staying with Rory in his castle, Dùndubhan, for a while now. This evening, Rory and I are in the sitting room enjoying hot cocoa. All right, I'm drinking cocoa. Rory prefers to sip whisky.

Then Lachlan bursts into the room. "Did ye tell her yet, Rory?"

My most taciturn brother turns his head to look at Lachlan. "I thought I was meant to wait for you."

"Well, I'm here now. So, tell the lass."

Rory faces me. "Lachlan, Aidan, and I had a teleconference earlier and reached a decision. You may go to America, but you will travel on my jet."

"*Our* jet," Lachlan corrects. "We share it. Or have ye conveniently forgotten that?"

"Aye, fine, *our* jet."

Did my brothers actually just agree to let me go to America? I think they did. "When can I leave?"

My brothers glance at each other again, and Lachlan sighs heavily. "Tomorrow morning."

"I'd rather leave tonight. Maybe my Prince Charming is waiting for me in America."

Rory's expression becomes rather grave. "I wish you weren't so dead-set on finding a man. It's bad enough that Aidan is living with a woman he just met, but I worry more for you than I do for him. With good reason."

"I know that, Rory. But you know I'm not an eejit. Besides, Aidan will pick me up at the airport and keep an eye on me for you."

"Then you've given up on the idea of staying at Erica's house in Chicago."

"No. But I can visit with Aidan and his lass, then go to Chicago for a weekend."

Lachlan rubs his jaw. "We've done all we can do, Rory. Jamie won't give up, and the best we can do is make sure she's in safe hands. Aidan's lass has offered to let Jamie stay with them at her house in Michigan. We all know Aidan won't let anything happen to Jamie. But you will wait until tomorrow."

I can't wait to fall in love. I've dreamed about my Prince Charming since I was a little girl, and that desire has become even stronger lately. The men I've dated left me feeling less than enthusiastic about my prospects for getting married and starting a family, but I can't give up yet. I need to do something drastic to change my life and achieve my goals.

And my brothers have finally agreed to help me do that.

I rush up to Lachlan and kiss his cheek, then do the same for Rory. Cannae help grinning. "Thank you so much. I love you both."

"We love you too, Jamie. And if some American *cacan* breaks your heart, we will hunt him down and batter him."

The evening after my brothers gave up on changing my mind, I stand on the tarmac at the Inverness airport surrounded by my family, while they hug me and haver about how much they'll miss me. My sisters, Catriona and Fiona, urge me to be careful but also wish me success in finding an American man. The fact that Lachlan married an American lass proved to be the final nail in the coffin of the idea that I shouldn't leave home for a holiday on another continent.

"Scottish men can be so bloody pigheaded," Fiona says. "Maybe we should all try Americans instead."

I nod with sarcastic gravity. "Oh, aye, Catriona should definitely try that. Her British Bastard broke her heart, so she might as well branch out into another country."

Our father overheard what I said and saunters over to us. "What's wrong with a good Scotsman? Plenty of those for you lasses to choose from."

Ma hooks her arm around Da's and gives him a patient smile. "Let Jamie make her own decisions, Niall. Besides, after testing out American men, she might well decide to marry a Scot after all."

"As long as she's happy, that's all that matters."

Lachlan walks up the stairs with me, keeping a light hold on my elbow as we climb to the open door of the private jet. He walks with me onto the plane too. Then he hugs me. "Be careful, *gràidh*. You've never left Scotland before, and America is much different from our home here in the Highlands. Aidan will take care of you, but…" He hugs me again and kisses the top of my head. "You are my baby sister. I will always worry about you."

"If I find the right man, you won't need to worry so much." I make a shooing motion. "Now go on, Lachie. I don't think Erica wants you to escort me all the way to Michigan."

"No, my wife wouldn't like that."

My brother shuffles over to the door, then pauses to glance back at me. He smiles a little, seeming a wee bit melancholy.

I smile and wave. He'll get over his worry once he knows I'm with Aidan.

Lachlan finally exits the jet, and a moment later, one of the pilots emerges from the cockpit to close the door.

I rush over to a sofa that lies up against the wall and kneel on the seat to watch out the windows as the plane begins to roll down the runway. My throat tightens. My eyes burn. I'm about to cry, but that's rubbish. A grown woman doesn't cry simply because she's leaving her home for the first time. I never went away to university in England like my siblings did, instead choosing to earn my degree close to home. I certainly haven't visited America before, though Cat had done that when she was a grad student.

Once the initial rush of excitement wears off, I realize just how dead boring a long flight to another country really is. Traveling alone is, well, rather lonely. The pilots take turns visiting with me, apparently because they feel sorry for the lassie who's traveling alone. I appreciate the effort, but it only makes me feel more isolated. I've always been surrounded by MacTaggarts, from my brothers and sisters to my many cousins.

After three hours, I need to talk to someone I know. But instead of ringing either of my sisters, I dial the number for my cousin Jack. He groans when he picks up the call, sounding as if he'd been asleep.

"Hello, Jack, it's Jamie."

"Who?" He yawns loudly. "Bloody hell, Jamie. It's after midnight."

"Sorry. I just wondered if—Oh, never mind."

"You rang me, so now you need to explain yourself. Are ye already feeling homesick? I heard you were off on an American adventure."

Leave it to a psychotherapist to realize that without me saying a word. "Aye, I'm a wee bit homesick. I've tried to sleep, but I feel restless."

"Of course you do, *gràidh*. You're excited and anxious at the same time, which is to be expected when you're away on a holiday in another country—on another continent."

"You always know how to make me feel better, Jack. You're a wonderful therapist."

He chuckles. "I appreciate the compliment. But I haven't done anything. You just needed a sounding board, and I was glad to serve that purpose for you. Now, let's both go to bed. Aye?"

"You're right. Good night, Jack."

"Good night, Jamie. And have fun in America—if Aidan will let you. I doubt he's pleased with your plan to find an American man to marry."

"Why would Aidan care? He's Don Juan MacTaggart, after all. I expect he'll be happy about my plan. Aidan did fly to America to find a lass for himself."

Jack chuckles again. "Och, Jamie, you don't understand brothers. Good night again, lass."

By the time I wake in the wee hours of the morning, we're already flying across Michigan on our way to the Upper Peninsula. I eat a quick breakfast, then gaze out the windows, too excited to simply relax on the sofa or read a magazine. The closer we come to the Houghton County Memorial Airport, the more excited I feel. My pulse has quickened. As the jet descends, I move onto a window seat and stare out at the landscape that reveals itself little by little. I see trees, but at first, I can't make out much detail. Then it all comes into view. I have never seen a forest as lush and gorgeous as the ones here in the Upper Peninsula of Michigan. I watch the waters of Lake Superior as they whisk by beneath the jet and see whitewater splashing and breakers crashing onto the shore. We fly over what looks like a lift bridge too.

My American adventure is about to begin.

Chapter Three

Gavin

This morning, I feel surprisingly good. Maybe I don't like that my sister is shacking up with a virtual stranger, but that's one damn good reason why I need to stick around until I either figure out that Aidan isn't a scam artist or I've beaten him to death with a tree branch and buried the body in the woods where no one will ever find it. Yeah, it's possible I'm overreacting. But Calli is my family. She's my baby sister, and without our parents around to watch out for her, I'm the only one who can protect her.

While I lie here in the hunting shack, with only a comforter as a mattress, I reminisce about yesterday. I'd returned to the house after stashing my stuff in the shack, and I'd walked in on Aidan smooching with my sister. When I cleared my throat deliberately, Calli scuttled away from the Scottish guy. But Aidan simply gazed at me steadily, as if he had no intention of explaining himself or apologizing for making out with my sister in my presence.

Not that doing it in private would make me happy either.

During dinner, I'd razzed Aidan some more, strictly to find out what his limits are. He doesn't seem to have a button I can push to make him fly off the handle. Okay, that's good to know. He also doesn't seem to give a damn what I think, though he clearly wants to reassure me that Calli is in safe hands with him. He didn't say that outright, but I could tell that was what he meant every time he talked about his family.

The guy has five siblings. *Five.* The MacTaggarts have an even lineup, with three brothers and three sisters. Today, I'll meet one of his relatives—his sister Jamie.

As I'd exited the house last night, I'd called out over my shoulder, "I'll be within earshot of the house, Romeo."

"I'm known as Don Juan MacTaggart, not Romeo."

"Whatever." I raised two fingers and aimed them at him, then at my own eyes. "I'll be watching you, MacTaggart."

Aidan had smiled with no small amount of sarcasm. "That's very comforting. I'll sleep better just knowing you're there."

While he was in the master bedroom screwing my sister.

I get dressed and head for the house, ready for another round of former Marine versus cocky Scot. But I know that this morning, Calli and Aidan will be heading for the airport to pick up his little sister. They had invited me to go with them, but that seemed kind of weird. I don't know Jamie. She might feel uncomfortable with a stranger standing there beside her brother.

How old is Jamie MacTaggart? I hadn't thought to ask yesterday. She's probably a cute little fifteen-year-old who has pigtails and wears a plaid skirt. Aidan's older brother, Rory, had let his sister fly to America on his private jet all alone. So maybe she's a little older than fifteen. I'll find out soon enough.

Now, I climb down from the little shack, which has a wooden ladder for accessing the interior. Then I jog the short distance to the house and try to open the sliding glass doors at the back side. It won't budge. Calli must have locked the doors overnight. I knock on the glass.

Calli emerges from the hallway dressed in a satin robe. She halts and peers at me from across the living room.

I'm standing here with one hand in my jeans pockets and the other knocking on the glass, waiting to be admitted into the house. The puppies race up to me from behind. I'd come through the yard gate and hadn't noticed Mandy and Misty. They must've been around the corner of the house, where there's a small area that's part of the yard. Now, they jump up and down while licking my hands and pawing at my jeans. Jeez, women were never this excited to see me. Calli's puppies have always been kind of hyper.

I wave at Calli.

Finally, my sister secures her robe more tightly around herself and trots over here to open the doors.

Misty starts bouncing up and down like a pogo stick, her feet lifting several inches off the ground with every bounce. The puppy manages to slather her tongue over my hand while still pogo-sticking around me.

I grimace. Slimy puppy saliva isn't my favorite thing. Who knows what these dogs have eaten today? Might be rotting rat carcasses or smelly insects.

Calli aims an overly cheerful smile at me. She's trying too hard for sure. "Morning, Gav. Are the girls being pests?"

"No, they're fine." The only pest in the vicinity is the asshat who seduced my sister. "You planning to let me in? Or is what's-his-name walking around buck naked in there?"

"Of course you can come in, Gavin."

She moves aside, waving for me to walk into the house.

I shuffle inside and throw Calli a sidelong glance.

My sister bites her lip and hunches her shoulders.

The puppies bound after me while I make a beeline for the kitchen bar and mutter, "So glad Mom and Dad aren't here to see this. Calli shacking up with a stranger."

Calli clearly didn't hear what I said, and I never intended for her to hear it. As much as I don't like this situation, I have no choice but to accept it for now. So, I let out an annoyed sigh and park my ass on the nearest stool, facing my sister.

Mandy and Misty had followed me into the house, and now, their ears perk up like they heard something. Their heads swivel toward the hallway in unison. Then the puppies take off in the direction of the spare bedroom.

They must have heard or smelled the Scottish asshat. I hope he slept alone last night, but I kind of doubt it. Something way more disturbing has happened, though, and I forget all about Don Juan. Surprise makes me stop blinking briefly, and I point at Calli's face. "You're blushing."

She lays a hand on her cheek, seeming as surprised as I am.

"Why are you blushing, Calli?" I wait for five seconds—yeah, I counted—and then rest one arm on the bar and drum my fingers on the surface. "You're sleeping with him, aren't you?"

My sister marches up to me and lifts her chin while trying to give me a tough stare. "Do you really want to talk about my sex life?"

Oh, shit. I should've thought about that before I asked if she was screwing Aidan. Because no, I do not want to hear about Calli's sex life. The very idea of that makes me a little queasy. "No, I don't need to hear about that."

"Then accept that it's none of your business."

I frown and tap one finger on the countertop. "What's wrong with you, C? For years, you didn't even date—as far as I know. When I called a week ago, you didn't say anything about a guy, and now you're shacked up with him. I don't understand, that's all."

Calli just stares at me.

The look of despair on her face shatters me, and I soften my tone. "I'm sorry, okay? Maybe it is none of my business. But I love you, Calli. You're the only family I've got—besides Tara, who's a good kid but kind of ditsy. You're supposed to be my level-headed sister, the one I can count on to make sense."

"Sorry I disappointed you. But you're acting like I committed a capital offense by getting involved with a man. I like Aidan. You've been spending time with him. Do you really think he's a Euro-trash gigolo taking advantage of me?"

I slump on the stool and release a long sigh. "No. I don't think that."

Barking erupts from down the hallway, a sure sign that Don Juan is about to waltz into the living room. Calli's expression shifts from anxious to excited in a heartbeat.

I gape at her. "Now you're smiling. I may not like you sleeping with Aidan, but I have to admit I've never seen you this happy before. Ever. When you look at him, you get…gushy."

Calli stares at me, eyes wide.

I nod slowly. "Yep, that's right. You moon over him, and I'm guessing you don't even realize you're doing it. Man, you've got it bad, don't you?"

She clamps her teeth down on her lips and veers her gaze to the kitchen cabinets.

Oh, yeah, I know exactly what's going on here. I can't help laughing a little bit, though it's not derisive. "At least promise me if you marry him, you won't move to Scotland."

Her gaze veers back to me. "I'm not marrying Aidan."

"No? You say that like there's no way in hell you'd even consider it. You always wanted to get married. I remember you acting out fake weddings between your Barbie and Ken dolls."

"That was a long time ago."

I tip my head to the side, studying her. "What happened to you, C? Whatever's going on with you, I hope you know you can tell me about it."

Her mouth opens, like she's about to speak.

But then Don Juan himself saunters into the living room, and any chance I had to get the truth out of Calli has vanished. For now, at least.

After breakfast, Calli and Aidan jump in the fancy car his brother had rented for him and head for the airport. The puppies and I watch bad talk shows on TV while we wait for the new guest to arrive. Eventually, I give up on the talk shows and return to my little cabin for a while, if only to get a brief break from the sweet but extremely rambunctious puppies.

I've just started to make my way back to the house when I hear the distinctive sound of gravel crunching on the driveway. Calli and the Scots must be pulling up. The puppies race into the house, making the dog door thwap, just as I reach the sliding glass doors. I push them open, stepping inside. Calli and Aidan stand near the front door, holding hands. But I can't focus on that for long enough to say something snarky. No, my full attention is consumed by the beautiful girl who giggles as Mandy and Misty lick her shapely ankles.

Who is that?

Her long, golden-brown hair shivers every time she moves her head, and her hazel eyes shimmer with flecks of emerald green. Damn, she's gorgeous. When she smiles, I swear I can feel the warmth of that expression infiltrating me.

"You can love me more later," the girl tells the puppies. Then she straightens, smoothing out her skirt, and turns toward me. "You must be Calli's brother. I'm Jamie, Aidan's sister."

I swallow hard and suddenly can't remember how to speak, not coherently, anyway. I might be speaking gibberish, but I can't focus on any of the words that come out of my mouth. "Hey. Nice to, uh, meet you. I'm Gavin. Douglas. Calli's brother, Gavin Douglas."

Jamie smiles at me, and the cutest dimples form in her cheeks. "Nice to meet you too, Gavin."

She must think I'm a complete moron. Jamie MacTaggart is not a pigtailed girl but a full-grown and voluptuous woman. I can't seem to get my brain in gear while I'm looking at her, which is something I've never experienced before. I've never seen a woman as beautiful and sweet as Aidan's little sister.

I suddenly realize I'm holding Jamie's hand. Did we shake hands? I've got no frigging idea. But her palm feels warm and soft, and that fact makes me wonder how warm and soft she is everywhere else. I swear she's gazing at me with the same desire that I've felt since the moment I laid eyes on her.

Aidan grasps Jamie's wrist and tugs, but she doesn't release my hand. His lips pucker, and he tugs again. "Let me show you to your room."

Yeah, he spoke those words in a tone that proves he's not as unflappable as he likes for me to think. Aidan is getting irritated. Well, now he knows how I felt when I found him shacking up with my baby sister.

But I still can't tear my focus away from Jamie.

Aidan drags Jamie away from me, forcing us to let go of each other's hands as he hauls her down the hallway. She keeps glancing back at me and smiling. Once the two of them disappear from view, Calli rounds on me.

She plants her hands on her hips, and her lips kink up on one side in a sly, smug smile. "Gee, Gav, looks to me like you're going gushy over Aidan's sister."

"What?" I blink several times quickly, but that only breaks about eighty percent of my trance. "I was being friendly to your guest, that's all."

"Uh-huh. Flirting is a requirement for proper etiquette?"

I splutter because I still can't think straight, and Calli's being ridiculous. "All I said was hello."

My sister grins. "No, you said 'uh, hey, nice to meet you, can I please shave your legs for you.' Right before you mooned at her."

"I did not say that."

"Okay, maybe I ad-libbed the shaving part. But you were stammering and gaping at her like you'd never seen a pretty girl before."

I clench my teeth. "I'm not the one getting naked with somebody I barely know."

"But you'd like to make time with Aidan's little sister."

"Well—" Damn, she's right. And I hate that. Maybe I don't like the Aidan-Calli situation, but I've pretty much lost all my leverage in that regard since the moment I saw Jamie. I shove my hands into my jeans pockets. "You're a grown-up, so you can do what you want."

Calli struggles not to grin at me again. "Gee, thanks, Gav."

No matter what Calli says, I never "mooned" at Jamie MacTaggart.

I might've gawked. A little. Hardly at all, really.

Jeez, I am so screwed.

Chapter Four

Jamie

od an Donais, Gavin Douglas is the handsomest and sexiest man I've ever seen. No film star could compete with his looks, his muscular body, or his voice. I could listen to him read the phone book, followed by a recitation of the Encyclopedia Britannica. Oh, aye, everything about Gavin turns me on. If Aidan likes Calli, then her brother must be a good person too. He's spent a day or two with Gavin and Calli, so he must have gotten to know the man with the beautiful, pale-brown eyes.

A sigh rushes out of me. I could gaze into Gavin's eyes all day long.

My brother virtually drags me into what looks like a guest bedroom. I got a glimpse of another, larger bedroom at the end of the hall, which must be the main suite. That means Calli sleeps in there. That realization brings up questions I need to ask my brother.

Aidan shuts the door behind us and frowns at me.

I set my hands on my hips. "Are you sleeping with Calli?"

"None of your business, Jamie."

"Ooh, Aidan the Magnificent is getting testy. This must be a first. After all, you're the cheerful one who never growls at anybody." I can't help smirking. "But you've fallen head over heels for Calli Douglas, and ye dinnae want to talk about that, do you?"

"Ahmno head over heels." He thumps the top of his head with one fist. "See? My head is still on top."

"Very funny. But I can't give up on harassing you. Might as well answer my question, or else you'll have no leverage to make me tell you anything."

My brother flattens his lips and squints at me for a moment. Then he bows his head and blows out a breath. *Mhac na galla.* You're right, but I still can't answer your question. It wouldn't be chivalrous to share that information."

"All right, I understand that. I'm sorry for poking my nose into your business, but you were being a bit overbearing."

"I'm sorry for that."

"Thank you." I tip my head to the side and study him. "You really like this lass, don't you? The man who loves women finally found one who makes him want more than a fling."

"Aye, I do feel that way about Calli."

I sit down on the bed, clasping my hands on my lap. "You said you'd find an American wife, and you did."

He sits down beside me. "Calli isn't my wife, not yet. And I dinnae know if she ever will be."

"The way she looks at you, I'd say it's a dead certainty you will marry her."

"What about you and Gavin?"

I roll my eyes. "Honestly, Aidan, I met the man thirty seconds ago. I'm attracted to him, but that's all."

"Aye, of course. I'm sorry." He pushes up off the bed. "We should go back out there."

I trail after Aidan as we exit the guest bedroom. He walks rather more swiftly than seems necessary, but I reckon he's anxious about me and Gavin—or maybe he's worried about whether Calli will ever marry him.

Gavin is nowhere in sight. That fact makes me feel a wee bit deflated.

But I recover quickly and sit on the sofa with Calli. "Sooo, we should get to know each other, Calli. Since you're going to be my sister-in-law."

Aidan throws his hands up, his jaw drops, and he flaps his head. "I didn't say a word to her."

"You didn't need to, Aidan. I have eyes, and ahmno an eejit. Besides, you told everyone you were coming to America to find a wife like Lachlan did."

Aidan shifts his attention to Calli, his expression almost pleading, as if he hopes she can save him from having to discuss the subject any further.

Calli speaks to me but keeps her focus on Aidan. "It's a bit early to think about that."

I lift my brows. "Aye, but Aidan has a way of convincing women to do almost anything."

"Does he now."

Aidan's jaw drops again as he shakes his head.

Calli puckers her lips, but it seems like a teasing expression.

I decide to take pity on the pair of them and change the subject. "Where's Gavin?"

"He's staying in the hunting cabin out in the woods," Calli tells me. "We'll see him again at lunch."

I sag against the sofa. No Gavin until lunch? I want to chat to him and… I don't know. Well, if I'm completely honest with myself, I want to beg him to shag me. I've never been the sort of lass who engages in casual sex, though. Something about Gavin makes me want to do all manner of wild things.

We could shag in that hunting cabin.

Bloody hell. What is wrong with me?

Since Aidan and Calli clearly need a bit of time alone to discuss things, I take a shower in the guest bedroom. Washing off all that travel grime feels wonderful, especially since the guest bathroom includes lovely little scented soaps and soft shower poufs.

I do see Gavin at lunch, though Aidan insists that I sit beside him at the table while Gavin and Calli sit on the opposite side. Neither man wants his sister to be within touching distance of the other. Our conversations revolve around boring things like the weather, the scenery, and the tourist destinations in the area. I would love to explore the Keweenaw Peninsula, which I've just learned is the name of this part of the Upper Peninsula of Michigan. And I now know all about the copper mining that used to take place in this region, beginning in ancient times and then starting up again thousands of years later in the eighteen hundreds.

I want to chat to Gavin alone. When Calli gives me a tight smile, I'm dead sure that she wants to be alone with Aidan too.

Calli gets what she wants when Aidan takes her into the master bedroom. They both seem tired, just like I am and Gavin must be too.

Gavin simply walks out the back door and disappears into the woods, carrying a large, battery-operated torch.

While I'm lying in bed, trying to sleep, I keep fantasizing about sneaking into that wee cabin so I can crawl under the covers and lick my way down his chest, lower and lower, until I reach his cock. Those fantasies make me so randy that I need to *fannadh*, but touching myself isn't as fulfilling as shagging Gavin would be. With a body like his, he could drive me to the heights of ecstasy. No man has ever done that for me. The laddies I've dated just wanted a quick poke, then they either left or rolled over and fell asleep.

Somehow, I know Gavin wouldn't be like that.

In the evening, we're all jeeked. It's been an exhausting but wonderful day, getting to know Calli and especially Gavin. He has a wry sense of humor that I love, and every time he looks at me, I feel like he wants to kiss me. I want that, for sure. Being this attracted to a man I met this morning seems irrational, but I dinnae care.

A big yawn splits my mouth open. Time for bed, alone.

I amble down the hallway and pop my head through the open doorway to Calli and Aidan's room, wishing them a good night. Then I shuffle into my room, shut the door, and collapse onto the bed. I almost forget to change into my pajamas, but quickly realize I don't want to sleep while fully clothed. The moment I've curled up under the covers, I fall asleep.

When I wake in the morning, I feel more refreshed than I have in ages. Maybe it's the clean Michigan air doing that to me. Dinnae care what the reason is. All right, maybe I do have a clue why I feel this way. The word starts with a G and ends with "avin."

I wander out of my room, heading for the kitchen. Maybe I'll cook breakfast for Calli and Aidan, to show my appreciation for the way they've handled my attraction to Gavin. Aidan clearly wanted to tell me to go home right away, but he didn't do it. He understands that I'm a grown woman and not a bloody eejit.

Something crackles under my foot just as I've reached the bar. It's a scrap of crumpled paper that was ripped from a larger sheet, but there's nothing on it. I bend over to pick it up.

"Good morning, Jamie. Thanks for the fantastic wake-up call."

The sound of Gavin's voice makes every hair on my body stand up. A thrill rushes through me, and I spin round to smile at him. "I didn't give you a wake-up call, since I had no idea you were here."

"Oh, you woke me up for damn sure." He skims his gaze over my body, clearly noting my pajamas that consist of short-shorts and a skimpy top that has spaghetti straps. My nipples are jutting too, thanks to the way his sexy voice affects me. Gavin licks his lips, then veers his attention to my face. "That's a view any man would love to see first thing in the morning."

When I had bent over, did he get a glimpse of my cleavage? Part of me hopes he got a full view of my tits. But it isn't fair. I haven't glimpsed any naughty bits of him.

I toss the paper into the rubbish bin and wave toward the kitchen. "I was just about to make breakfast for all of us."

He eyes me up and down again. "Would you like to go for a walk first? Our keepers aren't up yet."

"A walk would be lovely."

Gavin gives me a sensual smile and winks. "Might want to get dressed first. It's mating season out there, and your PJs would draw in all the horny bucks."

"I thought deer rutted in the fall. It's still summer."

He chuckles. "I'm sure you could make every male of every species as horny as hell. You've sure done that to me."

I can't believe we're discussing the rutting habits of animals. But oddly, I am getting randy. "Wait here while I get dressed. Then we'll go for a walk."

As I'm leaving the guest room, now fully clothed and ready for a nature hike, I bump into Aidan. He's just left the room he shares with Calli, and he discreetly shuts the door behind him.

"*Madainn mhath*, Jamie." He studies me briefly. "You seem even more cheerful than usual. Gavin must be in the house, aye?"

"He is." I fold my arms over my chest. "You're very relaxed and satisfied this morning, so Calli must be in that bedroom. Aye?"

"When did you become a *smuilceag*? My sweet little sister never would have discussed my sex life."

My brother just called me a chit. I am cheeky, but only because Aidan started it. "If ye dinnae want me to comment on your love life, then don't comment on mine."

"I'm glad to see you so happy, that's all I meant."

Lifting onto my toes, I kiss his cheek. "And I'm glad to see you so happy too."

We stroll into the living room together.

Gavin is sitting on a stool at the bar. When he sees Aidan, his brows lift. "Are you coming for a walk with us?"

"No, I'll stay here. Calli is still sleeping. But you two should go out there and enjoy the wilderness."

Calli emerges from the master bedroom then, dressed and wearing a soft smile. When she sees Aidan, her expression broadens into a glowing grin. My brother slips an arm round her waist, tugging her into his side. "Now that you're awake, *gràidh*, we should all have breakfast together. Gavin and Jamie can delay their walk until later."

I glance at Gavin, who shrugs. "Aye, we can wait. I'll make breakfast."

Gavin leaps off the stool. "I'll help you."

"Thank you."

He winces. "Fair warning. I'm not the best chef in the world."

I clasp his hand. "We don't need a five-star chef. The full Scottish breakfast isn't posh."

"Good. Then I'm definitely in."

Aidan and Calli snuggle up on the sofa to watch television while Gavin and I have fun cooking up a meal for the four of us. He might not be an expert cook, but he listens to my advice and instructions, following them precisely. Soon, we have a delicious breakfast feast ready to eat. We go out into the backyard to enjoy the food at the picnic table. Calli's dogs, Mandy and Misty, stay close by to snap up any tidbits that might fall onto the grass.

After breakfast, my brother suggests we should play Monopoly. Gavin and Calli don't understand why, not until Aidan tells them that Lachlan and Erica had played the game when they first met. It's become a sort of MacTaggart family legend. Aidan adds elements to the story that Lachlan never mentioned. I'm fair certain Calli and Gavin realize my brother is concocting a porky, but they play along for the fun of it.

We play six rounds of Monopoly. I win four of them. Gavin wins one, and Calli also wins one. Aidan couldn't get out of jail.

Gavin insists on making lunch alone. That surprises me, and I have to ask a question.

"I thought you didn't know how to cook," I say. "Just this morning, you told us that you aren't skilled at crafting meals."

"And it's true. But I can whip up a mean hamburger."

He does just that too. Gavin seasoned the ground beef with "secret ingredients" that he wouldn't divulge, not even to me. I leaned over to whisper into his ear that I'd make it worth his while if he shared the secret. But he only smirked and said, "You could torture it out of me, and I wouldn't mind at all."

Oh, aye, this man has captivated me. And I love it.

Chapter Five

Gavin

Aidan decided to stay in the house while I take the girls out into the fenced backyard to play with the puppies. They worship Jamie and can't seem to stop themselves from licking every inch of her exposed skin. I'd love to do that too, but in a different way. For a few minutes, the three of us take turns tossing a toy around for the puppies. Then Jamie and I start to excuse ourselves so we can enjoy that walk we'd planned on taking.

But Calli has a different suggestion. "Why don't you guys take the puppies with you? They love to get out of the yard, and I have retractable leashes for them."

I roll my eyes. "They'll probably yank us off our feet, using their leashes to drag us around while we're flat on our bellies."

"You love my girls, Gavin. Why else would you roll around on the ground tickling their tummies?"

Jamie laughs. "Gavin does that?"

"Absolutely. He's a softy at heart."

I aim a sarcastically stern look at her. "Don't spread that rumor, Calli. I have a badass rep to uphold."

Jamie nudges me with her elbow. "You don't need to uphold your reputation. Everyone who sees you knows you're a powerful man."

My sister puckers her lips like she's desperately trying not to smirk.

I squint at her. "You better not be laughing at me in your mind."

Calli's laughter splutters out of her.

Sighing, I shake my head at her. "I might need to disown you, C. No way can I have a sister who's a... What did you call it, Jamie?"

"A *smuilceag*. It means she's a cheeky chit."

"Yeah, that fits Calli to a tee."

Jamie eyes me sideways. "Do you even know what a chit is?"

"Hey, I've watched British TV shows. A chit is a sassy girl."

My sister never used to be quite so sarcastic, but I have to admit, I like this new side of her. She's a stronger person than she used to be, though I can still see traces of the fear she's been hiding for years. Calli has never wanted to talk about it. I know at least part of the reason for that fear stems from that guy Rade. For now, I won't interrogate her about that. Instead, I'll spend the afternoon strolling through the woods with the prettiest girl I've ever seen and the world's most insane puppies.

Calli goes into the house. I'm positive I don't want to know what she and Aidan will be getting up to while I'm enjoying an innocent walk with Jamie. Don Juan will probably screw my sister on the sofa.

"Are we away?" Jamie asks. "That means do you want to go yet?"

"Guess that's the Scottish way of saying that. It's cute." We already have the leashes on the puppies. I hand one leash to Jamie. "You can take Mandy. She's smaller and should be easier for you to handle. Misty can be a jumping bean and could knock you over if she catches you off guard."

"I can handle two wee pups."

A laugh snorts out of me. "These dogs are fifty times stronger than they look."

"Hmm, are you afraid you can't handle three girls?"

"Three?" I suddenly realize what she meant and can't resist taking the bait. "Mandy and Misty can be rambunctious, but you will be putty in my hands."

"I'd like that."

Once we reach the gate, I swing it open to let the three ladies go first. Then I slip my hand into Jamie's palm. Her head jerks up, and her lips curl into a sweetly surprised smile—and she threads her fingers with mine. I haven't even taken her on a real date. Maybe this is the backwards way of wooing a woman, but I don't give a damn. Doing it the so-called right way ended in heartbreak. I might have just met Jamie yesterday, but I already know she would never treat me the way Leanne did.

I lead my little harem down the widest path in these woods. Most game trails are pretty narrow, but the people who used to live in the house that Calli's been renting widened those trails. They must've liked to go for walks. The old hunting cabin, which is really more of a shack, had been built by a previous owner.

We talk about silly things, like movies and music. She informs me that bagpipes are the best instrument on earth, but I know she's only trying to test my limits of how Scottish I want to go. For her, I'd change my accent and wear a kilt every day. And yeah, I tell her that.

Jamie laughs, and it's the sweetest sound I've ever heard. "You don't need to go that far. Even my brothers don't wear kilts every day." She already had her arm hooked around mine, but now she snuggles up to me and rests her chin on my arm. "I would never want you to change your accent. I love the way you talk."

"Thanks. I love the way you talk too."

"You're so sweet, Gavin. I wouldn't have expected that from a former military man."

"Have you met a lot of those types?"

"Aye. I have cousins who served, like Munro, Logan, and Magnus. My friend Thane Buchanan also served." She studies me for a moment as we continue strolling through the woods. "They fought in combat situations. Were you sent to a war zone too?"

"Yeah, in Afghanistan."

"I had a feeling you must have seen combat. The men I know who were in the military have the same sort of reticence about their pasts."

Am I reticent? Well, I guess I must be. Never considered the possibility. But talking about my past isn't my favorite thing to do.

Jamie rests her cheek on my arm. "It's all right if you don't want to discuss it. We just met, so you have no reason to trust me with your secrets."

"What makes you think I have secrets?"

She smiles, and her cheeks dimple. "It's dead obvious, Gavin."

"Right. It would be. I'm good at being stoic, but hiding things never works out for me. I guess that's why my ex-wife left me." I stop dead, staring at empty space, as a chill sweeps over me. Why in the hell did I blurt that out? *I guess that's why my ex-wife left me.* I couldn't have sounded more pathetic if I'd started crying. "Uh, sorry. I shouldn't have said that. Just came out. Kinda ruins my image, doesn't it?"

"Oh, tosh." Jamie turns toward me, though she keeps holding my hand. "Having a painful past doesn't make you less of a man. My brother Lachlan used to think the same way, but Erica helped him move past all of that rubbish. Everyone knows his ex-wife was a rotten cow. Rory's first wife was that way too."

"Really? Huh. I kind of assumed all your brothers were like Aidan, annoyingly happy and good with the ladies."

"Aye, Aidan is a sweet man. But even he had some issues. I shouldn't share that with you, though, since it's Aidan's story, not mine."

"I get that." I realize something she just said, and it triggers my curiosity. "Rory's first wife? How many does he have?"

"Three ex-wives. He needs to find a good woman, but he's too afraid to step into the romance waters again."

I smirk. "He's probably worried a giant shark will eat him."

"So now lasses are sharks?" Jamie wags a finger at me and tsks. "Dinnae be a sexist, Gavin. I won't let you kiss me if you do."

Did she just suggest she might let me kiss her? Sounded that way. Damn, I want to kiss her so badly that I can almost taste it. I'd love to taste her, for sure. But I know she was joking.

I clasp her hand. "Let's keep walking while I tell you a little bit about me."

"You don't have to do that."

"I know. But I'd like to tell you, if you're comfortable with that."

"Of course."

We start ambling again, which is something I can honestly say I've never done before. Walking, sure. Hiking too. But never ambling. It feels good to be with someone who has no preconceived expectations and just wants to spend time with me.

Might as well dive into the shark-infested waters. "Before I can tell you about my ex-wife, Leanne, you need to understand what happened before my parents died. Calli is eight years younger than me, but she wound up taking care of me. That was later on, though. First, you should know that I joined the Marines straight out of high school, though I never imagined I'd wind up in combat. I wanted to serve my country, that was all. But I wound up getting deployed to Afghanistan."

Jamie holds my hand more firmly, but she doesn't speak.

"I, um, met Leanne..." My voice trails off, and I can't seem to convince my brain to let me say anything else. Memories of Afghanistan replay in my mind, showing me all the horrors in vivid detail. I stop walking and shut my eyes. "Can't talk about this. I'm sorry, Jamie."

"No need to be sorry. We hardly know each other, so it's none of my concern."

"Maybe we should go back to the house. I'm feeling wiped out all of a sudden."

Jamie doesn't complain or ask any questions. She just leads me back to the house. The puppies have even stopped bouncing around, like they can sense I'm not in a playful mood. I shouldn't get this way every time somebody mentions my military service, but I can't help it.

We walk back to the house faster than we had ambled away from it. That's not because Jamie wants to speed up. Once we reach the yard fence, I open the gate to let the puppies in, then shut it as Misty and Mandy race through the dog door into the house.

I grasp Jamie's upper arms. "Sorry about the sudden end to our nice little walk."

"No worries. I understand why you don't like to talk about your time in the Marines. I told you I have relatives and friends who have gone through similar things."

She's so damn sweet and empathetic that I need to make sure she understands. "I'm messed up, Jamie, and it's because of more than my military service or the fact that my marriage fell apart. My parents died five years ago, and I didn't handle it well. We just met, and I don't want you to get dragged down into my shit."

Jamie lays her palms on my chest. "That's my decision to make, not yours."

"I know. But—"

"Let me decide, Gavin."

I swallow hard and can't manage to say anything.

She moves closer with her body now inches away from mine. "Let's not discuss your past yet. I want to get to know you, but for now, I don't want to hear about your painful memories. We need to find out if we're compatible before we cross that bridge."

"You are a wonderful woman. Not sure I deserve you."

"I'm dead certain about that."

Her statement leaves me wondering whether she meant that she's positive I don't deserve her or that she believes I do deserve her. But like she said, we need to get better acquainted before we worry about that. She's gazing up at me with a serene expression, her hazel eyes glowing in the reflected sunshine, lighting up the green flecks in those irises.

I know I shouldn't ask, but…I can't help it. "Would you mind if I kissed you?"

"Not at all. I would love that."

How long has it been since I kissed any woman? Too damn long. I take hold of Jamie's upper arms and gently pull her closer until her body just barely touches mine. She tips her head back, exposing the slender column of her throat, and those hazel eyes shimmer with a deeper shade of brown, thanks to her pupils dilating. I could drown in those eyes and never want to be rescued.

She bites her bottom lip, releasing it so slowly.

I lower my head, brushing my nose against hers. Then I exhale a shallow breath and kiss her.

Jamie sags into me and fists her hand in my T-shirt. She exhales the sweetest little moan, and I tentatively slip my tongue between her lips. When she moans again, I take that as permission and push deeper into her mouth so I can coil my tongue around hers and tease the roof of her mouth with the tip. She wraps her arms around my waist. She must feel my dick hardening, but she doesn't shy away from that. Instead, she rocks her hips into me. I groan and delve deeper into her mouth, sliding my hands down to her ass.

"Dinner in five minutes!"

Though I hear those words, I can't understand the meaning or recognize who that is shouting at us. I go on kissing Jamie.

"Gavin! Jamie! Dinner in five minutes! If you don't get your butts in here, Aidan and I will eat everything, and you'll be grazing in the backyard with the squirrels."

Calli's voice finally penetrates my brain.

I reluctantly peel my mouth away from Jamie's lips. She seems a touch dazed, and I must look the same way. Kissing Jamie affected me like nothing else I've ever experienced before. I clear my throat. "Guess we'd better go into the house."

"Aye." That single syllable managed to convey everything I've been feeling too. "Aidan and Calli must have cooked for us. We wouldn't want to disappoint them."

I take Jamie's hand, leading her through the yard. As I reach for the handle on the sliding glass door, I pause to glance down at her. "Think I'd rather forage with the squirrels if it means I can kiss you more."

She grins. "I'd rather do that too."

But we head into the house instead. Sometimes being a mature adult really sucks.

Chapter Six

Jamie

In the morning, I wake up feeling so bloody fantastic that I almost can't believe I am awake. I must be dreaming, aye? There's no way Gavin actually kissed me, and that kiss absolutely could not have made me tingle and feel as if I might float away into outer space. But it did happen. I've kissed my fair share of men, but Gavin Douglas isn't just another lad. He's the sexiest, most virile, sweetest, and cleverest man I've ever known.

But, oh…that kiss.

I swear I can still taste him on my lips.

For a while, I simply lie here in my bed and revel in this feeling. I can't describe it, and I don't need to.

A knock rattles my door. "Rise and shine, Jamie. The rest of us are having breakfast, so if you want to eat, best get your erse out of bed."

"Haud yer wheesht, Aidan. I'll be there in a few minutes."

"Gavin might eat all the pancakes before you emerge from your cocoon."

"I need a shower first. So away and chew a brush, Don Juan."

My brother chuckles, and I hear his footfalls receding.

Aye, I essentially told him to sod off. Aidan was being bloody cheeky, so he can't blame me for cursing at him.

Ten minutes later, I walk out of my room having showered and dressed in record time. As I shuffle into the living room, I see Gavin and Aidan sitting on stools at the bar, chatting about who knows what while Calli watches them with an amused expression. Once I reach the kitchen area, I realize the men are discussing a very important subject.

Gavin smiles and winks at me, then slides an arm around my waist to pull me close. But he speaks to Aidan. "Come on, bro, you can't honestly believe that British soccer is better than American football."

"Americans don't play football. The rest of the world knows that the term football refers to the sport that involves a round ball that no one catches. They kick it about instead. Only American heathens call it 'soccer.' "

"Soccer is a sport for pansies. Try real football sometime, and we'll see how tough you really are. I'll even pay for your ticket so you can watch the Packers in action."

"Packers? Do you work in a factory?"

Gavin gives my brother a sarcastically disappointed look. "The Green Bay Packers. It's a football team."

"Isn't Green Bay in Wisconsin? I thought you were from Minnesota."

"Yeah, but I prefer the Packers. Just because I live in Minneapolis doesn't mean I'm required to support their team."

"How strange. If I decided to support Chelsea instead of Kilmarnock, I'd be run out of Scotland."

Gavin scrunches up his face. "What are Chelsea and Kilmarnock?"

"Football teams. Kilmarnock is in the Highlands."

"Uh-huh. Do you play so-called football?"

Aidan smirks. "Aye, but I prefer shinty."

Calli smacks two plates down on the bar, one for Aidan and one for Gavin. "Stuff your faces, boys. We girls are sick of listening to you two gab about sports. Aren't we, Jamie?"

"Oh, aye, we are."

Calli offers me a plate and a glass of orange juice, then she and I sit on the sofa to enjoy our breakfast and chat about much more interesting topics. We haver about how silly men are about sports as well as what we'd like to do today. The men don't seem to pay any attention to our conversation—until we begin to discuss what we should do today.

"Aidan and I should take you two on a tour of the Keweenaw Peninsula," Calli suggests. "The scenery is just gorgeous this time of year."

My brother crosses his arms over his chest as he turns his attention to Calli. "Why dinnae we let Gavin and Jamie go sightseeing on their own."

I can't help laughing. "Desperate to have a poke, eh?"

"Falbh a ghabhail do ghnùis airson cac."

Gavin lifts one brow. "And for those of us who don't speak Gaelic, that means…"

"Away and take your face for a shite."

The man who kissed me yesterday, and did it so thoroughly that I'm still weak in the knees, gives Aidan a hard stare. It's pure sarcasm, though. "Don't speak to a lady that way, asshat."

I kiss Gavin's cheek. "Dinnae worry about me. I can handle any of my brothers, even all three at once."

"Yeah, I'm sure you can."

Aidan glances down at Gavin's arm, the one wrapped around my waist. His lips pucker briefly, then he sighs. "Let's go sightseeing. Dinnae want to leave you two alone, since I dinnae want to walk in on you two snogging. Actually, I don't want that to happen when I'm not in the vicinity either. So just dinnae touch my sister at all."

Does Aidan think I haven't kissed Gavin yet? He knows full well that I am not a virgin, yet he keeps talking about me as if I'm an innocent wee lassie. I still remember the day I bumped into Aidan at a chemist's shop, and he realized I'd been about to buy a box of condoms. I think he nearly had a heart attack then.

The four of us jump into Aidan's car, which Lachlan had hired for him without Aidan's consent. It's a lovely convertible, so we put the top down to get the best view of the surroundings. Despite the suggestion that we would go sightseeing, we end up simply visiting a few shops in the nearby villages. Not that I mind. As long as Gavin is with me, I'm happy to browse the silly trinkets and postcards on display in the shops.

Aidan and Calli pretend to be browsing a different section of the shop, but their plan is dead obvious. They want to keep an eye on us while pretending not to do that. Aidan is a bad liar and a bad actor. Calli isn't much better.

Gavin leads me over to a display of socks and taps his finger on one pair. "I think your brother Rory would love these."

"Do you? Why is that? Since you haven't met Rory, I'm curious about your reasoning."

"You mentioned that Rory is known as the Ogre of Loch Fairbairn. That sounds like he's probably a Bigfoot in disguise." He taps the package of socks again. "And these must have been modeled after him."

I take a good look at the socks and can't help smiling. "There are several variations of these. Which one do you claim must be a depiction of my brother?"

Gavin crooks his thumb under his chin and taps one finger on his mouth. "It's probably the socks that show a Bigfoot being abducted by aliens."

"I must have overlooked that one."

He snatches a pair of socks off the rack and holds it out to me. "Here you go. Rory would love these, I'm sure."

Laughter splutters out of me, and other customers give me strange looks. But I dinnae care. I accept the socks and study the image on them. It does indeed show a spaceship beaming a light down on a Bigfoot. I thrust the socks at Gavin and feign being offended. "If you gave these to Rory, he'd hurl you all the way around the globe and back again."

"Damn. He's that strong, huh? Well, maybe I should pick a different gift for him. We could give Lachlan the socks."

"You would do better to give them to Aidan. He loves jokes."

"I have noticed that." Gavin leads me over to a different display, one that showcases novelty mugs. "Oh, yeah, this is definitely more Rory's style."

Laughter bursts out of me again, garnering more odd looks that I ignore. "You think the Steely Solicitor wants a cup that's painted with neon colors? Pink, blue, yellow, orange. Oh, aye, that's Rory's style."

"I thought so." He snags a scarf off another display and slings it around his neck. "See? If it looks good on me, it'll be Rory's style for sure."

"Aye, because you two have so much in common—never having met or spoken to each other." This time I struggle to restrain my laughter and partially succeed. "Neon shades flatter you, Gavin."

"Don't they? I look hot in anything, though." He snatches up a pink hat. "See? I was right."

He is adorable when he's playful. I can't stop myself from leaning into Gavin and gazing up at him with what must look like adoration. No man has ever done silly things just to make me smile, and no one else has ever made me feel so good.

Gavin decides against buying all but one of the trinkets. He insists on giving me the Bigfoot UFO socks.

I clasp them to my chest and flutter my lashes. "Oh, thank you, Gavin. I will cherish these and wear them every day."

"Yeah, Rory ought to love that."

When and if Gavin ever meets my brother, I might need to make sure Rory has drunk half a bottle of whisky first.

Gavin does buy the neon-colored mug—for Aidan. My youngest brother grins and thanks Gavin profusely, and also sarcastically. I show Aidan my new socks, and he sighs, telling me that I risk developing an incurable disease called Conspiracy Theory-itis if I continue to fraternize with an American.

"You'll catch it too," Gavin tells Aidan. "You're fraternizing with an American, you know—my baby sister."

"No, Calli is immune. The disease only affects former US Marines who are flirting with my sister."

"Ah, so it's one of those bioengineered things. You should write a paper on it for a medical journal."

Calli and I start walking out of the shop, and the men trail after us while continuing to exchange sarcastic comments. By the time we get back to Calli's house, it's lunchtime. I am unusually hungry. I reckon visiting kitschy shops takes more out of a person than it seems like it should. Having fun is tiring, but in a good way. We enjoy our afternoon meal in the backyard while sitting at the picnic table. Gavin and I are on one side with Calli and Aidan directly across from us. Aye, the meal includes a fair amount of teasing and laughter.

Once the meal is over, Aidan makes a bizarrely sudden announcement. "Calli and I are going for a drive. Alone."

Gavin aims a hard stare at my brother. "I'm watching you."

Aidan glances at me, then returns his attention to Gavin. "Got my eye on you too."

Though my brother attempted to look tough when he spoke those words, he couldn't pull it off. It's just not in his nature. I know he was teasing Gavin, anyway.

Aidan clears his throat. "We will be away overnight. Please do not destroy Calli's home in the meantime. You'll need to care for the puppies too."

I salute. "Aye-aye, Captain Don Juan."

He squints at me. "There will be no *coinbheineadh* while I'm away, and absolutely no *feis*. Dinnae want you to catch *olcas*."

"Aidan! *Mhac na galla*. This is beyond the pale. You're behaving like Rory would in this situation, assuming I'm a brainless bairn who needs to be told what not to do."

"Sorry." Aidan winces. "I suppose I am going a wee bit too far."

We all carry the remnants of our meal back into the house, then Aidan and Calli grab their bags and drive away in the car Lachlan had hired.

That means Gavin and I are alone. Completely alone.

We settle onto the sofa, side by side but without touching each other. I reckon we're both slightly nervous about being genuinely alone together for the first time.

He stretches his arm out across the sofa's back, turning slightly toward me. "What were those things Aidan said to you? The stuff that made you so mad."

"Aidan told me he doesn't want us to fondle each other, and that we should not have sex." I compress my lips and shake my head. "But then he added that he's worried I might get gonorrhea from having a poke with you."

Gavin's expression goes blank for a few seconds. Then he laughs with such enthusiasm that a wee bit of spittle sprays from his lips. "No wonder he said some of that stuff in Gaelic. I would've needed to pummel him if I'd known what it all meant. A gentleman defends a lady's honor."

"That's the sweetest threat I've ever heard."

He shimmies a wee bit closer and rests his arm over my shoulders. "Let's not talk about your brother or my sister for a while. We can pretend we're all alone on a deserted island, and we can do anything we want."

The way his voice grew softer and deeper makes my body awaken, setting off a tingle that spreads out and becomes a warm, liquid feeling. That sensation dives deep under my skin. I pull in a ragged breath, exhaling it as we gaze deep into each other's eyes. His pupils have grown larger, darkening his beautiful brown eyes. *Bod an Donais*, I want him like mad, want him more than I ever imagined I could want any man.

I unconsciously lick my lips as my gaze lands on his mouth. I suck in another ragged breath, but I can manage only a shallow one this time. My focus drops to his lap, and I swear I can see his cock thickening before my eyes into a bulge the grows rapidly. I gulp but can't get rid of the lump in my throat.

Gavin licks his lips, just like I had done. "Want dinner now? Or should we skip ahead to dessert?"

Oh, aye, I know what he means. The rough tone of his voice elicits a delicious desire that sets off a slick heat between my thighs. "Skip straight to dessert, please."

His mouth slides into a sensual grin. "Can't deny a lady what she wants."

Chapter Seven

Gavin

I trace my fingertips over her skin, and I can tell her nipples are stiffening. I raise my other hand to brush my thumb across her lips. "I loved kissing you yesterday, but I want a lot more than that. I've never been this attracted to a woman I just met. Something about you makes me want to hold you and kiss you and make love to you, consequences be damned."

Jamie rotates toward me the slightest bit, and her knees brush against mine. "Dinnae care about the consequences either. Aidan might not approve, but he's not my keeper. I'm a grown woman who wants to be made love to."

"By anyone in particular?"

"You, of course." I settle my hand on her thigh, then move it down until I reach the hem of her skirt. It's the same skirt she wore this morning during our shopping trip and all day after that. "I want to touch you, Jamie, right now. I'll take it slow, so I can feel every inch of your soft skin and watch your reactions to my touch."

"Please touch me that way. I'm aching to feel your skin on mine."

My breathing has become labored, simply because I crave this woman so intensely. "I bought condoms in that little shop where we picked out gifts for everybody. I was hoping you'd want what I want, but I never imagined your brother would leave us alone together like this."

"He wanted to shag Calli in private. I doubt Aidan bothered to think about anything else, and in the morning, he'll probably realize that he left me alone with you, the American wolf."

I wink. "I'm a Marine, ma'am, not a wolf."

"Stop talking and make love to me."

"Yes, ma'am."

I push my hand up her inner thigh, under her skirt, and suddenly realize she isn't wearing any nylons. That doesn't shock me. But when I move my hand higher, I get a real surprise. "No panties, eh? I thought you were a good girl."

"Why would ye think that? I'm letting a man I barely know touch me intimately, and I fully expect that you'll ravish me very soon."

"Absolutely." I cup her groin, feeling her wetness trickle onto my skin. "For the record, I love a good girl who goes bad in the bedroom."

While I pet her folds, she sags against the sofa and lets her lids drift half closed. I press my lips to hers and kiss her deeply, groaning when she curls her hand around my dick, massaging it through my jeans. "Unbutton your shirt for me, please. I don't have enough hands."

Jamie does what I asked, then arches her back to show off those gorgeous tits. They aren't large, but just the right size to fit in my palm—if I didn't have both my hands occupied right now. Well, I might not have a free hand, but I've got a mouth. So, I duck my head to latch on to her nipple and suckle it gently.

She gasps, throwing her head back.

I push a finger inside her, feeling all that hot, slippery cream coat my skin. I can smell the scent of it too, and that makes me hunger to taste her. Can't wait one second longer. While she arches her back and her mouth falls open, I slide off the sofa to kneel between her legs. I grasp the waistband of her skirt and drag it down her thighs little by little. She writhes and grips the back of the sofa. I toss her skirt away, not giving a damn where it lands, and shove her thighs apart so I can push my head between them and latch on to her clit.

The flavor of her makes me groan even more deeply than before.

I tease her nub with my front teeth until she cries out again, then start licking her folds fiercely, devouring every bit of her cream while she grasps my head with both hands and her knees curl up as if she's about to come.

Then I thrust a finger inside her, and she goes off. The spasms of her inner muscles try to milk my finger, but her sheath is too small. So, I shove two more fingers in there while I keep suckling her clit and those muscles clench my fingers over and over. Once she's done, she slumps and closes her eyes. Her lips relax into a satisfied smile, but I am still not done yet.

"Ready for more?" I ask. "If you're wiped out, I can go into the bathroom and finish myself off."

I start to rise, but she sets one leg on my shoulder to stop me.

Her eyes fly open. "No, Gavin, you will not finish yourself off."

"Then you want me to fuck you right here on the sofa."

She shakes her head. "Not yet. I want you to sit on the coffee table and pull your jeans down to your ankles."

Do I comply? You're damn straight I do. Jamie gives the sexiest orders.

I sit on the cool, smooth surface of the coffee table and wait to find out what Jamie wants to do to me. The sweet Scot kneels between my legs, then bends forward, positioning her mouth directly in front of my stiff dick.

No, she won't do *that*. Will she? We just met a couple of days ago, so she couldn't want to...

She takes my dick into her mouth, coiling her tongue around the crown.

"Fuck, Jamie..."

The hottest woman I've ever met clasps the base of my erection and pumps from both ends, sucking me off like nobody's business. I grip the table's edge hard enough to cause pain, but I don't care about that. When her hair falls over my lap, it tickles my skin and especially my dick.

I gasp. "Damn, Jamie, you'll give me a heart attack if you keep doing that."

She ignores what I said and begins to massage my inner thigh with her soft fingers. I'm breathing so hard that my ears start to ring, and I'm almost hyperventilating.

Jamie pulls away. "Want to shag now?"

"Hell yeah." I pick her up and rise. But when I try to walk, I almost fall over. "Whoops. Forgot I still have my pants around my ankles."

She smiles. "And you have your shoes on."

I glance down. "Shit. Gimme a minute to take care of this, uh, issue."

Jamie keeps on smiling while I set her on the sofa and fix my wardrobe malfunction. She doesn't seem like she's mocking me, though. Jamie acts like she thinks my problem is cute and slightly entertaining. My erection flaps around while I remove my jeans and shoes. Maybe that's what she thinks is funny. I have just enough wits leftover to remember to dig a condom packet out of my jeans pocket.

Now completely naked, I spread my arms. "Armed and ready for action."

"But I was enjoying the striptease. Get dressed again and perform your show more slowly this time."

"No can do. I'll pop my cork if I have to touch my own dick again to get it stuffed inside my jeans."

She taps her chin, pretending to consider the situation. "Then I suppose you should fuck me now."

Oh, thank goodness. Don't think I could wait much longer. I scoop her up again and glance around. "Where should we do it?"

"My room."

"Yes, ma'am. I'd salute, but that probably would make me drop you."

She has her arms looped around my neck, but now she rests her cheek on my chest. Jamie looks even sweeter while cradled in my arms with no skirt or panties on and her blouse hanging open. She had already been barefoot when we sat down on the sofa. I glance at her cute little toes, with their pink-painted nails, and seeing them oddly makes me need to fuck her immediately and as hard as possible.

Jamie tickles the nape of my neck. "Shouldn't you be doing something, Gavin?"

"What? Oh, yeah, sorry."

I head for the smaller bedroom, the one where Jamie has been sleeping. The door to the master suite is open. Normally, when I get a glimpse of that room, I get a pit in my stomach because I know my sister has been sleeping in there—with a Scottish guy she met less than two weeks ago. But the second I walk into Jamie's room, I forget all about that. I've never told anyone that I feel a twinge of anxiety when I think about my sister shacking up with Aidan MacTaggart.

But can't complain about it. Calli is happier than I've ever seen her, and that's because of Aidan.

I use my foot to push the covers out of the way, then gently lay Jamie down on the sheets. She starts to sit up, so she can remove her blouse, but I shake my head. She relaxes and lets me slide that shirt off. Jamie doesn't even complain when I toss the blouse away and it lands on a chair by the window.

For a moment, I just gaze at her naked body and the way the moonlight coming in through the window paints her skin with its pale shades. She looks like a goddess from ancient mythology, lying in wait for her lover. That would be me. So, why am I just standing here gawking at her? *Make love to her, you moron, right now.*

I climb onto the bed, straddling her body.

Her smile has softened, and now it's imbued with sensual overtones. I bend my head to kiss her softly, slowly, while my dick nudges her belly and she runs her hands up my arms. A faint moan whispers from her lips. I grab the condom I'd tossed onto the bedside table and cover myself with it. Jamie tries to help me, but I wave her hand away. If she touches my dick, I'll explode—and it'll take too damn long for me to recover enough to make love to her.

"You are so damn beautiful, Jamie. I love kissing you, and I love gorging myself on your cream."

I press my lips to her throat, then paint a trail down her skin straight to her belly button, where I flick my tongue inside her navel to tease her. She moans, her breaths coming faster and shallower. I nuzzle her mound before I kiss my way back up to her tits. The areola is as rosy red as her stiff peaks, and I can't resist taking all her nipple into my mouth so I can scrape my teeth over it and suckle the tip.

Jamie spreads her legs, inviting me to take her body.

"Not just yet," I murmur. "Got another idea first."

She smiles in that sexy way I love, and I know that means she wants whatever I want.

I rise to my knees. "Push your tits together for me, but not too tightly."

Jamie's brows lift, but she does what I said.

I grasp the headboard, leaning over her body, and thrust my dick between those gorgeous tits. She seems a little confused, but she gets the picture once I start pumping my hips, pushing my dick between her breasts the way I would fuck her. The moisture on my crown rubs off on her skin, and the very tip pokes out just below her breastbone.

She bites her lip. "Och, Gavin, you're making me so randy that I might come without you even shagging me."

"I *am* shagging you. But don't worry, this is only the appetizer."

While I speed up the pace, she makes little moaning grunts that get me even hotter for her. My dick throbs. If I don't fuck her the usual way very soon, I might spew all over her chest and throat. The thought of that steals my breath, but I don't want to go off like that the first time we have sex.

I pull away and crawl backward until I'm in position.

Jamie massages her tits, arching her back slightly.

She seriously wants to kill me with her sexiness, and that's fine by me. Since she still has her thighs spread for me, I slide my hands under her ass to lift it off the bed just enough to give me the perfect angle. Then I ease my cock inside her, doing it so gradually that my pulse accelerates and pounds in my ears, while Jamie clenches her pillow above her head and arches her back even more. Once I'm seated as deep inside her as I can get, it's time to let go.

I pull back, then thrust into her hard. I keep thrusting, deeply and powerfully, making the bed frame creak and the legs thump. Jamie wraps her thighs around me while I pick up the pace, grunting and gasping, lifting her thighs higher to go deeper. She thrashes her head while shouting things that might be words, but I can't understand any of it. Maybe it's in Gaelic. I know I'll come any second, so I rub her clit to make sure she hits that peak first.

Jamie's entire body freezes. Her mouth falls open, but she seems incapable of making even the tiniest sound. Then her inner muscles clench around me in wave after wave of spasms. She cries out. I fuck her harder as electricity surges down my spine, barreling straight into my cock, setting off rapid-fire spasms. I couldn't stop if I wanted to, and I come so hard that I squeeze my eyes shut and can't breathe while I punch into her twice more, then collapse on top of the incredible woman who just let me pummel her body.

I roll off her, flopping onto my back. My breaths come in staccato gasps, and sweat has beaded on my brow. Sex had never been this good with anyone else. Maybe it's the forbidden aspect making it hotter. Her brother doesn't like me getting intimate with Jamie, so we're even. But this isn't about Aidan and Calli anymore. It's about me and Jamie and what we could be together.

Will we work out in the end? Only time will tell.

Chapter Eight

Jamie

We both lie on our backs, gradually catching our breath. I gaze up at the ceiling for a wee while, unable to make any muscle in my body function properly, not even my eyes. I have never before had a poke with a man I've known for a few days. If anyone had asked me a week ago if I would behave this way, I would have laughed at them. But Gavin makes me feel so good in every way possible.

Eventually, I regain the ability to move and turn onto my side to gaze at the man who gave me this delicious afterglow. "That was bloody brilliant, Gavin."

"I'm assuming that means you liked it."

"No, I didn't like it. I loved it." I sling an arm across his torso and kiss his chest, loving that I can taste the salty sweetness of his perspiration. "I would love to do that again."

He chuckles, though the sound is ragged and breathless. "Yeah, I'd love to do that too, but a man needs a break to recover between bouts of earth-shattering sex."

"I know you need time before we can shag again. So, why don't we eat something decadent and chat to each other in the meantime?"

"Now that's a 'bloody brilliant' plan."

A laugh bubbles out of me, and I can honestly say I have never laughed this way before. It's a cross between a giggle and a hiccup. Dinnae care if I sound ridiculous. I never want this feeling to end.

Gavin heads for the kitchen while I scurry into the bathroom. I needed to empty my bladder about thirty seconds before Gavin gave me a fantastic orgasm on the sofa, but I couldn't speak to tell him so once he put his mouth on my *brillean*. I should have taken a brief trip to the bog when he carried me into the bedroom, but I was too aroused to give a toss. That means now I desperately need to relieve myself. Once I've done that, I trot out into the living room and veer around the bar. Gavin is facing away from me, cooking something on the stove.

I come up beside him and sniff the air. "What are you making? It smells divine."

"French toast sticks, bacon, and scrambled eggs. I might not be a great chef, but I rock the breakfast foods—day or night." He pushes something around in the frying pan while keeping his attention exclusively on me. "I figured we both needed a boatload of protein."

"Oh, aye. Give me gobs of protein, please."

He glances at my body. "You're still naked."

"So are you."

Gavin smirks. "I wasn't complaining. But I figured you'd want to at least put on a robe. Women usually don't like prancing around buck naked outside of the bedroom, especially in front of sliding glass doors."

"Dinnae care what anyone thinks of me. Besides, we're in the back of beyond. Not many keekers out here, I imagine."

He freezes in the midst of scrambling the eggs. "What in the world is a 'keeker'?"

"Someone who spies on other people."

"Oh, you mean a peeping tom."

"That's what Americans call it, aye? My sister-in-law Erica has taught me some American expressions, and I taught her a few Scottish ones."

Gavin pours the egg mixture into a pan, glancing away from me only for a second or two. "Is Erica the only Yank you've ever met?"

"No, I've met the occasional American."

"And did you dislike them all?"

I kiss his bicep and smile up at him. "No, I love Yanks. They know how to shag a lass."

"Damn straight we do. And Scottish lasses know how to shag Americans."

This is the most unusual after-sex conversation I've ever had. Most men want to brag about their prowess, but they don't compliment me.

Calli's puppies had been asleep in the master suite when Gavin and I left the bedroom. Now, they come tumbling out of the hall. Misty and Mandy weave around our feet several times, then leap up to plant their paws on our bellies. I can't resist them. So, I bend my knees to let them lick my chin. Gavin ruffles their hair and scratches their heads, but he's busy cooking and can't play with the furry pair.

After a moment, the puppies both barrel out the dog door.

Gavin glances at me sideways and grins. "I love the way you laugh and smile whenever the puppies assault you."

"Cannae help it. They're adorable." I peer out the sliding glass doors. "Should we call them back in? It is dark outside."

"They'll come back in a minute, then we can shut the dog door."

By the time Gavin has finished cooking our meal, Misty and Mandy have returned to the house. He shows me how to close the dog door, then we sit down on the sofa to eat. Aye, we're still naked. We feed each other and tease each other, and we even shove food into each other's mouths. When a bit of syrup dribbles down my chin, a drop of it lands on my chest.

Gavin licks it away.

The puppies have kept us company. Misty has tucked herself behind Gavin's feet on the floor, while Mandy chose to snuggle up in the corner of the sofa. They're both sleeping, but I don't feel drowsy at all. Gavin suggests we should watch TV for a while to see if we get tired. If not, then we will "have some more fun under the sheets or on top of them," as Gavin tells me. He also suggests we might "get dirty on every surface in the house" because Calli and Aidan will never know how we defiled the premises.

I could fall for this man. He makes me feel…so bloody good.

After the meal is over, and the puppies have eaten the leftovers, Misty and Mandy retreat to the master suite. Gavin says they do that because they always sleep in Calli's room and it makes them feel safe when she's away. That leaves us, the only humans in the house, alone in the living room. We've agreed to remain in the nude. It just feels right.

We've been watching a documentary about the mating habits of tropical birds, only because we couldn't find anything else to watch. Neither of us likes reality shows. But the documentary about birds has an odd effect on Gavin.

He has his arm draped across my shoulders. But now, he dips his head to whisper into my ear, "Something weird is happening to me. Watching this show about birds is making me so fucking horny."

"Aye, me too. It's very strange."

"Maybe we feel this way because the narrator keeps using the word copulate."

"Hmm, that could be the reason." I rotate my head toward him, and our lips brush against each other. "Or maybe you are just a very, very naughty man who cannae stop thinking about sex."

"That's a good point. But I'm naughty only because you are so hot."

I smirk. "You're blaming me? I might need to punish you for that."

"Your willing slave will do anything you want."

"Want to make good on the suggestion that we should get dirty on every surface in the house?"

"Oh, yeah, baby. Let's do it." He nods toward the television. "Should we leave the raunchy bird documentary on?"

I grin. "Why not?"

"Just let me go grab another condom. Got at least one more in the pocket of my jeans." He squints as he surveys the living room. "Where'd I leave my pants?"

"We tossed our clothes into a pile over there." I point toward the far corner of the room. "Stay right where you are. I'll get a condom for you."

I race over to the pile of clothing. While I hunt about for his jeans, Gavin makes catcalls.

"Look at that fine Scottish ass," he calls out. "Just watching those round, sweet tits bouncing is getting me hard. This is a much better show than the one on TV."

Having located my prize, I decide to tease him the way does with me. But instead of making suggestive comments, I hold the condom packet between my teeth and crawl across the floor on my hands and knees, purposely swaying my hips and tossing my hair.

Then I kneel directly in front of Gavin, working my jaw to make the condom packet flap.

Gavin chuckles. "You're the cutest hot chick I've ever met."

I flutter my lashes, flapping the packet again.

He plucks it away, then taps the packet on my nose. "Maybe we should try mating the cockatoo way. Remember how the boy climbed on top of the girl, who was lying on her tummy?"

I shimmy forward and lay my hands on his thighs. "The boy cockatoo also shoves his beak up the lass's erse. Not sure I want you to do that to me. It looked painful, though the lass didn't seem to mind."

"Good point. We aren't cockatoos, but they have given me another idea." He pulls me onto his lap. "Wanna screw outside under the light of the moon?"

"Do you mean in the yard? Or in the woods?"

"The yard. Might be wolves out there in the dark."

I kiss him softly. "Thank you for worrying about my safety while we have a poke."

He wraps his arms around me. "I'll watch out for your safety all the time, baby."

I never used to like it when a man called me "baby." But every time Gavin says that, I melt inside and want to wrap my entire body around him. I would've expected a tough man like Gavin Douglas to avoid getting sentimental or saying sweet, loving things. Of course, my only role models for ex-military men are my cousins Logan, Magnus, and Munro. They are not average lads. None of them would behave the way Gavin does with me, though to be fair, I haven't seen my cousins with women. Maybe they do behave in the same manner.

No, I can't picture Magnus the bounty hunter cuddling with a lass.

Gavin sneaks down the hall to check on the puppies, but they're still happily sleeping. We leave the dog door shut while we go outside, barefoot, and search for the best spot for having a poke. After examining the entire yard, he selects a location at last.

And I laugh. "You needed ten minutes to choose the most dead-obvious place? You want to shag on the grass."

"Yeah. I considered other spots, but they all had something that wasn't right—like rocks sticking up out of the dirt or a lack of a soft surface." He slings an arm around my waist and tugs me close. "Can't have you getting scrapes or cuts."

"That is so sweet, Gavin. Thank you for worrying about my skin."

We do wind up making love on the soft, cool grass, beneath the big tree that provides shade in the daytime. A clear, moonlit sky sheds its milky light on us, so we can see each other almost as well as in the daytime. The moon is full, after all. Gavin lavishes light kisses over my entire body, arousing me tenderly until my breaths quicken and my heart races. By the time he pushes his cock inside me, I'm on the verge of orgasm. But he knows exactly how to keep me on the edge without letting me come until he's ready for us both to do that.

Making love has never been so literal. I've fallen for him here on the lawn with the moon above us. We created a bond with our bodies.

In the afterglow, we lie on the grass on our backs, holding hands while the moon gradually sinks lower and lower in the sky. We joke and tease each other, but we also discuss more serious things—like what we want our lives to become. I tell Gavin about my current state of unemployment and how I haven't yet found a long-term career path. He listens without commenting while I ramble on about my life.

"All my relatives have tried to help me find a job, and I know they mean well. But none of my positions have lasted longer than five years. I'm not a wastrel. I want to be settled in my life, but most of all, I want to find the right man and settle down to have children."

I glance at Gavin, expecting him to seem uncomfortable because of what I said. But he simply gazes up at the stars with a serene expression.

"Gavin, are you awake?"

He turns his head to look at me. "Yeah, I'm awake. And I heard everything you said, but I was waiting to find out if you had more to say."

"Aren't you ready to leg it? I did talk about my desire to start a family."

"Leg it? What does that mean?"

"To run away."

"Oh, I see." He rolls onto his side and drapes an arm across my belly. "Not going to leg it anywhere except back into the house. And for the record, I'd love to have kids. My ex-wife wasn't really into the idea."

"But we barely know each other. You should be horrified."

Gavin lays a hand on my cheek to turn my head toward him. Then he rubs his thumb across my bottom lip. "I care about you, Jamie. Care a lot. I know we just met, and I should be freaked out by how quickly we've gotten close. But I can't feel anything bad when I'm with you. It's all good, and that's something I've never experienced before."

"Neither have I. The only serious boyfriend I ever had seemed like Prince Charming, but he mutated into a slimy toad." I place my hand over his on my cheek. "But somehow I know you would never become a cretin like that chancer."

"Thanks. Maybe I should have a T-shirt printed up with that endorsement on it. 'This guy is not a slimy toad.' I could make a fortune selling those shirts."

I love his sarcastic sense of humor. I love everything about him, actually. He's never mean, but he enjoys making sly jokes. Whenever he softly kisses me, I feel a pang in my chest.

Oh, aye. I am falling for Gavin Douglas.

Chapter Nine

Gavin

Jamie insists on making breakfast for us in the morning, just to prove that she's capable of doing that. I never thought she wasn't. But I've realized lately that she feels kind of inferior to her brothers and sisters. Catriona is an archaeologist, Rory is a solicitor, Lachlan is a financial adviser, Fiona runs a dress shop, and Aidan owns a construction company.

Well, that's what I assume—until I notice something strange about her grammar. She started out using the present tense but then shifted into past tense when she talked about Aidan and Catriona.

"What gives?" I ask as we're snuggled together on the sofa, having stuffed our faces with Jamie's excellent food. "It sounds like Catriona and Aidan don't have jobs anymore. You used the past tense when you mentioned them."

"Aye, it's true. They are both…seeking new opportunities."

"They're unemployed. You can just say it. I won't think they're massive losers because they're between jobs."

"What do you do for a living?"

I squirm and wince. "Well, I, uh…It's nothing interesting."

"Please tell me, Gavin. I'm currently unemployed, like Aidan and Cat, so you don't need to feel embarrassed to tell me about your job—or your lack of one, if that's the case."

"Oh, I've got a job. It sucks, though." I scratch my cheek and wince again. "I'm a sales rep for a company that sells emergency home recovery services."

"What does that mean? I've never heard of that sort of thing, so I'm interested in learning more."

"You really don't want to know more. It's boring as hell."

Jamie has been smiling sweetly at me ever since we sat down on the sofa. She seems to genuinely want to know about my job, and I don't want to get cagey about that. I've avoided telling her a lot of things about my past, so the least I can do is share this boring part with her.

"Basically, I talk to people on the phone all day long. Mostly, it's cold calling where I harass perfectly nice people and try to talk them into buying services they don't need. About sixty percent of my job is like that."

She just keeps on gazing at me like I'm Superman.

"But I do also work with customers who've experienced a residential disaster and call us for help. That's what the company calls it. Residential disasters. It means that if your sewer backs up or your septic system goes wonky, we're here for you. We also handle broken water pipes, mold problems, insect infestations, and other stuff."

Jamie studies me for a moment. "You expected me to be disgusted with your job, didn't you?"

"Yeah. Duh. I annoy people for a living."

"But you also give people the services they need in an emergency. I assume the company actually delivers on their promises and doesn't simply take the money and not do the work."

"No, our disaster recovery team does the work, and they always finish the job." I think my whole face is scrunching up now. And yeah, I'm using my baby sister's term for that expression. "But lately, most of what I do is cold calling. I hate that."

"Have you looked for another job?"

"Yeah. The job market is tight these days. Hard to find anything I'm qualified for."

"But you must have had other sorts of jobs in the past."

I slump against the sofa and sigh. "My only previous work experience was in the Marine Corps."

"Oh. But your job in the military must have given you some experience that you could leverage in the civilian world."

"My MOS was ground ordnance maintenance."

She bites one side of her lip. "What does that mean? I'm not well-versed in military jargon."

"MOS means military operational specialty. Basically, my specific job in the Corps which was ground ordnance maintenance. That means I inspected, repaired, and maintained weapons systems in the field." I let my head fall back against the sofa. "So you see, I don't have relevant experience for getting a civilian job. The only thing I could get was being a telemarketer." I snort. "And I only got that gig because the guy who interviewed me liked my voice. He said it would make people feel more at ease."

"Aye, that's a fact. I feel at ease whenever I'm with you." She kisses my cheek. "And you do have a lovely voice."

"Uh, thanks. I guess. My boss would agree with you, apparently."

"I've embarrassed you, haven't I? Sorry."

"Don't apologize. But no, I'm not embarrassed. I appreciate any compliments you want to give me, though I'll admit I'm not great at accepting things like that. Just not sure I deserve it."

She snuggles up to me and splays a hand on my chest. "I can think of several compliments I could give you that would probably make you blush."

"Doubt it. But it might be fun to let you try."

"That sounds like an invitation."

"Because it is. Do your best to make me blush."

She slides a hand up my inner thigh while giving me a sly smile. "You'll have to do better than that, Jamie."

"All right." She swings her leg over my thighs to squat on my lap. "Just wait, *gràidh*. I'll have you blushing soon."

"What did you just call me?"

"*Gràidh*. It means 'darling' in Gaelic."

"Thanks, baby. I love being called 'darling.' But I'm still not blushing, so you might as well give up and—"

Jamie thrusts a hand down to my groin, cupping my dick through my jeans, then she begins to massage me. "You gasped."

"Yeah. That's what happens when you take my dick in your palm, but it doesn't mean I'm embarrassed."

She puckers her lips and releases my dick. "I'll need to think on the problem for a wee bit longer."

"Your determination is cute." I move her off my lap, then pull her close. "Forget about making me blush. Let's make out instead."

Jamie grins. "That's a dead brilliant idea."

"When do you think Aidan and Calli will come home?"

"They didn't say. But it's nearly ten o'clock, so they might be back at any moment."

"No time to waste, then." I turn toward her and rest my arm across the sofa's back, then use my other arm to pull her firmly against my chest. "Time to make out."

We tip our heads toward each other at the same time, and we keep our eyes open for a few seconds after our lips meet. I've never kissed a woman this way before, but I love gazing into her hazel eyes from such close proximity. I can count every line in her irises and watch as her pupils dilate, darkening her eyes. Mine must be doing the same thing. Then we both shut our eyes at the same instant.

I grasp her hip while she thrusts a hand into my hair to cradle the back of my head. Our tongues thrust and tangle with each other. Her hair tickles my cheek. My pulse revs up, and my dick starts to thicken. I know kissing her will lead to screwing, and with my sister and her lover about to arrive at any moment, we should stop.

But I can't do it. Jamie tastes too damn good.

The front door bursts open.

Jamie and I both jump at the same time, tearing our mouths away from each other.

Aidan and Calli just walked into the house. My sister seems sheepish, but Aidan wears a thunderous expression that I didn't actually think the guy had in him. Well, I guess he does have a tough side after all. And seeing me kissing his sister brought it out in him.

Calli shuts the door and seizes Aidan's arm to stop him. He halts and glances at her sideways.

Jamie flings a hand up to cover her mouth, like she's trying to hide her swollen lips.

I pretend I have no idea what Aidan's upset about. Why? Just because. I'm sure Aidan "had a poke" with my sister several times last night, so I have every right to give him a hard time.

Calli aims her gaze at Don Juan. "Let's not overreact."

Strictly to maintain my I-don't-give-a-shit attitude, I get up and face my sister and her lover, with the sofa between us. "Hey, didn't think you'd be back so soon."

My sister rolls her eyes at me. "Duh. Figured you wouldn't be sucking face with Aidan's sister if you thought he was about to come home."

Aidan swerves his gaze to Calli and mouths, "Home?"

Her eyes flare wide. Her lips fall open. Her gaze flicks between me and the Scot.

Now I feel like punching someone—preferably a man with a Scottish accent. "You two are living together. I knew it."

"Not the way you mean. He sleeps here."

"With you."

"Honestly, we've already had this conversation." She tugs her shirt down, though it didn't need to be tugged. That's one of her tells. When Calli gets nervous because she's hiding something, she fusses with her clothes. "Aidan is not my boyfriend."

Aidan and I both snort and smirk at Calli. Hey, look at that. We finally agree on something. Jamie snorts and smirks too, though I wouldn't have expected that. She's on my side? I think so, which is kind of strange.

My sister lodges her hands on her hips and tries to scowl at us.

But we all glance at each other, nod, and then smile at Calli. Her shoulders slump, and her arms go slack.

Jamie springs off the sofa, clasps my hand, and puts on the biggest, brightest, phoniest smile—aimed at Calli. "Gavin's not my boyfriend either, then."

"Are all you Scottish people so snarky?" Calli asks.

Aidan throws an arm around her shoulders. "You like it. From me, at least."

Jamie looks at me, her smile becoming genuine. Then she faces Calli. "Would you mind if Gavin was my boyfriend?"

Calli's mouth falls open again, and I can tell she wants to say that yes indeed, she would mind. But my sister isn't stupid. And I'm sure she can tell how much I like Jamie. On top of that, Calli knows it would be hypocritical for her to demand that Jamie stop spending time with me when she's been shacking up with Aidan.

Surprisingly, he reaches that conclusion first. "It's all right. Let them have their fun."

I raise my brows. "Fun? I like Jamie a lot. It's more than a good time. Not like you and my sister, who've been having sex while she says you're not her boyfriend. At least I'm upfront about it."

Calli winces.

Aidan stiffens, narrowing his gaze. "Upfront? You snogged with my sister while I was away."

"You want I should do it in front of you?" I smirk. "All right, I will."

Then I drag Jamie into my arms and crush my mouth to hers. She dissolves into a human puddle, held up by my body. She moans a little, just enough to make my libido kick into high gear, and I struggle to tamp down my lustful instincts.

Aidan growls. Seriously, he does. "Why dinnae ye just tear her clothes off right in front of us?"

No, I would never embarrass Jamie like that. So, I release her. Jamie's cheeks have turned a sweet shade of rosy pink. She bites her lip and avoids looking at me.

Aw, shit. I *did* embarrass her. I hadn't meant to do that.

Calli rushes over to wrap an arm around Jamie's shoulders and pull her away from me. "Both of you, stop harassing the poor girl. Gavin, quit trying to annoy Aidan. And you Aidan, let your sister live her own life. At least she's not in Chicago trolling the clubs. My brother is a good man." She throws a reproving look at me. "Most of the time."

Aidan and I bow our heads. Yeah, we both behaved like asses. I peek up at Jamie, with my eyelashes as cover.

Then I hear her whisper something to Calli. "Will you be my honorary sister?"

"Wouldn't that make me Aidan's sister?"

"Not at all. But if you marry him, you could be my sister-in-law. Even better than honorary sister."

She glances at Aidan.

Don Juan blows out a big breath. "I'm sorry. Won't happen again."

I clear my throat. "Yeah, me too. Sorry."

Calli shakes her head at us. "I suppose we will accept your half-assed apologies."

Jamie glances at me and winks. "Aye, we will accept it."

I really, really want to make it up to Jamie. Not sure how to do that. But I can't leave without making things right with my sister.

She waves a hand at me, as if she read my mind. "Go. Take Jamie to dinner, make out with her in the car, whatever. You're adults, and we—" She aims a pointed look at Aidan—"will not interfere. Will we?"

"You have my word."

I walk up to my sister. "Calli, I am sorry for being such a jerk."

She gives me a slight smile. "I know you're sorry. Let's forget about it."

I claim Jamie's hand, leading her out the sliding glass doors. Once we're out of earshot and eyesight of Calli and Aidan, I stop to ask a question. "What would you like to do now? Go out to dinner? Have a picnic in the yard?"

"Would you show me that hunting cabin where you've been sleeping?"

"Sure thing. But it's not much of a cabin. There are no real amenities, just bare floors and a tiny bathroom. I've been bunking on the floor with just a sleeping bag. It's well-padded but still counts as roughing it."

"Dinnae care. I'd like to see it anyway."

"All righty, then."

We leave the yard and begin ambling down the path that leads to the cabin. But we keep glancing at each other at the same time, repeatedly, and smile too. Soon, we're picking up the pace, almost jogging in our zeal to get there and be alone again. I look at Jamie, and the way her hair flies around her face and her smile has become a brilliant grin, gives me a feeling I've never felt this strongly before.

I think I'm happy. And it's all because of Jamie.

Chapter Ten

Jamie

By the time we reach the cabin, we're both breathing so hard that we can barely speak. Maybe we hadn't needed to sprint all the way here. But we couldn't wait, so excited to be alone again that we would've run for miles to get here. Every time Gavin grinned at me, I felt as if my feet had lifted off the ground like helium balloons.

But we have a wee problem.

I study the structure before us. "This is the hunting cabin? It's in a tree."

"No, it's attached to the tree. Technically, it's a deer blind. But Calli told me that the guy who built this blind wanted more than a place to squat while he waited for deer to wander by so he could shoot them." Gavin waves up toward the wee structure. "He decided to live here too."

As I gaze up at the so-called cabin, I twist my lips into an expression that probably conveys my skepticism. "Are you sure the 'cabin' will hold us? It won't break and come crashing down on us? I dinnae care to become a human pancake."

"I would never let that happen to you." He clasps both my hands, facing me. "I've slept here since the day I arrived in Michigan, and I'm a lot heavier than you are. If this thing was in danger of collapsing, I wouldn't have brought you here."

"Aye, I know that. But I do have a slight issue with heights."

He chuckles, though the sound is full of affection. "Don't worry. I'll help you get up there. The cabin has stairs. They're around the side, where you can't see them."

"No ladder?"

Gavin shakes his head and makes a cross shape over his heart. "My word of honor."

I let him lead me around the side of the cabin. It does indeed have a set of stairs that lead up to the main part of the structure. But we do need to climb up through a sort of hatch in the floor to access the wee shack. Gavin gives my erse a shove with both hands. I appreciate the help, but I could have gotten in here without that. I'm sure he saw an opportunity to get his hands on my erse and couldn't resist.

Well, I might've done the same thing if he'd climbed in ahead of me. That man has a braw erse.

Once I've reached the top of the stairs and climbed in, I straighten and take in my surroundings. Aye, it is a genuine cabin. But I cannae admire the decor yet, not when Gavin just climbed in, and I got a fine view of his backside.

I sigh with mock wistfulness. "Och, Gavin, you do have a braw erse for sure. I could watch you crawling about on the floor for hours just to see those glutes flex."

He stands up and groans, rubbing his lower back. "Damn, climbing into this place always gives me a crick in my back."

"Would you like a rubdown?"

"Seriously?"

I nod.

His lips form a suggestive smile. "Yeah, I'd love that. Then I'll do the same for you."

"Undress, please."

He salutes. "Yes, ma'am."

While Gavin gets naked, I finally take in the full scope of the cabin. It has no living room or bedroom, only a single open space with a wee attached bathroom that is indeed quite small. I'm surprised Gavin can fit in there. The sleeping bag lies on the floor beside an oil lantern. The shack does have a kitchen, of a sort. If a body accepted that a wee wood stove can be a kitchen appliance too. Well, why not?

Gavin clears his throat deliberately.

I spin round to face him—and cannae help smiling in the same sly way he had done a moment ago. "You definitely look best starkers. You should become a nudist, so I can see you naked every day."

"Only if you do the same."

"Is that an order?"

"Yes, ma'am, it is."

I salute, then strip off my clothing faster than even I thought I could do it. Then I realize we have a problem. I hug myself and rub my arms. "It's a wee bit chilly in here."

"Shit. Sorry, I forgot to turn on the wood stove. Gimme a minute."

He excavates a throw blanket from his luggage and tosses it to me. While I sit cross-legged on the sleeping bag, he wraps the blanket around me. I pull my knees up to my chest, and he fires up the wood stove in record time.

Soon, warmth begins to fill the cabin.

Gavin kneels in front of me. "Bet I can warm you up a lot faster than a stove or a blanket."

"I'm dead sure you can." I toss the blanket away and lie down on the sleeping bag, on my back, stretched out in the middle. "Warm me up, Gavin."

He crawls onto our makeshift bed, straddling my body. His straight arms hold him up, so he's not actually touching me, not yet. "Would it freak you out if I said I'm falling in love with you?"

"No. I'm falling for you too."

He sits back on his heels and begins gliding his hands up and down my legs, taking it slow at first, then speeding up little by little. His motions create a delicious friction that arouses me and heats me up. By the time he moves his hands up to my belly, I'm already quite warm. He runs his palms over my entire torso, from my hips to my throat, all while carefully avoiding my breasts. The nipples had been taut from the cold, but now, they're stiff because this man knows how to turn me on so swiftly that it's breathtaking.

"Jamie, sweet Jamie. Wanna make love to you slowly this time."

"Please do. I love having a poke with you."

"Gotta say, I love Scottish slang. It's cute and dirty at the same time."

Suddenly, I experience a strong need to ask for something I've never wanted before. "Talk dirty to me, Gavin."

"Only if you call me Gav. That's my nickname, and I need to hear you calling me that while we fuck."

"All right, Gav. Talk dirty, please."

He molds his hands to my breasts and massages them slowly. "Feel free to beg all you want, baby."

I arch my back slightly, needing to feel his hands more firmly grasping my flesh. When he flicks his fingertip over my nipple, I gasp.

"You have the most beautiful tits in the world." He lies down beside me and resumes tracing his hands over my skin. "I'd love to pull one of those rosy peaks into my mouth and suckle until you start writhing. But I need to get you so turned on that your cream will be dribbling down your inner thighs."

"Oh, Gav, please do that."

He pets my mound, splaying his fingers through the hairs there. "Ah, fuck, Jamie. I can smell your cream now. Thought it would take longer, but you got wet right away. I love that about you. But I wanna see how drenched I can get you by using only my hands."

"Och, I'm begging you, do that to me."

Gavin glides his palms up and down my skin, covering every inch in slow increments. He begins with my throat, where he splays his fingers over my flesh and teases me with the tips. I wriggle and gasp. He drags that hand down my breastbone, all the way to the edge of my mound.

"Your skin is so damn soft, it's like silk." His voice has dropped to a husky murmur that makes me shiver a wee bit. "Need to spread your legs and push my head between them so I can lap up every little bit of your juices. I already know you taste like honey and cream and caramel."

Gavin slides his hand between my thighs but doesn't touch my folds or my mound. Instead, he runs his palm down one leg and back up the other, his touch so delicate that it heightens my desire even more. I'm almost shaking from the need to have him inside me.

"I changed my mind. Please fuck me now, Gav. Cannae stand this any longer, need you inside me."

"Oh, thank goodness. My dick's about to explode."

Though I successfully fight off the impulse to laugh at that statement, I can't stop myself from smiling. He seemed so relieved, and it was utterly adorable. But I won't tell him that. Not yet. Maybe after we shag.

But I do need to remind him of something. "Condom?"

"Shit, yeah, of course. Almost forgot again, didn't I?" He leaps up to find his clothes and get the condom. Then he joins me on the sleeping bag again, now straddling my body. "You are the most beautiful woman in the world. But more than that, you're the kindest, sweetest woman and one tough chick when it comes to dealing with your brother. You are amazing, Jamie."

Gavin lowers himself onto his elbows, placing his body in full contact with mine. He carefully avoids crushing me with his heavier weight. Then he begins to slide his length inside me little by little, brushing his lips across mine and exhaling his heated breath over my mouth. The friction of his skin against mine makes my heart beat faster even while his leisurely movements relax me. It seems contradictory, yet it's what I feel. No man has ever made love to me like this.

No one except Gavin.

I glide my hands up and down his back while I spread my thighs to give him more room. He gazes into my eyes unwaveringly, and I gaze into his in the same way. It's a sort of connection I've never experienced before, and I love it. I bend my knees, grazing my nails up and down his back as I lift my hips in a gentle rhythm to push his cock deeper inside me. Gavin groans deeply, his eyes drifting half closed. I close my eyes too, so I can revel in every sensation. I've grown even wetter with every passing second, so much so that I can hear the faint sucking sound as he takes my body.

He scrunches up his face. "Wanted to go slow, need to go faster."

"Anything you need. Just do it."

Gavin raises onto his straight arms and starts pumping into me with more force, though he still keeps the pace measured. Moment by moment, inch by inch, he speeds up his thrusts. I grip his biceps and lock my ankles behind his erse, holding on while he punches into me harder and faster until my body begins to slide up and down on the flat surface.

Wild, incoherent cries tumble from my lips.

He grits his teeth, and his lips peel back, as if he needs to come so badly that it hurts. I feel the same desperate need for release. With his cock pummeling me, I can't stop my body from pushing me over the edge. A long, keening cry spills from my lips and gradually rises in pitch and volume until it becomes a shrill scream. My inner muscles pulsate around him as I come, and suddenly, I've lost my voice. Can't breathe either. As he pounds into me a few more times, letting out harsh yells in time with his thrusts, I suddenly regain my voice enough to release a single cry.

"Gavin!"

Then we both collapse. He falls on top of me, but immediately shifts about as if he means to roll off my body.

I wrap my arms round him. "Dinnae move yet. I love the weight of you on top of me."

"Okay, I'll stay put. Let me know if I get too heavy for you."

"Gavin, you are the sweetest man in the world."

We spend the remainder of the day inside this wee cabin, naked for the entire time, while we chat and laugh and generally bask in the afterglow of incredible sex as well as our newly forged bond. I've never felt this deeply for any man, not even the ones I dated for several months. Gavin Douglas is not like anyone else, and I know I never want to say goodbye to him.

After our third round of hide-and-go-seek, during which Gavin pretended to hide under an invisible bed, we decide it's time to return to Calli's house. Gav looked bloody ridiculous when he curled up as if he actually were under a bed. I laughed so hard that my eyes watered. And when he crawled out of his supposed hiding place, he acted as if he had bumped his head on the imaginary bed frame.

And I laughed even harder.

We stroll back to the house hand in hand, glancing at each other often, smiling in the way couples in love do. I've seen that happen with other people, but never with me. Not until I met Gavin. Now everything has changed, and I'm beginning to see a future with him, unfolding from this moment on.

As we walk through the sliding glass doors, I sense that something isn't right. We both halt just inside the doorway, exchanging confused glances. Aye, he must feel the difference too. What is it, exactly?

"The puppies aren't bounding around," Gavin says. "I don't hear any noises at all in here. Aidan and Calli should be talking while Mandy and Misty try to slather their tongues all over them."

"Aye, something is different. I feel it too."

He grips my hand more firmly as we shuffle across the living room.

Calli and Aidan emerge from the hallway. Their expressions prove our suspicions were correct. Calli seems completely forlorn, while Aidan wears a stoic mask. I have never seen my brother look that way. Never.

"What's happened?" I ask.

"Pack your things," Aidan tells me. "We're going home first thing tomorrow."

I gawp at him. "Home? I don't want to leave yet. If Calli's going with you, then Gavin should come with us too."

"You and I are flying home. Calli and Gavin will stay here."

"But—"

"No arguments. Go pack your things—now."

Gavin's hand has tightened around mine so much that it almost hurts. He aims his steely stare at Aidan. "Tell us what's going on. We deserve that much."

Aidan sighs, and his shoulders sag. "Aye. Let's all sit down, and I'll explain everything."

Chapter Eleven

Gavin

I lead Jamie over to the sofa while Aidan and Calli sit in arm-chairs positioned at opposite sides of the sofa. They don't look at each other, except for the occasional furtive glance. The last time I saw my sister looking so dejected had been right after our parents died in a car crash. Now, Aidan and Calli explain every-thing to us.

Calli has a husband she never told me about. I knew she'd been friends with a guy called Rade back in college, but now I learn that he tricked my baby sister into marrying him so he could get a green card. That's marriage fraud, and he's held it over her for years. I never had a clue. After my time in Afghanistan, and our parents' deaths, I'd been useless. Calli's dilemma is my fault.

"No, Gavin, it's not your fault," Calli insists. "I made my own mistakes and believed the wrong man."

"But I should've been there for you. Instead, I made you handle all the funeral arrangements and deal with the life insurance com-pany. I'm your big brother, and I failed you."

I can tell Calli wants to argue with me, to convince me I'm wrong. But she must realize now isn't the time for that. She keeps quiet.

Aidan tells us about his rock-climbing accident, and how the girl he'd taken up a big mountain with him had nearly died in the rockslide that injured them both. She suffered the most severe wounds, though. He blames himself, of course, just like I blame myself for Calli's dilemma. Seona, the woman who was involved in the accident, now claims she's pregnant with Aidan's child. That's why he and Jamie need to go home.

Though I want to argue about that, I realize Aidan is upset about the Seona situation. He wants to take Jamie home with him because he needs to be with his family. I get that. But the thought of Jamie flying away from me makes my chest ache and my throat tighten. She means more to me than a casual fling. I want to spend the rest of my life with her.

We all try to sleep that night, but given our haggard expressions in the morning, I know none of us managed to get any rest. Breakfast becomes a silent movie. Might as well have turned the world into black and white. Jamie and Aidan spend most of the morning packing up their suitcases and stowing them in the trunk of Aidan's rented Mustang. Then they spend a while arguing out in the yard while Calli and I sit on the sofa, at opposite ends, watching them.

Jamie doesn't want to leave. I can tell that much just from watching her argue with Aidan.

Though I make lunch for all of us, we don't eat much. We avoid looking at each other too.

Now, it's time for Jamie and Aidan to leave.

Calli needs to say goodbye to him alone, and I get that. So, I lead Jamie out of the house. We halt beside the Mustang.

She clasps my hands. "Dinnae want to go."

"And I don't want you to go either. But your family needs you, and I've gotten to know you well enough that I can say with absolute certainty that you will never forgive yourself if you aren't there when Aidan needs you." I brush my thumb over her cheek. "He's your best friend. You told me that."

"You're right, I know. But I…" She raises onto her toes to look straight into my eyes. "I love you, Gavin."

"I love you too. And we will see each other again, that's a promise."

Aidan shambles out of the house, looking as dejected as I feel. He hides it pretty well, but guys can tell when one of our buddies is upset. We might not want to talk about it, but we can tell. Women aren't the only ones with insight into the human condition.

I give Jamie a quick, soft kiss. "I won't forget about you, not ever. You're the only one for me, and I'll fight for us. However long it takes, I'll wait."

Jamie and Aidan climb into the car.

I stand here watching while the only woman I've ever really loved rides out of my life. A hard pang hits me in the chest, and for a moment, I have trouble catching my breath. But I won't fall apart. The way I'd behaved five years ago, and for too long after that, will never happen again. I'll take care of my sister this time. She won't be alone.

And somehow, some way, I will reunite with Jamie.

Once the car has moved out of sight, I walk into the house.

Calli sits there in a lump on the floor, just under the window, with her legs splayed and her head bowed, sobbing.

I kick the door shut and crouch in front of her. "Jesus, Calli. What can I do?"

She shakes her head while tears pour down her cheeks.

Yes, I *will* take care of my sister this time. So, I sit down beside Calli, tug her close to my side, and throw my arm around her. When I rest my chin on her head, she sags against me, her sobs growing louder and stronger, shaking her entire body.

"It'll be okay, Calli. One day it'll be okay, I promise."

"He's gone." Her voice had cracked on the final syllable. "I lost him."

"One thing I've learned about Aidan is that he's not the kind of guy who gives up easily. He loves you like crazy, and that's how I know he'll do whatever it takes to get back to you."

She buries her face against my chest and keeps on sobbing.

I've never seen my sister like this. Never. Not even when Mom and Dad died. I think she's broken right now because she held in all that grief for our parents and the strain of knowing she'd violated the law to help Rade. Losing Aidan was the last straw, and she can't hold it together anymore. But I'm here for her this time, and I won't leave until she's okay. Screw my job. Calli needs me.

We sit here sprawled on the floor while her sobs gradually become silent tears, and eventually, she stops crying altogether. Even when that happens, she doesn't move away from me and keeps her face buried against my chest. But she does unclench her hand, the one that had been fisted in my shirt. I switch from rocking her gently to just combing my fingers through her hair.

I get why Calli fell apart. She's never really had a boyfriend, much less been in love. I've watched her with Aidan, so I know what they have is real. Maybe even the fairy-tale kind of love.

Do Jamie and I have that? Not sure, but I want to find out.

At last, Calli raises her head. "Sorry I got your shirt all wet."

"It's just a little damp. Don't worry about it." I still have one arm around her, and she doesn't seem to mind that. "How do you feel? Sorry, that's a dumb question."

"No, it isn't. I feel like somebody shoved a melon baller inside my chest and scooped out my heart."

"I know. I felt that way when Leanne left me, though not because I wanted her back. I didn't love her the way you love Aidan."

She almost smiles. "But you love Jamie that way, don't you?"

"Yeah, I think I do."

"Then don't let her go. I want you to be happy, Gav. One of us should be, at least."

I kiss the top of her head. "Let's make you happy, then worry about me and Jamie."

We both get up and get on with life the best we can. I stick around until the next day, but then Calli insists I need to go home so I won't lose my job. She seems genuinely okay, in relative terms, and I believe it when she tells me she'll get through this ordeal.

Once I get back to my little apartment in Minneapolis, the first thing I do is call Jamie. We talk for an hour, but we both feel a little awkward about being happy while my sister and her brother are miserable. As the days go by, our phone calls become less awkward and more fun. We make each other laugh and talk about when we might get together again. Since Jamie has two rich brothers, and those guys share a private jet, it seems likely that she won't need to fly commercial to come visit me.

I want to go to Scotland right now. I need to pull her into my arms and kiss her until she's weak in the knees. When I tell Jamie I want to book a flight, she reminds me that Rory and Lachlan co-own a jet. Duh, I knew that. I guess I forgot because I feel weird about letting her brothers transport me to Scotland for free, but the longer I go without seeing her in person, the less I care about who pays for it.

Still, I can't leave America yet. Calli still has her divorce proceedings to worry about. I made a promise to myself that I would be here for my sister until her ordeal is over, and I won't renege on that. For the first two weeks after Aidan and Jamie went back to Scotland, I provide moral support for Calli while she deals with Rade and the divorce. At least the bastard relented at last, granting her a divorce and offering a financial settlement. In seven weeks, she will be free to marry Aidan.

"Don't jump the gun, Gav," my sister tells me as we're walking out of the lawyer's office. "Aidan and I still don't know if Seona's baby is his."

"But you love him like crazy, and I can't believe the universe would smack you both down like that."

She shrugs. "Life can really suck. Just have to pick yourself up and keep going, right?"

"Exactly."

Calli halts just as we're exiting the building. "You should go see Jamie. Or she should come to you."

"Uh, that statement came out of nowhere."

"No, it didn't. Make yourself happy, Gavin." She rubs her arms as if she's cold, though it's a warm day. "I just wish this divorce could be over today."

"Yeah, I know. My offer to beat the holy living shit out of Rade still stands. Just say the word."

"I appreciate that, but I don't think it will be necessary."

That afternoon, I fly home to Minneapolis—and I take my sister's advice. I make myself happy by calling Jamie. We talk for two hours. It's not enough, but it'll do for now. Jamie is happy to hear that Calli is almost free of her husband, but she also informs me of news at her end.

"Aidan is not the father of Seona's baby. We just heard the results of the paternity test. After that, Seona admitted that she'd slept with another man while she was with Aidan. At least that drama is over."

"That's great. I'm sure Calli and Aidan are relieved."

"Aye, they are." Jamie hesitates, and I swear I can almost hear her biting her lip. Maybe I just recognize the tone of her silence. Okay, that's dumb. But she does make a flat humming sound right before she speaks again. "You haven't heard, have you?"

"Heard what?"

"Aidan wants to marry Calli, but she threw him over."

"What?" I bolt upright. I'd been slouching in my easy chair, but Jamie's statement shocked me to my core. "Why the hell would Calli do that?"

"Dinnae know. She said goodbye to Aidan and hung up on him."

"Aw, shit. She's panicking." I slump into my chair again. "I need to call Tara. This is a two-person job."

"What is?"

"Talking my sister out of screwing up her life because she's afraid Aidan will turn into Rade."

"Good. That's exactly what I hoped you would say." She sighs. "Aidan is miserable, and I'm sure Calli is too."

Three days later, Tara and I knock on Calli's front door. She's stunned to see us, but happy too. We spend a good part of the day just hanging out with Calli until she finally fesses up and tells us everything. Aidan had written her the most romantic letter I've ever read, talking about how much he loves her and how much he needs her in his life. In the letter, Aidan told Calli to let me and Tara read it. He's a smart guy. Sharing his words with us finally helped my sister shake off her fears and realize what she needs to do.

"Jamie says Aidan is heartbroken," I tell my sister, "but he's trying to hide it. You're the same way, and if you don't get your ass on a plane right away, I'll hogtie you and send you to Aidan in a FedEx box."

Not sure if that threat is what pushed her in the right direction, but ten minutes later, Calli leaps off the sofa and stands up straighter than she has in weeks. "I'm going to Scotland to get my man."

Tara, the goofball, grins and squeals, leaping up and down. Then she hauls Calli into a bear hug that must be squeezing the life out of her. I can't help myself. Two of my favorite people in the world are happy, and I need to join in. It becomes a group hug. Then Calli rushes into the bedroom to pack her bags. Tara and I drive her to the airport, just to make sure she doesn't chicken out.

But I know she won't. Calli has shed her fears at last.

Now, if only I could do the same...

Eight weeks later, I'm flying to Scotland via MacTaggart Air—along with Tara and her husband, Blake. Calli and Aidan greet us at the Inverness airport, where we climb into a limo provided by Rory and Lachlan for the three-hour drive to the village where most of the MacTaggarts live. Two days later, I watch my baby sister marry a Scotsman in a cute little church on the outskirts of Loch Fairbairn, and later, we all travel to Lachlan and Erica's farm for the outdoor reception.

The weather gods blessed us with sunshine and warmth today. But I'd feel warm even if it were raining. This is the first time I've seen Jamie in person since she left Michigan.

We might have sneaked away to a secluded spot behind the barn to have a "wee poke," as Jamie calls it. We stay quiet enough that nobody will hear us, though some people might've noticed us skulking away. So what? I'm with the woman I love, the sky is blue, and Jamie feels incredible. When she comes, I seal my mouth over hers to mute her cries, right before I come too. Yeah, I'd stashed a box of condoms in my suitcase and slipped three of them into the inside pocket of my suit jacket.

It's been too damn long since I made love to this woman.

As the reception winds down, Aidan invites me to go into the house and have a "dram" of Scottish whisky with him in the kitchen. I can guess his real reason for the invite. So, it's no surprise when he finally speaks.

"Jamie is my sister and my best friend," he tells me, like I didn't already know that. "Dinnae break her heart, or I'll have to batter you bloody."

"I have no intention of breaking Jamie's heart. I love her, and I promise not to hurt her."

"Good. Now keep that vow."

Aidan loves his sister and would do anything for her. I can relate. If Aidan had kicked Calli to the curb, I would have pummeled him for sure. And I will do my best to show her family that I mean it when I say I never want to hurt her.

Chapter Twelve

Jamie

After the wedding, Gavin tells me he can only stay for two more days. He needs to get back to his job in Minneapolis. I understand that, but we barely have time to get reacquainted before he leaves, and the time we have left doesn't seem like enough. That's because it isn't enough. He still lives in America, and I still live here in Scotland. I never imagined I would become entangled in an intercontinental romance with an American man. My family has always assumed I would marry a good Scottish laddie.

Are they disappointed that I chose Gavin Douglas? Not entirely. He would fit right in with my cousins Magnus and Logan, if he gave them the chance. But Gavin didn't do much socializing at the wedding.

Now it's time for him to leave me.

We stand on the tarmac at the Inverness airport, holding hands, face to face, while we both struggle to figure out how to say goodbye. I'd been happy for several days because he was here. I dinnae want him to go.

"Take me with you," I say. "Please, Gavin, I'll miss you too much."

"Won't your family be pissed that I whisked you away without any warning?"

"Dinnae give a toss. Aidan ran away to America, so why shouldn't I? The last time I did that, no one minded."

He pulls me close, wrapping his arms around me. "I love you, Jamie, and nothing will change that. You don't need to jump on a plane with me to prove you feel the same way. I know it's true."

I rest my forehead on his chest, suddenly feeling deflated.

Gavin kisses the top of my head. "I'll come back as soon as I can, promise."

"But you've nearly used up your vacation days."

"I'll still have weekends off."

Lifting my head, I loop my arms around his neck. "Kiss me so thoroughly that I'll forget you're leaving until after the plane takes off."

He tugs me more firmly into his body, lowers his head, and—

My mobile pings, alerting me to a new text.

I shut my eyes and shake my head. "*Mhac na galla.*"

"Are you going to check that?"

"No. Ugh, yes." I dig the mobile out of my purse and check the new text. "It's Aidan. He says…run away to America with Gavin. We all agreed you should."

Gavin grabs my mobile and types on the screen, then hands the device back to me. "There. I made the decision for you, so you couldn't come up with reasons not to do it."

I should be very annoyed with him, but instead, I grin. "Let's get on the bloody plane before Lachlan realizes what he's done."

"Thought Aidan texted you."

"Aye, but Lachlan would have told him to do it."

Gavin steals my mobile again so he can dump it into my purse. Then he sweeps me up in his arms and carries me up the stairs and into the jet. I'd only ever flown in this jet twice, when I went to America on a trip that would change my life and when Aidan and I had to go home. Since I don't have a job right now anyway, I might as well go away with Gavin.

The co-pilot emerges from the cockpit and seems not the least confused that I'm on board. One of my brothers must have alerted the pilots. Once the co-pilot has shut the door, he disappears into the cockpit again.

Gavin takes my hand, leading me to a sofa, and we both sit down. "What was that thing you said when your phone pinged you?"

"What thing?" I suddenly realize what he's asking. "Oh, you mean the phrase I used. *Mhac na galla* means 'son of a bitch.' It's a Gaelic curse."

"I see. That's cool." He slings an arm across the sofa's back and leans in closer. "Got any dirty Gaelic phrases?"

"Oh, aye. Want to hear some?"

"Absolutely."

I lean toward him to whisper, "This jet has a bedroom."

"Let's go in there, so you can talk dirty Gaelic to me in private. That will probably wind up with us fucking."

I pretend to pout. "That would be just awful."

We retire to the bedroom and spend a good portion of the six-hour flight to Minneapolis in that room, shagging and laughing, while I teach Gavin all the dirty Gaelic words I know. By the time we reach our destination, he has become quite good at pronouncing Gaelic, and I love the phrases he has chosen to use. Rory had arranged for a limousine to pick us up at the airport and drive us to Gavin's wee apartment.

He winces as he opens the door and seems to be delaying, as if he worries I'll run back to Scotland once I see his home. But he finally swings the door open, and I walk inside.

Gavin shuts the door, leaning back against it while I explore the small space.

When I'm done, I face him. "Ahmno horrified, Gavin. You can relax. This is a cozy apartment. You even have a comfortable recliner."

"Yeah, but you're used to living in a castle."

I approach him, settling my hands on his chest. "I love you, Gavin. That means I would live in an igloo in the arctic to be with you."

He relaxes and almost smiles. "You're really not disgusted with my tiny, cramped, rundown hovel?"

"Not in the least." I take his hand, leading him over to the twin-size bed. "I'm sure we can both fit on this mattress. Let's make love."

He grins.

And we both undress. He insists on giving me plenty of foreplay, though I would've been fine with going straight to the shagging. I love that he wants to give me more than a quick poke. Gavin genuinely worries about my pleasure. And when he uses a bit of dirty Gaelic, I grow so aroused that I dinnae know how much longer I can wait to have him inside me.

He kneels over me, straddling my thighs, and skims his hand up and down his stiff cock. "Damn, Jamie, you are so beautiful. Need to push my *bigealais* inside your *baltan* and fuck you until I *caith*."

I know he will always make sure I come before he does. I don't need to hear him say the words. We make the wee bed creak in an erotic rhythm that matches our movements, and when we come at the same time, it feels like destiny.

Dinnae care how bloody stupid that sounds.

A few days later, I go home.

I'd love to say that in the following months our relationship remains rock solid and angst-free. But lying to myself won't help matters. Our long-distance romance comes with hiccups and false starts and a growing sense that we're drifting away from each other. I dinnae want that. Gavin doesn't either, I know. But we can't seem to find our way back to those easy, sweet days in Michigan when everything seemed perfect.

Gavin has to work overtime more often than either of us would like. That means I don't visit him in America more than once a month, and he begins to find excuses for why he can't come to Scotland. Gradually, once a month visits become once every other month, and I know something is wrong.

But Gavin won't talk to me.

In the meantime, my brother Rory returns from a business trip to New Orleans with a surprise. He married an American woman, Emery, and has brought her home to meet the family. We're all stunned beyond words. Rory has known Emery for barely more than four days. And he never told us he'd met anyone. Gavin and I fell in love quickly, but we haven't tied the knot. More than nine months has elapsed since those lovely days in Michigan, yet still, we're only dating—the intercontinental way.

At least we speak on the phone regularly, though those conversations have become somewhat strained.

When Rory comes home with his new wife, I don't have time to think about Gavin and our relationship. Since I've been living at Dùndubhan, I'm one of the first family members to meet Emery. She's bonnie and sweet, but also feisty enough to handle my brother. Rory seems a bit shell-shocked, and that means he gets grumpy. That doesn't faze Emery at all.

I instantly adore my newest sister-in-law. We hit it off like a house on fire.

Once we're all inside the castle, Rory finally introduces me. He seemed to have forgotten I existed. *Bod an Donais*, he must be completely in love with her to be so scatterbrained.

I seize Emery's arm. "Let me give you the tour. This house is really a castle, do ye know? Built in the Middle Ages."

"I knew it was a castle, yeah, but Rory hasn't been forthcoming with the details."

While Rory scowls at me, I shepherd Emery down the hall. "We'll start the tour here."

"Stop," my brother exclaims. "I will show my wife our home, if you please, Jamie."

"No need to shout at me. Ahmno deaf, Rory."

"Why don't you go to bed?"

I snort, thanks to the fact I'm trying not to laugh at him. "Ahmno five years old. It's only seven o'clock."

Mrs. Darroch, the housekeeper has been observing our exchange with definite amusement. She has always treated Rory like a son, which means she doesn't shy away from giving him a verbal spanking. But she doesn't need to do that now. Emery takes over that duty, and she does it expertly.

Aye, Rory has finally found his soul mate. We all know that—except for Rory.

The next day, we hold a family gathering in the garden at Dùndubhan to celebrate Rory's marriage. That's when I learn that my brothers have conspired to give me a surprise. A large, sexy surprise.

Gavin is here.

I race up to him and fling my arms around his neck, hugging him tightly. "I've missed you so much, *mo chridhe*."

"Missed you too, baby." He kisses me, crushing his mouth to mine despite my brothers watching us. "Feels so good to be with you again and hold you again."

We keep our arms around each other as we follow my brothers into the garden where so many MacTaggarts have gathered, from my immediate family to my cousins and uncles and aunts. Gavin and I get separated. The next time I see him, he's on the other side of the garden talking to Emery and seems uncomfortable being in a crowd of MacTaggarts.

Too soon, it's time for Gavin to leave. Watching him climb onto a jet and go home to America… That breaks my heart every time. I do get to see him again three weeks later for Rory and Emery's official wedding ceremony, the one my mother insisted they must have. We all know Sorcha MacTaggart gets her way. Even Rory, the Steely Solicitor, cannae say no to Ma.

Naturally, my brothers made sure to not only invite Gavin to the wedding, but to insist that he must come. So now, I wait on the tarmac to greet the man I love. The second he steps off the stairs,

I throw myself at him, showering him with kisses and hugs. He reciprocates in a similar manner, but after our initial reunion, we both seem to have trouble getting back into the groove, as Gavin would say. That night, we make love with a new intensity, as if we worry this will be the last time we see each other.

But now, Rory and Emery's wedding ceremony is about to begin.

Gavin and I sit beside each other, and I cry when Rory kisses Emery. But then, the crowd disperses and heads for the ceilidh in the great hall. I get one spin round the room with Gavin before the ceilidh becomes a merry-go-round of dancing with my relatives.

Then I notice that Emery's sister, Hadley, doesn't join in the dancing. She has her hands full with her twin girls. When I suggest to Gavin that we should help Hadley, he agrees. Now, Emery's sister can dance with her husband, Cole, while Gavin and I entertain the bairns. Gavin makes ridiculous faces and speaks in a silly voice to make them laugh, and he even shows them a magic trick. I had no idea he could do magic. I'm as enthralled by his antics as the bairns are.

When Lachlan and Aidan approach us, wearing grave expressions, I know something is wrong.

"Rory has gotten buckled," Lachlan explains. "That word is hardly adequate to describe his condition, since he's passed out, but that's not the point right now. We need to drag Rory upstairs. Gavin, could you please let Emery know what's happened?"

"Sure thing."

My brothers lead a wee parade with Gavin bringing up the rear, then he veers away to find Emery and give her the bad news. What in the world is wrong with Rory? I can't believe he would behave this way. Then again, he has been off kilter ever since he married Emery.

Gavin and I enjoy one more night in the castle. After that, he flies home to America. I am alone again. Aye, my family does their best to keep my spirits up in Gavin's absence, but they're more concerned for Rory—and they should be.

But I'm no longer privy to my brother's gnashing teeth and snarling. I decided it was best for Rory and Emery to have the castle to themselves while they sort out their relationship. For now, I'll be staying at Aidan and Calli's house where I can spend time with my wee niece. Emery says goodbye to me, but Rory is holed up in his office, and I agree with Emery when she suggests I shouldn't bother my brother right now.

Rory behaves rather badly for some time after the wedding, as if he's determined to chase Emery away. But she refuses to give up on him. He almost loses Emery because of his boorish behavior but finally realizes he made a huge mistake. He loves her deeply, a fact recognized by everyone except Rory. Emery, being a sweet and also practical woman, understands that his previous marriages damaged him. That's why he pushed her away. But Rory has declared his love for her at last, and she comes home to Dùndubhan, never to leave again.

If Rory could find his soul mate, why can't I? Gavin might be the one, and I have a newfound resolve to make our relationship work.

How will I do that? By whatever means necessary. Aye, that might be a vague plan, but I can flesh it out later. For tonight, I simply need to share my loosely conceived plan with my sister Fiona. She's very clever and more mature than I am, in terms of her age and her temperament.

"You want to do what?" Fiona says. "You're off your head, Jamie."

"Why? Rory married a woman after knowing her for four days. My idea is nowhere close to as barmy as that."

"Och, Jamie. What makes you think Gavin will agree to do it?"

"Because he loves me. But I need an excuse to ask him, and Ma and Da's anniversary is the perfect opportunity."

Fiona clucks her tongue. "Be careful. This might blow up in your face."

"A chance I will gladly take."

"If you insist, then…go for it."

This is an insane plan, for certain. But as the saying goes, desperate times call for desperate measures. Gavin and I have been apart too often lately, and I miss him terribly. This is the only option.

I'm going to get my man.

Chapter Thirteen

Gavin

I'm sitting in my tiny apartment on a Friday night, wiped out from work and ready to hit the hay, half asleep already. Then someone rings my doorbell. I never realized that thing even worked. Nobody rings the bell. They just bang on the door instead. It's a sad commentary on the modern world when ringing a doorbell becomes too onerous a task for anyone to bother with. But who the heck is knocking at this hour? It's almost ten o'clock.

Yawning, I hoist my sorry ass out of my recliner and shuffle to the door. I pull it open without even thinking to look through the peephole.

Jamie grins at me. "Surprise!"

"What?" I gape at her, not sure if I'm awake or asleep. Then I feel drool on the corner of my mouth and realize this can't be a dream. I hastily wipe the saliva off with the hem of my T-shirt. "Jamie? I thought you couldn't make it here for another two weeks."

"I couldn't wait any longer. I miss you."

She leaps into my arms, trusting me to catch her. I do, of course, but I'm still kind of confused. For a moment, though, I just hold her and relish the warmth and softness of her body pressed to mine. It's been too damn long since we saw each other in person.

Finally, I set her down on her feet. "I've missed you too, Jamie. But why didn't you let me know you were coming? I would've picked you up at the airport."

"I wanted to surprise you." She gives me an impish smile. "Cannae do that if you know in advance."

"Uh, yeah, I get that."

She leans sideways to peer past my shoulder. "May I come in? Or do you have another girlfriend hiding in there?"

"Yeah, I'd better tell my three other girlfriends to skedaddle." I pick her up and carry her into the tin-can apartment, setting her down on the recliner. "Are you hungry? No, you probably ate on the plane. I mean, it comes with a gourmet chef, for pity's sake."

Jamie studies me for a moment. "Are you jealous that Rory and Lachlan lent me their jet to get me here?"

"No. Well, maybe." I drop onto the bed, which places me less than five feet away from her. "I'm tired, Jamie. I had a long week at work."

"Let's go to sleep, then. We can talk in the morning."

She jumps out of her chair and insists on pulling the covers back for me. Then the woman I adore casually strips and climbs onto the bed. I struggle to get undressed. My exhaustion makes it a lot more difficult, but eventually, I'm naked. So, I crawl onto the bed to lie down beside her.

I must've fallen asleep instantly, because the next thing I know, it's morning and I'm alone in bed. For a few seconds, I think Jamie must have snuck out in the middle of the night and gone back to Scotland. But then I hear sizzling sounds coming from the kitchen. I haven't opened my eyes yet. Jamie is humming a melodic tune, and I just lie here for a while listening to her. After a few minutes, her humming turns into singing as she softly croons a pretty tune that I know I've heard before, though I can't remember the name of it. Probably something Scottish. Jamie loves the traditional songs.

But I've never heard her sing before. She has a beautiful voice.

I drag my butt out of bed and get dressed. Jamie smiles when she realizes I'm up and awake, but she doesn't stop singing. Good. I want to hear more of her voice. I walk up to the kitchen island, which is more like an islet considering the mini size of everything in this apartment. There's only one stool at the island, but I pull that up to the counter and rest my arms on it, enjoying the serenade from a hot Scottish lass.

Jamie raises onto her tiptoes to lean across the islet and kiss me. "*Madainn mhath*, Gavin. That means good morning."

"Good morning to you too, Jamie. Are you starting me on a Gaelic language course?"

"Not officially. But I would love to teach you, if you're interested."

"Sure, sounds like fun. The only language I really know is English—the American version. I took Spanish in high school, since it was required, but I don't remember any of it these days."

Jamie slants across the counter to kiss me again. "Once I teach you Gaelic, you'll never forget it."

"I'm sure you're right. By the way, what was that song you were singing?"

"The Elfin Knight."

"Are you serious? Scots have a song about an elf who's a knight too? That doesn't sound like anything your brothers would sing about. Can't picture Lachlan riding an elf horse. He'd break its little back."

Jamie raises a spatula, aiming it at me. "Dinnae be sarcastic about a traditional folk song. Scots love The Elfin Knight. It's about a lass who is sitting on a hill when she hears the blare of an elf knight's horn and wishes he would come to her bedroom."

"A spicy Scottish folk song? I'm starting to like this. Tell me the rest."

"Dinnae remember the whole story. But I do recall that the elfin knight shows up in her bed chamber and makes some sort of deal with her that results in the lass marrying the knight. She performs tasks for him, though I can't remember the details offhand."

"So, he blows his horn to attract a girl, then screws her and gets her to do stuff for him. Do they live happily ever after?"

Jamie shrugs. "I reckon so."

"Damn, Scots are so weird."

"In the oldest version of the ballad, the lass has no choice in the matter. The elfin knight plans to defile her without her consent. I prefer the later version because the lass isn't a victim in that story."

"Yeah, I wouldn't like the older version either."

Jamie sets two plates on the island. "Let's eat."

I jump off the stool as she comes around to my side. Though she tries to push me back onto the stool, I'm bigger and can easily overwhelm her. I don't need to do that, however. She relents and sets her sexy little ass on the stool. I jump up to sit on the countertop.

We talk about that song some more, making jokes about it and generally enjoying ourselves. I hadn't realized how lonely I was until Jamie turned up last night. We talk on the phone a lot, but that's not the same thing as being together in person, in the same place. I've missed the hell out of her. Not sure how much longer I can stand to be away from her, but I can't ask Jamie to move to America for me. The MacTaggarts are all very close, especially Jamie and her brothers and sisters. Now that my sister lives in Scotland too, maybe I should move there.

To another country? Where the people speak so differently? I feel anxious just thinking about that.

Sure, I know Scots basically speak the same language as Brits and Americans. But they have strange slang, and there's the whole Gaelic issue. Jamie taught me some dirty Gaelic, but that won't help me in everyday life. I meant it when I said I'd love to learn the language. I'd probably suck at it, though. Despite learning Spanish in high school, the only phrase I remember is "*buenos dias.*" I think that means "good morning."

If I can't assimilate with the MacTaggarts...will Jamie dump me?

The lass in question raises one hand to touch my cheek. "What's fashing you, Gavin?"

Another Scottish word—"fash." I know that asking what's fashing me means she wants to know what's wrong, but hearing that term only brought home the reality of the language difference. Am I being a dick and a dope? Should I fall to one knee and beg her to marry me, damn the consequences? That's what I've wanted to do since the day we met.

"Well, Gav? What's fashing you? I'm asking—"

"I know what you're asking. What's bothering me is that when I think about us, I flash back to the day I met Aidan. He wasn't thrilled to find out that I was attracted to his sister." I down a mouthful of coffee a little too fast, making me cough. Jamie sits there serenely waiting for me to speak again. "I'm starting to feel like I'm the elfin knight who's trying to whisk you away from your family so I can do naughty things to you."

"Dinnae think the song mentions the lass's family."

"Yeah, but the knight was an outsider."

Jamie slides off the stool and wraps her arms around me. She presses her cheek to my belly, since she can't reach my chest when I'm sitting on the counter. "You *are* my knight, Gav. You swept me off my feet and made me feel like a maiden in one of those medieval romances."

I brush my fingers through her hair while she gazes up at me with the sweetest look on her face. "I don't want to disappoint you,

Jamie. Not sure your brothers will ever really accept me, not to mention all your cousins who probably want to murder me. Logan for sure would want that."

"He was a spy, but he's a sweet man at heart."

"If you say so. He gives me the 'I could kill you with one finger' look every time I see him."

Jamie lifts her head and pulls it back a touch. "Do you feel inadequate because the men in my extended family are tough?"

"Inadequate? No, I don't think so." Do I feel that way? Never really thought about it until Jamie mentioned the possibility. "Well, I don't know. Maybe I sort of, kind of feel that way."

She backs away, waving for me to jump off the island. Once I hop down, she grabs my hand. "Let's do something fun today. Something that will make you feel reinvigorated and full of machismo."

A laugh splutters out of me. "Machismo? Come on, Jamie, I'm not that much of a wuss. Am I?"

"Of course not. But I think you need to do something other than answering phone calls all day. Something that will remind you of what a virile, powerful, sexy, braw man you are."

The way her voice dropped to a lower key when she called me virile and all that other stuff... It makes me feel like a man again. Not that I ever felt like I wasn't a man. Jeez, even in my head I sound wimpy. Time to fix that issue.

I pull Jamie into my body. "Let's get wild together—in and out of bed."

We get on my computer and search for exciting things we can do together—outdoors. I decided we've done enough hanging out inside my apartment, and it's time to have an open-air adventure. Jamie agreed. Actually, she grinned, jumped up and down, and high-fived me three times. She also slapped my ass, but I slapped hers right back. Jamie calls it my "erse," though. It's the Scottish word for her cute little caboose.

Jamie laughs. "What did you just call my erse, Gav?"

"Your caboose. I could've used a variety of other terms for your cute ass. Booty, heinie, keister, patootie—"

"Puh-what-ee?" she says with a half-suppressed laugh.

"Patootie. It's an American thing."

"I see." She grabs my ass. "Whatever you call it, your erse is mine."

Yeah, I feel better already. There's nothing like teasing Jamie to make me feel good again.

Since it's a beautiful, warm late summer's day, we agree to go skydiving as our first adventure in what will become a two-day experience. Neither of us has ever done anything like this before. My job in the Marines had been ground-based. I was never a paratrooper. But maybe what I've really needed ever since I came back from Afghanistan was to jump out of my comfort zone—literally.

There's nobody I'd rather do that with than Jamie.

After receiving some training, we get to skydive tandem. I take the reins while Jamie just hangs on for the ride, strapped to my body. The minutes fly by thanks to the adrenaline boost brought on by sheer excitement, and I'm sure Jamie feels the same way. Then it's time for us to fly. We leap out of the plane, soaring through the sky, sailing down, down, down. I pull our chutes just like the instructor told us, and our descent slows but still gives us plenty of time to appreciate our view of the earth from high above. Then we touch down in the grassy field next to the airstrip.

Once we've ditched our chute, Jamie leaps on me with her arms and legs wrapped around me. Then she throws her head back and whoops.

I chuckle. "Guess you liked that, huh?"

"No, I bloody loved it!"

"Me too. But now we have a decision to make."

She slides down my body slowly until her feet hit the ground. "What should we do next. That's the decision."

"Exactly."

We return to my car and browse options on my cell phone, searching for something that's less of an adrenaline rush after our skydiving fun. We finally choose kayaking. A lot of places not far from Minneapolis offer those kinds of experiences, and the best part is that we won't require any training. We'll be able to just hop in a kayak and go. The company we select gives us a map with their recommended route, which will give us the chance to see lots of wildlife, including birds.

Jamie loves that. She's an outdoorsy girl. One of the first things I learned about her once we seriously started dating was that she loves bicycling through the villages of Loch Fairbairn and Ballachulish. I haven't had the chance to do that with her yet, but I'd love to.

I would go anywhere with this woman.

<h1 style="text-align:center">Chapter Fourteen</h1>

Jamie

Oh, I love kayaking with Gavin while surrounded by the most beautiful scenery I've ever seen in America. To be fair, I haven't seen much of this country. I wish I had suggested we do this months ago. Gavin has relaxed and become the man I knew when we first met—strong, clever, full of humor, and ready for anything that I want to try. Flying to America to see him had been the best thing I could've done for our floundering relationship. My surprise arrival had reawakened Gavin—and me too.

We're kayaking along the Chain of Lakes which, as the name implies, consists of three interconnected bodies of water. We visit all of them—Lake of the Isles, Lake Calhoun, and Lake Harriet—while enjoying the scenery and the wildlife. We see multiple species of geese as well as ducks and swans, not to mention land-based birds like partridges, pheasants, hawks, doves, and even eagles.

I just stop myself from shrieking when I see my first bald eagle. Dinnae want to scare it away. We don't have those birds in Scotland, and I love getting such a close-up view of America's most famous eagle species. Gavin even manages to take a picture of the bald eagle so I'll have a memento of our adventure today.

But I don't need a photograph to remember this day.

After enjoying a delicious lunch at a restaurant, we go on a self-guided walking tour of sights along the Mississippi River. I never knew just how wide the river is until I saw it in person. Pictures and films don't do it justice. Gavin suggests we should walk across the Stone Arch Bridge so I can get a better view of St. Anthony Falls. It's impressive, to say the least. The bridge used to be for trains only. Gavin tells me about that, and I try to pay attention to everything he says, but I keep getting distracted by the scenery.

My day with Gavin has been the best time we've ever had together.

The man I adore wants to take me to a posh hotel for the night, but I assure him he doesn't need to do that. I'm happy to stay at his apartment. But I soon realize that he suggested a hotel because he wants that, though he won't tell me that straight out. So, I relent and allow him to spoil me. If it makes him happy, which it clearly does, then it makes me happy too.

But now it's time for me to go home.

Gavin drives me to the airport, but I don't need to go through security. Having brothers who co-own a private jet has its perks, that's for dead sure. Gavin walks with me across the tarmac and even climbs onto the jet with me. Then he pulls me close and simply cradles my head to his chest as if he doesn't want to let me go. I feel that way about him too. The longer our relationship stays intercontinental, the more I feel as if we will never be able to get married and live in the same house, much less in the same country.

"I've got some vacation time left," Gavin tells me. "I could see if I can take four or five days off to go to Scotland."

My head pops up. "You want to do that?"

"Yeah. I mean, it's not like I've never gone there before. But it would be great to have more than two days with you."

"I would love that."

"Then it's settled. I'll find out how soon I can use those vacation days."

"Oh, Gav, thank you." I pepper kisses all over his face. "I love you so much."

Though I would never tell him so, all this traveling back and forth between America and Scotland has become exhausting. Now that Calli has married Aidan, and they live in the Highlands, I cannae see what's preventing Gavin from moving there too. His cousin Tara is married, so he wouldn't be abandoning her. Besides, he's lived away from Tara for a long time. Why won't Gavin even talk about the prospect of moving to Scotland? I know he'd love it there if he stopped worrying about everything.

We have occasionally discussed the possibility of one of us moving so we could be together. But the pain and guilt he still feels, about his parents and the way he abandoned Calli after their death, keeps him rooted in place. I know his military experience left him battered emotionally and physically. But he can't hold on to all that pain forever. Can he?

"We're about to take off," the co-pilot says. He's standing near the doorway, waiting for Gavin to leave.

I kiss him and smile. "Go on. We'll see each other soon."

He stares at me for a moment, then crushes me to his body, kissing me with such passionate desperation that I almost want to cry. Then he touches his head to mine and jogs down the stairs.

I watch out the window as Gavin keeps jogging away from the plane. He pauses only long enough to wave at me before he disappears from view.

Six hours later, I'm back in Scotland. Alone.

Well, all right, I'm not actually alone. I have my extended family to keep me company. I've been staying with Aidan and Calli ever since Rory married Emery, so I expect one or both of them to greet me when I walk out of the jet. But instead, Rory and Lachlan are there.

"What's wrong?" I ask as I approach them. "You look like you have bad news. Did Erica and Emery both boot you out of your homes?"

Rory rolls his eyes. "There is no bad news. And no, our wives have not booted us out of anywhere."

"Then why are you and Lachie here?"

Peripherally, I can see Lachlan grimacing—because I used his diminutive. But he doesn't speak up to complain.

"We've all agreed," Rory says, "that you shouldn't continue living with Aidan and Calli. You were never meant to be their permanent nanny."

"But I love spending time with the bairn."

"Aye. But we've decided you should go elsewhere."

"Such as where? The moon?"

Lachlan shakes his head. "No, ye cheeky lass. We want you to move in with Fiona and Cat."

"Oh, I see. Thank you for the offer, but I'd rather not stay with them. Fiona and Cat might feel slighted because I have a boyfriend and they don't."

"They dinnae care, I'm sure. What's the real reason you'd rather not stay with your sisters?"

"My boyfriend might be coming to visit, and I dinnae think Fiona or Cat wants to hear me and Gav shagging."

"*Bod an Donais*," Rory says miserably. "How many times have we asked you lasses not to bring up the subject of your love lives in front of us?"

"At least a hundred times."

Lachie and Rory whisper to each other for a moment, then Rory faces me. "You will be a guest at Dùndubhan for the time being."

"Thank you, Rory."

"What about me?" Lachlan says. "It was a joint decision."

"Aye, also thank you, Lachie. My brothers are so generous in the way they order their sisters about."

He squints at me, but Lachlan knows that won't fash me. Rory knows it too, but at least he has the sense not to let his displeasure show on his face.

I'd lived at Dùndubhan for nearly a year before Rory married Emery, so it's like coming home when I arrive at the castle again. Lachlan drives back to Ballachulish, to the farm he and Erica own just outside the village, while Rory and I head for Dùndubhan. The moment we enter the vestibule, Emery and Mrs. Darroch suddenly appear from the vicinity of the kitchen to greet us. Mrs. Darroch hugs me and kisses my cheek. But Emery is far more boisterous in her greeting.

She seizes me in a hug so firm that I gasp. "Oh, Jamie, we're so happy to have you at Dùndubhan again. And Lachlan called to tell us that Gavin might be coming for an extended visit. That's wonderful!"

"Aye, it is. Cannae wait to see him again, even though I just spent the weekend with him in Minneapolis."

"Being away from your honey is awful. When Rory went to Paris for a few days to attend a conference, I missed him like crazy." She aims a sly glance at her husband. "Of course, Rory was only trying to hide from me. The conference was a ruse."

Rory rolls his eyes, as he often does. "Em, dinnae tell lies to Jamie. It wasn't completely a ruse. I did learn new things at the conference."

"Uh-huh." She winks at him. "You learned how to avoid your wife."

"But I will never do that again. You are my soul mate, *mo chridhe*."

Rory MacTaggart just used the phrase soul mate. I cannae believe it. Though I know Emery has changed my brother's life and his attitudes toward everything, I hadn't expected him to announce that out loud.

If Lachlan and Rory could change… Maybe Gavin and I have a chance too.

Ten days later, I'm once again standing on the tarmac at the Inverness airport waiting for one of the pilots to open the jet's door. The moment Gavin steps out of the jet and onto the stairs, I rush toward the bottom of the steps. He jogs down them and pulls me into his arms, kissing me so thoroughly that I feel soft and warm and melty. Aye, Emery taught me the word melty. My newest sister-in-law is my favorite person in the world—after Gavin. No one will ever displace him in my heart.

He finally peels his lips away from mine. "So damn glad to see you, baby."

My heart swells at those simple words. "I couldn't sleep last night because I was so excited to see you again."

"Can we go straight to your bedroom and make love?"

I bite my lip and lift my brows. "We could do that in the car. Rory sent me here in a limousine that I know for a fact has a privacy partition."

He chuckles. "I love how hot you always are for me. That's a great idea. I've never done it in any kind of vehicle."

"Does a private jet count as a vehicle?"

"No, it's an airplane." He grasps my erse. "So, this will be a first for us."

"Brilliant! Take me to the limousine—and *in* the limousine, please."

He salutes. "Yes, ma'am."

Then he picks me up and carries me over to the waiting vehicle. The driver doesn't even bat an eye when Gavin asks for the privacy partition to be lowered. I reckon the driver has done that many times for clients who do business in the car, and perhaps even for randy lovers like me and Gavin.

We have three and a half hours to enjoy each other in this car.

Gavin slides a hand up my thigh, and even through my jeans, I swear I can feel the heat of his skin. "Wanna get naked? Or mess around with our clothes on?"

"I've never 'messed around' while fully clothed. So do whatever you want, Gav. I need you to fuck me, that's all."

"You are the best girl any man could hope to find."

He slides that hand up to my waistband. When he unhooks the button on my jeans, my breath catches. But when he pulls the zipper down slowly, my pulse accelerates and my skin grows sensitive, so much that the slightest touch drives me mad with desire for him.

Gavin pushes his hand inside my knickers, cupping me there. "Fuck, you're already wet for me. I can smell it and feel it all over my palm."

"Oh, God, I love the way this feels. Dinnae stop, Gav, please."

"I'm going to take it so slow that you'll be panting for me."

He gently separates my folds and glides one finger down to pet my clitoris. His fingers move so slowly and delicately that the sensation drives me mad, and I begin to thrust my hips without any conscious decision to do that. My body has a mind of its own. No, that's not true. Gavin commands my body, and I love letting him take control of me.

I slap my hands down on his thighs and grip them so tightly that he sucks in a sharp breath. Then my hands drift up to his hips. While he spreads his fingers to rub my folds, using only his thumb to torment my nub, I cannae stop myself from rubbing his cock through his jeans.

He's breathing as hard as I am. "Fuck, Jamie, don't do that unless you want me to come in my pants. I'd rather come inside you."

I peel my hand away. "Sorry. Couldn't help myself."

Gavin latches his mouth on to my breast, suckling it through my blouse. The fabric isn't enough of a barrier. While he goes on sucking my nipple, I grow so painfully aroused that I begin to pant and moan. Instead of gripping his cock, I clench the edge of the seat and squeeze my eyes shut, just waiting for the moment when he will push me over the edge.

"Come for me, baby, come for me now."

I throw my head back, my mouth open on a strangled cry—and I come. My muscles clench nothing, until he shoves two fingers inside me. He pumps them in and out, powerfully and swiftly, while he keeps suckling my nipple. That sends a pulse of pleasure barreling down my nerves, intensifying my orgasm.

He releases my nipple and seals his mouth over mine, swallowing my cries.

When it's over, I sag against the seat. My breaths come hard and fast, just like my heartbeats.

Someone knocks on the partition.

"*Mhac na galla,*" I hiss. "What the bloody hell is that?"

Gavin seems dazed as he stares at the partition.

"Sorry to bother you," the driver shouts through the barrier. "Just got news."

News? What? Dinnae understand the word. An incredible climax delivered by an incredible man will do that to a lass.

Gavin shakes off his confusion before I do. He shouts to the driver, "Just a minute." Then he turns to me. "Zip up, Jamie."

"Huh?" I blink rapidly and at last manage to clear my head. I zip up my jeans and shout to the driver, "You can lower the partition."

The barrier rolls down, revealing the driver's face inch by inch. His expression is a wee bit pinched. "I apologize for the interruption. Just got a text from your brother Rory. We're picking up another passenger."

"Passenger?" I glance at Gavin, but he simply shrugs. "Do you know who it is?"

"Aye. It's Evan MacTaggart."

"Oh. Well, thank you for letting us know."

"Should I raise the partition?"

"No, that won't be necessary." Because we won't be shagging in this car today.

Chapter Fifteen

Gavin

I can't believe this. Though I love giving Jamie orgasms, the driver's announcement has left me in a bad way. I'm so hard that I think my jeans might split open. Watching Jamie come always affects me that way. Still, I'm glad I could give her pleasure, even if I didn't get any myself. A gentleman always makes sure a lady has everything she wants and needs, no matter what.

Ten minutes later, when we reach an apartment building on the other side of Inverness, my stiff problem has softened considerably. Thank goodness. Jamie's cousin Evan has just climbed into the limo.

He sits down on the bench seat that faces us and smiles at Jamie. "It's good to see you, *gràidh*. Sorry we haven't seen each other more often, but my work has consumed me lately."

"No worries, Evan. We're all so proud of your accomplishments."

The guy seems a touch uncomfortable with Jamie's praise. But he shakes it off and looks at me. "You must be the American laddie who has stolen my cousin's heart."

I hold out my hand to him. "Gavin Douglas. Your cousin Aidan is married to my sister."

Evan shakes my hand. "Pleasure to meet you. I met Calli briefly at the wedding ceilidh for Rory and his new bride. Your sister is a lovely lass."

The three of us have a nice conversation for the first hour of our journey, but then Evan tells us he needs to do some work on his computer. He's some kind of tech genius, according to Jamie. I talk my "lass" into playing gin rummy with me to pass the time. Evan smirks at that suggestion, which I assume means he doesn't think we can play a card game on the backseat of a limo. But we have no trouble playing the game this way. Jamie and I sit sideways on the seat, facing each other, and we both sit cross-legged too.

So much for the tech genius knowing everything.

Maybe I do rib Evan a little bit, but he clearly doesn't mind. In fact, about two hours and fifteen minutes into our journey, he asks if he can get in on the gin rummy action. We play a three-way game with Evan sitting on the floor with his cards on the seat between me and Jamie. I'd kind of assumed Evan was an uptight geek, but he's actually pretty cool. Not the laugh-riot type of guy. But he can relax enough to enjoy a card game and even make a few jokes.

Jamie loves all of it. Every time she wins a hand, she throws her arms up and cheers—though she keeps her cries muted enough that the driver won't crash the car. Jamie has perfected the shrieking version of golf claps. It's the cutest thing ever.

We drop Evan off at his mom's house, then continue on to Dùndubhan. We both wind up taking a joint nap with my arm around her shoulders and her head on my chest, waking up only once we reach the castle. The driver gently rouses us. As we climb out of the limo, Rory and Emery emerge from the vestibule to greet us.

Jamie hugs them both. I hug Emery but shake Rory's hand. Guys like us don't do the hugging thing with each other.

Before we walk into the castle, I take a moment to enjoy the sunset. With my arm around Jamie, we both gaze up at the golden rays as they sink toward the horizon and streamers of deep pink and orange fill the sky. I've never been the type to study a sunset, but being with Jamie has turned me into a sentimental fool—and I don't care.

Mrs. Darroch has gone home, which means she walked across the courtyard to the little cottage alongside the walled garden. But she left us a great snack. The four of us enjoy the food the housekeeper made, but we don't talk about the elephant in the kitchen. That would be me and my relationship with Jamie. Our weekend in Minneapolis had been incredible, but now we're back in MacTaggart territory.

And I'm the invader.

Rory and Emery head up to the top floor, where they have a huge bedroom. Jamie and I will stay on the ground floor, in one of the bedrooms in the guest wing. That means we can make all the noise we want.

Tonight, though, we're too tired for sex.

In the morning, it's raining. No golden sunrise to match yesterday's golden sunset. Oh, well. I've got the human version of a stunning sunrise lying beside me in this bed. I wake up with Jamie snuggled against me. We're facing each other, so I can just lie here watching her while she sleeps and count the smattering of faint freckles on her cheeks.

She sighs and stretches, keeping her eyes shut.

I brush a lock of hair away from her face. "Good morning, baby."

Jamie slowly peels her lids open and gives me a sleepy-sexy smile. "Good morning, Gavin."

"What amazing adventures would you like to have today?"

"Let's go into Loch Fairbairn and visit Kirsty's shop."

"That would be the metaphysical shop, right? And Kirsty is one of your cousins."

"Aye. She has two sisters, Isla and Elspeth, as well as a brother, Logan."

"Yeah, I've met him. Not the sisters, though." I sit up and pat her bottom. "Time to get off your patootie and get dressed."

She laughs. "Had you ever actually used the word patootie before that morning in your apartment?"

"No. But I've decided it describes your ass perfectly."

"Hmm." She rolls onto her back and stretches languorously. "What should I call your erse? 'Caboose' is intriguing, but I think 'booty' suits you best."

"Scots don't have any words other than 'erse' to describe someone's heinie?"

"That's the only one I've ever used."

A fist raps on the bedroom door. "Rise and shine, Jamie and the American *cacan*. Breakfast will be served in the dining room in precisely eighteen minutes."

Oh, yeah, even if Rory wasn't the only other man in the castle this morning, I'd still know that was him. He's teasing me with the *"cacan"* thing. I know that word means "wee shit." I've been dating his sister, after all, and sweet Jamie loves to curse in Gaelic. Despite the way her brothers behave, I don't believe they want to chase me away. Why would Rory let me stay in his castle if he wanted me gone? No, I think he and his brothers just want to harass me to make sure I won't break Jamie's heart.

I never want to do that. And I admire her brothers for their commitment to protecting Jamie without directly interfering in our relationship. I have a sister too, and I would do anything I could to prevent Calli from getting hurt. Luckily, she married Aidan, a nice guy who I know would never hurt my sister.

Jamie and I get up and get dressed, then head for the dining room. It's just at the end of the guest-wing hallway, so we don't have far to walk. When we traipse into the dining room, Rory and Emery are already seated and waiting for us. Rory sits at the head of the table, naturally, with Emery at his right.

I pull out a chair for Jamie, and as she sits down, she smiles up at me.

Rory gives me an appreciative nod. Did I just gain a small measure of approval from the Steely Solicitor? I think maybe I did.

Jamie is sitting directly across from Emery, right next to Rory. I take the chair beside hers, and Emery winks at me. No idea what that means. Emery is very smart and kind, but she's also sorta weird. I guess it takes an unusual woman to tame a man like Rory.

We all have a nice conversation over breakfast, discussing mundane things—until Emery brings up Halloween.

She sets her arms on the table and smiles with a touch of mischief. "We need to throw a big Halloween party here at Dùndubhan."

Rory rolls his eyes. "Why, Em, do we need that?"

"For fun. You finally unleashed your wild side, and I'd bet you have never attended any kind of party, much less a costume bash."

"Aye, and there's a bloody good reason for that." He leans forward slightly and squints at his wife. "Because I despise parties."

"Oh, come on, Rory Baby. Let's have a big bash."

He squints harder. "I've repeatedly asked you never to call me that in front of other people."

Emery tries to suppress a laugh, but she winds up spluttering instead. "Everyone already knows I call you Rory Baby. The cat's out of that bag and scurrying around the house, scratching up all your precious furniture. Get over it, sweetie."

Damn, I love Emery more every time I see her. She's awesome.

I might be smirking now. Can't help it. Watching a blonde bombshell basically tell her much-larger husband to lighten up and grow a pair is one of the highlights of my life so far.

Rory relaxes and smiles, grasping his wife's hand so he can kiss it. "You're right, *mo gaoloch*. A Halloween ceilidh would give us an excuse to bring the entire clan together. I cannot promise I will enjoy every moment of it, but I will give it a go."

Emery grins and claps three times. "Yay! Thank you, Rory Baby. You're the sweetest."

He smiles with a touch of bemusement and relaxes in his chair.

Will Jamie and I ever have the kind of relationship these two have? Well, I can't really compare our relationships. Rory married Emery four days after they met in New Orleans. Jamie and I have been navigating an intercontinental romance for more than a year.

After breakfast, Jamie and I go for a walk. There's a trail on the far side of the castle that leads to the river. It's nice to spend some time outdoors with the lass I love, rather than just hanging out inside. Our weekend trips to see each other don't give us much of a chance to relax. We both feel compelled to find activities to do together, to make the most of our brief in-person visits.

Strolling with Jamie makes me feel like all that stress has vanished.

We sit down on the banks of the river, which Jamie tells me has no name. That's weird, but I'd rather focus on her than on finding out why Rory's river has no name. We have our arms around each other's waists as we amble long, listening to birdsongs and the rushing of the water. I can't help imagining us walking like this with our children. In my fantasy, we have two kids, a boy and a girl, but that brings up a question in my mind. If we have kids, will they speak with Scottish accents or American ones?

Don't care. I'll love them either way.

But will they be raised in Scotland? Will I need to get dual citizenship?

Jamie rubs her cheek on my arm. "What are you thinking about, Gavin? You seem very serious."

"No, it's nothing. Just lost in my own thoughts." I kiss the top of her head. "Maybe we should come up with potential names for the river, just for the heck of it."

Didn't I deftly change the subject? I don't want to explain my weird, silly thoughts to her, not yet. If we get engaged, maybe I will tell her.

"Are you sure everything is all right?" Jamie asks. "You know you can tell me anything."

"I swear it's nothing, honestly." Yeah, that didn't sound guilty at all. "Don't you like my idea that we should invent names for the river?"

"Aye, I do like that. It sounds like something Rory would positively hate, so we should definitely do it." She bumps into me on purpose, gazing up at me with the sweetest impish smile. "It would be fun to watch Rory's face turn bright red."

I chuckle. "You're a naughty lass, aren't you?"

"Aye. But you love that about me."

"Yep, always have, always will."

But more than that, I will love this woman forever. Unless she dumps me first. I don't mention that thought to Jamie. It's dumb and nothing but a passing worry.

We spend the remainder of my vacation days however Jamie wants. She insists I should tell her what I'd like to do, but I prefer to let her act as my tour guide to the Highlands. After all, this is her home. I love the way she lights up when she points out her favorite places on a map, so she can devise the best itinerary for our day trips. Every evening, we go back to Dùndubhan to have dinner with Rory and Emery—and whoever else might show up. Jamie's relatives have a way of just appearing suddenly in the dining room doorway. It's kind of weird, but I've gotten used to it.

Mostly, it's her immediate family who magically appear. But I have met a few of her cousins, of which there a shocking number around these parts.

"Oh, aye," she agrees when I share my thoughts with her. "There are MacTaggarts everywhere. We're a wee bit like ants. We emerge from under a rock to crawl about and overtake you when we're least expected. Sort of like the blob in that old science fiction film."

"Your metaphors are weird and kind of sinister, but I think that's cute."

She kisses my cheek. That's what Jamie does whenever I say something that she labels "barmy," but she's even cuter when she informs me that I might be "off my head" if I think danger is adorable.

But soon, it's time for me to fly home. I do have a job, after all, though I'd much rather stay here with Jamie. She offers to go home with me, though I assure her that's unnecessary. We can talk on the phone, after all, or even do video calls. After six days with Jamie in Scotland, I feel refreshed and ready to go.

Everything gets back to normal, but not for long.

Six weeks after I came back from the Highlands, my boss calls me into his office. I can tell by the look on his face that he isn't about to give me a promotion or a raise. By the time he stops babbling meaningless boss-talk, I've already guessed what he wants to tell me. All that's left is for him to say the words.

"I'm sorry, Gavin. I have to let you go."

"Yeah, I figured."

"The company has been going through a rough time, financially, and we need to cut the wheat from the chaff." He hands me an actual pink slip and actually expects me to take it. "I truly am sorry. You've been a dedicated employee, but your sales volume was lower than that of other associates."

Since he's still thrusting that pink piece of paper at me, I give up and take it.

My former boss looks obviously relieved, like he expected me to karate kick him in the nuts. "Please gather your personal items and relinquish your badge at the security station downstairs."

"Uh-huh."

I trudge out of his office and collect up the few items on my desk that belong to me. Then I trudge downstairs to hand my employee badge to a stern pseudo-cop who analyzes it for several seconds before he tells me I can leave.

Yeah, my life is so amazing. How can I tell Jamie I'm an unemployed loser? She doesn't have a job either, but I would never ask her to support me while I hunt for another crappy position. What am I qualified for? Ground ordnance maintenance isn't a popular search on job sites. It's a military thing. And my years of working for Rapid React didn't qualify me for anything other than annoying innocent people with cold calls.

Tomorrow, I'm supposed to fly to Scotland for the weekend. I'd been looking forward to that for weeks, but now the only news I can give her is that I'm an unemployed loser. The worst part of all is that I bought an engagement ring for her. I decided to pop the question this weekend.

Now, I don't know if I should. Jamie deserves better than a screwed-up guy who doesn't even have a job. My secondary present for her isn't really a gift at all. Just something I thought might be useful.

None of that matters anymore. My life just got flushed down an industrial toilet.

Chapter Sixteen

Jamie

A sigh of pleasure whispers out of me as I walk into the Loch Fairbairn café at precisely ten o'clock, just as Gavin had asked me to do. We have never needed a timetable for our dates, but lately, he has seemed uneasy and a wee bit uncertain too. About what? Us? Me? My family? I know my brothers can be intimidating, but not to Gavin. He's a strong, braw man who would never run away from a fight.

Not that my brothers have ever tried to literally chase him away.

Just inside the café doors, I halt. Does my hair look all right? Maybe I should get out my comb and run it through my hair one last time. I have a feeling this might be the day when Gavin pops the big question. Dinnae know why I feel that way. My heart believes it, though. I glance down at my flower-print skirt and peasant blouse. It looks fine. I look fine. *No more dawdling, you silly lass.*

I march across the café with my skirt swishing and my head held high as I wend my way around the tables and chairs to reach Gavin. I grin at him.

He jumps up to pull a chair out for me. Though he smiles, it's rather subdued and seems almost anxious. He can't worry I'll say no to his proposal, can he?

Once we're both seated, he clasps his hands on the tabletop—and begins to wring them.

"Are you all right, Gav?"

"Uh, yeah, sure." He moves his hands to his lap. "You look really pretty today."

"Thank you."

He chose a table in the outdoor section of the café, beneath a striped awning, as if he wants as much privacy as possible. But now he fidgets and keeps glancing about like he's worried a boulder might crash down on his head from the clear blue sky.

I scoot my chair closer to his. "You dinnae seem all right. What's fashing you?"

"Nothing, I swear." He grasps the seat of my chair to pull it closer to him. Our faces are now within kissing distance, and his expression has become relaxed. But the way he licks his lips, coupled with his darkening irises, tells me he wants to snog. "Mind if I kiss you for an hour or two?"

"As long as you want, *mo chridhe.*"

Gavin presses his mouth to mine, molding our lips to each other in the most languid and sensual manner, until I'm melting for him. When he slips his tongue between my lips, I sag into him. A soft wee moan whispers out of me. *Bod an Donais*, I love kissing this man. He tastes like coffee with two creams and three sugars, which is odd since I know he takes his coffee black with one sugar. Why did he change his preference?

That's the way I like my coffee, though.

With his mouth still touching mine, he gazes straight into my eyes. "Did you notice the coffee flavor? I know you don't like it when I kiss you after I've drunk black coffee."

"You did that for me? Och, Gav, you are the sweetest man."

"Anything for you, baby."

We go back to kissing, oblivious of anything that might be occurring around us. Nothing matters except the two of us inside this wee bubble of romance. We go on reveling in the kiss for so long that I lose track of time. This feels wonderful, especially since we haven't made love in three months. He always has an excuse for that, and it's usually work stress. But here, while we're enjoying each other's lips, none of that matters anymore.

At last, Gavin slowly pulls away, though his eyes remain closed. He exhales a long sigh before finally opening his eyes.

I glance round the café without moving my head, expecting to see other customers glaring at us and our flagrantly romantic display. But no one has paid any mind to us. We might as well have become invisible. Beyond our wee bubble of solitude, the sun shines and showers its warmth on us. Inside the café, Halloween decorations hang from the ceiling and from the awning, and still more decorate the tables and even the counter just inside the doorway.

Gavin finally pulls away, though only slightly.

I smile with my lips closed, which probably makes my cheeks dimple. "You must have something important to say, otherwise you'd never stop kissing me after only a few minutes."

Gavin loves to kiss me for so long that I lose track of time, and I love it when he does that. But now, he gazes at me steadily, as if he's considering how to start saying whatever it is he clearly wants to tell me. Abruptly, his expression turns anxious, and he swallows hard enough that I can see the movement in his throat. He winces the tiniest bit.

My smile falters. "What's wrong, Gav?"

"Nothing, I—Uh, well, see…"

"You can tell me, whatever it is." I peck a light kiss on his lips. "Do you trust me?"

He gulps again and stops blinking. "You know I do."

"Then tell me. I'm tougher than I look."

He just stares at me.

Is proposing such a difficult thing to do? I wouldn't think so, but then, I am not a man. They can be such numpties about love sometimes. "You think about it while I powder my nose."

"Your nose looks fine to me."

I laugh softly, charmed by his statement because it's such an innocently barmy thing to say. "It's a polite way of telling you I need to piss."

His brows shoot up, though I can't imagine that he's shocked that I used a vulgar word. Gavin hears me curse all the time.

I rise from my chair and kiss his forehead. "I'll be a minute."

After a brief trip to the restroom, I swiftly make my way through the café. I feel lighter today, as if I might float up into the sky. This has been the best day I've had in a long time, and I just know Gavin has something up his sleeve. But when I walk into the outdoor patio, I see him sitting at our table with his head bowed and his hands tightly clasped on the tabletop. Then he rubs his eyes.

Maybe he's just a wee bit anxious about popping the question.

"Here I am," I announce as I reclaim my seat beside Gavin. "What was it you wanted to talk about?"

He sits up straighter and lifts his chin.

"You okay?" I ask, tipping my head to study him. "The flight from America has you knackered, doesn't it? We can talk later."

"No," he snaps. "Now. We should, uh, talk now. I'm going home tomorrow."

I know that already. Why did he feel the need to remind me? Nerves, I assume. So, I lean toward him. "Go on, Gavin. I'm listening."

He winces again. Then he surreptitiously shoves a hand into his trouser pocket. Well, not that surreptitiously since I saw him do it. He clearly hoped I wouldn't notice.

Go on, Gavin, just do it. Ask me. He must know I'll say yes. How could he believe otherwise?

He yanks an object out of his pocket and…thrusts a slender, flat rectangular object at me. "This is for you. It's so you can get miles to use for travel expenses."

Miles? What the bloody sodding hell is he havering about? I gawp at the credit card he just offered me, unable to move or speak for several seconds that feel like hours. I gingerly accept the credit card, holding the very edge of one corner between my thumb and forefinger. I cannae help curling my lip, though not from disgust. It's from utter confusion. "I don't need miles, Gavin. We both fly on Rory's jet."

His face blanches. His eyes nearly bulge out of their sockets. His lips work as if he cannae cobble together even one sentence. And he clamps his fingers around the ring box. "I got one of those credit cards where you earn miles with every purchase. Made you an authorized user on it. This'll, uh, help pay for—expenses. When you visit me."

"You said this already." My lips begin to quiver. My pulse races, though not in a good way, and I feel the first sting of tears in my eyes. "I reminded you I don't need a bloody credit card. Is this why you brought me here? To a romantic restaurant? This is the important thing you needed to tell me? After eighteen months together, this is all you think I'm worth."

He shakes his head slowly, minutely, while his eyes remain wide. He says nothing.

Tears trickle down my cheeks even while I want to grab him by the throat and bash his head onto the table repeatedly. I love him, and he claims to love me. If that's true, how could he hand me a credit card as if it's a wonderful gift? He must have realized I'd assume he meant to ask me to marry him. After all these months, nearly two years together, this is what he thinks of me? I need a fucking credit card? No, I need *him*. I want to spend the rest of my life with Gavin Douglas. Yet he just smacked me in the face, metaphorically.

"You're an eejit, Gavin. A *bod ceann* and an eejit, and I'm done."

"Jamie—"

I leap out of my chair so quickly that it topples over, but I can't worry about that or anything right now. I fling the credit card at him. It lands on his lap. "I cannae do this anymore, Gavin. It's over."

"What?"

"I'm breaking up with you." I enunciate each word with knife-like precision, even while my throat tightens and tears pour down my cheeks. "Goodbye, forever."

While Gavin just sits there gawping at me, I rush out of the café and down the sidewalk, swerving down the side street where I'd parked my car. As I collapse onto the driver's seat and shut the door, I can no longer hold back my anguish. I cover my face with my hands and sob. But I only do that for a moment, then I realize that crying willnae help at all. So, I wipe away my tears and blow my nose.

In the rearview mirror, I can see my own face. My eyes are red, and my face is blotchy. *Mhac na galla*. This isn't the way I behave. I'm always cheerful and optimistic, but Gavin Douglas has taken all of that away from me. I still love him. I always will. But I dinnae know if we can ever repair the damage he caused simply by offering me a sodding credit card.

No, I will not let Gavin ruin my day or my outlook on life.

After a few moments of rest, I study myself in the mirror again. No more bloodshot eyes. No more blotchy face. I look like myself again.

But I still have a dilemma. Where should I go? Home? That means Aidan and Calli's house. I'd moved back in with them recently. Ugh, no, I can't run there. I might look better now, but I still feel like rubbish. Maybe a wee walk might refresh me. I climb out of my car and return to the corner where the café is. Gavin's car is gone, so at least I won't need to worry about bumping into him.

I am alone.

That solitary thought spurs the tears to gather once again in my eyes. *Bloody hell*. Look what Gavin has done to me. I march off down the street, away from the café, while I sniffle and wipe tears away from my eyes. Rory's office is two blocks away. I'll go there. Maybe my taciturn brother will offer to hunt down Gavin and batter him senseless. No, I dinnae want that. Because the worst part of all is that I will always love him, even if we never reconcile.

Gavin Douglas is the love of my life, that ersehole. How could he do this to me?

As I march down the pavement toward Rory's office, I experience something I have never felt before. I think it's what people call an epiphany. Usually, those are a good thing, aren't they? Mine is bloody awful. I've just realized that my relationship with Gavin must have been doomed from the start. His emotional damage has stood between us like a concrete wall ever since the day we met. He can't adjust to living in Scotland. He's made that clear, though he never specifically said so. My brothers might have found their true loves, but I am not that lucky.

Unless…

As I push through the door to Rory's outer office, I realize that I'm still conflicted about Gavin and always will be unless something changes. The only way this will end without both our hearts getting shattered is if he makes the next move.

Please, Gavin, fight for me.

How did Gavin win back Jamie?
Experience the rest of their story in
***Gift-Wrapped in a Kilt* (Hot Scots, Book Four).**

Love the

Hot Scots

series?

Visit
AnnaDurand.com

to subscribe to her newsletter
for updates on forthcoming books in the series
&
to receive exclusive content!

Anna Durand is a bestselling, multi-award-winning author of contemporary and paranormal romance. Her books have earned bestseller status on every major retailer and wonderful reviews from readers around the world. But that's the boring spiel. Here are the really cool things you want to know about Anna!

Born on Lackland Air Force Base in Texas, Anna grew up moving here, there, and everywhere thanks to her dad's job as an instructor pilot. She's lived in Texas (twice), Mississippi, California (twice), Michigan (twice), and Alaska—and now Ohio.

As for her writing, Anna has always invented stories in her head, but she didn't write them down until her teen years. Those first awful books went into the trash can a few years later, though she learned a lot from those stories. Eventually, she would pen her first romance novel, the paranormal romance *Willpower*, and she's never looked back since.

To get exclusive content, join Anna's Facebook group, Anna's Romance Addicts, or sign up for her newsletter.

Visit AnnaDurand.com to sign up.

www.ingramcontent.com/pod-product-compliance
Lightning Source LLC
Chambersburg PA
CBHW071205210726
48293CB00002B/293